# FIFTY DEGREES BELOW

Kim Stanley Robinson was born in 1952 and, after travelling and working around the world, has now settled in his beloved California. He is widely regarded as the finest science fiction writer working today, noted as much for the verisimilitude of his characters as the meticulously researched hard science basis of his work. He has won just about every major sf award there is to win and is the author of the massively successful and lavishly praised Mars series.

By Kim Stanley Robinson

# Fifty Degrees Below

## KIM STANLEY ROBINSON

HarperCollins*Publishers*

HarperCollins*Publishers*
77–85 Fulham Palace Road,
Hammersmith, London W6 8JB

www.harpercollins.co.uk

This paperback edition 2006
1

First published in Great Britain by
HarperCollins*Publishers* 2005

ISBN 10: 0-00-714891-7
ISBN 13: 978-0-00-714891-2

Set in Sabon

Printed and bound in Great Britain by
Clays Ltd, St Ives plc

# Acknowledgments

Thanks for always generous help from:

Jürgen Atzgerstorfer, Terry Baier, Willa Baker, Guy Guthridge, George Hazelrigg, Charles Hess, Tim Highham, Neil Koehler, Rachel Park, Ann Russell, Tom St. Germain, Michael Schlesinger, Mark Schwartz, Jim Shea, Gary Snyder, Mark Thiemens, Buck Tilley, and Paul J. Werbos.

# Contents

# ONE

# *Primate In Forest*

Nobody likes Washington D.C. Even the people who love it don't like it. Climate atrocious, traffic worse: an ordinary midsized gridlocked American city, in which the plump white federal buildings make no real difference. Or rather they bring all the politicians and tourists, the lobbyists and diplomats and refugees and all the others who come from somewhere else, often for suspect reasons, and thereafter spend their time clogging the streets and hogging the show, talking endlessly about their non-existent city on a hill while ignoring the actual city they are in. The bad taste of all that hypocrisy can't be washed away even by the food and drink of a million very fine restaurants. No – bastion of the world government, locked vault of the world bank, fortress headquarters of the world police; Rome, in the age of bread and circuses; no one can like that.

So naturally when the great flood washed over the city, wreaking havoc and leaving the capital spluttering in the livid heat of a wet and bedraggled May, the stated reactions were various, but the underlying subtext often went something like this: HA HA HA. For there were many people around the world who felt that justice had somehow been served. Capital of the world, thoroughly trashed: who wouldn't love it?

*Of course the usual things were said by the usual parties. Disaster area, emergency relief, danger of epidemic, immediate restoration, pride of the nation, etc. Indeed, as capital of the world, the President was firm in his insistence that it was everyone's patriotic duty to support rebuilding, demonstrating a brave and stalwart response to what he called 'this act of climatic terrorism.' 'From now on,' the President continued, 'we are at a state of war with nature. We will work until we have made this city even more like it was than before.'*

*But truth to tell, ever since the Reagan era the conservative (or dominant) wing of the Republican party had been coming to Washington explicitly to destroy the federal government. They had talked about 'starving the beast,' but flooding would be fine if it came to that; they were flexible, it was results that counted. And how could the federal government continue to burden ordinary Americans when its center of operations was devastated? Why, it would have to struggle just to get back to normal! Obviously the flood was a punishment for daring to tax income and pretending to be a secular nation. One couldn't help thinking of Sodom and Gomorrah, the prophecies specified in the Book of Revelation, and so on.*

*Meanwhile, those on the opposite end of the political spectrum likewise did not shed very many tears over the disaster. As a blow to the heart of the galactic imperium it was a hard thing to regret. It might impede the ruling caste for a while, might make them acknowledge, perhaps, that their economic system had changed the climate, and that this was only the first of many catastrophic consequences. If Washington was denied now that it was begging for help, that was only what it had always done to its environmental victims in the past. Nature bats last – poetic justice – level playing field – reap what you sow – rich arrogant bastards – and so on.*

*Thus the flood brought pleasure to both sides of the aisle.*

And in the days that followed Congress made it clear in their votes, if not in their words, that they were not going to appropriate anything like the amount of money it would take to clean up the mess. They said it had to be done; they ordered it done; but they did not fund it.

The city therefore had to pin its hopes on either the beggared District of Columbia, which already knew all there was to know about unfunded mandates from Congress, to the extent that for years their license plates had proclaimed 'Taxation Without Representation;' or on the federal agencies specifically charged with disaster relief, like FEMA and the Army Corps of Engineers and others that could be expected to help in the ordinary course of their missions (and budgets).

Experts from these agencies tried to explain that the flood did not have a moral meaning, that it was merely a practical problem in city management, which had to be solved as a simple matter of public health, safety and convenience. The Potomac had ballooned into a temporary lake of about a thousand square miles; it had lasted no more than a week, but in that time inflicted great damage to the infrastructure. Much of the public part of the city was trashed. Rock Creek had torn out its banks, and the Mall was covered by mud; the Tidal Basin was now part of the river again, with the Jefferson Memorial standing in the shallows of the current. Many streets were blocked with debris; worse, in transport terms, many Metro tunnels had flooded, and would take months to repair. Alexandria was wrecked. Most of the region's bridges were knocked out or suspect. The power grid was uncertain, the sewage system likewise; epidemic disease was a distinct possibility.

Given all this, certain repairs simply had to be made, and many were the calls for full restoration. But whether these calls were greeted with genuine agreement, Tartuffian assent, stony indifference, or gloating opposition, the result was the same; not enough money was appropriated to complete the job.

*Only the essentials were dealt with. Necessary infrastructure, sure, almost; and of course the nationally famous buildings were cleaned up, the Mall replanted with grass and new cherry trees; the Vietnam Memorial excavated, the Lincoln and Jefferson Memorials recaptured from their island state. Congress debated a proposal to leave the high-water mark of greenish mud on the sides of the Washington Monument, as a flood-height record and a reminder of what could happen. But few wanted such a reminder, and in the end they rejected the idea. The stone of the great plinth was steam-cleaned, and around it the Mall began to look as if the flood had never happened. Elsewhere in the city, however . . .*

It was not a good time to have to look for a place to live.

And yet this was just what Frank Vanderwal had to do. He had leased his apartment for a year, covering the time he had planned to work for the National Science Foundation; then he had agreed to stay on for a second year. Now, only a month after the flood, his apartment had to be turned over to its owner, a State Department foreign service person he had never met, returning from a stint in Brazil. So he had to find someplace else.

No doubt the decision to stay another year had been a really bad idea.

This thought had weighed on him as he searched for a new apartment, and as a result he had not persevered as diligently as he ought to have. Very little was available in any case, and everything on offer was prohibitively expensive. Thousands of people had been drawn to D.C. by a flood that had also destroyed thousands of residences, and damaged thousands more beyond immediate repair and reoccupation. It was a real seller's market, and rents shot up accordingly.

Many of the places Frank had looked at were also physically repulsive in the extreme, including some that had been thrashed by the storm and not entirely cleaned up: the bottom of the barrel, still coated with sludge. The low point in this regard came in one semi-basement hole in Alexandria, a tiny dark place barred for safety at the door and the single high window, so that it looked like a prison for troglodytes; and two thousand a month. After that Frank's will to hunt was gone.

Now the day of reckoning had come. He had cleared out and cleaned up, the owner was due home that night, and Frank had nowhere to go.

It was a strange sensation. He sat at the kitchen counter in the dusk, strewn with the various sections of the *Post*. The 'Apartments for Rent' section was less than a column long, and Frank had learned enough of its code by now to know that it held nothing for him. More interesting had been an article in the day's Metro section about Rock Creek Park. Officially closed due to severe flood damage, it was apparently too large for the over-extended National Park Service to be able to enforce the edict. As a result the park had become something of a no-man's land, 'a return to wilderness,' as the article had put it.

Frank surveyed the apartment. It held no more memories for him than a hotel room, as he had done nothing but sleep there. That was all he had needed out of a home, his life proper having been put on hold until his return to San Diego. Now, well . . . it was like some kind of premature resuscitation, on a voyage between the stars. Time to wake up, time to leave the deep freeze and find out where he was.

He got up and went down to his car.

Out to the Beltway to circle north and then east, past the elongated Mormon temple and the great overpass graffiti referencing it: GO HOME DOROTHY! Get off on Wisconsin, drive in toward the city. There was no particular reason for him to visit this part of town. Of course the Quiblers lived over here, but that couldn't be it.

He kept thinking; Homeless person, homeless person. You are a homeless person. A song from Paul Simon's 'Graceland' came to him, the one where one of the South African groups kept singing, *Homeless; homeless, Da da da, da da da da da*

6

*da . . .* something like, *Midnight come, and then you wanna go home.* Or maybe it was a Zulu phrase. Or maybe, as he seemed to hear now: *Homeless; homeless; he go down to find another home.*

Something like that. He came to the intersection at the Bethesda Metro stop, and suddenly it occurred to him why he might be there. Of course – this was where he had met the woman in the elevator. They had gotten stuck together coming up from the Metro; alone together underground, minute after minute, until after a long talk they had started kissing, much to Frank's surprise. And then when the repair team had arrived and they were let out, the woman had disappeared without Frank learning anything about her, even her name. It made his heart pound just to remember it. Up there on the sidewalk to the right, beyond the red light – there stood the very elevator box they had emerged from. And then she had appeared to him again, on a boat in the Potomac during the height of the great flood. He had called her boat on his cell phone, and she had answered, had said, 'I'll call. I don't know when.'

The red light turned green. She had not called and yet here he was, driving back to where they had met as if he might catch sight of her. Maybe he had even been thinking that if he found her, he would have a place to stay.

That was silly; an example of magical thinking at its most unrealistic. And he had to admit that in the past couple of weeks he had been looking for apartments in this area. So it was not just an isolated impulse, but a pattern of behavior.

Just past the intersection he turned into the Hyatt driveway. A valet approached and Frank said, 'Do you know if there are any rooms available here?'

'Not if you don't got a reservation.'

Frank hurried into the lobby to check anyway. A receptionist shook her head: no vacancies. She wasn't aware of the situation at any other hotel. The ones in their chain were full all over the metropolitan area.

7

Frank got back in his car and drove onto Wisconsin heading south, peering at the elevator kiosk when he passed it. She had given a fake name on the Metro forms they had been asked to fill out. She would not be there now.

Down Wisconsin, past the Quibler's house a couple of blocks over to the right. That was what had brought him to this part of town, on the night he and the woman got stuck in the elevator. Anna Quibler, one of his colleagues at NSF, had hosted a party for the Khembali ambassador, who had given a lecture at NSF earlier that day. A nice party. An excess of reason is itself a form of madness, the old ambassador had said to Frank. Frank was still pondering what that meant, and if it were true, how he might act on it.

But he couldn't visit Anna and her family now. Showing up unannounced, with no place to go – it would have been pitiful.

He drove on. *Homeless, homeless – he go down to find another home.*

Chevy Chase looked relatively untouched by the flood. There was a giant hotel above Dupont Circle, the Hilton; he drove down Wisconsin and Massachusetts and turned up Florida to it, already feeling like he was wasting his time. There would be no rooms available.

There weren't. 'Homeless, homeless. Midnight come, and blah blah blah blah blahhhh.'

He drove up Connecticut Avenue, completely without a plan. Near the entrance to the National Zoo damage from the flood suddenly became obvious, in the form of a mud-based slurry of trash and branches covering the sidewalks and staining the storefronts. Just north of the zoo, traffic stopped to allow the passage of a backhoe. Street repairs by night, in the usual way. Harsh blue spotlights glared on a scene like something out of Soviet cinema, giant machines dwarfing a cityscape.

Impatiently Frank turned right onto a side street. He found

an empty parking spot on one of the residential streets east of Connecticut, parked in it.

He got out and walked back to the clean-up scene. It was still about 90 degrees out, and tropically humid. A strong smell of mud and rotting vegetation evoked the tropics, or Atlantis after the flood. Yes, he was feeling a bit apocalyptic. He was in the end time of something, there was no denying it. *Home-less; home-less.*

A Spanish restaurant caught his eye. He went over to look at the menu in the window. Tapas. He went in, sat down and ordered. Excellent food, as always. D.C. could almost always be relied on for that. Surely it must be the great restaurant city of the world.

He finished his meal, left the restaurant and wandered the streets, feeling better. He had been hungry before, and had mistaken that for anxiety. Things were not so bad.

He passed his car but walked on east toward Rock Creek Park, remembering the article in the *Post*. A return to wilderness.

At Broad Branch Road Frank came to the park's boundary. There was no one visible in any direction. It was dark under the trees on the other side of the road; the yellow streetlights behind him illuminated nothing beyond the first wall of leaves.

He crossed the street and walked into the forest.

The flood's vegetable stench was strong. Frank proceeded slowly; if there had been any trail here before it was gone now, replaced by windrows of branches and trash, and an uneven deposition of mud. The rootballs of toppled trees splayed up dimly, and snags caught at his feet. As his eyes adjusted to the darkness he came to feel that everything was very slightly illuminated, mostly no doubt by the luminous city cloud that chinked every gap in the black canopy.

He heard a rustle, then a voice. Without thought he slipped

behind a large tree and froze there, heart pounding.

Two voices were arguing, one of them drunk.

'Why you buy this shit?'

'Hey you never buy anything. You need to give some, man.'

The two passed by and continued down the slope to the east, their voices rasping through the trees. *Home-less, home-less*. Their voices had reminded Frank of the scruffy guys in fatigues who hung out around Dupont Circle.

Frank didn't want to deal with any such people. He was annoyed; he wanted to be out in a pure wilderness, empty in the way his mountains out west were empty. Instead, harsh laughter nicotined through the trees like hatchet strokes. 'Ha ha ha harrrrrr.' There went the neighborhood.

He slipped off in a different direction, down through windrows of detritus, then over hardened mud between trees. Branches clicked damply underfoot. It got steeper than he thought it would, and he stepped sideways to keep from slipping.

Then he heard another sound, quieter than the voices. A soft rustle and a creak, then a faint crack from the forest below and ahead. Something moving.

Frank froze. The hair on the back of his neck was standing up. Whatever it was, it sounded big. The article in the *Post* had mentioned that many of the animals from the National Zoo had not yet been recaptured. All had been let loose just before the zoo was inundated, to give them a chance of surviving. Some had drowned anyway; most had been recovered afterward; but not all. Frank couldn't remember if any species in particular had been named in the article as being still at large. It was a big park of course. Possibly a jaguar had been mentioned.

He tried to meld into the tree he was leaning against.

Whatever it was below him snapped a branch just a few trees away. It sniffed; almost a snort. It was big, no doubt about it.

Frank could no longer hold his breath, but he found that if he let his mouth hang open, he could breathe without a sound. The tock of his heartbeat in the soft membrane at the back of his throat must surely be more a feeling than a sound. Most animals relied on scent anyway, and there was nothing he could do about his scent. A thought that could reduce one's muscles to jelly.

The creature had paused. It huffed. A musky odor that wafted by was almost like the smell of the flood detritus. His heart tocked like Captain Hook's alarm clock.

A slow scrape, as of shoulder against bark. Another branch click. A distant car horn. The smell now resembled damp fur. Another crunch of leaf and twig, farther down the slope.

When he heard nothing more, and felt that he was alone again, he beat a retreat uphill and west, back to the streets of the city. It was frustrating, because now he was intrigued, and wanted to explore the park further. But he didn't want to end up one of those urban fools who ignored the reality of wild animals and then got chomped. Whatever that had been down there, it was big. Best to be prudent, and return another time.

After the gloom of the park, all Connecticut seemed as garishly illuminated as the work site down the street. Walking back to his car, Frank thought that the neighborhood resembled one of the more handsome Victorian districts of San Francisco. It was late now, the night finally cooling off. He could drive all night and never find a room.

He stood before his car. The Honda's passenger seat tilted back like a little recliner. The nearest streetlight was down at the corner.

He opened the passenger door, moved the seat all the way back, lowered it, slipped in and sat down. He closed the door, lay back, stretched out. After a while he turned on his side and fell into an uneasy sleep.

For an hour or two. Then passing footsteps woke him. Anyone could see him if they looked. They might tap the window to see if he was okay. He would have to claim to be a visiting reporter, unable to find a room – very close to the truth, like all the best lies. He could claim to be anyone really. Out here he was not bound to his real story.

He lay awake, uncomfortable in the seat, pretty sure he would not be able to fall back asleep; then he was lightly under, dreaming about the woman in the elevator. A part of his mind became aware that this was unusual, and he fought to stay submerged despite that realization. He was speaking to her about something urgent. Her face was so clear, it had imprinted so vividly: passionate and amused in the elevator, grave and distant on the boat in the flood. He wasn't sure he liked what she was telling him. Just call me, he insisted. Give me that call and we can work it out.

Then the noise of a distant siren hauled him up, sweaty and unhappy. He lay there a while longer, thinking about the woman's face. Once in high school he had made out with a girl in a little car like this one, in which the laid-back seat had allowed them somehow to lie on each other. He wanted her. He wanted to find her. From the boat she had said she would call. I don't know how long, she had said. Maybe that meant long. He would just have to wait. Unless he could figure out some new way to hunt for her.

The sky was lightening. Now he definitely wouldn't be able to fall back asleep. With a groan he heaved himself up, got out of the car.

He stood on the sidewalk, feeling wasted. The sky was a velvet gray, seeming darker than it had in the middle of the night. The air was cool. He walked east again, back into the park.

Dew polished the thick gray foliage. In the diffuse low light the wet leaves looked like a forest of wax. Frank slowed down. He saw what looked like a trail, perhaps an animal trail. There were lots of deer in the park, the article had said. He could hear the sound of Rock Creek, a burbling that as he descended overwhelmed the city sounds, the perpetual grumble of trucking. The sky was lightening fast, and what had seemed to him cloud cover was revealed as a clear pale sky. Dim greens began to flush the grays. The air was still cool.

It turned out that in this area Rock Creek ran at the bottom of a fairly steep ravine, and the flood had torn the sidewalls away in places, as he saw when he came to a sudden drop-off. Below him, bare sandstone extruded roots like ripped wiring. He circled above the drop, dodging between low trees.

From a little clearing he could suddenly see downstream. The flood in spate had torn the little canyon clear. Everything that had been down there before – Beach Road, the small bridges and buildings, the ranger station, the picnic areas – all of it was gone, leaving a raw zone of bare sandstone, flat mud, thrashed grass, downed timber, and stubborn trees that were either clinging to life or dead in place. Many trees had been knocked over and yet held on by a few roots, forming living snags piled high with mud and trash. A larger snag downstream looked like a giant beaver dam, creating a dirt-brown pond.

The sky stood big and blue overhead, a tall dome that seemed to rise as the day lightened. Muddy Rock Creek burbled noisily down its course, spilling from one foamy brown stretch to the next.

At the far edge of the pond a heron strode slowly, its knees bending backward. Long body, long legs, long neck, long head, long beak. A great blue heron, Frank guessed, though this one's dark gray feathers looked more green than blue. A kind of dinosaur. And indeed nothing could have looked more pterodactylic. Two hundred million years.

Sunlight blazed green at the tops of the trees across the ravine. Frank and the heron stood attentively, listening to unseen smaller birds whose wild twittering now filled the air. The heron's head cocked to one side. For a time everything was as still as bronze.

Then beyond the twittering came a different sound, fluid and clear, rising like a siren, like a hook in the flesh:

*Ooooooooooooooooooop!*

National Science Foundation, Arlington Virginia, basement parking lot, seven AM. A primate sitting in his car, thinking things over. As one of the editors of *The Journal of Sociobiology* Frank was very much aware of the origins of their species. The third chimp, as Diamond had put it. Now he thought: chimps sleep outdoors. Bonobos sleep outdoors.

Housing was ultimately an ergonomic problem. What did he really need? His belongings were here in the car, or upstairs in his office, or in boxes at UCSD, or in storage units in Encinitas, California, or down the road in Arlington, Virginia. The fact that stuff was in storage showed how much it really mattered. By and large he was free of worldly things. At age forty-three he no longer needed them. That felt a little strange, actually, but not necessarily bad. Did it feel good? It was hard to tell. It simply felt strange.

He got out of his car and took the elevator to the third floor, where there was a little exercise room, with a men's room off its entryway that included showers. In his shoulder bag he carried his laptop, his cell phone, his bathroom kit, and a change of clothes. The three shower stalls stood behind white curtains, near an area with benches and lockers. Beyond it extended the room containing toilets, urinals, and a counter of sinks under a long mirror.

Frank knew the place, having showered and changed in it many times after runs at lunch with Edgardo and Kenzo and Bob and the others. Now he surveyed it with a new regard. It was as he remembered: an adequate bathroom, public but serviceable.

14

He undressed and got in one of the showers. A flood of hot water, almost industrial in quantity, washed away some of the stiffness of his uncomfortable night. Of course no one would want to be seen showering there every day. Not that anyone was watching, but some of the morning exercisers would eventually notice.

A membership in some nearby exercise club would provide an alternative bathroom.

What else did one need?

Somewhere to sleep, of course. The Honda would not suffice. If he had a van, and an exercise club membership, and this locker room, and his office upstairs, and the men's rooms up there . . . As for food, the city had a million restaurants.

What else?

Nothing he could think of. Many people more or less lived in this building, all the NSF hardcores who spent sixty or seventy hours a week here, ate their meals at their desks or in the neighborhood restaurants, only went home to sleep – and these were people with families, with kids, homes, pets, partners!

In a crowd like that it would be hard to stick out.

He got out of the shower, dried off (a stack of fresh white towels was there at hand), shaved, dressed.

He glanced in the mirror over the sink, feeling a bit shy. He didn't look at himself in mirrors anymore, never met his eye when shaving, stayed focused on the skin under the blade. He didn't know why. Maybe it was because he did not resemble his conception of himself, which was vaguely scientific and serious, say Darwinesque; and yet there in the glass getting shaved was always the same old sun-fried jock.

But this time he looked. To his surprise he saw that he looked normal – that was to say, the same as always. Normative. No one would be able to guess by his appearance that he was sleep-deprived, that he had been thinking

15

some pretty abnormal thoughts, or, crucially, that he had spent the previous night in his car because he no longer had a home.

'Hmm,' he told his reflection.

He took the elevator up to the tenth floor, still thinking it over. He stood in the doorway of his new office, evaluating the place by these new inhabitory criteria. It was a true room, rather than a carrel in a larger space, so it had a door he could close. It boasted one of the big inner windows looking into the building's central atrium, giving him a direct view of the big colored mobile that filled the atrium's upper half.

This view was unfortunate, actually. He didn't want to look at that mobile, for not too long ago he had found himself hanging upside down from it, in the middle of the night, working desperately to extricate himself from an ill-conceived and poorly executed break-and-enter job. He had been trying and failing to recover a poorly-worded resignation letter he had left for Diane Chang, the NSF director. It was an incident he would really rather forget.

But there the mobile hung, at the new angle which Frank had given to it and which no one had noticed, perhaps a reminder to – to what? To try not to do stupid things. To think things through before attempting them. But he always tried to do that, so the reminder was unnecessary. Really, the mobile outside his window was a disadvantage. But drapes could be installed.

There was room for a short couch against one wall, if he moved the bookcase there to the opposite corner. It would then be like a kind of living room, with the computer as entertainment center. There was an ordinary men's room around the corner, a coffee nook down the hall, the showers downstairs. All the necessities. As Sucandra had remarked, at dinner once at the Quiblers', tasting spaghetti sauce with a wooden spoon: Ahhhh – what now is lacking?

Same answer: Nothing.

It had to be admitted that it made him uneasy to be contemplating this idea. Unsettled. It was deranged, in the literal sense of being outside the range. Typically people did not choose to live without a home. No home to go home to; it was perhaps a little crazy.

But in some obscure way, that aspect pleased him too. It was not crazy in the way that breaking into the building through the skylight had been crazy; but it shared that act's commitment to an idea. And was it any crazier than handing well over half of your monthly take-home income to pay for seriously crappy lodging?

Nomadic existence. Life outdoors. So often he had thought about, read about, and written about the biological imperatives in human behavior – about their primate nature, and the evolutionary history that had led to humanity's paleolithic lifestyle, which was the suite of behaviors that had caused their brains to balloon as rapidly as they had; and about the residual power of all that in modern life. And all the while, through all that thinking, reading, and writing, he had been sitting at a desk. Living like every other professional worker in America, a brain in a bottle, working with his fingertips or his voice or simply his thoughts alone, distracted sometimes by daydreams about the brief bursts of weekend activity that would get him back into his body again.

That was what was crazy, living like that when he held the beliefs he did.

Now he was considering acting in accordance with his beliefs. Something else he had heard the Khembalis say at the Quiblers', this time Drepung: If you don't act on it, it wasn't a true feeling.

He wanted these to be true feelings. Everything had changed for him on that day he had gone to the Khembali ambassador's talk, and then run into the woman in the elevator, and afterward talked to Drepung at the Quiblers' party, and then, yes, broken into the NSF building and tried to recover his resignation. Everything had changed! Or so it had felt; so it felt still. But for it to be a true feeling, he had to act on it.

Meaning also, as part of all these new behaviors, that he had to meet with Diane Chang, and work with her on coordinating NSF's response to the climate situation that was implicated in the great flood and many other things.

This would be awkward. His letter of resignation, which Diane had never directly acknowledged receiving, was now an acute embarrassment to him. It had been an irrational attempt to burn his bridges, and by all rights he should now be back in San Diego with nothing but the stench of smoke behind him. Instead, Diane appeared to have read the letter and then ignored it, or rather, considered how to use it to play him like a fish, and reel him back into NSF for another year of service. Which she had done very skillfully.

So now he found that he had to stifle a certain amount of resentment as he went up to see her. He had to meet her secretary Laveta's steely eye without flinching; pretend, as the impassive black woman waved him in, that all was normal. No way of telling how much she knew about his situation.

Diane sat behind her desk, talking on the phone. She gestured for him to sit down. Graceful hands. Short, Chinese-American, good-looking in an exotic way, businesslike but friendly. A subtly amused expression on her face when she listened to people, as if pleased to hear their news.

As now, with Frank. Although it could be amusement at his resignation letter, and the way she had jiu-jitsued him into staying at NSF. So hard to tell with Diane; and her manner, though friendly, did not invite personal conversation.

'You're into your new office?' she asked.

'My stuff is, anyway. It'll take a while to sort out.'

'Sure. Like everything else these days! What a mess it all is. I have Kenzo and some of his group coming this morning to tell us more about the Gulf Stream.'

18

'Good.'

Kenzo and a couple of his colleagues in climate duly appeared. They exchanged hellos, got out laptops, and Kenzo started working the Power Point on Diane's wall screen.

All the data, Kenzo explained, indicated stalls in what he called the 'thermohaline circulation.' At the north ends of the Gulf Stream, where the water on the surface normally cooled and sank to the floor of the Atlantic before heading back south, a particularly fresh layer on the surface had stalled the downwelling. With nowhere to go, the water in the current farther south had slowed to a halt.

What was more, Kenzo said, just such a stall in the thermohaline circulation had been identified as the primary cause of the abrupt climate change that paleoclimatologists had named the Younger Dryas, a bitter little ice age that had begun about eleven thousand years before the present, and lasted for a few thousand years. The hypothesis was that the Gulf Stream's shutdown, after floods of fresh water coming off the melting ice cap over North America, had meant immediately colder temperatures in Europe and the eastern half of North America. This accounted for the almost unbelievably quick beginning of the Younger Dryas, which analysis of the Greenland ice cores revealed had happened in only three years. Three years, for a major global shift from the worldwide pattern that climatologists called warm-wet, to the worldwide pattern called cool-dry-windy. It was such a radical notion that it had forced climatologists to acknowledge that there must be nonlinear tipping points in the global climate, leading to general acceptance of what was really a new concept in climatology: abrupt climate change.

'What caused the stall again?' Diane said.

Kenzo clicked to the next slide, an image of the Earth portraying the immense ice cap that had covered much of the northern hemisphere throughout the last ice age. The end of that one had arrived slowly, in the old-fashioned linear way, melting the top of the ice cap and creating giant lakes that rested on the remaining ice. These lakes had been held in place by ice dams that were themselves melting, and when the dams had at last given way, extraordinarily large floods of fresh water had rushed down into the ocean, emptying volumes as large as the Great Lakes in a matter of weeks. Signs left on the landscape indicated this had happened down the watersheds of the St. Lawrence, the Hudson, and the Mississippi, and out west, a lake covering most of Montana had drained down the course of the Columbia River several times, leaving an area in Washington called the scablands which gave eloquent testimony to the power of these floods to tear into the bedrock. Presumably the same thing had happened on the East Coast, but the signs had mostly been submerged by rising sea levels or the great eastern forest, so that they were only now being discerned.

Frank, looking at the map on the screen, thought of how Rock Creek had looked that morning at dawn. Theirs had been a very tiny flood relative to the ones Kenzo was describing, and yet the watershed was devastated.

So, Kenzo continued, fresh water, dumped into the North Atlantic all at once, appeared to block the thermohaline cycle. And nowadays, for the last several years, the Arctic Ocean's winter sea ice had been breaking up into great fleets of icebergs, which then sailed south on currents until they encountered the Gulf Stream's warm water, where they melted. The melting zones for these icebergs, as a map on the next slide made clear, were just above the northern ends of the Gulf Stream, the so-called downwelling areas. Meanwhile the Greenland ice cap and glaciers were also melting much faster than had been normal, and running off both sides of that great island.

'How much fresh water in all that?' Diane asked.

Kenzo shrugged. 'The Arctic is about ten million square kilometers. The sea ice lately is about five meters thick. Not all of that drifts into the Atlantic, of course. There was a paper that estimated that about twenty thousand cubic kilometers of fresh water had diluted the Arctic over the past thirty years, but it was plus or minus five thousand cubic kilometers.'

'Let's get better parameters on that figure, if we can,' Diane said.

'Sure.'

They stared at the final slide. The implications tended to stall on the surface of the mind, Frank thought, like the water in the north Atlantic, refusing to gyre down. The whole world, ensconced in a global climate mode called warm and wet, and getting warmer and wetter because of global warming caused by anthropogenically released greenhouse gases, could switch to a global pattern that was cold, dry, and windy. And the last time it happened, it had taken three years. Hard to believe; but the Greenland ice core data were very clear, and the rest of the case equally persuasive – one might even say, in science's distinctive vocabulary of levels of certainty, compelling.

When Kenzo and his team had left, Diane turned to Frank. 'What do you think?'

'It looks serious. It may get people to take action.'

'Except by now it may be too late.'

'Yes.'

They considered that in silence for a few moments, and then Diane said, 'Let's talk about your second year here, how to organize it to get the most out of you.'

That was a pretty blunt way to put it, given Diane's manipulations, but Frank was careful not to express any resentment. 'Sure,' he said. It had been documented that if you forced your face to take on pleasant expressions, your mood tended helplessly to follow. So, small smile of acceptance; pull chair up to desk.

They worked their way down a list Diane had made identifying areas where NSF might do something to deal with the impacts of abrupt climate change. As they did Frank saw that Diane was well ahead of him in thinking about these matters, which he found a little surprising, although of course it made sense; otherwise why would she have wanted him to stay another year? His letter would not have been what brought her the news of NSF's ineffectiveness in dealing with a crisis situation.

She spoke very quickly. Slightly fog-minded, Frank struggled to keep up, looking at her more closely than ever before. Of course every face was inscrutable in the end. Diane's was dramatically planed, cheekbones, forehead, and jaw all distinct and somehow angled to each other. Formal; formidable. Asian dragon lady, yes. She drew the eye. She was about ten years Frank's senior, he had gathered; a widow, he had heard; had been NSF head for a long time, Frank wasn't sure how long. Famous for her incredibly long work days. They used to call people like her workaholics before everyone got up to speed and the concept had gone away. Once Edgardo had said of Diane, she makes Anna look like a slacker, and Frank had shuddered, because Anna was a veritable maniac for work. Anything beyond that pretty much had to be insane. And this was who he was going to be working for.

Well, fine. He had not stayed in D.C. to fool around. He too wanted to work long hours. And now it was clear he would have Diane's ear and her support, therefore the co-operation of anyone needed at NSF; things would therefore get done. That was the only thing that would make staying in Washington bearable.

He focused on her list:

- Coordinate already existing federal programs
- Establish new institutes and programs where necessary
- Work with Sophie Harper, NSF's congressional liaison officer, to contact and educate all the relevant Congressional

committees and staffs, and help craft appropriate legislation
- Work with the Intergovernmental Panel on Climate Change, the UN Environmental Program, its Millennial Project, and other international efforts
- Identify, evaluate and rank all potential climate mitigation possibilities: clean energy, carbon sequestration, etc.

This last item, to Frank, would create the real *Things To Do* list.

'We'll have to go to New York and talk to people about that stuff,' Diane said.

'Yes.'

It would be interesting to watch her there. Asian martial arts were often about turning one's opponents' force against them. Certainly she had floored Frank that way. Maybe the rest of the world would follow.

But reviewing the list, he felt a surge of impatience. He tried to express this to Diane politely: he didn't want to spend his extra year starting studies. He wanted to find where small applications of money and effort could trigger larger actions. He wanted to *do* things. If the weather was going to heat up, he wanted to cool it. If vice versa, then vice versa. He wanted to identify a viable new energy generation system, he wanted to sequester billions of tons of carbon, he wanted to minimize human suffering and the loss of other species. He wanted impossible things! Quickly he scribbled a new list for their mutual inspection:

- direct climate mitigation
- carbon sequestration (bio, physical)
- water cycle interventions
- clean renewable energy (biomass, solar, wave, tide, wind)
- political action
- a new paradigm (permaculture)

Diane read the list. Her expression of subtle amusement became a full smile, perfectly scrutable.

'You think big.'

'Well, it's a big situation. I mean even the Gulf Stream stall is only a proximate cause. The ultimate causes have to do with the whole situation. Carbon, consumption, population, technology, all that. We'll have to try to take all that on if we're going to actually do something.'

'There are other agencies working on these things. In fact, lots of this isn't really our purview.'

'Yes, well, but – we are the National Science Foundation,' emphasizing the words. 'It isn't really clear yet just how big a purview such an organization should have. Given the importance of science in this world, you could argue that it should be pretty much everything. But for sure it should be the place to coordinate the scientific effort. Beyond that, who knows? It's a new situation.'

'True,' she said, still smiling at him in her amused way. 'Well, okay! Let's go get some lunch and talk about it.'

Frank tried to conceal his surprise. 'Sure.'


The hotel above the Ballston Metro offered a buffet lunch that was so fancy that it redefined the concept. The restaurant was cool and quiet, decorated in the finest American Hotel Anonymous. Diane appeared to know it well, and to have a hidden corner table reserved. She filled a big plate with salad and some strips of seared flank steak, and took no bread. Iced tea without sugar. She was dressed in a businesslike skirt and heavy silk blouse, and Frank saw as he followed her that it was all perfectly tailored and fitted, and looked expensive. She moved gracefully, looked strong. Usually Frank's eye was not attracted to short women, but when it happened it was a matter of proportion, a kind of regal bearing. She wore flat shoes, and did not seem attentive to herself. Probably, judging by her food, thought of herself as overweight. But she looked good.

The irrepressible sociobiologist that was always theorizing inside Frank wondered if he was experiencing some bias here, given that she was a powerful alpha female, and his boss. Perhaps all alpha females were somehow physically impressive, and this part of their alpha-ness; it was generally true of males.

They sat, ate, spoke of other things. Frank asked about her kids.

'Grown up and moved out. It's easier now.' She spoke offhandedly, as if talking about a matter that did not really concern her. 'How could it not be.'

'For a while it must have been busy.'

'Oh yes.'

'Where were you before NSF?'

'University of Washington. Biophysics. Then I got into administration there, then at triple A S, then NIH. Now here.' She shrugged, as if to admit that she might have gone down a wrong path somewhere. 'What about you? What brought you to NSF?'

Well, I gambled with equity that wasn't entirely mine, lost it, went through a break-up, needed to get away . . .

It wasn't a story he wanted to tell. Maybe no one's story could really be told. She had not mentioned her late husband, for instance. She would understand if he only spoke of his scientific reasons for coming to NSF: new work in bio-algorithms, needed a wider perspective to see what was out there, a year visiting NSF good for that – and so on.

She nodded, watching him with that amused expression, as if to say, I know this is only part of the story but it's still interesting. He liked that. No wonder she had risen so high. Alpha females pursued different strategies than alpha males to achieve their goals; their alpha-ness derived from different social qualities.

'What about your living situation?' she asked. 'Were you able to stay in the place you had?'

Startled, Frank said, 'No. I was renting from a State Department guy who came back.'

'So you managed to find another place?'

'Yes . . . For the moment I'm in a temporary place, and I've got some leads for a permanent one.'

'That's good. It must be tough right now, with the flood.'

'That's for sure. It's gotten very expensive.'

'I bet. Let me know if we can help with that.'

'Thanks, I will.'

He wondered what she meant, but did not want to ask. 'One thing I'm looking into is joining an exercise club around here, and Anna mentioned that you went to one?'

'Yes, I go to the Optimodal.'

'Do you like it?'

'Sure, it's okay. It's not too expensive, and it has all the usual stuff. And it's not just kids showing off. Most days I just get on a treadmill and go.' She laughed. 'Like a rat on a wheel.'

Just like at work, Frank didn't say.

'Actually I've been trying more of the machines,' she added. 'It's fun.'

Frank got the address from her, and they went back to the serving area for pie and ice cream (her portion small), and talked a bit more about work. She never made even the slightest hint of reference to his letter of resignation. That was strange enough to disturb his sense of being in a normal professional relationship. It was as if she were in some way holding it over him.

Then, walking in the covered walkway above the street to the NSF building, she said, 'Let's set up a regular meeting between us for every two weeks, and add more if you need to. I want to be kept up on what you're thinking.'

Quickly he glanced down at her. She kept looking at the glass doors they were approaching.

'That's the best way to avoid any misunderstandings,' she went on, still not looking at him. Then, as they reached the doors to their building, she said, 'I want something to come of this.'

'Me too,' he assured her. 'Believe me.'

They approached the security desk. 'So what will you do first?' she asked, as if something had been settled between them.

'To tell the truth, I think I'll go see about joining that health club.'

She grinned. 'Good idea. I'll see you there sometimes.'

He nodded. 'And, as far as the working committee, I'll start making calls and setting it up. I'd like to get Edgardo on it too, if you think that would be okay.'

She laughed. 'If you can talk him into it.'

So. Frank returned to his office, collecting his thoughts. A workman was there installing a power strip on the newly exposed wall behind his desk, and he waited patiently until the man left. He sat at the desk, swiveled and looked out the window at the mobile in the atrium.

He had spent the night in his car and then lunched with the director of the National Science Foundation, and no one was the wiser. He did feel a little spacy. But when appearances were maintained, no one could tell. Nothing obvious gave it away. One retained a certain privacy.

Remembering a resolution he had made that morning, he picked up the phone and called the National Zoo.

'Hi, I'm calling to ask about zoo animals that might still be at large?'

'Sure, let me pass you to Nancy.'

Nancy came on and said hi in a friendly voice, and Frank told her about hearing what seemed like a big animal, near the edge of the park at night. 'Do you have a list of zoo animals still on the loose?'

'Sure, it's on our website. Do you want to join our group?'

'What do you mean?'

'There's a committee of the volunteer group, FONZ? Friends of the National Zoo. You can join that, it's called the Feral Observation Group.'

'The FOG?'

'Yes. We're all in the FOG now, right?'

'Yes.'

She gave him the website address, and he checked it out. It turned out to be a good one. Some 1500 Fonzies already. There was a page devoted to the Khembalis' swimming tigers, and on the FOG page, a list of the animals that had been spotted, as well as a separate list for animals missing since the flood and not yet seen. There was a jaguar on this list. And gibbons had been seen, eight of them, white-cheeked gibbons, along with three siamangs. Almost always in Rock Creek Park.

'Hmmm.' Frank recalled the cry he had heard at dawn, pursued the creatures through the web pages. Gibbons and siamangs both hooted in a regular dawn chorus; siamangs were even louder than gibbons, being larger. Could be heard six miles rather than one.

It looked like being in FOG might confer permission to go into Rock Creek Park. You couldn't observe animals in a park you were forbidden to enter. He called Nancy back. 'Do FOG members get to go into Rock Creek Park?'

'Some do. We usually go in groups, but we have some individual permits you can check out.'

'Cool. Tell me how I do that.'

He left the building and walked down Wilson and up a side street, to the Optimodal Health Club. Diane had said it was within easy walking distance, and it was. That was good; and the place looked okay. Actually he had always preferred getting his 'exercise' outdoors, by doing something challenging. Up until now he had felt that clubs like these were mostly just another way to commodify leisure time, in this case changing

28

things people used to do outdoors, for free, into things they paid to do inside. Silly as such.

But if you needed to rent a bathroom, they were great.

So he did his best to remain expressionless (resulting in a visage unusually grim) while he gave the young woman at the desk a credit card, and signed the forms. Full membership, no. Personal trainer ready to take over his thinking about his body but without incurring any legal liability, no way. He did pay extra for a permanent locker in which to store some of his stuff. Another bathroom kit there, another change of clothes; it would all come in useful.

He followed his guide around the rooms of the place, keeping his expressionless expression firmly in place. By the time he was done, the poor girl looked thoroughly unsettled.

Back at NSF he went into the basement to his Honda.

A great little car. But now it did not serve the purpose. He drove west on Wilson for a long time, until he came to the Honda/Ford/Lexus dealer where he had leased this car a year before. In this one aspect of the fiasco that was remaining in D.C., his timing was good; he needed to re-up for another year, and the eager salesman handling him was happy to hear that this time he wanted to lease an Odyssey van. One of the best vans on the road, as the man told him as they walked out to view one. Also one of the smallest, Frank didn't say.

Dull silver, the most anonymous color around, like a cloak of invisibility. Rear seat removal, yes; therefore room in back for his single mattress, now in storage. Tinted windows all around the back, creating a pretty high degree of privacy. It was almost as good as the VW van he had lived in for a couple of Yosemite summers, parked in the Camp Four parking lot enjoying the stove and refrigerator and pop-top in his tiny motor home. Culturally the notion of small vehicle as home had crashed since then, having been based on a beat/hippie idea of frugality that had lost out to the usual American excess, to the point of being made illegal by a Congress bought by the auto industry. No stoves allowed in little vans, of course! Had to house them in giant Rvs.

But this Odyssey would serve the purpose. Frank skimmed the lease terms, signed the forms. He saw that he might need to rent a post office box. But maybe the NSF address would do.

Walking back out to take possession of his new bedroom, he and the salesman passed a line of parked SUV – tall fat station wagons, in effect, called Expedition or Explorer, absurdities for the generations to come to shake their heads at in the way they once marveled at the finned cars of the fifties. 'Do people still buy these?' Frank asked despite himself.

'Sure, what do you mean? Although now you mention it, there is some surplus here at the end of the year.' It was May. 'Long story short, gas is getting too expensive. I drive one of these,' tapping a Lincoln Navigator. 'They're great. They've got a couple of TVs in the back.'

But they're stupid, Frank didn't say. In prisoner's dilemma terms, they were always-defect. They were America saying Fuck Off to the rest of the world. Deliberate waste, in a kind of ritual desecration. Not just denial but defiance, a Götterdämmerung gesture that said: If we're going down we're going to take the whole world with us. And the roads were full of them. And the Gulf Stream had stopped.

'Amazing,' Frank said.

His drove his new Odyssey directly to the storage place in Arlington where he had rented a unit. He liked the feel of the van; it drove like a car. In front of his storage unit he took out its back seats, put them in the oversized metal-and-concrete closet, less than half full with his stuff; took his single mattress out and laid it in the back of the van. Perfect fit. He could use the same sheets and pillows he had been using in his apartment.

'Home – less, home – less. Ha ha ha, ha ha ha ho ho ho.'

He could sort through the rest of his stored stuff later on. Possibly very little of it would ever come out of boxes again.

He locked up and drove to the Beltway, around in the jam to Wisconsin Avenue, down into the city. The newly ritualized pass by the elevator kiosk at Bethesda. Now he could have dropped in on the Quiblers without feeling pitiful, even though in most respects his circumstances had not changed since the night before; but now he had a plan. And a van. And this time he didn't want to stop. Over to Connecticut, down to the neighborhood north of the zoo, turn onto the same street he had the night before. He noted how the establishing of habits was part of the homing instinct.

Most streets in this neighborhood were permit parking by day and open parking by night, except for the one night a week they were cleaned. Once parked, the van became perfectly nondescript. Equidistant from two driveways; streetlight near but not too near. He would learn the full drill only by practicing it, but this street looked to be a good one.

Out and up Connecticut. Edward Hopper tableaux, end of the day. The streetwork waiting on the sidewalks for rush hour to be over and the night work to begin. It was mostly retail on this part of Connecticut, with upscale apartments and offices behind, then the residential neighborhood, no doubt extremely expensive even though the houses were not big. Like anywhere else in D.C., there were restaurants from all over the world. It wasn't just that one could get Ethiopian or Azeri, but that there would be choices: Hari food from southern Ethiopia, or Sudanese style from the north? Good, bad or superb Lebanese?

Having grown up in southern California, Frank could never get used to this array. These days he was fondest of the Middle Eastern and Mediterranean cuisines, and this area of

Northwest was rich in both, so that he had to think about which one he wanted, and whether to eat in or do take-out. Eating alone in a restaurant he would have to have something to read. Funny how reading in a restaurant was okay, while watching a laptop or talking on a cell phone was not. Actually, judging by the number of laptops visible in the taverna at the corner of Connecticut and Brandywine, that custom had already changed. Maybe they were reading from their laptops. That might be okay. He would have to try it and see how it felt.

He decided to do take-out. It was dinner time but there was still lots of light left to the day; he could take a meal out into the park and enjoy the sunset. He walked on Connecticut until he came on a Greek restaurant that would put dolmades and calamari in paper boxes, with a dill yogurt sauce in a tiny plastic container. Too bad about the ouzo and retsina, only sold in the restaurant; he liked those tastes. He ordered an ouzo to drink while waiting for his food, downing it before the ice cubes even got a chance to turn it milky.

Back on the street. The taste of licorice enveloped him like a key signature, black and sweet. Steamy dusk of spring, hazed with blossom dust. Sweatslipping past two women; something in their sudden shared laughter set him to thinking about his woman from the elevator. Would she call? And if so, when? And what would she say, and what would he say? A licorish mood, an anticipation of lust, like a wolf whistle in his mind. Vegetable smell of the flood. The two women had been so beautiful. Washington was like that.

The food in his paper sack was making him hungry, so he turned east and walked into Rock Creek Park, following a path that eventually brought him to a pair of picnic tables, bunched at one end of a small bedraggled lawn. A stone fireplace like a little charcoal oven anchored the ensemble. The muddy grass was uncut. Birch and sycamore trees overhung the area. There had been lots of picnic areas in the park, but most had been located down near the creek and so presumably had been washed away. This one was set higher, in a little hollow next to Ross Drive. All of them, Frank recalled, used to be marked by big signs saying CLOSED AT DUSK. Nothing like that remained now. He sat at one of the tables, opened up his food.

He was about halfway through the calamari when several men tromped into the glade and sat at the other table or stood before the stone fireplace, bringing with them a heavy waft of stale sweat, smoke, and beer. Worn jackets, plastic bags: homeless guys.

Two of them pulled beer cans out of a paper grocery bag. A grizzled one in fatigues saluted Frank with a can. 'Hey man.'

Frank nodded politely. 'Evening.'

'Want a beer?'

'No thanks.'

'What's a matter?'

Frank shrugged. 'Sure, why not.'

'Yar. There ya go.'

Frank finished his calamari and drank the offered Pabst Blue Ribbon, watching the men settle around him. His benefactor and two of the others were dressed in the khaki camouflage fatigues that signified Vietnam Vet Down On Luck (Your Fault, Give Money). Sure enough, a cardboard sign with a long story scrawled in felt-tip on it protruded from one of their bags.

Next to the three vets, a slight man with a dark red beard and pony-tail sat on the table. The other three men were black, one of these a youth or even a boy. They sat down at Frank's table. The youngster unpacked a box that contained a chess set, chessboard, and timer. The man who had offered Frank a beer came over and sat down across from the youth as he set the board. The pieces were cheap plastic, but the timer looked more expensive. The two started a game, the

kid slapping the plunger on his side of the timer down after
pauses averaging about fifteen seconds, while the vet usually
depressed his with a slow touch, after a minute or more had
passed, always declaring 'Ah fuck.'

'Want to play next?' the boy asked Frank. 'Bet you five
dollars.'

'I'm not good enough to play for money.'

'Bet you that box of squid there.'

'No way.' Frank ate on while they continued. '*You* guys
aren't playing for money,' he observed.

'He already took all I got,' the vet said. 'Now I'm like
pitching him batting practice. He's dancing on my body, the
little fucker.'

The boy shook his head. 'You just ain't paying attention.'

'You wore me out, Chessman. You're beating me when I'm
down. You're a fucking menace. I'm setting up my sneak
attack.'

'Checkmate.'

The other guys laughed.

Then three men ran into their little clearing. 'Hi guys!' they
shouted as they hustled to the far end of the site.

'What the hell?' Frank said.

The big vet guffawed. 'It's the frisbee players!'

'They're always running,' one of the other vets explained.
He wore a VFW baseball cap and his face was dissolute and
whiskery. He shouted to the runners: 'Hey who's winning!'

'The wind!' one of them replied.

'Evening, gentlemen,' another said. 'Happy Thursday.'

'Is that what it is?'

'Hey who's *winning*? Who's *winning*?'

'The wind is winning. We're all winning.'

'That's what you say! I got my money on you now! Don't
you let me down now!'

The players faced a fairway of mostly open air to the north.

'What's your target?' Frank called.

The tallest of them had blue eyes, gold-red dreadlocks, mostly gathered under a bandana, and a scraggly red-gold beard. He was the one who had greeted the homeless guys first. Now he paused and said to Frank, 'The trashcan, down there by that light. Par four, little dogleg.' He took a step and made his throw, a smooth uncoiling motion, and then the others threw and they were off into the dusk.

'They run,' the second vet explained.

'Running frisbee golf?'

'Yeah some people do it that way. Rolfing they call it, running golf. Not these guys though! They just run without no name for it. They don't always use the regular targets either. There's some baskets out here, they're metal things with chains hanging from them. You got to hit the chains and the frisbees fall in a basket.'

'Except they don't,' the first vet scoffed.

'Yeah it's a finicky sport. Like fucking golf, you know.'

Down the path Frank could see the runners picking up their frisbees and stopping for only a moment before throwing again.

'How often do they come here?'

'A lot!'

'You can ask them, they'll be back in a while. They run the course forward and back.'

They sat there, once or twice hearing the runners call out. Fifteen minutes later the men did indeed return, on the path they had left.

Frank said to the dreadlocked one, 'Hey, can I follow you and learn the course?'

'Well sure, but we do run it, as you see.'

'Oh yeah that's fine, I'll keep up.'

'Sure then. You want a frisbee to throw?'

'I'd probably lose it.'

'Always possible out here, but try this one. I found it today, so it must be meant for you.'

35

'Okay.'

Like any other climber, Frank had spent a fair amount of camp time tossing a frisbee back and forth. He much preferred it to hackysack, which he was no good at. Now he took the disk they gave him and followed them to their next tee, and threw it last, conservatively, as his main desire was to keep it going straight up the narrow fairway. His shot only went half as far as theirs, but he could see where it had crashed into the overgrown grass, so he considered it a success, and ran after the others. They were pretty fast, not sprinting but moving right along, at what Frank guessed was about a seven-minute mile pace if they kept it up; and they slowed only briefly to pick up their frisbees and throw them again. It quickly became apparent that the slowing down, throwing, and starting up again cost more energy than running straight through would have, and Frank had to focus on the work of it. The players pointed out the next target, and trusted he would not clock them in the backs of their heads after they threw and ran off. And in fact if he shot immediately after them he could fire it over their heads and keep his shot straight.

Some of the targets were trash cans, tree trunks, or big rocks, but most were metal baskets on metal poles, the poles standing chest high and supporting chains that hung from a ring at the top. Frank had never seen such a thing before. The frisbee had to hit the chains in such a way that its momentum was stopped and it fell in the basket. If it bounced out it was like a rimmer in golf or basketball, and a put-in shot had to be added to one's score.

One of the players made a putt from about twenty yards away, and they all hooted. Frank saw no sign they were keeping score or competing. The dreadlocked player threw and his frisbee too hit the chains, but fell to the ground. 'Shit.' Off they ran to pick them up and start the next hole. Frank threw an easy approach shot, then tossed his frisbee in.

'What was par there?' he asked as he ran with them.

'Three. They're all threes but three, which is a two, and nine, which is a four.'

'There's nine holes?'

'Yes, but we play the course backward too, so we have eighteen. Backward they're totally different.'

'I see.'

So they ran, stopped, stooped, threw, and took off again, chasing the shots like dogs. Frank got into his running rhythm, and realized their pace was more the equivalent of an eight or nine-minute mile. He could run with these guys, then. Throwing was another matter, they were amazingly strong and accurate; their shots had a miraculous quality, flying right to the baskets and often crashing into the chains from quite a distance.

'You guys are good!' he said at one tee.

'It's just practice,' the dreadlocked one said. 'We play a lot.'

'It's our religion,' one of the others said, and his companions cackled as they made their next drives.

Then one of Frank's own approach shots clanged into the chains and dropped straight in, from about thirty yards out. The others hooted loudly in congratulation.

On his next approach he focused on throwing at the basket, let go, watched it fly straight there and hit with a resounding clash of the chains. A miracle! A glow filled him, and he ran with an extra bounce in his step.

At the end of their round they stood steaming in the dusk, not far from the picnic area and the homeless guys. The players compared numbers, 'twenty-eight,' 'thirty-three,' which turned out to be how many strokes under par they were for the day. Then high fives and handshakes, and they began to move off in different directions.

'I want to do that again,' Frank said to the dreadlocked guy.

'Any time, you were keeping right with us. We're here most days around this time.' He headed off in the direction of the homeless guys, and Frank accompanied him, thinking to return to his dinner site and clear away his trash.

The homeless guys were still there, nattering at each other like Laurel and Hardy: 'I did not! *You* did. I did not, *you* did.' Something in the intonation revealed to Frank that these were the two he had heard the night before, passing him in the dark.

'Now you wanna play?' the chess player said when he saw Frank.

'Oh, I don't know.'

He sat across from the boy, sweating, still feeling the glow of his miracle shot. Throwing on the run; no doubt it was a very old thing, a hunter thing. His whole brain and body had been working out there. Hunting, sure, and the finding and picking up of the frisbees in the dusk was like gathering. Hunting and gathering; and maybe these were no longer the same activities if one were hunting for explanations, or gathering data. Maybe only physical hunting and gathering would do.

The homeless guys droned on, bickering over their half-assed efforts to get a fire started in the stone fireplace. A piece of shit, as one called it.

'Who built that?' Frank asked.

'National Park. Yeah, look at it. It's got a *roof*.'

'It looks like a smoker.'

'They were idiots.'

'It was the WPA, probly.'

Frank said, 'Isn't this place closed at dusk?'

'Yeah right.'

'The whole fucking *park* is closed, man. Twenty-four seven.'

'Closed for the duration.'

'Yeah right.'

'Closed until further notice.'

'Five dollar game?' the youngster said to Frank, rattling the box of pieces.

Frank sighed. 'I don't want to bet. I'll play you for free.' Frank waved at the first vet. 'I'll be more batting practice for you, like him.'

'Zeno ain't never just batting practice!'

The boy's frown was different. 'Well, okay.'

Frank hadn't played since a long-ago climbing expedition to the Cirque of the Unclimbables, a setting in which chess had always seemed as inconsequential as tiddly-winks. Now he quickly found that using the timer actually helped his game, by making him give up analyzing the situation in depth in favor of just going with the flow of things, with the shape or pattern. In the literature they called this approach a 'good-enough decision heuristic,' although in this case it wasn't even close to good enough; he attacked on the left side, had both knights out and a great push going, and then suddenly it was all revealed as hollow, and he was looking at the wrong end of the end game.

'Shit,' he said, obscurely pleased.

'Told ya,' Zeno scolded him.

The night was warm and full of spring smells, mixing with the mud stench. Frank was still hot from the frisbee run. Some distant gawking cries wafted up from the ravine, as if peacocks were on the loose. The guys at the next table were laughing hard. The third vet was sitting on the ground, trying to read a *Post* by laying it on the ground in front of the fitful fire. 'You can only *see* the fire if you lie on the ground, or look right down the smoke hole. How stupid is that?' They rained curses on their miserable fire. Chessman finished boxing his chess pieces and took off.

Zeno said to Frank, 'Why didn't you play him for money, man? Take him five blow jobs to make up for that.'

'Whoah,' Frank said, startled.

Zeno laughed, a harsh ragged bray, mocking and aggressive, tobacco-raspy. '*HA ha ha.*' A kind of rebuke or slap.

He had the handsome face of a movie villain, a sidekick to someone like Charles Bronson or Jack Palance. 'Ha ha – what you think, man?'

Frank bagged his dinner boxes and stood. 'What if I had beat him?'

'You ain't gonna beat him.' With a twist of the mouth that added, asshole.

'Next time,' Frank promised, and took off.


Primate in forest. Warm and sweaty, full of food, beer and ouzo; still fully endorphined from running with the frisbee guys. It was dark now, although the park wore the same nightcap of noctilucent cloud it had the night before, close over the trees. It provided enough light to see by, just barely. The tree trunks were obvious in some somatic sense; Frank slipped between them as if dodging furniture in a dark house he knew very well. He felt alert, relaxed. Exfoliating in the vegetable night, in the background hum of the city, the click of twigs under his feet. He swam through the park.

An orange flicker glimpsed in the distance caused him to slow down, change direction, approach it at an angle. He hid behind trees as he approached. He sidled closer, like a spy or a hunter. It felt good. Like the frisbee run, but different. He got close enough to be sure it was a campfire, at the center of another brace of picnic tables. Here they had a normal fire ring to work with. Faces in the firelight: bearded, dirty, ruddy. Homeless guys like the ones behind him, like the ones on the street corners around the city, sitting by signs asking for money. Mostly men, but there was one woman sitting at this fire, knitting. She gave the whole scene a domestic look, like something out of Hogarth.

After a while Frank moved on, descending in darkness through the trees. The gash of the torn ravine appeared below him, white in the darkness. A broad canyon of sandstone, brilliant under the luminous cloud. The creek was a black ribbon cutting through it. Probably the moon was near full, somewhere up above the clouds; there was more light than the city alone could account for. Both the cloud ceiling and the newly torn ravine glowed, the sandstone like sinuous naked flesh.

A truck, rumbling in the distance. The sound of the creek burbling over stones. Distant laughter, a car starting; tinkle of broken glass; something like a dumpster lid slamming down. And always the hum of the city, a million noises blended together, like the light caught in the cloud. It was neither quiet, nor dark, nor empty. It definitely was not wilderness. It was city and forest simultaneously. It was hard to characterize how it felt.

Where would one sleep out here?

Immediately the question organized his walk. He had been wandering before, but now he was on the hunt again. He saw that many things were a hunt. It did not have to be a hunt to kill and eat animals. Any search on foot was a kind of hunt. As now.

He ranged up and away from the ravine. First in importance would be seclusion. A flat dry spot, tucked out of the way. There, for instance, a tree had been knocked over in the flood, its big tangle of roots raised to the sky, creating a partial cave under it – but too damp, too closed in.

Cobwebs caught his face and he wiped them away. He looked up into the network of black branches. Being up in a tree would solve so many problems . . . That was a prehominid thought, perhaps caused merely by craning his neck back. No doubt there was an arboreal complex in the brain crying out: Go home, go home!

He ranged uphill, moving mostly northward. A hilltop was another option. He looked at one of the knolls that divided Rock Creek's vestigial western tributaries. Nice in some ways; flat; but as with root hollows, these were places where all manner of creatures might take refuge. The truth was that the best nooks were best for everything out there. A distant crash in the brush reminded him that this might include the zoo's jaguar.

He would need to make some daytime explorations, that was clear. He could always stay in his van, of course, but this felt more real. Scouting trips for the Feral Observation Group. We're all in the fog now, Nancy had said. He would spend some of his time hunting for animals. A kind of return to the paleolithic, right here in Washington D.C. Repaleolithization: it sounded very scientific, like the engineers who spoke of amishization when they meant to simplify a design. Landscape restoration inside the brain. The pursuit of happiness; and the happiness was in the pursuit.

Frank smiled briefly. He realized he had been tense ever since leaving the rented apartment. Now he was more relaxed, watchful but relaxed, moving about easily. It was late, he was getting tired. Another branch across the face and he decided to call it a night.

He made his way west to Connecticut, hit it at Fessenden, walked south on the sidewalk blinking in the flood of light. It might as well have been Las Vegas or Miami to him now, everything blazing neon colors in the warm spring night. People were out. He strolled along among them. The city too was a habitat, and as such a riot of sensation. He would have to think about how that fit in with the repaleolithization project, because the city was a big part of contemporary society, and people were obviously addicted to it. Frank was himself, at least to parts of it. The technological sublime made everything magical, as if they were all tripping with the shaman – but all the time, which was too much. They had therefore lost touch with reality, gone mad as a collective.

And yet this street was reality too. He would have to think about all this.

When he came to his van no one was in sight, and he slipped inside and locked the doors. It was dark, quiet, comfortable. Very much like a room. A bit stuffy; he turned on the power, cracked the windows. He could start the engine and power the air conditioner for a while if he really needed to.

He set his wristwatch alarm for 4:30 AM, afraid he might sleep through the dawn in such a room. Then he lay down on his familiar old mattress, and felt his body start to relax even further. Home sweet home! It made him laugh.

At 4:30 his alarm beeped. He squeezed it quiet and slipped on his running shoes and got out of the van before his sleepiness knocked him back down. Out into the dawn, the world of grays. This was how cats must see, all the grays so finely gradated. A different kind of seeing altogether.

Into the forest again. The leafy venation of the forest air was a masterpiece of three-dimensionality, the precise spacing of everything suggesting some kind of vast sculpture, as in an Ansel Adams photo. The human eye had an astonishing depth of field.

He stood over the tawny sandstone of Rock Creek's newly burnished ravine, hearing his breathing. It was barely cool. The sky was shifting from a flat gray to a curved pale blue.

'Ooooooooooop!'

He shivered deep in his flesh, like a horse.

The sound came from overhead; a rising 'oooooooooo' that then suddenly fell. Something like the cooing of a dove, or the call of a coyote. A voice, or a kind of siren – musical, unearthly, bizarre. Glissandos up and down. Voices, yes. Gibbons and/or siamangs. Frank had heard such calls long ago, at the San Diego Zoo.

It sounded like there were several of them now. 'Ooooop! Oooooooooooop! Ooooooooooooop!'

Lows to highs, penetrating and pure. The hair on Frank's neck was sticking out.

He tried it himself. 'Ooooooop!' he sang, softly. It seemed

43

to fit in. He could do a fair imitation of one part of their range. His voice wasn't as fluid, or as clear in tone, and yet still, it was somewhat the same. Close enough to join in unobtrusively.

So he sang with them, and stepped ever so slowly between the trees, looking up trying to catch a glimpse of them. They were feeding off each other's energy, sounding more and more rambunctious. Wild animals! And they were celebrating the new day, there was no doubt about it. Maybe even celebrating their freedom. There was no way to tell, but to Frank it sounded like it.

Certainly it was true for him – the sound filled him, the morning filled him, spring and all, and he bellowed 'Oooooooopee oop oop!' voice cracking at its highest. He longed to sing higher; he hooted as loudly as he could. The gibbons didn't care. It wasn't at all clear they had even noticed him. He tried to imitate all the calls he was hearing, failed at most of them. Up, down, crescendo, decrescendo, pianissimo, fortissimo. An intoxicating music. Had any composer ever heard this, ever used this? What were people doing, thinking they knew what music was?

The chorus grew louder and more agitated as the sky lightened. When sunlight pierced the forest they all went crazy together.

Then he saw three of them in the trees, sitting on high branches. He saw their long arms and longer tails, their broad shoulders and skinny butts. One swung away on arms that were as long as its body, to land on a branch by another, accept a cuff and hoot some more. Again their raucous noise buffeted Frank. When they finally quieted down, after an earsplitting climax, the green day was upon them.

**Senator Phil Chase said,** 'You know, it's not a question of you being right and me being wrong.'

'Of course not,' Charlie Quibler replied.

Phil grinned. 'We all agreed that global warming was real.'

'Yes, of course we did.'

'No!' Joe Quibler murmured as he drowsed on Charlie's back.

Phil laughed to hear it. 'You've got a lie detector there.'

'Going off all the time, in this company.'

'Ha ha. Looks like he's waking up.'

Charlie glanced over his shoulder. 'I better start walking.'

'I'll join you. I can't stand any more of this anyway.'

They were at the Vietnam Memorial, attending a ceremony to mark its reopening. Phil, a veteran who had served as an Army reporter in Saigon for a year, had said a few words; then the President had shown up, but only near the end, the feeling among his people being that this was one memorial that would be better left buried in the mud. After that Phil was forgotten by the press on hand, which did not surprise him; but Charlie could tell by the slight tightness at the corner of his mouth that the calculated back of the hand to Vietnam had irritated him.

In any case they were free to leave. Normally Phil would have been whisked by car up the Mall to his offices, but a cancellation had opened a half-hour slot in his schedule. 'Let's go say hi to Abe,' he muttered, and turned them west. Offering this gift of time to Charlie; it was as close to an apology as Charlie would ever get.

A month earlier, right before the flood, Charlie had helped craft a giant bill for Phil, designed to jumpstart a real engagement with the climate change problem. Then, in the last phase of intense committee negotiations, Phil had dismantled the bill to get a small part of it passed, effectively destroying the rest. He had promised Charlie he wouldn't, but he had; and had done so without warning Charlie he was going to.

At the time Charlie had been furious. Phil had shrugged him off. 'I am only doing the necessary,' he said, in his version of an Indian accent. 'I must first be doing the necessary.'

But Charlie did not believe it had been necessary. And it did not help that since the flood Phil had been widely hailed as a prophet on the climate issue. Phil had laughed at this little irony, had thanked Charlie, had ignored with aplomb all Charlie's explicit and implied I-told-you-sos. 'It's all really a compliment to you, Charles – to you and your unworkable brilliance.'

'Um hmm,' Charlie said. 'Yeah right.'

He was enjoying the situation too much to invent his side of the banter. Two old colleagues, out for a walk to the Lincoln Monument; it was the rarest thing in town.

Landscaping equipment dotted the newly restored bank of the Potomac, and the background buzz of the city was augmented by their noise. The violent diesel huffing and puffing might have startled some sleeping children awake, but it served as a lullaby to Joe Quibler; the noise of trucks shifting gears on Wisconsin was his usual soporific, and he loved all big grinding sounds. So now he snoozed happily on, head nestled into the back of Charlie's neck as they approached the memorial.

This part of the Mall had been twenty feet under the rush of the Potomac during the flood, and being landfill to begin with it had not put up very much resistance to the spate;

much of it had been torn away, leaving the Lincoln Memorial an island in the stream. 'Check it out,' Charlie said to Phil, pointing up at the big white foursquare building. There was a dark horizontal line partway up it. 'High water mark. Twenty-three feet above normal.'

Phil frowned at the sight. 'You know, the goddammed House is never going to appropriate enough money to clean up this city.'

Senators and their staffs often had an immense disdain for the House of Representatives. 'True.'

'It's too much like one of their Bible prophecies, what was that one?'

'Noah's flood? Revelation?'

'Maybe. Anyway they're loving it. No way they're going to allocate money to interfere with God's judgment. That would be bad. That would be worse than, than *what* – than *raising taxes*!'

'Joe'll wake up if you yell like that.'

'Sorry. I'll calm down.'

Joe rolled his head on Charlie's neck. 'No,' he said.

'Ha,' Phil said, grinning. 'Caught in another one.'

Charlie could just glimpse the boy's red cheek and furrowed brow. He could feel Joe's agitation; clearly he was once more locked into one of his mighty dreams, which from his sleeping scowls and jerks appeared to be fierce struggles, filled with heartfelt *Nos*. Joe awakened from them with big sighs of relief, as if escaping to a quieter, lesser reality, a kind of vacation cosmos. It worried Charlie.

Phil noticed Joe's distress, patted his damp head. Step by broad step they ascended the Memorial.

To Phil this place was sacred ground. He loved Lincoln, had studied his life, often read in the nine volumes of his collected works. 'This is a good place,' he said as he always did when visiting the memorial. 'Solid. Foursquare. Like a dolmen. Like the Parthenon.'

'Especially now, with all the scaffolding.'

Phil looked in at the big statue, still stained to the knees, a sight that made him grimace. 'You know, this city and the Federal government are synonymous. They stand for each other, like when people call the administration "the White House". What is that, metonymy?'

'Metonymy or synecdoche, I can never remember which.'

'No one can.' Phil walked inside, stopped short at the sight of the stained inner walls. 'Damn it. They are going to let this city sink back into the swamp it came out of.'

'That's synecdoche I think. Or the pathetic fallacy.'

'Pathetic for sure, but how is it *patriotic*? How do they *sell that*?'

'Please Phil, you're gonna wake him up. They have it both ways, you know. They use code phrases that mean something different to the Christian right than to anyone else.'

'Like the beast will be slain or whatnot?'

'Yes, and sometimes even more subtle than that.'

'Ha ha. Clerics, everywhere you look. Ours are as bad as the foreign ones. Make people hate their government at the same time you're scaring them with terrorists, what kind of program is that?' Phil drifted through the subdued crowd toward the left wall, into which was incised the Gettysburg Address. The final lines were obscured by the flood's high water mark, a sight which made him scowl. 'They had better clean this up.'

'Oh they will. He was a Republican, after all.'

'Abraham Lincoln was no Republican.'

'Hello?'

'The Republicans in Congress hated him like poison. The goddammed Copperheads did everything they could to sabotage him. They cheered when he was killed, because then they could claim him as a martyr and rip off the South in his name.'

'Limited value in hitting them with that now.'

'But it's still happening! I mean whatever happened to

government of the people by the people and for the people not perishing from this earth?' Pointing at the marred lines on the wall, looking as heavily symbolic as an image in a Cocteau film.

'An idea that lost?' Charlie said, spurring him on.

'Democracy *can't* lose. It *has* to succeed.'

'"Democracy will never succeed, it takes up too many evenings."'

'Ha. Who said that?'

'Oscar Wilde.'

'Please. I mean, I see his point, but don't quote Oscar Wilde to me when I'm trying to think like Abraham Lincoln.'

'Wilde may be more your level.'

'Ha ha.'

'Wilde was witty just like that.'

'Ha ha *ha*.'

Charlie gave up tweaking Phil in favor of contemplating the mud-stained statue of the sixteenth president. It was a great work: massive, brooding, uneasy. The big square-toed boots and obviously handmade broadcoat somehow evoked the whole world of the nineteenth century frontier. This was the spirit that America had given to the world – its best gesture, its exemplary figure.

His oversized hands were dirty. The great bearded head looked sadly over them. The whole interior space of the building had a greatness about it – the uncanny statue, the high square ceiling, the monumental lettering of the speeches on the side walls, the subdued people visiting it. Even the kids there were quiet and watchful.

Perhaps it was this that woke Joe. He yawned, arched back in his seat, whacked Charlie on the head. 'Down! Down!'

'Okay okay.'

Charlie went back outside to let him down. Phil came along, and they sat on the top step and let Joe stretch his legs behind them.

49

A TV crew was working at the bottom of the steps, filming what looked to be a story on the memorial's reattachment to land. When the reporter spotted them, he came up to ask Phil if he would make a comment for the program.

'My pleasure,' Phil said. The reporter waved his crew over, and soon Phil was standing before the camera in a spot where Lincoln loomed over his left shoulder, launching into one of his characteristic improvs. 'I'm sick of people putting Washington down,' he said, waving a hand at the city. 'What makes America special is our constitution, and the laws based on it – it's our *government* that makes America something to be proud of, and that government is based here. So I don't like to see people wrapping themselves in the flag while they trash the very country they pretend to love. Abraham Lincoln would not stand for it –'

'Thanks, Senator! I'm sure we can use that. Some of it, anyway.'

'I should hope so.'

Then a shout of alarm came from inside the building, causing Charlie to shoot to his feet and spin around, looking for Joe – no luck. 'Joe!' he cried, rushing inside.

Past the pillars he skidded to a halt, Phil and the TV crew crashing in behind him. Joe was sitting up on Lincoln's knee, far above them, looking around curiously, seemingly unaware of the long drop to the marble floor.

'*Joe!*' Charlie tried to catch his attention without causing him to topple off. 'Joe! Don't move! Joe! Stay there!'

How the hell did you get up there, he didn't add. Because Lincoln's marble chair was smooth and vertical on all sides; there was no way up it even for an adult. It almost seemed like someone had to have lifted him up there. Of course he was an agile guy, a real monkey, very happy on the climbing structures at Gymboree. If there was a way, he had the will.

Charlie hustled around the statue, hoping to find Joe's route up and follow it himself. There was no way. 'Joe! Stay right there! Stay right there till we get you!'

A group was gathering at Lincoln's feet, ready to catch Joe if he fell off. He sat there looking down at them with an imperial serenity, completely at ease. The TV cameraman was filming everything.

The best Charlie could think to do was to request a boost from two willing young men, and clamber onto their shoulders as they stood on Lincoln's right boot and wrapped their arms around his calf. From there Charlie could reach up with his arms and almost reach Joe, although at that point it was a balancing act, and things were precarious. He had to talk Joe into toppling over into his hands, which of course took a while, as Joe was clearly happy where he was. Eventually, however, he tipped forward and Charlie caught him, and let him down between his legs onto the two young men and a nest of hands, before falling back himself into the arms of the crowd.

The crowd cheered briefly, then gave them a little round of applause. Charlie thanked the two young men as he collected the squirming Joe from other strangers.

'Jesus, Joe! Why do you *do* these things?'

'Look!'

'Yeah yeah, look. But how the hell did you get up there?'

'Up!'

Charlie took some deep breaths, feeling a bit sick to his stomach. If the TV station ran the story, which they probably would, and if Anna saw it, which she probably wouldn't, then he would be in big trouble. But what could you do? He had only taken his eye off him for a second!

Phil got back in front of the camera with them, heightening the chances it would make it to the news. 'This is my young friend Joe Quibler and his father Charlie, a member of my staff. Good job, you guys. You know, citizens like Joe are the ones we have to think about when we consider what sort of world we're going to be handing along to them. That's what government is, it's making the world we want to give to our kids. People should think about that before they put down Washington D.C. and our country's government. Lincoln would not approve!'

Indeed, Lincoln stared down at the scene with a knowing and disenchanted air. He looked concerned about the fate of the republic, just as Phil had implied.

The reporter asked Phil a few more questions, and then Phil signaled that he had to go. The TV crew shut down, and the little crowd that had stayed to watch dissipated.

Phil phoned his office to get a car sent, and while they waited he shook some hands. Charlie roamed the sanctum with Joe in his arms, looking for routes up to the great American's lap. There were some disassembled scaffolds stacked on their sides against the back wall of the chamber, behind Lincoln and next to an inner pillar; it was just conceivable that Joe had monkeyed up those. Easier than doing a dirretissima up Lincoln's calf, but still. It was hard to figure.

'God damn, Joe,' Charlie muttered. 'How do you do this stuff?'

Eventually he rejoined Phil, and they stood on the steps of the memorial, holding Joe by the hand between them and swinging him out toward the reflecting pools, causing Joe to laugh helplessly.

Phil said, 'You know, we're swinging him right over the spot Martin Luther King stood on when he gave his "I Have a Dream" speech. He is really touching all the bases today.'

Charlie, still a little bit shaky with relief, laughed and said, 'Phil, you should run for President.'

Phil grinned his beautiful grin. 'You think so?'

'Yes. Believe me, I don't want to say it. It would mean endless hassle for me, and I haven't got the time.'

'You? What about me?' Phil was looking back up into the building.

'Endless hassle for you too, sure. But you already live that way, right? It would just be more of the same.'

'A lot more.'

'But if you're going to run for high office at all, you might as well make the biggest impact you can. Besides you're one of the only people in the world who can beat the happy man.'

'You think so?'

'I do. You're the World's Senator, right? And the world needs you, Phil. I mean, when the hyperpower goes crazy what are the rest of us going to do? We need help. It's more than just cleaning up the city here. More even than America. It's the whole world needs help now.'

'A godawful fate,' Phil murmured, looking up at the somber and unencouraging Lincoln. A bad idea, Lincoln seemed to be saying. Serious business. Copperheads striking at heel and head. You put your life on the line. 'I'll have to think about it.'

# TWO

# Abrupt Climate Change

The ground is mud. There are a few sandstone rocks scattered here and there, and some river-rounded chunks of amber quartzite, but for the most part, mud. Hard enough to walk on, but dismal to sit or lie on.

The canopy stands about a hundred feet overhead. In the summer it is a solid green ceiling, with only isolated shafts and patches of sunlight slanting all the way to the ground. The biggest trees have trunks that are three or four feet in diameter, and they shoot up without thinning, putting out their first major branches some forty or fifty feet overhead. There are no evergreens, or rather, no conifers. No needles on the ground, no pinecones. The annual drift of leaves disintegrates entirely, and that's the mud: centuries of leaf mulch.

The trees are either very big or very small, the small ones spindly and light-starved, doomed-looking. There are hardly any medium-sized trees; it is hard to understand the succession story. Only after Frank joined FOG did he learn from one of his associates that the succession was in fact messed up, its balance thrown off by the ballooning population of white-tailed deer, whose natural predators had all been eradicated. No more wolf or puma; and so for generations now the new young trees had been mostly eaten by deer.

Big or small, all the trees were second or third growth; the whole watershed had been clear-cut before the Civil War, and during the war the guns of Fort DeRussey, at the high point of the park near Military Road and Oregon Avenue, had a clear shot in all directions, and had once fired across the gorge at a Confederate scouting party.

The park was established in 1890, and developed with the help of the great designer Frederick Law Olmstead; his sons' firm wrote a plan at the end of the First World War that guided the park through the rest of the twentieth century. Now, in the wake of the flood, it appeared to have reverted to the great hardwood forest that had blanketed the eastern half of the continent for millions of years.

The muddy forest floor was corrugated, with any number of small channels appearing in the slope down to Rock Creek. Some of these channels cut as deep as thirty feet, but they always remained mud troughs, with no stony creekbeds down their middles. Water didn't stay in them after a rain.

The forest appeared to be empty. It was easy to hike around in, but there was little to see. The animals, both native and feral, seemed to make efforts to stay concealed.

There was trash all over. Plastic bottles were the most common item, then glass bottles, then miscellaneous: boxes, shoes, plastic bag scraps . . . one plastic grocery bag hung in a branch over Rock Creek like a prayer flag. Another high-water mark.

There were many more signs of the flood. Most of the park's roads, paths, and picnic areas had been located down by the creek, and so were now buried in mud or torn away. The gorge walls were scarred by landslides. Many trees had been uprooted, and some of these had been caught by the Boulder Bridge, forming a dam there that held a narrow lake upstream. The raw sandstone walls undercut by this lake were studded with boulders emerging from a softer matrix. All over the forest above these new cliffs, windrows of downed trees, root balls, branches and trash dotted the forest floor.

The higher roads and trails had survived. The Western Ridge Trail extended the length of the park on its eponymous ridge, and was intact. The nine numbered cross-trails running down from the ridge trail into the gorge now all ended abruptly at some point. Up north near the Maryland border, the Pinehurst Branch Trail was gone, its creekbed ripped like the main gorge.

Before the flood there had been thirty little picnic areas in the park, ten of them reserved for use by permit. The higher ones were damaged, the dozen on the creek gone. Almost all of them had been paltry things, as far as Frank could determine in the aftermath – small clearings with picnic tables, fireplaces, a trashcan. Site 21 was the worst in the park, two old tables in perpetual gloom, stuck at the bottom of a damp hollow that ran right onto Ross Drive. With that road closed to traffic, of course, it had gained some new privacy. Indeed in the mud under one table Frank found a used condom and an item of women's pink underwear, Disney brand, picture of Ariel on waistband, tag saying Sunday. Hopefully they had had a blanket with them. Hopefully they had had fun. The condom seemed a good sign.

East of site 21 the drop to the creek was steep. The big trees that had survived overhung the water. Sandstone boulders as big as cars stood in the stream. There was no sign of the gravel path the map indicated had run up the western bank, and only short stretches of Beach Drive, a two-lane car road which had paralleled it on the eastern side. Above a flat-walled boulder, set crosswise in the stream, tall trees canted out over the creek into the open air. Across the ravine was a steep wall of green. Here the sound of the creek was louder than the sound of the city. If Beach Drive stayed closed to traffic, as it looked like it would, then water would remain the loudest sound here, followed by insects. Some birds were audible. The squirrels had grey fluffy backs, and stomachs

57

*covered with much finer fur, the same gold-copper color as the lion tamarins still missing from the zoo.*

*There were lots of deer, white-tailed in name and fact, big-eared, quick through the trees. It was a trick to move quietly through the forest after them, because small branches were everywhere underfoot, ready to snap in the mud. People were easier to track than deer. The windrows were the only good place to hide; the big tree trunks were broad enough to hide behind, but then you had to look around them to see, exposing yourself to view.*

*What would the forest look like in the autumn? What would it look like in winter? How many of the feral animals could survive a winter out?*

**It turned out that** Home Depot sold a pretty good treehouse kit. Its heavy-duty hardware allowed one to collar several floor beams securely to trunk or major branches, and after that it was a simple matter of two-by-fours and plywood, cut to whatever dimensions one wanted. The rest of the kit consisted mostly of fripperies, the gingerbread fill making a Swiss Family allusion that caused Frank to smile, remembering his own childhood dreams: he had always wanted a treehouse. But these days he wanted it simple.

Getting that was complicated. For a while he left work as early as he could and drove to one edge of the park or another, testing routes and parking places. Then it was off into the park on foot, using a Potomac Appalachian Trail Club map to learn it. He hiked all the trails that had survived, but usually these were just jumping-off points for rambles in the forest and scrambles in the gorge.

At first he could not find a tree he liked. He had wanted an evergreen, preferably in a stand of other evergreens. But almost every tree in Rock Creek Park was deciduous. Beech, oak, sycamore, ash, poplar, maple – he couldn't even tell which was which. All of them had tall straight trunks, with first branches very high, and crowns of foliage above that. Their bark had different textures, however, and by that sign – bark corrugated in a vertical diamond pattern – he decided that the best trees were probably chestnut oaks.

There were many of these upstream from site 21. One of

them canted out and overhung the creek. It looked as if its upper branches would have a nice view, but until he climbed it he wouldn't know.

While making his reconnaissances he often ran into the frisbee golfers, and when he did he usually joined them. In running the course they always passed site 21, and if the homeless guys were there the second vet, whose name was Andy, would shout his abrasive welcome: 'Who's *winning*? Who's *winning*?' The frisbee players usually stopped to chat for a moment. Spencer, the player with the dreadlocks, would ask what had happened lately, and sometimes get an earful in response. Then they were off again, Spencer in the lead, dreadlocks flying under bandana, Robin and Robert following at speed. Robin sounded like some kind of deist or animist, everything was alive to him, and after his throws he always shouted instructions to his frisbee or begged for help from the trees. Robert spoke more in the style of a sports announcer commenting on the play. Spencer spoke only in shrieks and howls, some kind of shaman language; but he was the one who chatted with the homeless guys.

During one of these pass-bys Frank saw that Chessman was there, and under Zeno's baleful eye he offered to come back and play him for money. Chessman nodded, looking pleased.

So after the run Frank returned, toting a pizza in a box and a sixpack of Pabst. 'Hey the doctor's here,' Zeno said in his heavy joking tone. Frank ignored that, sat down and lost ten dollars to the boy, playing the best he could but confirming his impression that he was seriously outclassed. He said little, left as soon as it seemed okay.

The first time he climbed his candidate chestnut oak he had to use crampons, ice axe, and a telephone linesman's pole-climbing kit that he had from his window-washing days, dug out of the depths of his storage locker. Up the tree at dawn, kicking in like a telephone lineman, slinging up the strap and leaning back in his harness, up and up, through the scrawny understory and into the fork of the first two big branches. It was nice to be able to sink an ice axe in anywhere one liked; an awkward climb, nevertheless. It would be good to confirm a tree and install a ladder.

Up here he saw that one major branch curved out over the creek, then divided into two. That fork would provide a foundation, and somewhat block the view from below. He only needed a platform a bit bigger than his sleeping bag, something like a ledge bivouac on a wall climb. There was a grand view of the ravine wall opposite him, green to a height considerably higher than he was. Glimpses of the burbling creek downstream, but no view of the ground directly below. It looked good.

After that he parked and slept in the residential neighborhood to the west, and got up before dawn and hiked into the forest carrying lumber and climbing gear. This was pretty conspicuous, but at that time of day the gray neighborhood and park were completely deserted. It was only a ten-minute hike in any case, a drop through forest that would usually be empty even at the busiest time of a Sunday afternoon.

He only needed two dawn patrols to install a climbing ladder, wound on an electric winch that he reeled up and down using a garage-door remote he found at Radio Shack. After that the two-by-sixes, the two-by-fours, and two three-by-five sheets of half-inch plywood could be hauled up using the ladder as a winch cable. Climb the ladder with the miscellaneous stuff, ice axing into the trunk for balance, backpack full of hardware and tools.

Collar around trunk; beams on branches; plywood floor; low railing, gapped for the ladder. He maneuvered slowly around the trunk as he worked, slung in a self-belay from a piton nailed above him. Cirque du Soleil meets Home Improvement. Using woodscrews rather than nails reduced the sound of construction, while also making the thing stronger.

Every day an hour's work in the green horizontal light, and all too soon it was finished, and then furnished. A clear plastic tarp stapled and glued to the trunk overhead served as a see-through roof, tied out to branches on a slant to let the rain run off. The opening in the rail, the winch screwed down to the plywood just inside it. Duffel bag against the trunk holding rolled foam mattress, sleeping bag, pillow, lantern, gear.

Standing on the platform without his sling one morning, in the slanting light that told him it was time to drive to work, he saw that the thing was built. Too bad! He would have liked the project to have lasted longer.

Driving across town that morning, he thought, Now I have two bedrooms, in a modular home distributed throughout the city. One bedroom was mobile, the other in a tree. How cool was that? How perfectly rational and sane?

Over in Arlington he drove to the NSF basement parking lot, then walked over to Optimodal Exercise to shower.

Big, new, clean, blazingly well-lit; it was a shocking contrast to the dawn forest, and he always changed at his locker feeling a bit stunned. Then it was off to the weight room.

His favorite there was a pull-down bar that gave his lats a workout they otherwise would not get. Low weight, high reps, the pull like something between swimming and climbing. A peaceful warm-up, on his knees as if praying.

Then over to the leg press. Here too he was a low-weight high-rep kind of guy, although since joining the club it had occurred to him that precisely the advantage of a weight room over the outdoors was the chance to do strength work. So now he upped the weight, for a few hard pushes at the end of the set.

Up and down, back and forth, push and pull, all the while taking in the other people in the room: watching the women, to be precise. Without ever actually focusing on them. Lifting, running, rowing, whatever they did, Frank liked it. He had a thing for jock women that long predated his academic interest in sociobiology. Indeed it seemed likely that he had gotten into the latter to explain the former – because for as long as he could remember, women doing sports had been the ultimate stimulus to his attraction. He loved the way sports moves became female when women did them – more graceful, more like dance – and he loved the way the moves revealed the shapes of their bodies. Surely this was another very ancient primate pleasure.

At Optimodal this all remained true even though there was not a great deal of athleticism on display. Often it was a case of non-athletes trying to 'get in shape,' so that Frank was covertly observing women in various stages of cardiovascular distress. But that was fine too: sweaty pink faces, hard breathing; obviously this was sexy stuff. None of that bedroom silliness for Frank – lingerie, make-up, even dancing – all that was much too intentional and choreographed, even somehow confrontational. Lovelier by far were women unselfconsciously exerting themselves in some physical way.

'Oh hi Frank.'

He jumped a foot.

'Hi Diane!'

She was sitting in a leg press seat, now grinning: 'Sorry, I startled you.'

'That's all right.'

'So you did join.'

'Yes, that's right. It's just like you said. Very nice. But don't let me interrupt you.'

'No, I was done.'

She took up a hand towel and wiped her brow. She looked different in gym clothes, of course. Short, rounded, muscular; hard to characterize, but she looked good. She drew the eye. Anyway, she drew Frank's eye; presumably everyone was different that way.

She sat there, barefoot and sweaty. 'Do you want to get on here?'

'Oh no, no hurry. I'm just kind of waking myself up to tell the truth.'

'Okay.'

She blew a strand of hair away from her mouth, kicked out against the weight ten times, slowing down in the last reps. She smelled faintly of sweat and soap. Presumably also pheromones, estrogens, estrogenlike compounds, and perfumes.

'You've got a lot on the stack there.'

'Do I?' She peered at the weights. 'Not so much.'

'Two hundred pounds. Your legs are stronger than mine.'

'I doubt that.'

But it was true, at least on that machine. Diane pressed the two hundred ten more times; then Frank replaced her and keyed down the weights. Diane picked up a dumbbell and did some curls while he kicked in his traces. She had very nice biceps. Firm muscles under flushed wet skin. Absence of fur made all this so visible. On the savannah they would have been watching each other all the time, aware of each other as bodies.

He wondered if he could make an observation like that to Diane, and if he did, what she would say. She had surprised him often enough recently that he had become cautious about predicting her.

She was looking at the line of runners on treadmills, so Frank said, 'Everyone's trying to get back to the savannah.'

Diane smiled and nodded. 'Easy to do.'

'Is it?'

'If you know that's what you're trying for.'

'Hmmm. Maybe so. But I don't think most people know.'

'No. Hey, are you done there? Will you check me on the bench press? My right elbow kind of locks up sometimes.'

So Frank held the handle bar outside her hand. A young

woman, heavily tattooed on her arms, waited for the machine to free up.

Diane finished and Frank held out a hand to help her. She took it and hauled herself up, their grips tightening to hold. When she was up the young woman moved in to replace her, but Diane took up a towel and said, 'Wait a second, let me wipe up the wet spot.'

'Oh I hate the wet spot,' the young woman said, and immediately threw a hand to her mouth, blushing vividly. Frank and Diane laughed, and seeing it the young woman did too, glowing with embarrassment. Diane gave the bench a final flourish and handed it over, saying, 'There, if only it were always that easy!'

They laughed again and Frank and Diane moved to the next machine. Military press, leg curls; then Diane looked at her watch and said, 'Oops, I gotta get going,' and Frank said 'Me too,' and without further ado they were off to their respective locker rooms. 'See you over there.' 'Yeah, see you.'

Into the men's room, the shower, ahhhh. Hot water must have been unusual in the hominid world. Hot springs, the Indian Ocean shallows. Then out on the street, the air still cool, feeling as benign as he had in a long time. And Diane emerged at the same time from the women's locker room, transformed into work mode, except wetter. They walked over to NSF together, talking about a meeting they were scheduled to attend later in the day. Frank arrived in his office at eight AM as if it were any ordinary morning. He had to laugh.

The meeting featured a presentation by Kenzo and his team to Diane, Frank's committee, and some of the members of National Science Board, the group that oversaw the Foundation in somewhat a board of directors style, if Frank understood it correctly. By the time Frank arrived, a large false-color map of the North Atlantic was already on the screen. On it the red flows marking the upper reaches of the Gulf Stream broke apart and curled like new ferns, one near Norway, one between Iceland and Scotland, one between Iceland and Greenland, and one extending up the long channel between Greenland and Labrador.

'This is how it used to look,' Kenzo said. 'Now here's the summer's data from the Argos buoy system.'

They watched as the red tendrils shrank in on themselves until they nearly met, at about the latitude of southern Ireland. 'That's where we're at now, in terms of temperature. Here's surface height.' He clicked to another false-colored map that revealed what were in effect giant shallow whirlpools, fifty kilometers wide but only a few centimeters deep.

'This is another before map. We think these downwelling sites were pretty stable for the last eight thousand years. Note that the Coriolis force would have the currents turning right, but the land and sea-bottom configurations make them turn left. So they aren't as robust as they might be. And then, here's what we've got now – see? The downwelling has clearly shifted to southwest of Ireland.'

'What happens to the water north of that now?' Diane asked.

'Well – we don't know yet. We've never seen this before. It's a fresh water cap, a kind of lens on the surface. In general, water in the ocean moves in kind of blobs of relative freshness or salinity, you might say, blobs that mix only slowly. One team identified and tracked the great salinity anomaly of 1968 to '82, that was a huge fresher blob that circled in the North Atlantic on the surface. It made one giant circuit, then sank on its second pass through the downwelling zone east of Greenland. Now with this fresh water cap, who knows? If it's resupplied from Greenland or the Arctic, it may stay there.'

Diane stared at the map. 'So what do you think happened to cause this fresh water cap?'

'It may be a kind of Heinrich event, in which icebergs float south. Heinrich found these by analyzing boulders dropped to the sea floor when the icebergs melted. He theorized that anything that introduces more fresh water than usual to the far North Atlantic will tend to interfere with downwelling there. Even rain can do it. So, we've got the Arctic sea ice break-up as the main suspect, plus Greenland is melting much more rapidly than before. The poles are proving to be much more sensitive to global warming than anywhere else, and in the north the effects look to be combining to freshen the North Atlantic. Anyway it's happened, and the strong implication is that we're in for a shift to the kind of cold-dry-windy climate that we see in the Younger Dryas.'

'So.' Diane looked at the board members in attendance. 'We have compelling evidence for an ocean event that is the best-identified trigger event for abrupt climate change.'

'Yes,' Kenzo said. 'A very clear case, as we'll see this winter.'

'It will be bad?'

'Yes. Maybe not the full cold-dry-windy, but heck, close enough. The Gulf Stream used to combine with Greenland to make a kind of jet stream anchor, and now the jet stream is likely to wander more, sometimes shooting straight down the continents from the Arctic. It'll be cold and dry and windy all over the northern hemisphere, but especially in the eastern half of North America, and all over Europe.' Kenzo gestured at the screen. 'You can bet on it.'

'And so . . . the ramifications? In terms of telling Congress about the situation?'

Kenzo waved his hands in his usual impresario style. 'You name it! You could reference that Pentagon report about this possibility, which said it would be a threat to national security, as they couldn't defend the nation from a starving world.'

'Starving?'

'Well, there are no food reserves to speak of. I know the food production problem appeared to be solved, at least in some quarters, but there were never any reserves built up. It's just been assumed more could always be grown. But take Europe – right now it pretty much grows its own food. That's six hundred and fifty million people. It's the Gulf Stream that allows that. It moves about a petawatt northward, that's a million billion watts, or about a hundred times as much energy as humanity generates. Canada, at the same latitude as Europe, only grows enough to feed its thirty million people, plus about double that in grain. They could up it a little if they had to, but think of Europe with a climate suddenly like Canada's – how are they going to feed themselves? They'll have a four or five hundred million person shortfall.'

'Hmm,' Diane said. 'That's what this Pentagon report said?'

'Yes. But it was an internal document, written by a team led by an Andrew Marshall, one of the missile defense crowd. Its conclusions were inconvenient to the administration and it was getting buried when someone on the team slipped it to *Fortune* magazine, and they published it. It made a little stir at the time, because it came out of the Pentagon, and the possibilities it outlined were so bad. It was thought that it might influence a vote at the World Bank to change their investment pattern. The World Bank's Extractive Industries Review Commission had recommended they cut off all future investment in fossil fuels, and move that same money into clean renewables. But in the end the World Bank board voted to keep their investment pattern the same, which was ninety-four percent to fossil fuels and six percent to renewables. After that the Pentagon report experienced the usual fate.'

'Forgotten.'

'Yes.'

'We don't remember our reports either,' Edgardo said. 'There are several NSF reports on this issue. I've got one here called "Environmental Science and Engineering for the 21st Century, The Role of the National Science Foundation." It called for quadrupling the money NSF gave to its environmental programs, and suggested everyone else in government and industry do the same. Look at this table in it – forty-five percent of Earth's land surface transformed by humans – fifty percent of surface freshwater used – two thirds of the marine fisheries fully exploited or depleted. Carbon dioxide in the atmosphere thirty percent higher than before the industrial revolution. A quarter of all bird species extinct.' He looked up at them over his reading glasses. 'All these figures are worse now.'

Diane looked at the copy of the page Edgardo had passed around. 'Clearly ignorance of the situation has not been the problem. The problem is acting on what we know. Maybe people will be ready for that now. Better late than never.'

'Unless it is too late,' Edgardo suggested.

Diane had said the same thing to Frank in private, but now she said firmly, 'Let's proceed on the assumption that it is never too late. I mean, here we are. So let's get Sophie in, and prepare something for the White House and the congressional committees. Some plans. Things we can do right now, concerning both the Gulf Stream and global warming more generally.'

'We'll need to scare the shit out of them,' Edgardo said.

'Yes. Well, the marks of the flood are still all over town. That should help.'

'People are already fond of the flood,' Edgardo said. 'It was an adventure. It got people out of their ruts.'

'Nevertheless,' Diane said, with a grimace that was still somehow cheerful or amused. Scaring politicians might be something she looked forward to.

Given all that he had to do at work, Frank didn't usually get away as early as he would have liked. But the June days were long, and with the treehouse finished there was no great rush to accomplish any particular task. Once in the park, he could wander up the West Ridge Trail and choose where to drop deeper to the east, looking for animals. Just north of Military Road the trail ran past the high point of the park, occupied by the site of Fort DeRussey, now low earthen bulwarks. One evening he saw movement inside the bulwarks, froze: some kind of antelope, its russet coloring not unlike the mounded earth, its neck stretched as it pulled down a branch with its mouth to strip off leaves. White stripes running diagonally up from its white belly. An exotic for sure. A feral from the zoo, and his first nondescript!

It saw him, and yet continued to eat. Its jaw moved in a rolling, side-to-side mastication; the bottom jaw was the one that stayed still. It was alert to his movements, and yet not skittish. He wondered if there were any general feral characterists, if escaped zoo animals were more trusting or less than the local natives. Something to ask Nancy.

Abruptly the creature shot away through the trees. It was big! Frank grinned, pulled out his FOG phone and called it in. The cheap little cell phone was on something like a walkie-talkie or party line system, and Nancy or one of her assistants usually picked up right away. 'Sorry, I don't really know what it was.' He described it the best he could. Pretty lame, but what could he do? He needed to learn more. 'Call Clark on phone 12,' Nancy suggested, 'he's the ungulate guy.' No need to GPS the sighting, being right in the old fort.

He hiked down the trail that ran from the fort to the creek, paralleling Military Road and then passing under its big bridge, which had survived but was still closed. It was nice and quiet in the ravine, with Beach Drive gone and all the roads crossing the park either gone or closed for repairs. A sanctuary.

Green light in the muggy late afternoon. He kept an eye out for more animals, thinking about what might happen to them in the abrupt climate change Kenzo said they were now entering. All the discussion in the meeting that day had centered on the impacts to humans. That would be the usual way of most such discussions; but whole biomes, whole ecologies would be altered, perhaps devastated. That was what they were saying, really, when they talked about the impact on humans: they would lose the support of the domesticated part of nature. Everything would become an exotic; everything would have to go feral.

He walked south on a route that stayed on the rim of the damaged part of the gorge as much as possible. When he came to site 21 he found the homeless guys there as usual, sitting around looking kind of beat.

'Hey, Doc! Why aren't you playing frisbee? They ran by just a while ago.'

'Did they? Maybe I'll catch them on their way back.'

Frank regarded them; hanging around in the steamy sunset, smoking in their own fire, empties dented on the ground around them. Frank found he was thirsty, and hungry.

'Who'll eat pizza if I go get one?'

Everyone would. 'Get some beer too!' Zeno said, with a hoarse laugh that falsely insinuated this was a joke.

Frank hiked out to Connecticut and bought thin-crusted pizzas from a little stand across from Chicago's. He liked them because he thought the owner of the stand was mocking the thick pads of dough that characterized the pizzas in the famous restaurant. Frank was a thin-crust man himself.

Back into the dusky forest, two boxes held like a waiter. Then pizza around the fire, with the guys making their usual desultory conversation. The vet always studying the *Post*'s federal news section did indeed appear well-versed in the ways of the federal bureaucracy, and he definitely had a chip on his shoulder about it. 'The left hand don't know what the right one is doing,' he muttered again. Frank had already observed that they always said the same things; but didn't everybody? He finished his slice and crouched down to tend their smoky fire. 'Hey someone's got potatoes burning in here.'

71

'Oh yeah, pull those out! You can have one if you want.'

'Don't you know you can't cook no potato on no fire?'

'Sure you can! How you do think?'

Frank shook his head; the potato skins were charred at one end, green at the other. Back in the paleolithic there must have been guys hanging out somewhere beyond the cave, guys who had offended the alpha male or killed somebody by accident or otherwise fucked up – or just not been able to understand the rules – or failed to find a mate (like Frank) – and they must have hunkered around some outlier fire, eating lukewarm pizza and making crude chitchat that was always the same, laughing at their old jokes.

'I saw an antelope up in the old fort,' he offered.

'I saw a tapir,' the *Post* reader said promptly.

'Come on Fedpage, how you know it was a tapir.'

'I saw that fucking *jaguar,* I swear.'

Frank sighed. 'If you report it to the zoo, they'll put you in their volunteer group. They'll give you a pass to be in the park.'

'You think we need a pass?'

'We be the ones giving them a pass!'

'They'll give you a cell phone too.' That surprised them.

Chessman slipped in, glancing at Frank, and Frank nodded unenthusiastically; he had been about to leave. And it was his turn to play black. Chessman set out the board between them and moved out his king's pawn.

Suddenly Zeno and Andy were arguing over ownership of the potatoes. It was a group that liked to argue. Zeno was among the worst of these; he would switch from friendly to belligerent within a sentence, and then back again. Abrupt climate change. The others were more consistent. Andy was consistently abrasive with his unfunny humor, but friendly. Fedpage was always shaking his head in disgust at something he was reading. The silent guy with the silky dark red beard was always subdued, but when he spoke always complained, often about the police. Another regular was older, with faded blond-gray hair, pockmarked face, not many teeth. Then there was Jory, an olive-skinned skinny man with greasy black hair and a voice that sounded so much like Zeno's that Frank at first confused them when listening to their chat. He was if anything even more volatile than Zeno, but had no friendly mode, being consistently obnoxious and edgy. He would not look at Frank except in sidelong glances that radiated hostility.

Lastly among the regulars was Cutter, a cheery, bulky black guy, who usually arrived with a cut of meat to cook on the fire, always providing a pedigree for it in the form of a story of petty theft or salvage. Adventures in food acquisition. He often had a couple of buddies with him, knew Chessman, and appeared to have a job with the city park service, judging by his shirts and his stories. He more than the others reminded Frank of his window-washing days, also the climbing crowd – a certain rowdy quality – life considered as one outdoor sport after the next. It seemed as if Cutter had somewhere else as his base; and he had also given Frank the idea of bringing by food.

Chessman suddenly blew in on the left flank and Frank resigned, shaking his head as he paid up. 'Next time,' he promised. The fire guttered out, and the food and beer were gone. The potatoes smoldered on a table top. The guys slowed down in their talk. Redbeard slipped off into the night, and that made it okay for Frank to do so as well. Some of them made their departures into a big production, with explanations of where they were going and why, and when they would likely return again; others just walked off, as if to pee, and did not come back. Frank said, 'Catch you guys,' in order not to appear unfriendly, but only as he was leaving, so that it was not an opening to any inquiries.

Off north to his tree. Ladder called down, the motor humming like the sound of his brain in action.

The thing is, he thought as he waited, nobody knows you. No one can. Even if you spent almost the entirety of every day with someone, and there were people like that – even then, no. Everyone lived alone in the end, not just in their heads but even in their physical routines. Human contacts were parcellated, to use a term from brain science or systems theory; parcelled out. There were:

1) the people you lived with, if you did; that was about a hundred hours a week, half of them asleep;
2) the people you worked with, that was forty hours a week, give or take;
3) the people you played with, that would be some portion of the thirty or so hours left in a week.
4) Then there were the strangers you spent time with in transport, or eating out or so on. This would be added to an already full calendar according to Frank's calculations so far, suggesting they were all living more hours a week than actually existed, which felt right. In any case, a normal life was split out into different groups that never met; and so no one knew you in your entirety, except you yourself.

One could, therefore:

1) pursue a project in paleolithic living,
2) change the weather,
3) attempt to restructure your profession, and
4) be happy,

all at once, although *not* simultaneously, but moving from one thing to another, among differing populations; behaving as if a different person in each situation. It could be done, because *there were no witnesses*. No one saw enough to witness your life and put it all together.

Through the lowest leaves of his tree appeared the

aluminum-runged nylon rope ladder. One of his climbing friends had called this kind of ice-climbing ladder a 'Miss Piggy', perhaps because the rungs resembled pig iron, perhaps because Miss Piggy had stood on just such a ladder for one of her arias in 'The Muppets' Treasure Island.' Frank grabbed one of the rungs, tugged to make sure all was secure above, and started to climb, still pursuing his train of thought. The parcellated life. Fully optimodal. No reason not to enjoy it; and suddenly he realized that he *was* enjoying it. It was like being a versatile actor in a repertory theater, shifting constantly from role to role, and all together they made up his life, and part of the life of his time.

Cheered by the thought, he ascended the upper portion of his Miss Piggy, swaying as little as possible among the branches. Then through the gap, up and onto his plywood floor.

He hand-turned the crank on the ladder's spindle to bring the ladder up after him without wasting battery power. Once it was secured, and the lubber's hole filled with a fitted piece of plywood, he could relax. He was home.

Against the trunk was his big duffel bag under the tarp, all held in place by bungee cords. From the duffel he pulled the rolled-up foam mattress, as thick and long as a bed. Then pillows, mosquito net, sleeping bag, sheet. On these warm nights he slept under the sheet and mosquito net, and only used his down bag as a blanket near dawn.

Lie down, stretch out, feel the weariness of the day bathe him. Slight sway of the tree: yes, he was up in a treehouse.

The idea made him happy. His childhood fantasy had been the result of visits to the big concrete treehouse at Disneyland. He had been eight years old when he first saw it, and it had bowled him over: the elaborate waterwheel-powered bamboo plumbing system, the bannistered stairs spiraling up the trunk, the big living room with its salvaged harmonium, catwalks to the separate bedrooms on their branches, open windows on all four sides . . .

His current aerie was a very modest version of that fantasy, of course. Just the basics; a ledge bivouac rather than the Swiss family mansion, and indeed his old camping gear was well-represented around him, augmented by some nifty car-camping extras, like the lantern and the foam mattress and the pillows from the apartment. Stuff scavenged from the wreckage of his life, as in any other Robinsonade.

The tree swayed and whooshed in the wind. He sat on his thick foam pad, his back holding it up against the trunk. Luxurious reading in bed. Around him laptop, cell phone, a little cooler; his backpack held a bathroom bag and a selection of clothing; a Coleman battery-powered lantern. In short, everything he needed. The lamp cast a pool of light onto the plywood. No one would see it. He was in his own space, and yet at the same time right in the middle of Washington D.C. One of the ferals in the ever-encroaching forest. 'Ooooop, oop oop ooooop!' His tree swayed back and forth in the wind. He switched off his lamp and slept like a babe.

Except his cell phone rang, and he rolled over and answered it without fully waking. 'Hello?'

'Frank Vanderwal?'

'Yes? What time is it?' And where am I?

'It's the middle of the night. Sorry, but this is when I can call.' As he was recognizing her voice, she went on: 'We met in that elevator that stuck.'

Already he was sitting up. 'Ah yeah of course! I'm glad you called.'

'I said I would.'

'I know.'

'Can you meet?'

'Sure I can. When?'

'Now.'

'Okay.'

Frank checked his watch. It was three in the morning.

'That's when I can do it,' she explained.

'That's fine. Where?'

'There's a little park, near where we first met. Two blocks south of there, a block east of Wisconsin. There's a statue in the middle of the park, with a bench under it. Would that be okay?'

'Sure. It'll take me, I don't know, half an hour to get there. Less, actually.'

'Okay. I'll be there.'

The connection went dead.

Again he had failed to get her name, he realized as he dressed and rolled his sleeping gear under the tarp. He brushed his teeth while putting on his shoes, wondering what it meant that she had called now. Then the ladder finished lowering and down he went, swaying hard and holding on as he banged into a branch. Not a good time to fall, oh no indeed.

On the ground, the ladder sent back up. Leaving the park the streetlights blazed in his eyes, caged in blue polygons or orange globes; it was like crossing an empty stage set. He drove over to Wisconsin and up it, then turned right onto Elm Street. Lots of parking here. And there was the little park she had mentioned. He had not known it existed. It was dark except for one orange streetlight at its north end, near a row of tennis courts. He parked and got out.

Mid-park a small black statue of a female figure held up a black hoop. The streetlight and the city's noctilucent cloud illuminated everything faintly but distinctly. It reminded Frank of the light in the NSF building on the night of his abortive b-and-e, and he shook his head, not wanting to recall that folly; then he recalled that that was the night they had met, that he had broken into the NSF building specifically because he had decided to stay in D.C. and search for this woman.

And there she was, sitting on the park bench. It was 3:34 AM and there she sat, on a park bench in the dark. Something in the sight made him shiver, and then he hurried to her.

She saw him coming and stood up, stepped around the bench. They stopped face to face. She was almost as tall as he was. Tentatively she reached out a hand, and he touched it with his. Their fingers intertwined. Slender long fingers. She freed her hand and gestured at the park bench, and they sat down on it.

'Thanks for coming,' she said.

'Oh hey. I'm so glad you called.'

'I didn't know, but I thought . . .'

'Please. Always call. I wanted to see you again.'

'Yes.' She smiled a little, as if aware that *seeing* was not the full verb for what he meant. Again Frank shuddered: who was she, what was she doing?

'Tell me your name. Please.'

'. . . Caroline.'

'Caroline what?'

'Let's not talk about that yet.'

Now the ambient light was too dim; he wanted to see her better. She looked at him with a curious expression, as if puzzling how to proceed.

'What?' he said.

She pursed her lips.

'What?'

She said, 'Tell me this. Why did you follow me into that elevator?'

Frank had not known she had noticed that. 'Well! I . . . I liked the way you looked.'

She nodded, looked away. 'I thought so.' A tiny smile, a sigh: 'Look,' she said, and stared down at her hands. She fiddled with the ring on her left ring finger.

'*What?*'

'You're being watched.' She looked up, met his gaze. 'Do you know that?'

'No! But what do you mean?'

'You're under surveillance.'

Frank sat up straighter, shifted back and away from her. 'By whom?'

She almost shrugged. 'It's part of Homeland Security.'

'What?'

'An agency that works with Homeland Security.'

'And how do you know?'

'Because you were assigned to me.'

Frank swallowed involuntarily. 'When was this?'

'About a year ago. When you first came to NSF.'

Frank sat back even further. She reached a hand toward him. He shivered; the night seemed suddenly chill. He couldn't quite come to grips with what she was saying. 'Why?'

She reached farther, put her hand lightly on his knee. 'Listen, it's not like what you're thinking.'

'I don't know what I'm thinking!'

She smiled. The touch of her hand said more than anything words could convey, but right now it only added to Frank's confusion.

She saw this and said, 'I monitor a lot of people. You were one of them. It's not really that big of a deal. You're part of a crowd, really. People in certain emerging technologies. It's not direct surveillance. I mean no one is watching you or anything like that. It's a matter of tracking your records, mostly.'

'That's all?'

'Well – no. E-mail, where you call, expenditures – that sort of thing. A lot of it's automated. Like with your credit rating. It's just a kind of monitoring, looking for patterns.'

'Uh huh,' Frank said, feeling less disturbed, but also reviewing things he might have said on the phone, to Derek Gaspar for instance. 'But look, why me?'

'I don't get told why. But I looked into it a little after we met, and my guess would be that you're an associational.'

'Meaning?'

'That you have some kind of connection with a Yann Pierzinski.'

'Ahhhhh?' Frank said, thinking furiously.

'That's what I think, anyway. You're one of a group that's being monitored together, and they all tend to have some kind of connection with him. He's the hub.'

'It must be his algorithm.'

'Maybe so. Really I don't know. I don't make the determinations of interest.'

'Who does?'

'People above me. Some of them I know, and then others above those. The agency is pretty firewalled.'

'It must be his algorithm. That's the main thing he's worked on ever since his doctoral work.'

'Maybe so. The people I work for use an algorithm themselves, to identify people who should be tracked.'

'Really? Do you know what kind?'

'No. I do know that they're running a futures market. You know what those are?'

Frank shook his head. 'Like that Poindexter thing?'

'Yes, sort of. He had to resign, and really he should have, because that was stupid what he was doing. But the idea of using futures markets itself has gone forward.'

'So they're betting on future acts of terrorism?'

'No no. That was the stupid part, putting it like that. There's much better ways to use those programs. They're just futures markets, when you design them right. They're like any other futures market. It's a powerful way to collate information. They out-perform most of the other predictive methods we use.'

'That's hard to believe.'

'Is it?' She shrugged. 'Well, the people I work for believe in them. But the one they've set up is a bit different than the standard futures market. It's not open to anyone, and it isn't even real money. It's like a virtual futures market, a simulation. There are these people at MIT who think they have it working really well, and they've got some real-world results they can point to. They focus on people rather than events, so really it's a people futures market, instead of commodities or ideas. So Homeland Security and associated agencies like ours have gotten interested. We've got this program going, and now you're part of it. It's almost a pilot program, but it's big, and I bet it's here to stay.'

'Is it legal?'

'It's hard to say what's legal these days, don't you think? At least concerning surveillance. A determination of interest usually comes from the Justice Department, or is approved by it. It's classified, and we're a black program that no one on the outside will ever hear about. People who try to publish articles about idea futures markets, or people futures markets, are discouraged from doing so. It can get pretty explicit. I think my bosses hope to keep using the program without it ever causing any fuss.'

'So there are people betting on who will do innovative work, or defect to China, or like that?'

'Yes. Like that. There are lots of different criteria.'

'Jesus,' Frank said, shaking his head in amazement. 'But, I mean – who in the hell would bet on me?'

She laughed. 'I would, right?'

Frank put his hand on top of hers and squeezed it.

'But actually,' she said, turning her hand and twining her fingers with his, 'at this point, I think most of the investors in the market are various kinds of diagnostic programs.'

Now it was Frank's turn to laugh. 'So there are computer programs out there, betting I am going to become some kind of a security risk.'

She nodded, smiling at the absurdity of it. Although Frank realized, with a little jolt of internal surprise, that if the whole project were centered around Pierzinski, then the programs might be getting it right. Frank himself had judged that Pierzinski's algorithm might allow them to read the proteome directly from the genome, thus giving them any number of new gene therapies, which if they could crack the delivery problem had the potential of curing outright many, many diseases. That would be a good in itself, and would also be worth billions. And Frank had without a doubt been involved with Yann's career, first on his doctoral committee and then running the panel judging his proposal. He had impacted Yann's career in ways he hadn't even intended, by sabotaging his application so that Yann had gone to Torrey Pines Generique and then Small Delivery Systems, where he was now.

Possibly the futures market had taken notice of that.

Caroline was now looking more relaxed, perhaps relieved that he was not outraged or otherwise freaked out by her news. He tried to stay cool. What was done was done. He had tried to secure Pierzinski's work for a company he had ties to, yes; but he had failed. So despite his best (or worst) efforts, there was nothing now he needed to hide.

'You said MIT,' he said, thinking things over. 'Is Francesca Taolini involved with this?'

A surprised look, then: 'Yes. She's another subject of interest. There's about a dozen of you. I was assigned to surveil most of the group.'

'Did you, I don't know . . . do you record what people say on the phone, or in rooms?'

'Sometimes, if we want to. The technology has gotten really powerful, you have no idea. But it's expensive, and it's only fully applied in some cases. Pierzinski's group – you guys are still under a much less intrusive kind of thing.'

'Good.' Frank shook his head, like a dog shaking off water. His thoughts were skittering around in all directions. 'So . . . you've been watching me for a year. But I haven't done anything.'

'I know. But then . . .'

'Then what?'

'Then I saw you on that Metro car, and I recognized you.

I couldn't believe it. I had only seen your photo, or maybe some video, but I knew it was you. And you looked upset. Very . . . intent on something.'

'Yes,' Frank said. 'That's right.'

'What happened? I mean, I checked it out later, but it seemed like you had just been at NSF that day.'

'That's right. But I went to a lecture, like I told you.'

'That's right, you did. Well, I didn't know that when I saw you in the Metro. And there you were, looking upset, and so – I thought you might be trailing me. I thought you had found out somehow, done some kind of back trace – that's another area I've been working on, mirror searching. I figured you had decided to confront me, to find out what was going on. It seemed possible, anyway. Although it was also possible it was just one of those freak things that happen in D.C. I mean, you do run into people here.'

'But then I followed you.' Frank laughed briefly.

'Right, you did, and I was standing there waiting for that elevator, thinking: What is this guy going to *do* to me?' She laughed nervously, remembering it.

'You didn't show it.'

'No? I bet I did. You didn't know me. Anyway, then the elevator stuck –'

'You didn't stop it somehow?'

'Heck no, how would I do that? I'm not some kind of a . . .'

'James Bond? James Bondette?'

She laughed. 'It is *not* like that. It's just surveillance. Anyway there we were, and we started talking, and it didn't take long for me to see that you didn't know who I was, that you didn't know about being monitored. It was just a coincidence.'

'But you said you knew I had followed you.'

'That's right. I mean, it seemed like you had. But since you didn't know what I was doing, then it had to be, I don't know . . .'

'Because I liked the way you looked.'

She nodded.

'Well, it's true,' Frank said. 'Sue me.'

She squeezed his hand. 'It's okay. I mean, I liked that. I'm in a kind of a bad . . . Well anyway, I liked it. And I already liked you, see? I wasn't monitoring you very closely, but closely enough so that I knew some things about you. I – I had to monitor some of your calls. And I thought you were funny.'

'Yes?'

'Yes. You are funny. At least I think so. Anyway, I'm sorry. I've never really had to think about what I do, not like this, not in terms of a person I talk to. I mean – how horrible it must sound.'

'You spy on people.'

'Yes. It's true. But I've never thought it has done anybody any harm. It's a way of looking out for people. Anyway, in this particular case, it meant that I knew you already. I liked you already. And there you were, so, you know . . . it meant you liked me too.' She smiled crookedly. 'That was okay too. Guys don't usually follow me around.'

'Yeah right.'

'They don't.'

'Uh huhn. The man who knew too little, watched by the spy who knew even less.'

She laughed, pulled her hand away, punched him lightly on the arm. He caught her hand in his, pulled her to him. She leaned into his chest and he kissed the top of her head, as if to say, I forgive you your job, I forgive the surveillance. He breathed in the scent of her hair. Then she looked up, and they kissed, very briefly; then she pulled away. The shock of it passed through him, waking him up and making him happy. He remembered how it had been in the elevator; this wasn't like that, but he could tell she remembered it too.

'Yes,' she said thoughtfully. 'Then we did that. You're a handsome man. And I had figured out why you had followed me, and I felt – oh, I don't know. I *liked* you.'

'Yes,' Frank said, still remembering the elevator. Feeling the kiss. His skin was glowing.

She laughed again, looking off at her memories. 'I worried afterward that you would think I was some kind of a loose woman, jumping you like I did. But at the time I just went for it.'

'Yes you did,' Frank said.

They laughed, then kissed again.

When they stopped she smiled to herself, pushed her hair off her forehead. 'My,' she murmured.

Frank tried to track one of the many thoughts skittering back into his head. 'You said you were in a kind of a bad?'

'Ah. Yes. I did.'

The corners of her mouth tightened. She pulled back a bit. Suddenly Frank saw that she was unhappy; and this was so unlike the impression he had gained of her in the elevator that he was shocked. He saw he did not know her, of course he did not know her. He had been thinking that he did, but it wasn't so. She was a stranger.

'What?' he said.

'I'm married.'

'Ahh.'

'And, you know. It's bad.'

'Uh oh.' But that was also good, he thought.

'I . . . don't really want to talk about it. Please. But there it is. That's where I'm at.'

'Okay. But . . . you're out here.'

'I'm staying with friends tonight. They live nearby. As far as anyone knows, I'm sleeping on their couch. I left a note in case they get up, saying I couldn't sleep and went out for a run. But they won't get up. Or even if they do, they won't check on me.'

'Does your husband do surveillance too?'

'Oh yeah. He's much further up than I am.'

'I see.'

Frank didn't know what to say. It was bad news. The worst news of the night, worse than the fact that he was under surveillance. On the other hand, there she was beside him, and they had kissed.

'Please.' She put a hand to his mouth, and he kissed her fingertips. He tried to swallow all his questions.

But some of these questions represented a change of subject, a move to safer ground. 'So – tell me what you mean exactly when you say surveillance? What do you do?'

'There are different levels. For you, it's almost all documentary. Credit cards, phone bills, e-mail, computer files.'

'Whoah.'

'Well, hey. Think about it. Physical location too, sometimes. Although mostly that's at the cell phone records level. That isn't very precise. I mean, I know you're staying over off of Connecticut somewhere, but you don't have an address listed right now. So, maybe staying with someone else. That kind of stuff is obvious. If they wanted to, they could chip you. And your new van has a transponder, it's GPS-able.'

'Shit.'

'Everyone's is. Like transponders in airplanes. It's just a question of getting the code and locking on.'

'My Lord.'

Frank thought it over. There was so much information out there. If someone had access to it, they could find out a tremendous amount. 'Does NSF know this kind of stuff is going on with their people?'

'No. This is a black-black.'

'And your husband, he does what?'

'He's at a higher level.'

'Uh oh.'

'Yeah. But look, I don't want to talk about that now. Some other time.'

'When?'

'I don't know. Some other time.'

'When we meet again?'

She smiled wanly. 'Yes. When we meet again. Right now,' lighting up her watch and peering at it, 'shit. I have to get back. My friends will be getting up soon. They go to work early.'

'Okay . . . You'll be okay?'

'Oh yeah. Sure.'

'And you'll call me again?'

'Yes. I'll need to pick my times. I need to have a clear space, and be able to call you from a clean phone. There's some protocols we can establish. We'll talk about it. We'll set things up. But now I've gotta go.'

'Okay.'

A peck of a kiss and she was off into the night.


He drove his van back to the edge of Rock Creek Park, sat in the driver's seat thinking. There was still an hour before dawn. For about half an hour it rained. The sound on the van's roof was like a steel drum with only two notes, both hit all the time.

Caroline. Married but unhappy. She had called him, she had kissed him. She knew him, in some sense; which was to say, she had him under surveillance. Some kind of security program based on the virtual wagers of some MIT computers, for Christ's sake. Perhaps that was not as bad as it first sounded. A pro forma exercise. As compared to a bad marriage. Sneaking out at three in the morning. It was hard to know what to feel.

With the first grays of dawn the rain stopped, and he got out and walked into the park. Bird calls of various kinds: cheeps, trills; then a night thrush, its little melodies so outrageous that at first they seemed beyond music, they were to human music as dreams were to art – stranger, bolder, wilder. Birds singing in the forest at dawn, singing, *The rain has stopped! The day is here! I am here! I love you! I am singing!*

It was still pretty dark, and when he came to the gorge overlook he pulled a little infrared scope he had bought out of his pocket, and had a look downstream to the waterhole. Big red bodies, shimmering in the blackness; they looked like some of the bigger antelopes to Frank, maybe the elands. Those might bring the jaguar out. A South American predator attacking African prey, as if the Atlantic had collapsed back to this narrow ravine and they were all in Gondwanaland together. Far in the distance he could hear the siamangs' dawn chorus, he assumed; they sounded very far away. Suddenly something inside his chest ballooned like a throat pouch, puffed with happiness, and to himself (to Caroline) he whispered, 'ooooooooop! oooooooop!'

He listened to the siamangs, and sang under his breath with them, and fitted his digital camera to the night scope to take some IR photos of the drinking animals for FOG. In the growing light he could see them now without the scope. Black on gray. He wondered if the same siamang or gibbon made the first call every morning. He wondered if its companions were lying on branches in comfort, annoyed to be awakened; or if sleeping in the branches was uncomfortable, and all of them thus ready and waiting to get up and move with the day. Maybe this differed with animal, or circumstance – as with people – so that sometimes they snoozed through those last precious moments, before the noise became so raucously operatic that no one could sleep through it. Even at a distance it was a thrilling sound; and now it was the song of meeting Caroline, and he quit trying not to spook the big ungulents at the waterhole and howled. 'OOOOOOOOP! OoooooooooOOOOOOOOP OOP! OOP!'

He felt flooded. He had never felt like this before, it was some new emotion, intense and wild. No excess of reason for him, not any more! What would the guru say about this? Did the old man ever feel like this? Was this love, then, and him encountering it for the first time, not ever knowing before what it was? It was true she was married. But there were worse entanglements. It didn't sound like it was going to last. He could be patient. He would wait out the situation. He would have to wait for another call, after all.

Then he saw one of the gibbons or siamangs, across the ravine and upstream, swinging through branches. A small black shape, like a big cat but with very long arms. The classic monkey shape. He caught sight of white cheeks and knew that it was one of the gibbons. White-cheeked gibbons. The whoops had sounded miles away, but they might have been closer all along. In the forest it was hard to judge.

There were more of them, following the first. They flew through the trees like crazy trapeze artists, improvising every swing. Brachiation: amazing. Frank photographed them too, hoping the shots might help the FOG people get an ID. Brachiating through the trees, no plan or destination, just free-forming it through the branches. He wished he could join them and fly like Tarzan, but watching them he knew just what an impossible fantasy that was. Hominids had come down out of the trees, they were no longer arboreal. Tarzan was wrong, and even his treehouse was a throwback.

Upstream the three eland looked up at the disturbance, then continued to drink their fill. Frank stood on the overlook, happily singing his rising glissando of animal joy, 'ooooooooooop!'

And speaking of animals, there was a party at the re-opened National Zoo, scheduled for later that very morning.

**The National Zoo, perched** as it was on a promontory overlooking a bend in the Rock Creek gorge, had been hammered by the great flood. Lipping over from the north, the surge had rushed down to meet the rise of the Potomac, and the scouring had torn a lot of the fencing and landscaping away. Fortunately most of the buildings and enclosures were made of heavy concrete, and where their foundations had not been undercut, they had survived intact. The National Park system had been able to fund the repairs internally, and given that most of the released animals had survived the flood, and been rounded up afterward rather easily (indeed some had returned to the zoo site as soon as the water subsided), repairs had proceeded with great dispatch. The Friends of the National Zoo, numbering nearly two thousand now, had pitched in with their labor and their collective memory of the park, and the reconstructed version now opening to the public looked very like the original, except for a certain odd rawness.

The tiger and lion enclosure, at the southern end of the park, was a circular island divided into four quadrants, separated by a moat and a high outer wall from the human observers. The trees on the island had survived, although they looked strangely sparse and bedraggled for June.

On this special morning the returning crowd was joined by the Khembali legation, on hand to repeat their swimming tigers' welcoming ceremony, so ironically interrupted by the flood. The Quiblers were there too, of course; one of the

90

tigers had spent two nights in their basement, and now they felt a certain familial interest.

Anna enjoyed watching Joe as he stood in his backpack on Charlie's back, happy to be up where he could see properly, whacking Charlie on the sides of the head and shouting 'Tiger? Tiger?'

'Yes, tiger,' Charlie agreed, trying blindly to catch the little fists pummeling him. 'Our tigers! Swimming tigers!'

A dense crowd surrounded them, ooohing together when the door to the tigers' inner sanctum opened, and a few moments later the big cats strode out, glorious in the morning sun.

'Tiger! Tiger!'

The crowd cheered. The tigers ignored the commotion. They padded around on the washed grass, sniffing things. One marked the big tree in their quadrant, protected from claws if not from pee by a new wooden cladding, and the crowd said 'Ah.' Nick explained to the people around him that these were Bengal tigers that had been washed out to sea in a big flood of the Brahmaputra, not the Ganges; that they had survived by swimming together for an unknown period of time, and that the Brahmaputra's name changed to the Tsangpo after a dramatic bend upstream. Anna asked if the Ganges too hadn't been flooding at least a little bit. Joe jumped up and down in his backpack, nearly toppling forward over Charlie's head. Charlie listened to Nick, as did Frank Vanderwal, standing behind them among the Khembalis.

Rudra Cakrin gave a small speech, translated by Drepung, thanking the zoo and all its people, and then the Quiblers.

'Tiger tiger tiger!'

Frank grinned to see Joe's excitement. 'Ooooop!' he cried, imitating the gibbons, which excited Joe even more. It seemed to Anna that Frank was in an unusually good mood. Some of the FONZies came by and gave him a big round button that said FOG on it, and he took another one from them and pinned it to Nick's shirt. Nick asked the volunteers a barrage of questions about the zoo animals still on the loose, at the same time eagerly perusing the FOG brochure they gave him. 'Have any animals gotten as far as Bethesda?'

Frank replied for the FONZies, allowing them to move on in their rounds. 'They're finding smaller ones all over. They seem to be radiating out the tributary streams from Rock Creek. You can check the website and get all the latest sightings, and track the radio signals from the ones that have been tagged. When you join FOG, you can call in GPS locations for any ferals that you see.'

'Cool! Can we go and look for some?'

'I hope so,' Frank said. 'That would be fun.' He looked over at Anna and she nodded, feeling pleased. 'We could make an expedition of it.'

'Is Rock Creek Park open yet?'

'It is if you're in the FOG.'

'Is it safe?' Anna asked.

'Sure. I mean there are parts of the gorge where the new walls are still unstable, but we would stay away from those. There's an overlook where you can see the torn-up part and the new pond where a lot of them drink.'

'Cool!'

The larger of the swimming tigers slouched down to the moat and tested the water with his huge paw.

'Tiger tiger tiger!'

The tiger looked up. He eyed Joe, tilted back his massive head, roared briefly at what had to be the lowest frequencies audible to humans, or even lower. It was a sound mostly felt in the stomach.

'Ooooooh,' Joe said. The crowd said the same.

Frank was grinning with what Anna now thought of as his true smile. 'Now *that's* a vocalization,' he said.

Rudra Chakrin spoke for a while in Tibetan, and Drepung then translated.

'The tiger is a sacred animal, of course. He stands for

courage. When we are at home, his name is not to be said aloud; that would be bad luck. Instead he is called King of the Mountain, or the Big Insect.'

'The Big Insect?' Nick repeated incredulously. 'That'd just make him mad!'

The larger tiger, a male, padded over to the tree and raked the new cladding, leaving a clean set of claw marks on the fresh wood. The crowd ooohed again.

Frank hooted. 'Hey, I'm going to go see if I can set the gibbons off. Nick, do you want to join me?'

'To do what?'

'I want to try to get the gibbons to sing. I know they've recaptured one or two.'

'Oh, no thanks. I think I'll stay here and keep watching the tigers.'

'Sure. You'll be able to hear the gibbons from here, if they do it.'

Eventually the tigers flopped down in the morning shade and stared into space. The zoo people made speeches as the crowd dispersed through the rest of the zoo. Some pretty vigorous whooping from the direction of the gibbons' enclo-sure nevertheless did not sound quite like the creatures them-selves. After a while Frank rejoined them, shaking his head. 'There's only one gibbon couple that's been recovered. The rest are out in the park. I've seen some of them. It's neat,' he told Nick. 'You'll like it.'

Drepung came over. 'Would you join our little party in the visitors' center?' he asked Frank.

'Sure, thanks. My pleasure.'

They walked up the zoo paths together to a building near the entry on Connecticut. Drepung led the Quiblers and Frank to a room in back, and Rudra Cakrin guided them to seats around a round table under a window. He came over and shook Frank's hand: 'Hello, Frank. Welcome. Please to meet you. Please to sit. Eat some food, drink some tea.'

Frank looked startled. 'So you *do* speak English!'

The old man smiled. 'Oh yes, very good English. Drepung make me take lessons.'

Drepung rolled his eyes and shook his head. Padma and Sucandra joined them as they passed out sample cups of Tibetan tea. The cross-eyed expression on Nick's face when he smelled his cup gave Drepung a good laugh. 'You don't have to try it,' he assured the boy.

'It's like each ingredient has gone bad in a completely different way,' Frank commented after a taste.

'Bad to begin with,' Drepung said.

'Good!' Rudra exclaimed. 'Good stuff.'

He hunched forward to slurp at his cup. He did not much resemble the commanding figure who had given the lecture at NSF, Anna thought, which perhaps explained why Frank was regarding him so curiously.

'So you've been taking English lessons?' Frank said. 'Or maybe it's like Charlie said? That you spoke English all along, but didn't want to tell us?'

'Charlie say that?'

'I was just joking,' Charlie said.

'Charlie very funny.'

'Yes . . . so you are taking lessons?'

'I am scientist. Study English like a bug.'

'A scientist!'

'I am always scientist.'

'Me too. But I thought you said, at your lecture, that rationality wasn't enough. That an excess of reason was a form of madness.'

Rudra consulted with Drepung, then said, 'Science is more than reason. More stronger.' He elbowed Drepung, who elaborated:

'Rudra Cakrin uses a word for science that is something like devotion. A kind of devotion, he says. A way to honor, or worship.'

'Worship what, though?'

Drepung asked Rudra, got a reply. 'Whatever you find,' he said. 'Devotion is a better word than worship, maybe.'

Rudra shook his head, looking frustrated by the limited palette of the English language. 'You *watch*,' he said in his gravelly voice, fixing Frank with a glare. '*Look*. If you can. Seems like healing.'

He appealed again to Drepung. A quick exchange in Tibetan, then he forged on. 'Look and heal, yes. Make better. Make worse, make better. For example, take a *walk*. Look *in*. In, out, around, down, up. Up and down. Over and under. Ha ha ha.'

Drepung said, 'Yes, his English lessons are coming right along.'

Sucandra and Padma laughed at this, and Rudra scowled a mock scowl, so unlike his real one.

'He seldom sticks with one instructor for long,' Padma said.

'Goes through them like tissues,' Sucandra amplified.

'Oh my,' Frank said.

The old man returned to his tea, then said to Frank, 'You come to our home, please?'

'Thank you, my pleasure. I hear it's very close to NSF.'

Rudra shook his head, said something in Tibetan.

Drepung said, 'By home, he means Khembalung. We are planning a short trip there, and the rimpoche thinks you should join us. He thinks it would be a big instruction for you.'

'I'm sure it would,' Frank said, looking startled. 'And I'd like to see it. I appreciate him thinking of me. But I don't know how it could work. I'm afraid I don't have much time to spare these days.'

Drepung nodded. 'True for all. The upcoming trip is planned to be short for this very reason. That is what makes it possible for the Quibler family also to join us.'

Again Frank looked surprised.

Drepung said, 'Yes, they are all coming. We plan two days to fly there, four days on Khembalung, two days to get back. Eight days away. But a very interesting week, I assure you.'

'Isn't this monsoon season there?'

The Khembalis nodded solemnly. 'But no monsoon, this year or two previous. Big drought. Another reason to see.'

Frank nodded, looked at Anna and Charlie: 'So you're really going?'

Anna said, 'I thought it would be good for the boys. But I can't be away from work for long.'

'Or else her head will explode,' Charlie said, raising a hand to deflect Anna's elbow from his ribs. 'Just joking! Anyway,' addressing her, 'you can work on the plane and I'll watch Joe. I'll watch him the whole way.'

'Deal,' Anna said swiftly.

'Charlie very funny,' Rudra said again.

Frank said, 'Well, I'll think it over. It sounds interesting. And I appreciate the invitation,' nodding to Rudra.

'Thank you,' Rudra said.

Sucandra raised his glass. 'To Khembalung!'

'No!' Joe cried.

# THREE

# *Back To Khembalung*

*One Saturday Charlie was out on his own, Joe at home with Anna, Nick out with Frank tracking animals. After running some errands he browsed for a bit in Second Story Books, and he was replacing a volume on its shelf when a woman approached him and said, 'Excuse me, can you tell me where I can find William Blake?'*

*Surprised to be taken for an employee (they were all twenty-five and wore black), Charlie stared blankly at her.*

*'He's a poet,' the woman explained.*

*Now Charlie was shocked; not only taken for a Second Story clerk, but for the kind who did not know who William Blake was?*

*'Poetry's back there,' he finally got out, gesturing weakly toward the rear of the store.*

*The woman slipped past him, shaking her head.*

*Fire fire burning bright! Charlie didn't say.*

*Don't forget to check the oversized art books for facsimiles of his engravings! he didn't exclaim.*

*In fact he's a lot better artist than poet I think you'll find! Most of his poetry is trippy gibberish, I think you'll find! He didn't shout.*

His cell phone rang and he snatched it out of his pocket. 'William Blake was out of his mind!'

'Hello, Charlie? Charlie is that you?'

'Oh hi Phil. Listen, do I look to you like a person who doesn't know who William Blake was?'

'I don't know, do you?'

'Shit. You know, great arias are lost to the world because we do not speak our minds. Most of our best lines we never say.'

'I don't have that problem.'

'No, I guess you don't. So what's up?'

'I'm following up on our conversation at the Lincoln Memorial.'

'Oh yeah, good! Are you going to go for it?'

'I think I will, yeah.'

'Great! You've checked with your money people?'

'Yes, that looks like it will be okay. There are an awful lot of people who want a change.'

'That's for sure. But, you know ... do you really think you can win?'

'Yes, I think so. The feedback I've been getting has been positive. But ...'

'But what?'

Phil sighed. 'I'm worried about what effect it might have on me. I mean – power corrupts, right?'

'Yes, but you're already powerful.'

'So it's already happened, yes, thank you for that. But it's supposed to get worse, right? Power corrupts, and absolute power corrupts absolutely? Was it William Blake who said that?'

'That was Lord Acton.'

'Oh yeah. But he left out the corollary. Power corrupts, absolute power corrupts absolutely, and a little bit of power corrupts a little bit.'

'I suppose that must be so.'

'And everyone has a little bit of power.'

'Yes, I suppose.'

'So we're all a little bit corrupt.'

'Hmm –'

'Come on, how does that not parse? It does parse. Power corrupts, and we all have power, so we're all corrupt. A perfect syllogism, if I'm not mistaken. And in fact the only people we think of as not being corrupt are usually powerless. Prisoners of conscience, the feeble-minded, some of the elderly, saints, children –'

'My children have power.'

'Yes, but are they perfectly pure and innocent?'

Charlie thought of Joe, faking huge distress when Anna came home from work. 'No, they're a little corrupt.'

'Well there you go.'

'I guess you're right. And saints have power but aren't corrupt, which is why we call them saints. But where does that leave us? That in this world of universal corruption, you might as well be President?'

'Yes. That's what I was thinking.'

'So then it's okay.'

'Yes. But the sad part is that the corruption doesn't just happen to the people with power. It spreads from them. They spread it around. I know this is true because I see it. Every day people come to me because I've got some power, and I watch them debase themselves or go silly in some way. I see them go corrupt right before my eyes. It's depressing. It's like having the Midas touch in reverse, where everything you touch turns to shit.'

'The solution is to become saintlike. Do like Lincoln. He had power, but he kept his integrity.'

'Lincoln could see how limited his power was. Events were out of his control.'

'That's true for us too.'

'Right. Good thought. I'll try not to worry. But, you know.

*I'm going to need you guys. I'll need friends who will tell me the truth.'*

*'We'll be there. We'll call you on everything.'*

*'Good. I appreciate that. Because it's kind of a bizarre thing to be contemplating.'*

*'I'm sure it is. But you might as well go for it. In for a penny in for a pound. And we need you.'*

*'You'll help me with the environmental issues?'*

*'As always. I mean, I've got to take care of Joe, as you know. But I can always talk on the phone. I'm on call any time – oh for God's sake here she comes again. Look Phil I'd better get out of here before that lady comes to tell me that Abraham Lincoln was a president.'*

*'Tell her he was a saint.'*

*'Make him your patron saint and you'll be fine bye!'*

*'That's bye Mr President.'*

**Under surveillance.**

After he had come down from the euphoria of seeing Caroline, talking to her, kissing her, planning to meet again – Frank was faced with the unsettling reality of her news. Some group in Homeland Security had him under surveillance.

A creepy thought. Not that he had done anything he needed to hide – except that he had. He had tried to sink a young colleague's grant proposal, in order to secure that work in a private company he had relations with; and the first part of the plan had worked. Not that that was likely to be what they were surveiling him for – but on the other hand, maybe it was. The connection to Pierzinski was apparently why they were interested in him in the first place. Evidence of what he had tried to do – would there be any in the records? Part of the point of him proceeding had been that nothing in what he had done was in contradiction to NSF panel protocols. However, among other actions he was now reviewing, he had made many calls to Derek Gaspar, CEO of Torrey Pines Generique. In some of these he had perhaps been indiscreet.

Well, nothing to be done about that now. He could only focus on the present, and the future.

Thinking about this in his office, Frank stared at his computer. It was connected to the internet, of course. It had virus protections, firewalls, encryption codes; but for all he knew, there were programs more powerful still, capable of finessing all that and probing directly into his files. At the very least, all his e-mail. And then phone conversations, sure. Credit rating, sure, bank records, all other financial activity – all now data for analysis by participants in some kind of virtual futures market, a market trading in newly emerging ideas, technologies, researchers. All speculated on, as with any other commodity. People as commodities – well, it wouldn't be the first time.

He went out to a local cyber-cafe and paid cash to get on one of the house machines. Seating himself before it with a triple espresso, he looked around to see what he could find.

The first sites that came up told the story of the case of the Policy Analysis Market proposal, which had blown up in the face of DARPA, the Defense Advanced Research Projects Agency, some time before. John Poindexter, of Iran-Contra fame, had set up a futures market in which participants could bet on potential events in the Middle East, including possibilities like terrorist attacks and assassinations. Within a week of announcing the project Poindexter had been forced to resign, and DARPA had cut off all funds not just for the PAM project, but for all research into markets as predictive tools. There were protests about this at the time, from various parties convinced that markets could be powerful predictors, distilling as they did the collective information and wisdom of many people, all putting their money where their mouths were. Different people brought different expertise to the table, it was claimed, and the aggregated information was thought to be better able to predict future performance of the given commodity than any individual or single group could.

This struck Frank as bullshit, but that was neither here nor there. Certainly the market fetishists who dominated their culture would not give up on such an ideologically correct idea just because of a single public relations gaffe. And indeed, Frank quickly came on news of a program called ARDA, Advanced Research and Development Activity, which had become home to both the Total Information Awareness program and the ideas future market. ARDA had been funded as part of the 'National Foreign Intelligence Program,' which was part of an intelligence agency that had not been publicly identified. 'Evidence Extraction,' 'Link Discovery,' 'Novel Intelligence from Massive Data'; all kinds of data-mining projects had disappeared with the futures market idea down this particular rabbit hole.

Before it left public view along with the rest of this kind of thing, the idea futures market concept had already been fine-tuned to deal with first iteration problems. 'Conditional bidding' allowed participants to nuance their wagers by making them conditional on intermediary events. And – this jumped out at Frank as he read – 'market makers' were added to the system, meaning automated bidders that were always available to trade, so that the market would stay liquid even when there were few participants. The first market maker programs had lost tremendous amounts of money, so their programmers had refined them to a point where they were able to compete successfully with live traders.

Bingo. Frank's investors.

The whole futures market concept had then gone black, along with ARDA itself. Wherever it was now, it undoubtedly included these programs that could trade in the futures of researchers and their ideas, predicting which would prosper by using the collective pooling of information envisioned in the Total Information Awareness concept, which had dreamed of collating all the information everywhere in the datasphere.

So: virtual markets, with virtual participants, creating virtual results, tracked by real people in real security agencies. All part of the newly secure environment as envisioned in the Homeland Security acts. That these people had chosen a Nazi title for their enterprise was presumably more a tribute to their ignorance and stupidity than to any evil intent. Nevertheless it was not reassuring.

Briefly Frank wondered if he could learn enough to do some reverse transcription, and use this system against itself. Google-bombing was one method that had successfully distorted the datasphere, placing information in ways that caused it to radiate out through the system inaccurately. That particular method had been countered by blockers, but other methods remained out there, using the cascading recombinant math that was part of the algorithm family that both Frank and Yann Pierzinski studied. Pierzinski was the young hotshot, blazing out into new territory; but it was Frank who had recognized what his newly powerful algorithm might do in the real world. Now maybe he had identified another potential application. Yann never would; he was one of those mathematicians who just didn't care about other stuff. There were theorists and there were engineers, and then there were the few who straddled the two realms, identifying the theories that were most likely to bear fruit in real-world accomplishment, and could suggest to engineering types how they might go about implementing things. That was Frank's ability as he saw it, and now he wondered how one might formulate the problem for a mathematician, and then an engineering team . . .

Frank almost called Edgardo, as a fellow realm-straddler, to ask him what he knew; because among other factors, Edgardo had come to NSF from DARPA. DARPA was like NSF, in that it staffed itself mostly with visiting scientists, although DARPA stints were usually three to four years rather than one or two. Edgardo, however, had only lasted there a year. He had never said much about why, only once remarking that his attitude had not been appreciated. Certainly his views on this surveillance matter would be extremely interesting –

But of course Frank couldn't call him. Even his cell phone might be bugged; and Edgardo's too. Suddenly he recalled that workman in his new office, installing a power strip.

Could a power strip include a splitter that would direct all data flowing through it in more than one direction? And a mike and so on?

Probably so. He would have to talk to Edgardo in person, and in a private venue. Running with the lunchtime runners would give him a chance at that; the group often strung out along the paths.

He needed to know more. Already he wished Caroline would call again. He wanted to talk to everyone implicated in this: Yann Pierzinski – meaning Marta too, which would be hard, terrible in fact, but Marta had moved to Atlanta with Yann and they lived together there, so there would be no avoiding her. And then Francesca Taolini, who had arranged for Yann's hire by a company she consulted for, in the same way Frank had hoped to. Did she suspect that Frank had been after Yann? Did she know how powerful Yann's algorithm might be?

He googled her. Turned out, among many interesting things, that she was helping to chair a conference at MIT coming soon, on bioinformatics and the environment. Just the kind of event Frank might attend. NSF even had a group going already, he saw, to talk about the new federal institutes.

Meet with her first, then go to Atlanta to meet with Yann – would that make his stock in the virtual market rise, triggering more intense surveillance? An unpleasant thought; he grimaced.

He couldn't evade most of this surveillance. He had to continue to behave as if it wasn't happening. Or rather, treat his actions as also being experiments in the sensitivity of the surveillance. Visit Taolini and Pierzinski, sure, and see if that gave his stock a bump. Though he would need detailed information from Caroline to find out anything about that.

He e-mailed the NSF travel office and had them book him flights to Boston and back. A day trip ought to do it.

\* \* \*

Some mornings he woke to the sound of rain ticking onto his roof and the leaves. Dawn light, muted and wet; he lay in his sleeping bag watching grays turn silver. His roof extended far beyond the edges of his plywood floor. When he had all the lines and bungee cords right, the clear plastic quivered tautly in the wind, shedding its myriad deltas of water. Looking up at it, Frank lay comfortably, entirely dry except for that ambient damp that came with rain no matter what one did. Same with all camping, really. But mostly dry; and there he was, high in the forest in the rain, in a rain forest canopy, encased in the splashing of a million drips, and the wet whoosh of the wind in the branches, remaining dry and warm watching it all. Yes, he was an arboreal primate, lying on his foam pad half in his sleeping bag, looking through an irregular bead curtain of water falling from the edge of his roof. A silvery green morning.

Often he heard the other arboreal primates, greeting the day. These days they seemed to be sleeping on the steep slope across the creek from him. The first cry of the morning would fill the gorge, low and liquid at first, a strange cross between siren and voice. It never failed to send a shiver down his spine. That was something hardwired. No doubt the hominid brain included a musical capacity that was not the same as its language capacity. These days people tended to use their musical brains only for listening, thus missing the somatic experience of making it. With that gone the full potential of the experience was lost. 'Oooooop!' Singing, howling; it all felt so good. 'Ooooh-oooooooooooo-da.'

Something else to consider writing about. Music as primate precursor to language. He would add it to his list of possible papers, already scores if not hundreds of titles long. He knew he would never get to them, but they ought to be written.

He had extended his roof to cover the cut in the railing and floor through which he dropped onto his rope ladder, and so he was able to descend to the ground without getting very wet.

Onto the forest floor, not yet squishy, out to his van, around D.C. on the Beltway, making the first calls of the day over his headset. Stop in at Optimodal, singing under his breath, 'I'm optimodal, today – optimodal, today!' Into the weight room, where, it being six AM, Diane was working on one of the leg machines. Familiar hellos, a bit of chat about the rain and her morning calls, often to Europe to make use of the time difference. It was turning out to be a very cool summer in Europe, and rainstorms were being welcomed as signs of salvation; but the environmental offices there were full of foreboding.

Shower, change, walk over to NSF with Diane. Amazing how quickly people developed sets of habits. They could not do without them, Frank had concluded. Even his improvised life was full of them. It might be said that now he had an array of habits that he had to choose from, a kind of menu. Up to his office, check phone messages and e-mail, get coffee, start on the messages that needed action, and the making of a daily *Things To Do* list out of the standing one on the whiteboard. Bit of breakfast when his stomach reminded him it was being neglected.

One of his *Things To Do* was to attend another of Diane's meetings late that morning, this one attended by various division heads, including Anna, and some members of the Science Board.

Diane had been busy organizing her own sense of the climate problem, structuring it in the broadest terms possible. First, however, she had some good news to share; the appropriations committees in Congress had streamlined approval of two billion dollars for NSF to engage with climate issues as soon as possible. 'They want us to take action, they said, but in a strictly scientific manner.'

Edgardo snorted. 'They want a silver bullet. Some kind of technical fix that will make all the problems go away without any suffering on Wall Street.'

'That doesn't matter,' Diane said. 'They're funding us, and we'll be making the determinations as to what might work.'

She clicked to the first of her Power Point pages. 'Okay. Global environmental problem, having to do with habitat degradation and a hundred parts per million rise in atmospheric carbon, resulting in species loss and food insecurity. You can divide it into land, ocean, and atmosphere. On land, we have loss of topsoil, desertification, and in some places, flooding. In the oceans, we have sea level rise, either slow because of general warming, already happening, or else fast, as a result of the West Antarctic ice sheet detaching. Probability of the Antarctic ice sheet coming off is very hard to calculate. Then also thermohaline circulation, in particular the North Atlantic stall in the great world current. Also fisheries depletion, also coral reef loss. The oceans are more of a source of trouble than we're used to thinking. In the atmosphere, carbon dioxide build-up of course, very well known, but also methane and other more powerful greenhouse gases.'

She clicked to the next slide. 'Let's start with atmosphere, particularly the carbon dioxide aspect. Now up to 400 parts per million, from 280 before the industrial revolution. Clearly, we need to slow down how much $CO_2$ we're putting into the atmosphere, despite the industrialization of China, India, and many other places. Then also, it would be interesting to see if we could remove and sequester from the atmosphere any significant amounts of $CO_2$ that are already up there. Drawdown studies, these are sometimes called.

'What's putting carbon into the atmosphere? The bulk of it comes from energy production and cars. We've been burning fossil fuels to create electricity and to move us and our stuff around. If we had cleaner technologies to create electricity and to power transport, we would put less carbon in the air. So, we need cleaner cars and cleaner energy production. There's been a lot of work done on both fronts, with some very exciting possibilities explored, but bottom line, the oil and car industries are very big, and they work together to obstruct research and development of cleaner technologies that might replace them. Partly because of their lobbying here in D.C., research into cleaner technologies is under-funded, even though some of the new methods show real promise. Some are even ready to go, and could make a difference very rapidly, but are still too expensive to compete financially, especially given the initial costs in installing a new infrastructure, whatever it might be.

'So. Given this situation, I think we have to identify the two or three most promising options in each big carbon area, energy and transport, and then immediately support these options in a major way. Pilot projects, maybe competitions with prizes, certainly suggested tax structures and incentives to get private enterprise investing in it.'

'Make carbon credits really expensive,' Frank said.

'Make *gas* really expensive,' Edgardo said.

'Yes. These are more purely economic or political fixes. We will run into political resistance on those.'

'You'll run into political resistance on all these fronts.'

'Yes. But we have to work for everything that looks like it will help, political resistance or not. More and more I'm convinced that this will have to be a multi-disciplinary effort, in the largest sense. The front is very broad, and we can't avoid the awkward parts just because they've got difficulties. I was just mentioning them.'

She clicked to her next slide. 'Cars. It takes about ten years to replace the fleet of cars on the road, so we need to start now if anything is to be done in a relevant time period. Fuel cell cars, electric, hydrogen. Also, there are some things we could do right away with the current models. Increase fuel efficiency, of course. Could be legislated. Also, fuel flexibility. There is a device that could be added to every conventional car that would enable it to burn gas, ethanol or methanol. Adds only a couple hundred dollars per vehicle. It too could be legislated to be a requirement. This would have a national security aspect, which is to say, if we are unexpectedly cut off from foreign oil supplies, everyone could still burn ethanol in their cars, and we wouldn't be completely crippled.'

'Ethanol still puts carbon into the atmosphere,' Frank pointed out.

'Yes, but it's made from biological material that has been drawn down from the atmosphere when the plant material grew. On the plant's death it was going to rot and enter the atmosphere as carbon anyway. If you burn it and put it in the atmosphere, you can then also draw it back down in the plants that you use for later fuel, so that it becomes a closed-loop system where there is no net gain of carbon in the atmosphere, even though you have moved lots of transport. Whereas burning oil and coal adds new carbon to the atmosphere, carbon that was very nicely sequestered before we burned it. So ethanol is better, and it's available right now, and works in current cars. Most of the other technologies for cleaner power are a decade away in terms of research and development. So it's nice that we have something we can deploy immediately. A bridge technology. Clearly this should happen right now.'

'If it weren't for the political obstructions.'

'Yes. Maybe this is an issue where we have to try to educate Congress, the administration and the people. Think about how we might do that. But now, on to cleaner energy production.' Diane clicked slides again. 'Here again we already have proven options, in the form of all the renewables, many of them working and ready to be expanded. Wind, geothermal, solar, and so on.

'The one with tremendous potential for growth is of course solar power. The technological difficulties in transferring sunlight to electricity are complicated enough that there are competing designs for improvement, still struggling to show superiority over the other methods. So one thing we can do is to help identify which ones to pursue with a big effort. Photovoltaic research, of course, but also we need to look at these flexible mirror systems, directing light to heatable elements that transform the heat into electricity. Further down the line, there is also the prospect of space solar, gathering the sunlight in space and beaming it down.'

'Wouldn't that require help from NASA?'

'Yes, NASA should be part of this. A really big booster is a prerequisite for any conceivable space solar, naturally.'

'And what about DOE?'

'Well, perhaps. We have to acknowledge that some federal agencies have been captured by the industries they are supposed to regulate. Clearly the Department of Energy is one of these. They should have been taking the lead on clean energy, but they began as the Atomic Energy Commission, so for a while they would only look at nuclear, and now they are creatures of the oil industry. So they have been obstructions to innovation for many years. Whether that can change now, I don't know. I suspect the only good that can come from them is some version of clean coal. If coal can be gasified, it's possible its carbon and methane could be captured and sequestered before burning. That would be good, if they can pull it off. But beyond that, the unfortunate truth is that DOE is more likely to be one of the impediments to our efforts than a help. We will have to do what we can to engage them, and dance around any obstacles they might set up.'

She clicked again. 'Now, carbon capture and sequestering. Here, the hope is that ways can be found to draw down some of the $CO_2$ already in the atmosphere. That could be a big help, obviously. There are proven mechanical means to do this, but the scale of anything we could afford to build is much too small. If anything's going to work, it almost certainly will have to be biological. The first and most obvious method here is to grow more plants. Reforestation projects are thus helpful in more ways than one, as stabilizing soil, restoring

111

habitat, growing energy, and growing building materials, all while drawing down carbon. Poplars are often cited as very fast growers with a significant drawdown possibility.

'The other biological method suggested would involve some hypothetical engineered biological system taking more carbon out of the atmosphere than it does now. This brings biotech into the game, and it could be a crucial player. It might have the possibility of working fast enough to help us in the short term.'

For a while they discussed the logistics of initiating all the efforts Diane had sketched out so far, and then Anna took over the Power Point screen.

She said, 'Another carbon sequestration, in effect, would be to *not* burn oil that we would have using our current practices. Meaning conservation. It could make a huge difference. Since the United States is the only country living at American consumption levels, if we here decided to consume less, it would significantly reduce world consumption levels.'

She clicked to a slide titled *Carbon Values*. It consisted of a list of phrases:

- conservation, preservation (fuel efficiency, carbon taxes)
- voluntary simplicity
- stewardship, right action (religion)
- sustainability, permaculture
- leaving healthy support system for the subsequent generations

Edgardo was shaking his head. 'This amishization, as the engineers call it – you know, this voluntary simplicity movement – it is not going to work. Not only are we fond of our comforts and toys, and lazy too, but there is a fifty billion dollar a year industry fighting any such change, called advertising.'

Anna said, 'Maybe we could hire an advertising firm to

design a series of voluntary simplicity ads, to be aired on certain cable channels.'

Edgardo grinned. 'Yes, I would enjoy to see that, but there is a ten trillion-a-year economy that also wants more consumption. It's like we're working within the body of a cancerous tumor. It's hopeless, really. We will simply charge over the cliff like lemmings.'

'Real lemmings don't actually run off cliffs,' Anna quibbled. 'People might change. People change all the time. It just depends on what they want.'

She had been looking into this matter, which she jokingly called macrobioinformatics: researching, refining and even inventing various rubrics by which people could evaluate their consumption levels quantitatively, with the idea that if they saw exactly what they were wasting, they would cut back and save money. The best known of these rubrics, as she explained, were the various 'ecological footprint' measurements. These had been originally designed for towns and countries, but Anna had worked out methods for households as well, and now she passed around a chart illustrating one method, with a statistical table that illustrated her earlier point that since Americans were the only ones in the world living at American consumption levels, any reduction here would disproportionately shrink the total world footprint.

'The whole thing should be translated into money values at every step,' Edgardo said. 'Put it in the best way everyone in this culture can understand, the cost in dollars and cents. Forget the acreage stuff. People don't know what an acre is anymore, or what you can expect to extract from it.'

'Education, good,' Diane said. 'That's already part of our task as defined. And it will help to get the kids into it.'

Edgardo cackled. 'Okay, maybe they will go for it, but also the economists should be trying to invent an honest accounting system that doesn't keep exteriorizing costs. When you exteriorize costs onto future generations you can make any damn

113

thing profitable, but it isn't really true. I warn you, this will be one of the hardest things we might try. Economics is incorrigible. They call it the dismal science but actually it's the happy religion.'

Frank tended to agree with Edgardo's skepticism about these kinds of social interventions; and his own interests lay elsewhere, in the category Diane had labeled 'Mitigation Projects.' Now she took back the Power Point from Anna and clicked to a list which included several of the suggestions Frank had made to her earlier:

1) establishing one or more national institutes for the study of abrupt climate change and its mitigation, analogous to Germany's Max Planck Institutes.
2) establishing grants and competitions designed to identify and fund mitigation work judged crucial by NSF.
3) reviewing the already existing federal agencies to find potentially helpful projects they had undertaken or proposed, and coordinate them.

All good projects, but it was the next slide, 'Remedial Action Now,' that was the most interesting to Frank. One of the obvious places to start here was with the thermohaline circulation stall. Diane had gotten a complete report from Kenzo and his colleagues at NOAA , and her tentative conclusion was that the great world current, though huge, was sensitive in a nonlinear way to small perturbations. Which meant it might respond sensitively to small interventions if they could be directed well.

So, Diane concluded, this had to be investigated. How big a sea surface was critical to downwelling? How precisely could they pinpoint potential downwelling sites? How big a volume of water were they talking about? If they needed to make it saltier in order to force it to start sinking again, how much salt were they talking about? Could they start new downwellings in the north where they used to happen?

Kenzo's eyes were round. He met Frank's gaze, waggled his eyebrows like Groucho. Pretty interesting stuff!

'We have to do something,' Diane declared, without glancing at Frank. He thought: she's been convinced. I was at least part of that. 'The Gulf Stream is an obvious place to look at remediation, but there are lots of other ideas for direct intervention, and they need to be evaluated and prioritized according to various criteria – cost, effectiveness, speed, all that.'

Edgardo grinned. 'So – we are going to become global biosphere managers. We are going to terraform the Earth!'

'We already are,' Diane replied. 'The problem is we don't know how.'

**Later that day Frank** joined the noon running group, going with Edgardo and Kenzo down to the gym to dress and join Bob and Clark, from the Antarctic program on the seventh floor. The group was sometimes larger than this, sometimes smaller. They ran various routes, usually on old rail beds now converted into bike and running trails all through the area. Their usual lunchtime special ran parallel to Route 66 east for a while, then back around the curve of the Potomac and west back to NSF.

They ran at talking speed, which for this group meant about an eight-minute mile pace. A lot of the talking came from Edgardo, riffing on one thing or another. He liked to make connections; he liked to question things. He didn't believe in anything. Even the scientific method was to him a kind of ad hoc survival attempt, a not-very-successful concoction of emergency coping mechanisms. Which belief did not, however, keep him from working maniacally on every project thrown his way, nor from partying late almost every night at various Latin venues. He was from Buenos Aires originally, and this, he said, explained everything about him. 'All of us porteños are the same.'

'There's no one like you, Edgardo,' Bob pointed out.

'On the contrary. In Buenos Aires everyone is like me. How else could we survive? We've lived the end of the world ten times already. What to do after that? You just put Piazzolla on the box and dance on, my friend. You laugh like a fool.'

You certainly do, Frank didn't say. Of course Edgardo also did mathematics with applications in quantum computing, cryptology, and bio-algorithms, the last of which was the only aspect of his work that Frank understood. It was clear to him that at DARPA Edgardo must have had his fingers in all kinds of pies, subjects that Frank was much more interested in now than he had ever been before.

Where it paralleled Highway 66 the running path became a thin concrete walk immediately north of the freeway, between the cars and the soundwall, with only a chain link fence separating them from the roaring traffic to their right. The horribleness of it always made Edgardo grin. At midday when they usually ran it was totally exposed to the sun, but there was nothing for it but to put your head down and sweat through the smog.

'You really should run with an umbrella hat on like I do.' Edgardo looked ridiculous with this tall contraption on his saturnine head, but he claimed it kept him cool.

'That's what hair is for, right?'

'Male pattern baldness has taken that away as an option for me, as I am sure you have noticed.'

'Wouldn't that make baldness maladaptive?'

'Maladaptive in more ways than heat control, my friend.'

'Did you read that book, *Why We Run*? Explains how everything about us comes from adaptations to running? Even hair staying on the tops of our heads?'

Edgardo made a rude noise. '*Why We Run*, *Why We Love*, *Why We Reason*, all these are the same, they are simply titles for the bestseller list.'

'*Why We Run* was good,' Frank objected. 'It had stuff on the physiology of endurance. And it talked about how lots of native peoples ran animals down, over a matter of several days, even deer and antelope. The animals were faster, but the chase group would keep on pounding away until they wore the animals out.'

117

'Tortoise and hare.'

'I'm definitely a tortoise.'

'I'm going to write one called *Why We Shit*,' Edgardo declared. 'I'll go into all the details of digestion, and compare ours to other species, and describe all the poisons we take in and then have to process or pass through, or get poisoned by. By the time I'm done no one will ever want to eat again.'

'So it could be the next diet book too.'

'That's right! Atkins, South Beach, and me. The Alfonso Diet. Eat nothing but information! Digest that for once and never shit at all.'

'Like on Atkins, right?'

They left 66 for the river, passed through trees, and then the sun beat down on them again.

'What did you think of Diane's meeting?' Frank asked Edgardo when they were bringing up the rear.

'That was pretty good,' Edgardo said. 'Diane is really going for it. Whoever heads these agencies can make a lot of difference in how they function, I think. There are constraints on what each agency does, and the turf battles are fierce. But if an agency head were to get an idea and go after it aggressively, it could get interesting. So it's good to have her pushing. What's going to surprise her is what vicious opposition she's going to get from certain other agencies. There are people out there really committed to the status quo, let us say.'

They caught up with Bob and Kenzo and Clark, who were discussing the various odd climate interventions they had heard proposed.

Bob said, 'I like the one about introducing a certain bacterial agent to animal feed that would then live in the gut and greatly reduce methane production.'

'Animal Flatulence Avoidance Feed! AF AF – the sound of Congress laughing when they hear about that one.'

'But it's a good idea. Methane is a much stronger greenhouse gas than CO2, and it's mostly biologic in origin. It wouldn't be much different than putting vitamin A in soy sauce. They've done that and saved millions of kids from rickets. How is it different?'

They laughed at Bob, but he was convinced that if they acted boldly, they could alter the climate deliberately and for the good. Kenzo wasn't so sure; Edgardo didn't think so.

'Just think of it as something like the Manhattan Project,' Bob said. 'A war against disaster. Or like Apollo.'

Edgardo was his usual acid bath. 'I wonder if you are fantasizing physically or politically.'

'Well we obviously can change the atmosphere, because we have.'

'Yes, but now we've triggered abrupt change. Global warming is a problem that could have taken centuries to fix, and now we have three years.'

'Maybe less!' Kenzo bragged.

'Well, heck,' Bob said, unperturbed. 'It'll be a matter of making things up as we go along.'

Frank liked the sound of that.

They ran in silence for a while. Fleeting consciousness of the pack; immersion in the moment. Slipping slickly in your own sweat.

'Hotter than hell out here.'


After these runs Frank would shower and spend the afternoons working, feeling sharper than at any other time of the day. Mornings were for talking and prepping, afternoons were for work. Even algorithm work, where the best he could do these days was try to understand Yann's papers, now growing scarcer as Small Delivery made his work confidential.

There was always more to do than there was time to get it done, so he pitched in to the items on the list and set his watch's alarm for five, a trick he had picked up from Anna, so he would not forget and work deep into the evening. Then he cranked until it beeped. These hours disappeared in a subjective flow where they felt like minutes.

More work was accomplished than there is time to tell, ranging from discussions in house to communications with other people in other organizations, to the endless Sisyphean labor of processing jackets, which is what they called the grant proposals, never mind they were all onscreen now. No matter how high in the Foundation a person got, and no matter how important his or her other tasks might be, there was always the inevitable question from above: how many jackets did you process today? And so really there was no conceivable end to the work that could be done. Given Diane's interests now, there could never be enough networking with the outside world, and this of course brought Frank news of what everyone else was doing; and sometimes in the afternoons, first listening to a proposal to genetically engineer kelp to produce bulbs filled with ready-to-burn carbohydrates, then talking for an hour with the UNEP officer in town to plan a tidal energy capture system that placed a barge on a ratcheted piling in the tidal zone, then conferring with a group of NGO science officers concerning the Antarctic microwave project, and then speaking to people in an engineering consortium of government/university/industry groups about cheap efficient photovoltaics, he would come out of it to the high beeping of his watch alarm, dizzy at the touch of the technological sublime, feeling that a good array of plans existed already – that if they could enact this array, it would go a long way toward averting catastrophe. Perhaps they were already in the process of doing so. It was actually hard to tell; so much was happening at any one time that any description of the situation had some truth in it, from 'desperate crisis, extinction event totally ignored' to 'minor problems robustly dealt with.' It was therefore necessary to forge on in ignorance of the whole situation.

He put the finishing touches on the RFP for the Maxes,

while also reassuring those in the NSF hard core who felt that the Foundation was thereby creating its own evolutionary successors. It was easy in these arguments to see the way people thought of agencies in terms of human qualities, so that the agencies ended up behaving in the world like individuals in terms of power, will, skills and effectiveness. Some were amazingly effective for their size, others were permanently hampered by personality and history. NSF's ten billion a year made it a fairly small player on the national and world stage, but it was in a critical position, like the coxswain on a rowing team. It could coordinate the other scientific bodies, and to a certain extent industry; and exerting itself in that way, as it was now under Diane's direction, there seemed to be some kind of tail-wagging-dog possibilities not unsupported even by the most reputable and straightforward of cascade mathematics. All the suprahuman personalities represented by the various scientific bodies were mutually reinforcing each other now, in a kind of ad hoc team surge against the problem at hand. Anna had already helped them to identify the scientific infrastructural elements currently in place in the federal government and internationally, and transfer-of-infrastructure programs initiated as a result of her studies were already getting assistance and equipment. In Frank's mind, when he thought about it, science itself began to look like a pack on the move, big shadowy figures loping across the cave wall into the fray.

So he did his part, working hard in the building, learning about the West Antarctic Ice Sheet and its potential detachment from its seabed perch. Learning of plans to run oil tankers and other shipping over the pole from Japan to Scotland and Norway and back, halving the distance and making the Arctic Sea a trading lake like the Mediterranean –

Then his watch alarm would go off, surprising him again, and it was off into the long green end of the day, livid and

121

perspiring. Happy at the sudden release from the sitting at desk, the abstract thinking, the global anxiety (cave painting, Atlas figure, desperate effort to hold world aloft).

Because all that was only part of the optimodal project! Looking for animals, playing chess with Chessman, reading in the restaurants, sleeping in his tree . . .

These summer days usually cooled off a little in the last hour before dark. The sun disappeared into the forest, and then in the remaining hour or two of light, if Frank had managed to get over to Rock Creek Park in time, he would join the frisbee golfers, and run through the shadows throwing a disk and chasing it. Chasing the other players. Frank loved the steeplechase aspect of it, and the way it made him feel afterward. The things it taught him about himself: once he was running full tilt and a stride came down on a concealed hole with only his toes catching the far side, but by the time he was aware of that his foot and leg had stiffened enough that he had already pushed off using only the toes. How had he done that? No warning, instant reaction, how had there been time? In thousandths of a second his body had sensed the absence of ground, stiffened the appropriate muscles by the appropriate amount, and launched into an improvised solution, giving him about the same velocity a normal stride would have had.

Another time the reverse happened, and he stepped on a hidden bump under the front of his foot. But he knew that only after he had already given up on the stride and was catching himself on the other foot, thus saving himself a sprained ankle.

Things like this happened all the time. So just how fast *was* the brain? It appeared to be almost inconceivably fast, and in those split seconds, extremely creative and decisive. Indeed, running steeplechase and watching what his body did, especially after unforeseen problems were solved, Frank had to conclude that he was the inadvertent jailer of a mute genius.

His running foot would come down on nothing at all, he would fly forward in a tuck and roll, somersault back to his feet and run on as if he had practiced the move for years, only better – how could it be? Who did that?

Eleven million bits of data per second were taken in at the sensory endings of the nervous system, he read. In each second all incoming data were scanned, categorized, judged for danger, prioritized, and reacted to, this going on continuously, second after second; and at the same time his brain was doing all that unconsciously, in his conscious mentation he could be singing with the birds, or focusing on a throw, or thinking about what it meant to be under surveillance. Parallel processing of different activities in the parcellated mind, at different speeds, taking from near instantaneous to a matter of years, if not decades.

Thus the joy of running in the forest, giving him little glimpses of the great unconscious Mind.

Throwing was just as fun as running, or even more so, being more conscious and easier to notice. He looked, aimed, calculated, tried for a certain result. It had none of running's effortless adjustment, it was much more erratic and imprecise. Still, when the disk flew through the trees to its target and crashed into the chains and fell in a basket, it shared some of the miraculous quality of his tumbles; it did not seem physically possible. And if he thought about it too much he could not do it, his throws immediately degenerated into waldo approximations. You had to 'play unconscious,' letting unfelt parts of the brain do the calculating, while still consciously directing that the throws be attempted.

So he played on, in a kind of ecstatic state. There was some quality to the game that seemed to transcend sports as he had known them; not even climbing resembled it. Surely it was closely analogous to the hominid hunting and gathering experience that was central to the emergence of humanity. As Frank ran the park with the guys he sometimes thought about how it might have gone: I throw. I throw the rock. I throw the rock at the rabbit. I throw the rock at the rabbit in order to kill it. If I kill the rabbit I will eat it. I am hungry. If I throw well I will not be hungry. A rock of fist size was thrown *just so* (the first scientist). Rock of *just this size*, of *just this weight*, was thrown at *just under the full velocity of which one was capable*, at a trajectory *beginning just above horizontal*. It hit the rabbit in the leg but the rabbit ran away. When a rock hits a rabbit in the head it will usually stop. Hypothesis! Test it again!

The players collapsed at the end, sat around the final hole puffing and sweating.

'Forty-two minutes ten seconds,' Robert read from his watch. 'Pretty good.'

'We were made to do this,' Frank said. 'We evolved to do this.'

The others merely nodded.

'*We* don't do it,' Robin said. 'The gods do it through us.'

'Robin is pre-breakdown of the bicameral mind.'

'Frisbee is Robin's religion.'

'Well of course,' Robin said.

'Oh come on,' Spencer scolded, untying his fiery dreads from their topknot. 'It's bigger than that.'

Frank laughed with the others.

'It is,' Spencer insisted. 'Bigger and older.'

'Older than religion?'

'Older than *humanity*. Older than *homo sapiens*.'

Frank stared at Spencer, surprised by this chiming with his evolutionary musings. 'How do you mean?'

Spencer grabbed his gold disk by its edge. 'There's a prehistoric tool called the Acheulian hand axe. They were made for hundreds of thousands of years without any changes in design. Half a million years! That makes it a lot older than *homo sapiens*. It was a *homo erectus* tool. And the thing is, the archeologists named them hand axes without really knowing what they were. They don't actually look like they would make good hand axes.'

'How so?' Frank said.

'They're sharpened all the way around, so where are you going to hold the thing? There isn't a good place to hold it if you hit things with it. So it couldn't have been a hand axe. And yet there are millions of them in Africa and Europe. There are dry lakebeds in Africa where the shorelines are coated with these things.'

'Bifaces,' Frank said, looking at his golf disk and remembering illustrations in articles he had read. 'But they weren't round.'

'No, but almost. And they're flat, that's the main thing. If you were to throw one it would fly like a frisbee.'

'You couldn't kill anything very big.'

'You could kill small things. And this guy Calvin says you could spook bigger animals.'

'Hobbes doesn't agree,' Robert put in.

'No *really*!' Spencer cried, grinning. 'This is a *real theory*, this is what archeologists are saying now about these bifaces. They even call it the killer frisbee theory.'

The others laughed.

'But it's *true*,' Spencer insisted, whipping his dreads side-to-side. 'It's *obviously* true. You can *feel* it when you throw.'

'You can, Rasta man.'

'*Everyone* can!' He appealed to Frank: 'Am I right?'

'You are right,' Frank said, still laughing at the idea. 'I sort of remember that killer frisbee theory. I'm not sure it ever got very far.'

'So? Scientists are not good at accepting new theories.'

'Well, they like evidence before they do that.'

'Sometimes things are just too obvious! You can't be throwing out a theory just because people think frisbees are some kind of hippie thing.'

'Which they are,' Robert pointed out.

Frank said, 'No. You're right.' Still, he had to laugh; listening to Spencer was like seeing himself in a funhouse mirror, hearing one of his theories being parodied by an expert mimic. The wild glee in Spencer's blue eyes suggested there was some truth to this interpretation. He would have to be more careful in what he said.

But the facts of the situation remained, and could not be ignored. His unconscious mind, his deep mind, was at that very moment humming happily through all its parcellations. It was a total response. Deep inside lay an ancient ability to throw things at things, waiting patiently for its moment of redeployment.

'That was good,' he said as he got up to leave.

'Google Acheulian hand axes,' Spencer said. 'You'll see.'

The next day Frank did that, and found it was pretty much as Spencer had said. Certain anthropologists had proposed that the rapid evolutionary growth of the human brain was caused by the mentation necessary for throwing things at a target; and a subset of these considered the bifaced hand axes to be their projectiles of choice, 'killer frisbees,' as one William Calvin indeed called them. Used to stampede animals at waterholes, he claimed, after which the hominids pounced on animals knocked over by the rush. The increase in predictive power needed to throw the flattened rocks accurately had led to the brain's frontal lobe growth.

Frank still had to laugh, despite his will to believe. As one of the editors of the *Journal of Sociobiology* he had seen a lot of crazy theories explaining hominid evolution, and he recognized immediately that this was another specimen to add to the list. But so what? It was as plausible as most of the others, and given his recent experiences in the park, more convincing than many.

He stared at a website photo of a hand axe as he thought about his life in the park. He had written commentaries for the *Journal* suggesting that people would be healthier if they lived more like their paleolithic ancestors had. Not that they should starve themselves from time to time, or needed to kill all the meat they ate – just that incorporating more paleolithic behaviors might increase health and well-being. After all, a fairly well-identified set of behaviors, repeated for many generations, had changed their ancestors a great deal; had created the species *homo sapiens*; had blown their brains up like balloons. Surely these were behaviors most likely to lead to well-being now. And to the extent they neglected these behaviors, and sat around inside boxes as if they were nothing but brains and fingertips, the unhealthier and unhappier they would be.

Frank clicked to this commentary and its list of all the paleolithic behaviors anthropologists had ever proposed as a stimulant to the great brain expansion. How many of these behaviors was he performing now?

- talking (he talked much of the day)
- walking upright (he hiked a lot in the park)
- running (he ran with Edgardo's group and the frisbee guys)
- dancing (he seldom danced, but he did sometimes skip along the park trails while vocalizing)
- singing ('Home-less, home-less, ooooooooooop!')
- stalking animals (he tracked the ferals in the park for FOG)
- throwing things at things (he threw his frisbees at the baskets)
- looking at fire (he looked at the bros' awful fire)
- having sex (well, he was trying. And Caroline had kissed him)
- dealing with the opposite sex more generally (Caroline, Diane, Marta, Anna, Laveta, etc.)
- cooking and eating the paleolithic diet (research this; hard to cook in his treehouse, but not impossible)
- gathering plants to eat (he did not do that; must consider)

127

• killing animals for food (he did not want to do that, but frisbee golf was the surrogate)
• experiencing terror (he did not want to do that either)

It appeared by these criteria that he was living a pretty healthy life. The paleolithic pleasures, plus modern dental care; what could be nicer? Optimodal in the best possible sense.

He went back to the Acheulian hand axe link list, and checked out a commercial site called Montana Artifacts. It turned out that this site offered for sale an Acheulian axe found near Madrid, dated at between 200,000 and 400,000 years old. 'Classic teardrop shaped of a fine textured gray quartzite. The surface has taken a smooth lustrous polish on the exposed faces. Superb specimen.' One hundred and ninety-five dollars. With a few taps on his keyboard Frank bought it.

**Primates in airplanes. Aack!**

Flying now made Frank a little nervous. He gripped his seat arms, reminded himself of the realities of risk assessment, fell asleep. He woke when they started descending toward Logan. Landing on water, whoah – but no. The runway showed up in the nick of time, as always.

Then into Boston, a city Frank liked. The conference was at MIT, with some meetings across the river at Boston University.

Quickly Frank saw that getting an opportunity to talk in private with Dr Taolini would be hard. She was involved with the organization of the event, and much in demand. The one time Frank saw her alone, in the hall before her own presentation, she was talking on her cell phone.

But she saw him and waved him over, quickly ending her call. 'Hello, Frank. I didn't know you were going to be here.'

'I decided to come at the last minute.'

'Good, good. You're going to tell us about these new institutes?'

'That's right. But I'd like to talk to you one-on-one about them, if you have the time. I know you're busy.'

'Yes, but let's see . . .' checking her cell phone's calendar. 'Can you meet me at the end of my talk?'

'Sure, I'm going to be there anyway.'

'That's very nice.'

Her talk was on algorithms for reading the genomes of

methanogens. She spoke rapidly and emphatically, very used to the limelight: a star, even at MIT, which tended to be an all-star team. Stylish in a gray silk dress, black hair cut at shoulder length, framing a narrow face with distinct, even chiseled features. Big brown eyes under thick black eyebrows, roving the audience between slides, conveying a powerful impression of intelligence and vivacity, of pleasure in the moment.

After her talk many people, mostly men, clustered around her with what seemed to Frank a more-than-scientific interest. Turning to answer a question she saw him and smiled. 'I'll be just a minute.' Tiny rush of pleasure at that; ha ha, I get to take the beauty away, ooooop!

Her voice was low and scratchy, indeed it would be nasal if it weren't so low. A kind of oboe or bassoon sound, very attractive. Some kind of accent, maybe Boston Italian, but so faint it was impossible for Frank to identify.

Then the others had been dealt with, and he was the only one left. He smiled awkwardly, feeling alert and on edge.

'Nice talk.'

'Oh thanks. Shall we go outside? I could use some coffee and maybe a bite.'

'Sure, that would be nice.'

They walked out into the bright sunlight on the Charles. Francesca suggested a kiosk on the other side of the Mass. Ave. bridge, and Frank followed her onto it happily; Boston's river was full of light, open to the wind. It had good feng shui.

They talked about the dedicated institutes that NSF was planning, and Francesca said she had done a post-doc at the Max Planck in Bremen and been impressed. Then they reached the kiosk, bought lattes and scones, walked back onto the bridge. Frank stopped to look at a women's eight, sculling underneath them like a big water bug. He would have liked to linger there, but Francesca shivered.

'I get cold out here,' she said. 'It's like Byrd said – the coldest he ever got was on the bridges over the Charles.'

'Byrd the polar explorer?'

'Yes. My husband did work on the Greenland ice cores, and he likes to read the polar classics. He told me Byrd said that, because I was always complaining about how cold I get.'

'Well okay, back to land then.'

'There's some benches in the sun just over there.' She pointed.

'Didn't Byrd fake getting to the poles?'

She laughed. 'Maybe that explains why here is the coldest he ever got.'

'No, but didn't he?'

'I don't know, but he definitely wintered on the Ross Ice Shelf.'

'You couldn't do that now.'

'Sure you could. There are people living on the big pieces of it still floating around. That's what Jack tells me. Icebergs as big as Massachusetts, and so people have settled on them.'

'Fun. What does he do?'

'Paleoclimatology. He's been studying the Younger Dryas for a long time now.'

'Really! That's the climate we're dropping into again, I hear.'

'Yes. He's often away giving talks about it. It's quite a scramble with the kids.'

'I bet. How many do you have?'

'Two. Angie is eight, Tom is five.'

'Wow. You must be busy.'

'Yes, it's totally crazy.'

They sat on a bench looking out at the river, eating their scones and talking. She was a beautiful woman. Frank had not fully noticed this during the panel meeting at NSF. Of course he was well aware of the famous experiment in which an attractive woman approached men on a bridge with some question that allowed her plausibly to ask the men to call

131

her later, after which seventy percent of the men on the bridge had called, as compared to only thirty percent accosted in the same way in a park. So, very possibly this was another example of the bridge effect. But whatever. She looked good. Black tangled curls framing sharp Mediterranean features; neat intilting teeth; all of a piece, stylish and intelligent. If you were to play the game of choosing which movie star should play her, you'd have to go right to one of the ultimate Italian exotics, a middle-aged Sophia Loren or Claudia Cardinale.

A joy even to watch her eat; and at this observation Frank could not help remembering another paper, on human female sexual attractiveness, which had argued that even facial beauty consisted of signs of reproductive prowess, symmetry revealing undamaged DNA, widely spaced eyes meaning good eyesight, and prominent cheekbones and a gracile jaw indicating 'masticatory efficiency' – at which point in Frank's reading of the paper Anna had looked in his door to see why he was laughing so hard.

'If you can chew your food well, it's sexy!' he had informed her, and handed her the article while he continued to chortle convulsively. Sociobiology could be so stupid! Anna too had laughed, her gorgeous mirth pealing through the halls.

Frank grinned again thinking of it, watching Francesca sip her latte. No doubt she masticated very efficiently. And had legs fast enough to escape predators, hips wide enough to give birth safely, mammary glands generous enough to feed infants, yes, sure, she had quite a figure, as far as one could tell under her dress – and of course one could tell pretty damned well. She would certainly have many successful offspring, and therefore was beautiful. All so much crap! No *reductio ad absurdum* was more absurd.

'Yes, it's very busy,' she was saying between mastications, in response to a question he didn't remember asking; she appeared to be unaware of his train of thought, but maybe not; he might be staring. 'It works out – usually – but it feels so crazy. I don't know how, but –' swallow – 'things just seem to get busier and busier.'

Frank nodded as he chewed. 'It's true,' he said. 'True for me, and I'm not even married.'

She grinned. 'But that can make you even busier, right?' Leaning into his shoulder slightly with hers, giving him a conspiratorial bump.

Startled, Frank had to agree. There were lots of ways to be busy, he said, and his days were very full. She sipped her latte, looking relaxed and somehow pleased. Not flirtatious, but expansive. She could do what she wanted; what man was going to object? She licked coffee from her upper lip, neat pink tongue like a cat's. For sure the symmetry-as-beauty hypothesis was wrong; Frank had a tendency to zero in on the asymmetries in other people's faces, and he had often noted how it was precisely the asymmetry that drew or hooked the eye, that tugged at it like a magnet. As now, seeing the way Francesca's sharp nose tilted very slightly to the left then back. Magnetic.

Of course he was envious of her too. Lab, tenure, home, partner, children: she had it all. And seemed relaxed and happy, despite her talk about the crazy pace. Fulfilled. As Frank's mom would have said, in one of her most annoying formulations, 'she has it all put together, doesn't she?' At this point in his life Frank doubted that anybody on Earth 'had it all put together' in the way his mom meant. But if anyone did, this woman might.

So: Frank chatted on happily, full of admiration, respect, envy, doubt, resentment, suspicion, and a lust that was perhaps bridge-induced but nevertheless real. He had to mask that part. She would be used to seeing it in men, no doubt. Non-conscious regions of the mind were very sensitive to that.

He would also have to be very circumspect when it came to inquiring about her business affairs. This was one way of characterizing what he had come up to do, and she was done with her scone, and no doubt would soon suggest returning to her duties, so now was the time.

But it was a subject that scientists did not often discuss at academic meetings, as it was too much like prying into matters of personal income. How are you turning your scientific work into money? How much do you make? These questions weren't asked.

He tried a roundabout course. 'Is the teaching load heavy here?'

It was.

'Do you have any administrative duties?'

She did.

'And you do some consulting too, I think you said?'

'Yes,' she said, looking slightly surprised, as she had not said any such thing. 'Just a little. It doesn't take much time. A company in London, another in Atlanta.'

Frank nodded. 'I used to do some of that in San Diego. The biotechs can use all the help they can get. Although they seem to have a hard time turning lab results into products. Like the stuff we evaluated on that panel last fall.'

'Right, that was interesting.'

This was likely to be mere politeness talking. But then she glanced at him, went on: 'I saw one proposal there that I thought was a good one, that the panel ended up turning down.'

'Yes?'

'Yes. By a Yann Pierzinski.'

'Oh yes. I remember. That was a good one. I was the outside member of his doctoral committee at Caltech. He does really interesting work.'

'Yes,' she said. 'But the panel didn't agree.'

'No, I was surprised at that.'

'Me too. So when Small Delivery told me they were looking for a biomathematician, I recommended him.'

134

'Oh, is that what happened.'

'Yes.'

Her irises were a kind of mahogany color, speckled with lighter browns. Was this the face of what science could become, so vivacious and sophisticated?

'Well,' he said carefully, 'good for him. I liked his proposal too.'

'You didn't seem to at the time.'

'Well – I was on his doctoral committee. And I try not to be one of the evaluators in my panels anyway.'

'No?'

'No. I just run the panel. I don't want to sway anyone.'

'Then you must have to be careful which proposals you assign to Stuart Thornton,' she said with a brief ironic smile.

'Oh I don't know!' he said defensively, startled. 'Do you think so?'

'Hmm.' She watched him.

'I guess I know what you mean. It was probably a mistake to invite him on the panel at all. But, you know.' He waved a hand: people legitimately on the cutting edge deserved to be asked, no matter their personalities.

She frowned very slightly, as if she did not agree, or did not like him pretending she did not know what he had done.

Frank forged on. 'Anyway it sounds like Yann ended up all right, thanks to you.'

'Yes. Hopefully so.' She sipped her latte. Her fingers were long, her fingernails polished with a clear gloss. A thin wedding band was the only jewelry she wore. Frank looked down, unwilling to meet her sharp gaze. Her shoes were open-toed, her toenails colored pink. Frank had always considered toenail polish to be a kind of intelligence test that its users had embarrassingly and publicly failed; but here was Dr Taolini, tenured at MIT, a member of National Academy of Sciences, exposing pink toenails to the world without embarrassment. He would have to rethink some of his opinions.

'Still,' he said tentatively, 'even though Yann has ended up all right, I'd like to get him into one of these new institutes.'

'Maybe you can,' she said. 'Multiple appointments aren't that unusual anymore.'

'In academia, anyway. Do you think his contract would allow for that kind of thing?'

She shrugged, made a little gesture of her own; how should I know, I'm just a consultant.

He had learned what he was going to learn about her connection to Yann. Pressing further would look weird. She basked in the windy sun, would soon want to go back in to the conference.

He could ask her outright if she knew anything about the surveillance. He could share what he knew. It was another prisoner's dilemma: they both knew things the other could probably benefit from knowing, but it was a risk to bring them up; the other might defect. The safest thing was to defect preemptively. But Frank wanted to try the more generous strategies these days, and so he wanted to tell her: we're being watched by Homeland Security, in a surveillance clustered around Pierzinski. Did you know? Why do you think that is? What do you think is going on?

But then she could very justifiably ask, how do you know? And then he would be stuck. He could not say, because I've fallen in love with a spook who kissed me in an elevator, and she told me all about it. That just wasn't something he wanted to say to this woman.

Although in another way he did; it would be great to be close enough to this person to confide in her. She might laugh, might lean into his shoulder again, to draw out more of the tale.

But in fact he wasn't that close to her. So he couldn't talk about it.

A different approach occurred to him. 'I'm getting interested in finding algorithms or other rubrics for sorting through the various climate proposals we've gotten, to see if some are worth jumping on right now. Ways of checking not only the physical possibilities, which is the easy part in some senses, but also the economic and political viability of the plans.'

'Yes?' she said, interested.

'I read about something I think came out of MIT, of course there's a million things coming out of MIT, but maybe you've heard of this one, a kind of ideas futures market? You gather a group of stakeholders, and sort the ideas by how much money people are willing to risk on them?'

'Yes, do you mean that simulation program they've written, for market makers?'

'Yes,' Frank said. 'I guess so.'

She said, 'I heard about it. To me it sounds like one of those situations where simulation misses the point. You might need real experts risking real money, to get the kind of feedback a futures market is supposed to give you.'

'Yes, I wondered about that myself.'

'So, I don't know. You should talk to Angelo Stavros.'

'What department?' Frank said, getting out his phone to tap it in; then suddenly he recalled that his phone might be fully surveiled.

'Economics – but what is it?' She was watching him closely now, and he couldn't be sure if she knew more about the idea futures market or not.

'I was just thinking you're probably right. In the end it's going to take the usual analysis of the options, like we always have done before.'

'Another panel, you mean.'

'Yes,' he laughed ruefully, 'I suppose so.'

Her smile was suddenly wicked, and over it her eyes blazed, they *italicized* her words: 'Better not invite Thornton.'

He walked the north shore of the Charles, enjoying the wind that ruffled the water.

So. Francesca Taolini appeared to have guessed what he had tried to do on that panel. Maybe putting Thornton on a panel was too blatant, like throwing a rock – thus drawing her attention, perhaps even sparking extra interest in Pierzinski's proposal.

This realization was a shock, small but profound, like the shove of shoulder to shoulder. Balance thrown off. Presumably it would come back after a while. Meanwhile a shudder, an itch, an ache. In short, *desire*.

He found that he had become a seer of beauty in women. On the river path in Boston it was mostly expressed as youth and intelligence. That made sense; sixty degree-giving institutions, some three hundred thousand college students; that meant a surplus of at least 150,000 more nubile young women than ordinary demographics would suggest. Maybe that was why men stayed in Boston when their college years were over, maybe that explained why they were so intellectually hyperactive, so frustrated, so alcoholic, such terrible drivers. It all seemed right to Frank. He was full of yearning, the women on the river walk were all goddesses set loose in the sun. The image of Francesca Taolini even somehow made him angry; she had flirted with him casually, toyed with him. He wanted his Caroline to call him again, he wanted to kiss her and more. He wanted her.

Back in Rock Creek Park it was not like that. Frank hiked in to the picnic tables late that night, and Zeno saw him and bellowed, 'Hey it's the Professor! Hey, wanna buy a fuck? She'll do it for five dollars!'

The guys jeered at this, while the woman sitting in their midst rolled her eyes and continued to knit. She'd heard it all before. Blond, square, stoical; Zeno and the rest were in fact pleased to have her there, they just showed it in stupid ways.

'No thank you,' Frank said, and pulled a six pack from a grocery bag to stop Zeno's foolery before it went any further.

138

The woman shook her head when offered a beer. 'Day sixty-five,' she said to Frank with a brief gap-toothed smile. 'Day sixty-five, and here I am still hanging out with these bozos.'

'Yarrr!' they cheered.

'Congratulations,' Frank said.

'On what,' Zeno quipped, 'staying sober, or hanging with us?'

High humor in the park.

There were very few women to be seen out there, Frank thought as he sat at her table; and those he saw seemed sad drabs, just barely getting by. Homelessness was hard on anyone, but seemed to damage them more. They could not pretend it was some kind of adventure.

And yet the economy insisted on a minimum of five percent unemployment, to create the proper 'wage pressure.' Millions of people who wanted jobs went unhired and therefore couldn't afford a home, therefore suffered from 'food insecurity,' so that businesses could keep wages low. These people.

Unlike Frank. He was a dilettante here, dabbling, slumming. Choice made all the difference. He could have found a place to rent, he could have afforded a deposit and moved in. Instead he hung out tinkering with their crappy fire, then playing chess with Chessman, losing four games but making the last of them a real donnybrook. And when Chessman departed with his twenty, Frank got up and hiked into the night, made sure no one was following, went to his tree, called down Miss Piggy, and climbed up into his treehouse, there to lie down on the best bed in the world, and read by the light of his Coleman lantern, in the clatter of the wind in the leaves. Let the wind blow the world out of his hair. Rockabye baby, in the tree top. It was a relief to be there after the strangeness of the day.

Was curly hair adaptive? Tangled curls, black as a crow's wing?

He wanted her.

Damn it anyway. Sociobiology was a bad habit you could never get rid of. Once it invaded your thoughts it was hard to forget that human beings were apes, with desires shaped by life on the savannah, so that every move in lab politics or boardroom maneuvers became clearly a shove for food or sex, every verbal put-down from a male boss like the back of the hand from some hairy silverback, every flirt and dismissal from a woman like the head-turning-aside baboon, refusing acknowledgment, saying You don't get to fuck me and if you try my sisters will beat you up; and every acquiescence like the babs who accidentally had their pink butts stuck out when you went by, saying I'm in estrus you can fuck me if you want, shouldering you companionably or staring off into space as if bored –

But the problem was, thinking of interactions with other people in this way was not actually very *helpful* to him. For one thing it could often reduce him to speechlessness. Like at the gym for instance, my Lord if that was not the savannah he didn't know what was – and if that was the primal discourse, then he'd rather pass, thank you very much, and be a solitary. He was too inhibited to just lay it out there, and too honest to try to say it in euphemistic code. He was too self-conscious. He was too chicken. There was an awesome power in sex, he wanted it to go right. He wanted it to be part of a whole monogamy. He wanted love to be real. Science could go fuck itself!

Or: become useful. Become a help, for God's sake. It was the same in his personal life as it was for the world at large; if science wasn't helping then it was a sterile waste of time. It had to help or it was all for naught, and the world still nothing but a miserable fuck-up. And him too.

**The party traveling to** Khembalung had grown to ten: the Quiblers and Frank, Drepung, Sucandra, Padma, and Rudra Cakrin, and the Khembali woman Qang, who ran the embassy's big house in Arlington.

Dulles to LA to Tokyo to Bangkok to Calcutta to Khembalung; for two days they lived in long vibrating rooms in the air, taking short breaks in big rooms on the ground. They ate meals, watched movies, went to the bathroom, and slept. In theory it should have been somewhat like a rainy weekend at home or a bad film festival.

However, Charlie thought, a rainy weekend at the Quibler household could be a royal pain in the ass. It was not a good idea to confine Joe for that long. At home they would make things for him to do, find ways for him to let off some steam. They would go out in the rain and party. Now that was not an option.

They had flown business class, courtesy of the Khembalis, which gave them more room, though Anna could not help being concerned about the expense. Charlie told her not to worry about it, but she knew the Khembali budget and Charlie didn't. She never found it reassuring when someone who knew less about a situation than she did told her not to worry about it.

On the first plane Joe wanted to investigate every nook and cranny, and so Charlie followed him around, returning the smiles of those passengers who did in fact smile. Joe ran a route like a long figure 8, chanting 'Airplane! Airplane!

Airplane!' When the food and drink carts filled the aisles he had to be lifted into his seat, struggling as he declared 'Airplane! Truck!' (The drink cart). 'People!' Eventually he ran out of gas and fell asleep curled in his seat next to Rudra Cakrin, who nodded off over him, occasionally holding Joe's wrist or ankle between two gnarled fingers. Anna sat on the other side of Joe, using up her laptop battery all in one go. Across the aisle from her Charlie sat down and pulled out the seatback phone to make some calls. Anna tried to ignore him and work, but she heard him say hi to Wade Norton, a colleague down in Antarctica, and listened in.

'You saw twin otters? How did you know they were twins? . . Oh. Uh huh. You saw Roosevelt Island, nice. How could that be the first time anyone has seen it? . . . Oh! . . . How many meters? . . . Where'd all the ice go? . . . Wow. Jesus. That is a lot . . . Is that the beginning of the . . . the West Antarctic Ice Sheet, right I know. Sea level and all. How big is this piece? Wow . . . Yeah, of course. We'll be fine. We won't be there but a few days anyway.'

Charlie listened for a while. Then: 'Hey, Roy! I'm glad you were able to click in. What's up? . . . Andrea doesn't? Hey does that mean you two are speaking to each other again? Ha ha . . . No, I don't suffer under any illusions there, but Phil doesn't listen to you guys either . . . Oh right. From the South Pole, I'm sure . . . I thought you said she was a giant . . . Six foot four sounds giant to me . . . You are not, you're six feet at the most! Elevator shoes . . . She'd be what, six ten? Yeah. Ha . . . No, I think it's his to lose! The happy man is like Hoover, and none of the other Republicans are happy men. They're Angry Men. They've had the White House and Congress for so long it's made them bitter. It's just such an effort making it look like their program makes sense. It makes them angry and resentful. No. It's not a process you want to follow to its natural end. I agree . . . No, Phil would be fine. He'd love it. It's us who would suffer, you know . . . Well, because I thought it was a good idea! What else are we going to do anyway? We've got to try something, and Phil is our best shot . . . I know. I know . . . Yeah, just ride it . . . Well, the more fool you! I'm off to Shambala and Wade is at the South Pole. You can have D.C., ha!'

He rang off, leaned back looking pleased.

'You're making trouble,' Anna observed.

'Yes. Someone's got to do it.'

Hours later they floated down over the green fields of Japan, a startling sight if you were expecting nothing but Tokyolike cityscapes. Then out of their seats, up a jet way, feeling slightly deranged; running around an airport acting as marshal or warden to a two year-old minimum-security prisoner; then they were in another plane and rumbling into the air again, with another long day facing them. Nick kept on reading Carlyle's *History of the French Revolution*. Charlie and Anna kept trading off the pursuit of the indefatigable Joe, Anna having given up making Charlie do it all, as they had both known she would. Besides her battery was too low for her to keep working.

Joe seemed intent on confirming what Anna kept telling him, that this plane was identical to the one they had been on before. Except on this one the passengers seemed less amused by an exploratory bang on the knee.

Bangkok's airport hotel, tall and white, stood over its big pool in intense sunlight. Dazed wandering after Joe in the turquoise shallows, trying to stay awake and unsunburnt, trying to keep Joe out of the deep end. The water was too warm. Then back to a cool room, sleep, but then the alarm oh my, middle of the night, ultra groggy, pack up and off to the airport again to face its long lines, and get on what looked like the same plane. Except on this one, orchids were pinned to the back of every seat. Joe ate his before they could stop him. Anna went into her laptop's encyclopedia to see if it could have been toxic. Apparently it could, but Joe showed no ill effects, and Charlie ate a petal of his orchid too, in Anna's view merely compounding the problem with a very poorly designed follow-up experiment.

Nick had finished all his books, and now he listened as Charlie told Frank about Phil Chase running for president. Frank said, 'What about you, Nick? Who do you think should be President?'

Nick's brow furrowed, and Frank glanced at Anna – yes, she could feel that same frown in the muscles of her own forehead. Nick was often his mother's son. Now Frank watched him ponder, and Anna thought, It's the oblivious confronting the oblivious: Frank unaware of being condescending, Nick unaware of being condescended to. Maybe that meant it wasn't happening.

'Well you see,' Nick said, 'in Switzerland the executive branch is a seven-person council? And its members are voted in by the legislature. It means there's diverse views in the executive branch, and it doesn't dominate the other branches as much. Most Swiss people don't even know the actual president's name! He just like runs the council meetings.'

'That's a good idea,' Frank said.

'The Swiss have lots of good ideas. We've been studying them in world gee.'

'Oh I see. You'll have to tell me more about them.'

'It isn't easy to amend the Constitution,' Charlie warned them.

Nick and Frank knew this. Nick said, 'Maybe someone could run for president and tell everybody that if he won, he was going to like appoint a council to do his job.'

'Like Reagan!' Charlie said, laughing.

'It's still a good idea,' Frank said.

Then their plane was descending again.

In Calcutta they zombied through a reception at the Khembali legation, dreaming on their feet; all except Joe, who slept on Charlie's back; then they tumbled into beds, feeling the joy of horizontality; then the alarm went off again. 'Ah God.' It was almost like being at home.

Back to the airport, off in a little sixteen-seater so loud that it made Joe squeal with joy. Up and east, over the mind-boggling combined delta of the Ganges and the Brahmaputra, the world's largest delta, also a good percentage of Bangladesh. Looking down at it, Charlie shouted to Anna, 'I'll never call Washington D.C. a swamp again!' Green-brown islands in a brown-green sea. The delta patterns ran south, and they flew down one brown-green channel until the islands lay more diffusely, also lower, many half-submerged, with drowned coastlines visible in shallows. The water ahead shifted in distinct jumps from brown-green to jade to sea blue.

One of the outermost islands, right on the border of the jade sea and the blue, had a shoreline accentuated by a brown ring. As they descended, the interior of this island differentiated into patterns of color, then into fields, roads, rooftops. In the final approach they saw that the brown ring was a dike, quite broad and fairly high. Suddenly it appeared to Anna as if the land inside the dike was slightly lower than the ocean around it. She hoped it was only an optical illusion.

Joe had mashed his face and hands against the window, looking down at the island and burbling: 'Oh! My! Big truck! Big house! Ah fah. Oh! My!'

Frank, who had successfully slept through three-quarters of the flight, sat up on the other side of Joe, regarding him with a smile. 'Ooooooooop!' he gibboned, egging him on. Joe cackled to hear it.

Touchdown.

They were greeted as they came off the plane by a large group of men, women, and children, all dressed in their finery, which meant ceremonial garb better suited to the roof of the world than the Bay of Bengal; and on closer examination Anna saw that the fabrics of many of the robes and headdresses wafted on the stiff hot sea breeze, being diaphanous cotton, silk, and nylon, though they were Tibetan in color and design. That was Khembalung in a nutshell.

Rudra Cakrin descended the plane first, with Drepung right behind him. A triumphant *blaaaaaaaaaaaa* of brass long horns shattered the air so violently it seemed it might squeeze out rain. This was the brazen sound that had alerted Anna to the existence of the Khembalis in the first place, on the day of their arrival in the NSF building.

Everyone receiving them bowed; they looked down upon the black hair and colorful headgear of several hundred people. Joe goggled to see it, mouth hanging open in a perfect O.

Descending into this throng they were surrounded by their hosts, including two women from the Khembalung Institute of Higher Learning, who introduced themselves to Anna; she had been corresponding with them by e-mail. They took the visitors in hand, leading them slowly through the crowd and introducing them to many of the people they passed.

Soon they were through the airport's little building, and bundled into a van that drove them east on a broad, palm-lined boulevard of dusty white concrete. On each side extended flat fields, divided by rows of trees or shrubbery. Small building complexes stood under drooping palm trees. Many of the plants looked desiccated, even brown.

'There has been drought for two years,' one of their guides explained. 'This is the third monsoon season without rain, but we have hopes it will come soon. All South Asia has been suffering from these two bad monsoons in a row. We need the rain.'

Anna had heard a lot about this from her contacts with ABC, the 'Asian Brown Cloud' study, which was trying to determine if the long-term persistence of particulates in the air of south Asia – mysterious in their exact origins, although clearly linked to the industrialization and deforesting in the region – had any causal effect on the drought.

In any case it made for a rather drab and stunted landscape. No plants they saw were native to the island, they were told as they drove through the dust cloud of the bus before theirs. Everything was tended; even the ground itself had been imported, to raise the island a meter or two higher. Nick asked where the extra ground had come from, and they told him that a few surrounding islands had been dredged up and deposited here, also used to provide the raw material for the dike. It had all been done under the direction of Dutch engineers some fifty years before. Very little had been done since then, as far as Anna had been able to determine. The dike was in sight through the trees wherever they went, raising the horizon a bit, so that it felt a little like driving around in a very large roofless room, blasted with hazy harsh sunlight, the sky like a white ceiling. The inner wall of the dike had been planted with flowerbeds that when in bloom would show the usual colors of the Tibetan palette – maroon and saffron, brown and bronze and red, all gone or muted now but the blue and black patches, which were made of painted stones.

In a little town they got out of the van and crossed a broad pedestrian esplanade. The sea breeze poured over them in a hot wave, briny and seaweedy. The smell of the other Sundarbans, perhaps.

'Will we see more swimming tigers?' Nick inquired. He observed everything with great interest, looking cool in his sunglasses. Joe had refused to wear his. He was taking in the scene so avidly he was in danger of giving himself whiplash, trying to see everything at once. Anna was pleased to see this curiosity from the boys; clearly America had not yet jaded them to the beauty and sheer difference of the rest of the world.

Their guides took them in the biggest building, the Government House. It was darker inside, and with their sunglasses on, seemed at first black. By the time they had taken off sunglasses and adjusted to the relative gloom, they found Joe had run off ahead of them. The room displayed the post-and-beam construction characteristic of Himalayan buildings, and the rough-hewn posts in each corner were hung with demon masks.

They followed Joe over to one of these collections. Each mask grimaced rotundly, almost exploding with fury, pain, repugnance. Stacked vertically they looked like a totem pole from a tribe of utter maniacs. Joe was embracing the bottom of the pole.

'Oooh! Oooh! Big – big – big –'

Big what, he could not say. His mouth hung open, his eyes bugged out; they could have molded a new mask portraying astonishment directly from his face.

Frank laughed. 'These are his kind of people.'

'He probably thinks it's a stack of mirrors,' Charlie said.

'Quit it,' Anna said. 'Don't be mean.'

Charlie and Nick leaned their faces in to take photos of themselves on each side of Joe, eyes bugged, tongues thrust out and down. Hopefully they were not offending their hosts. But looking around Anna saw that the guides were smiling.

'They're masks that hide your face but show your insides,' Charlie said. 'This is what we're all really like inside.'

'No,' Anna said.

'Oh come on. In your feelings? In your dreams?'

'I certainly hope not. Besides, where's the good feelings?'

She had been thinking of perhaps the curiosity mask, or the striving-for-accuracy mask, but Charlie gave her a Groucho look and indicated with his eyebrows the paintings on the beams between wall and ceiling, which included any number of improbably entwined couples. Frank was frankly checking them out, nodding as if they confirmed some sociobiological insight only he could formulate, bonobo Buddhism or something like that. Anna snorted, pretty sure that the tantrically horny painters had to have been fantasizing elements of female flexibility, among other endowments. Maybe six arms made it easier to position oneself. Or perhaps there was no gravity in nirvana; which would also explain all the perfectly round tits. She wondered what Joe would make of those, being still a breast man of the first order. But for now he remained too fixated on the demon masks to notice them.

Then they were joined by more scientists from the Khembalung Institute of Higher Learning. There were introductions all around, and Anna shook hands, pleased to see all her correspondents at last, just as shockingly real and vivid as the demon masks. Frank joined them, and for a while they chatted about NSF and their various collaborations. Then Frank and Anna and Nick left Charlie and Joe in Government House, and followed their new hosts through rooms and across a courtyard to the Institute itself, where the new labs that NSF had helped to fund and build were still under construction. Outside one of the rooms was a statue of the Buddha, standing with one hand raised before him palm outward, in a gesture like a traffic cop saying STOP.

'I've never seen him look like that.'

'This is, what say, the Adamantine Buddha,' one of her pen pals said. 'The Buddha is represented in a number of different ways. He is not always meditating or laughing. When there is bad going on, the Buddha is as obliged to stop it as anyone else who sees it. And, you know, since bad things happen fairly regularly, there has always been a figure to represent the Buddha's response.'

Nick said, 'He looks like a policeman.'

Their guide nodded. 'Police Inspector Sakyamuni. Who insists that we all must resist the three poisons of the mind, fear, greed, and anger.'

'So true,' Anna said. Frank was nodding also, lost in his thoughts.

'This aspect of Buddha-nature is also the one represented in the statues on the dike, of course.'

'Can we go on it?' Frank and Nick asked together.

'Of course. We're very near it here.'

They finished their tour and joined the rest of their group outside, on a lawn surrounded on three sides by buildings, on the fourth, to the east, by the inner wall of the dike. The wall was a tilted lawn in this area, bisected by a set of broad stone steps leading to its top. Frank and Anna and Nick followed some of their guides up these steps; Charlie and Joe appeared below, and Joe began to run around on the grass.

On top they emerged into a stiff onshore wind. Out to sea lay a white fleet of tall clouds. A big statue of the Adamantine Buddha faced seaward, hand outstretched. From beside him they had a good view of both sea and land, and Anna felt herself lurch a little. 'Wow,' Nick said.

It was as it had appeared from the plane during their approach: the land inside the dike was slightly lower than the ocean surrounding it. It was no illusion; their eyesight and inner ear confirmed it.

'Holland is like this in some places,' Frank said to Anna as they followed Nick and the guides. 'Have you ever seen the dikes?'

'No.'

'Some of the polders there are clearly lower than the North Sea. You can walk the dikes, and it's the strangest sight.'

'So it's true?' Anna asked, waving at Khembalung. 'I mean – it looks like it must be.'

One of their guides turned and said, 'Unfortunately it is true. When the land is drained, there is a resulting subsidence. Dry land is heavier, and sinks, and then the water wicks up into it. We have gone through cycle after cycle.'

Anna shivered despite the hot wind. She felt faintly queasy and off-balance.

'Try looking only one way at a time.'

Anna tried, setting her back to the island. Under a pastel blue clouds flew in from the southwest. The sea bounced to the blue horizon, waves with whitecaps rolling in. Such a big world. Their guides pointed at the clouds, exclaiming that they looked like the beginning of the monsoon; perhaps the drought would end at last!

They walked along the dike, which was clearly old. A heavy bar mesh at the waterline had rusted away, so that the boulders held in by the mesh were slumping, and in places had fallen. Their guides told them that dike maintenance was done with human labor and the little machinery they had, but that there were structural repairs needed that they could not afford, as they could see. Frank jumped onto the waist-high outer wall, setting a bad example for Nick, who immediately followed it.

Sucandra and Padma came up the broad stone staircase, and when they saw Frank and Nick on the retaining wall they called to them. 'Hello! Look, the monsoon may be coming!'

They topped the wall and fell in with them. 'We wanted to show you the mandala. Hello, Mingma, you have met our visitors, we see.'

Back down on the dusty grass Charlie and Joe had been joined by Rudra, Drepung, and a group of Khembali youth who were creating a mandala on a giant wooden disk that lay on the lawn. 'Let's go down and see,' Sucandra suggested, and they walked down the steps and out of the brunt of the wind. It certainly felt humid enough to rain.

The biggest sand mandalas took about a week to complete, Mingma told them. Long brass funnels were held by the artists just an inch or so over the pattern, and when the funnels were rubbed with sticks, thin lines of colored sand fell from them. The colorists worked on their knees, scarcely breathing, rubbing the funnels rhythmically, gently, their faces down near the ground to watch the emerging line of sand; then with a quick tilt of the funnels they would stop the flow and sit back and turn to the others, to crack a joke or laugh at someone else's.

When the design was completely colored in, there would be a ceremony to celebrate the various meanings it held, and then it would be carried to the long shallow reflecting pool in front of Government House, and tipped into the water.

'A real launch party,' Charlie noted.

'It signifies the impermanence of all things.'

To Anna that seemed like a waste of the art. She did not like the impermanence of all things, and felt there was already enough in the world to remind her of it. She liked to think that human efforts were cumulative, that something in every effort was preserved and added to the whole. Perhaps in this case that would be the mandala's pattern, which would remain in their minds. Or maybe this art was a performance rather than an object. Maybe. What she wanted out of art was something that lasted. If their art did not have that, it seemed like a waste of effort to her.

Over on the other side of the mandala, Joe and Rudra were standing before a group of monks, and Rudra was chanting intently in his deep gravelly voice, a happy gleam in his eye. Those around him repeated the last word of every sentence, in a kind of shout or singing. Joe stamped his foot in time, crying 'No!' in unison with the rest of them. He hadn't even noticed Anna was there.

Then suddenly he took off directly toward the sand mandala, fists clenched and swinging like a miniaturized John Wayne. Anna cried out 'Joe!' but he did not hear her. The Khembalis actually made way for him, some of them with arms outstretched as if to create a better corridor. 'Joe!' she cried again more sharply. 'Joe! Stop!' He hesitated for a second, at the edge of the circle of brilliant color, then walked out onto it.

'JOE!'

No one moved. Joe stood peacefully at the center of the mandala, looking around.

Anna rushed down the steps to the edge of the circle. Joe's footprints had blurred some lines, and grains of colored sand were now out of place, scattered brilliantly in the wrong fields. Joe was looking very pleased with himself, surveying the pattern under his feet, a pattern made of colors almost precisely the same as the colors of his building blocks at home, only more vibrant. He spotted Rudra, and thrust an arm out to wave at him. 'Ba!' he declared.

'Baaaa,' Rudra replied, putting his hands together and bowing.

Joe held his pose, not unlike that of the Adamantine Buddhas, with a kind of Napoleonic grandeur. Charlie, standing now beside Anna, shook his head. 'Ya big old hambone,' he muttered.

Joe dropped his arm, made a gesture at all the people watching him. A few drops of rain spattered down out of the low clouds bowling in from sea, and the Khembalis oohed and ahhed as they felt it and looked up.

Joe took off again, this time in the direction of the reflecting pool. Anna rushed around the circle of people to cut him off, but she was too late; he walked right into the shallows. 'Joe!' she called out, to no effect. Joe turned and confronted the crowd that had followed him, standing knee-deep in the water. It was sprinkling lightly but steadily now, the rain warm on Anna's face, and all the Khembalis were smiling. Enough colored sand had stuck to Joe's feet that vermilion and yellow blooms spread in the water around him.

'Rgyal ba,' Rudra declared, and the crowd repeated it. Then: 'Ce ba drin dran-pa!'

'What is he saying?' Anna asked Drepung, who now stood beside her, as if to support her if she fainted, or perhaps to stop her if she started in after Joe. Charlie stood on her other side.

'All hail,' Drepung said. He looked older to Anna, his round face and little mouth finally at home. She had seen that he was clearly a well-known and popular figure here.

Joe stood in the shallows regarding the crowd. He was happy. The Khembalis were indulging him, enjoying him. The warm rain fell on them like a balm. Suddenly Anna felt happy; her little tiger saw that he was among friends, somehow, and

153

at last he stood in the world content, relaxed, even serene. She had never seen him look like this. She had wanted so much for him to feel something like this.

Charlie, on the other hand, felt his stomach go tense at the sight of Joe in the pool. All his worries were being confirmed. He took a deep breath, thinking Nothing has changed, you knew this already – they're thinking he's one of their tulkus. That doesn't mean that it's true.

He couldn't imagine what Anna was making of all this.

Standing beside each other, the two of them both felt the discrepancy in their reactions. And they sensed as well that their characteristic moods or responses were here reversed, Anna pleased by a Joe anomaly, Charlie worried.

Uneasily they glanced at each other, both thinking This is backwards, what's going on?

'Big rain!' Joe exclaimed, looking up, and the crowd sighed appreciatively.

That night the visitors collapsed on the beds in their rooms, even Joe, and slept from the early evening through the night and well into the next morning. It had rained the whole time, and when they went back out after breakfast they found the island transformed; everything was drenched, with standing water everywhere. The Khembalis were very happy to see it, however, so they split up into groups and took off in the rain as planned. Joe and Nick were first taken to the school to see classes and playground games. Everywhere he went Joe was made much of, and he was left free to commune with every demon mask they passed, directing diatribes in his private language at some of them. In the afternoon Nick left his group and joined Anna at the institute, where she was talking to her pen pals and the other scientists there. Charlie spent his time in Government House, talking to officials brought to him by Padma.

Frank was gone; they didn't know how he was spending

his time, although once in passing Anna saw him in conversation with Sucandra and some of the local monks. Later she saw him on the dike, walking the berm path with Rudra Cakrin. Judging from his talk at dinner, he had also spent time discussing agriculture out in the fields. But mostly he seemed to Anna like a religious pilgrim, eager for instruction and enlightenment, absorbed, distant, relaxed; very unlike his manner back in Washington.

Next afternoon they visited the zoo, located in a big park at the northwest quadrant of the island. Many of the animals and birds of the Sundarbans were represented. The elephants had a large enclosure, but the largest enclosure of all was the tigers'. Many of the big cats had been swept to sea by one flood or another, and rescued by Khembali patrol boats. Now they lived in an enclosure thick with stands of elephant grass and saal trees, fronted by a big pond cut by a curving glass retaining wall, so that when the tigers went swimming they could be seen underwater. Their abrupt foursquare dives and subsequent splayed strokes turned feline grace unexpectedly aquatic, and underwater their fur streamed like seaweed. 'Tiger! Tiger! Big big *tiger*!'

At the end of that wet day they sat in a big hall and ate a meal anchored by curried rice. Nick was served a special order of plain rice, arranged by Drepung, but Joe was fine with the curry. Or so it seemed during the meal; but that night in their room he was fractious, and then, after a long nursing session, wide awake. Jet lag, perhaps. The monsoon rains were coming down hard, the drumming of it on the roof quite loud. Joe began to complain. Anna was asleep on her feet, but Charlie was out entirely, so she had to zombie on, hour after hour, mumbling replies to Joe's cheerful jabberwocking. She was on the verge of a collapse when a knock came at the door, and Frank looked in.

'I can't sleep, and I could hear you were up with Joe. I wondered if you wanted me to play with him for a while.'

155

'Oh God bless you,' she cried. 'I was just about to melt.' She fell on the couch and shut her sandy eyes. For a while her brain continued to turn, as her body dove into sleep and dragged her consciousness down with it.

'Nick sleeping. Da sleeping. Mama sleeping.'

'That's right.'

'Wanna play?'

'Sure. What you got here, trains? What about some airplanes, shouldn't you have some airplanes?'

'Got planes.'

'Good. Let's fly, let's fly and fly.'

'Fly!'

'Hey, those are your tigers! Well, that's okay. Flying tigers are just right for here. Watch out, here he comes!'

'Tiger fly!'

Anna stitched the meandering border between sleep and dreams, in and out, up and down. Frank and Joe passed toys back and forth.

In the hour before dawn a hard knock battered their door, throwing Anna convulsively to her feet. She had been dreaming of the tigers' fluid swimming, up in the sky –

It was Drepung, looking agitated. 'I'm sorry to disturb you, my friends, but a decision has been made that we must all evacuate the island.'

This woke them all, even Charlie who was usually so slow to rouse. Frank turned on all the lights, and they packed their bags while Drepung explained the situation.

'The monsoon has returned, as you have seen,' he said. 'This is a good thing, but unfortunately it has come at a time of especially high tides, and together with the storm surge, and the low air pressure, sea level is extremely high.' He helped the comatose Nick into a shirt. 'It's already higher on the dikes than is judged fully safe, higher than we have seen for many years, and some weaknesses in it are being exposed. And now we have been informed that the monsoon or something else has caused the breaking of ice dams in the drainage of the Brahmaputra.' He looked at Charlie: 'These big glacial lakes are a result of global warming. The Himalayan glaciers are melting fast, and now lots of ice dams that create lakes behind them are giving way under these monsoon rains, adding greatly to the run-off. The Brahmaputra is already over-flowing, and much of Bangladesh is faced with flooding. They called with the alarm from Dhaka just a short while ago.' He checked his watch. 'Just an hour ago, good. It goes fast. The surge of high water will arrive soon, and we are already at our limit. And as you have seen, the island is lower than the sea even at the best of times. This is a problem with using dikes for protection. If the dike fails, the result can be severe. So we must leave the island.'

'How?' Anna exclaimed.

'Don't worry, we have ferries at the dock enough for all. Always docked here for this very purpose, because the danger is ever-present. We have used them before, when the rivers flood or there are high tides. Any of them can flood us. The island is just too low, and unfortunately, getting lower.'

'And sea level is getting higher,' Charlie said. 'I heard from a friend in Antarctica that a piece of the West Antarctic Ice Sheet came off a few days ago. Every time that happens sea level rises by whatever extra amount of water the ice displaces.'

'Interesting,' Drepung said. 'Perhaps that explains why we are already at the safety level on the dike.'

'How much time do we have?' Anna said.

'Two or three hours. This is more than enough time for us.' He sighed nevertheless. 'We prefer that our guests leave by heli-copter in a situation like this, but to tell the truth the helicopter went to Calcutta last night, to bring out the ABC officials to meet you. So now it appears you should join us on the ferries.'

'How many people live here again?' Charlie asked as he threw their bathroom bags into his backpack.

'Twelve thousand.'

'Wow.'

'Yes. It is a big operation, but all will be well.'

'What about the zoo animals?' Nick asked. By now their bags were packed, and Nick was dressed and looking wide awake.

'We have a boat for them too. It's a difficult procedure, but there is a team assigned to it. People with circus experience. They call their act, "Noah Goes Fast". How about you, are you ready?'

They were ready. Joe had watched all the action with a curious eye; now he said, 'Da? Go?'

'That's right, big guy. We're off on another trip.'

Outside it was raining harder than ever, the cloud cover somewhat broken and flying north on a strong wind. They hustled into a van and joined a little traffic jam on the island's main road. All the crowded vans turned north toward the dock. Joe sat in Anna's lap looking out the window, saying 'Ba? Ba?'

Charlie was on his phone. 'Hey Wade!' he said, and Anna bent her head to try and catch what he was saying. 'How big was that berg? . . . No kidding. Have they calculated the displacement yet? . . . Oh okay. Yeah, not that much, but we've got a situation here, a monsoon flood and a full-moon tide . . . Shit. Okay.'

He clicked off.

'What?' Anna said.

'Wade says the piece of the ice sheet that came off probably displaced enough water to raise sea level by a centimeter or two.'

'God that must be a big iceberg,' Anna said. 'Think of sea level going up a centimeter everywhere around the world.'

'Yes. Although apparently it's only a little piece of the total ice sheet. And once it starts coming apart there's no telling how fast it might go.'

'My Lord.'

They sat bracketing the boys. Nick was wide-eyed, but appeared too surprised by all the activity to formulate his usual barrage of questions. Their van joined the line out to the southern stretch of the dike. Drepung leaned forward from his seat to show them the screen of his cell phone, which now displayed a tiny image of the upper end of the Bay of Bengal and the lower delta of the Ganges and Brahmaputra. This satellite photo had rendered altimetry data in false coloration to show river and sea level departures from the norm, with the brilliant spectral band ranging from the cool blues and greens of normality to the angry yellows, oranges, and reds of high water. Now the right side of the delta ran red, the left side orange and then yellow. And the whole Bay of Bengal was light orange already.

Drepung put a fingertip to the screen, looking very serious. 'See that little blue dot there? That's us. We are low. Orange all around us. That mean a couple meters higher than normal.'

Charlie said, 'That's not so bad, is it?'

'The dike is maxed out. They're saying now that they don't think it will be able to handle this flood surge.' He leaned back to take a call on his cell phone. Then: 'Now they tell me that the helicopter is on its way, and will be here before the ferries can be loaded. We would very much appreciate it if you would take the helicopter back to Calcutta.'

'We don't want to take space you might need,' Charlie said.

'No, that's just it. It will be easier for us if you are away. No break in the routine at the docks.'

Their van turned around and drove back toward town. Now they were going against the traffic, and could speed south and then west out the road to the airport. Once there they circled around the terminal, directly out onto the wet tarmac near the helo's landing site.

'Another twenty minutes,' Drepung said. Joe began to wail, and they let him down to run around. From time to time they looked at Drepung's handheld and got the image of the delta, in real time but false color. The coming of day made it harder to see, but the whole delta was now orange, and the blue areas denoting islands were distinctly smaller. 'The Sundarbans,' Drepung said, shaking his head. 'They are really meant to be amphibious.'

Then a helicopter thwacked out of the dawn sky. 'Good,' Drepung said, and led them off the concrete pad, onto a flat field next to it. They watched the big helicopter drop down through the clouds in a huge noise and wind of its own making, settling down on its pad like an oversized dragonfly. Joe howled at the sight. Charlie picked him up and felt the child clutch at him. They waited to be signaled over to the helo. Its blades continued to rotate, chopping the air at a speed allowing them to make out a speed of rotation, whether real or not they could not say.

'Down!' Joe shouted in Charlie's ear. 'Down! Down! Down! Down!'

'Let him down for a second,' Anna said. 'There's time, isn't there?'

Drepung was still at their side. 'Yes, there's time.'

Men in dark green uniforms were getting off the helicopter. Charlie put Joe down on the ground. Immediately Joe struck out for the helo, and Charlie followed, intent on stopping him. He saw that Joe's feet had sunk into what must have been very soft ground; and water was quickly seeping into his prints. Charlie picked him up from behind, ignored his wails as he returned to the others. He looked back; Joe's watery prints caught little chips of the dawn light, looking like silver coins.

Then it was time to board. Joe insisted on walking himself, kicking furiously when held by either Charlie or Anna, shrieking 'Down let down *let down*!' So they let him down and held him hard by the hands and walked forward, Nick on the other side of Anna, all ducking instinctively under the high but drooping blades that guillotined the air so noisily overhead.

In the helicopter it was a bit quieter. There were a few

people already in the short rows of seats, and in the next half hour they were joined by others, about half of them Westerners, the rest perhaps Indians, including a bevy of wide-eyed schoolgirls. The Quiblers and Frank greeted each in turn, and the school girls gathered to dote on Joe in their musical English. He hid his head from them, clung hard to Anna. Charlie looked out a little window beside them, set low so that right now he could see little more than the puddles on the concrete.

The noise of the engines got louder and up they lifted, tilting back and then forward, a strange sensation for anyone used to airplanes.

Out the lower window they caught a glimpse of the dike when they were just above its height, and there was the sea right there beyond it, lipping at the very top of the berm. The uncanny sight remained burned in their minds as the helo banked and they lost the view.

They made a rising turn over the island, and the view came back and went away, came back and went away. Joe leaned from Anna's arms to the window, trying to see better. Nick was looking out the same window from the seat behind. The sea was a dark brown, and on the island everything was soaked, gray-green fields lined with standing water – trees, rooftops, the plaza with the reflecting pool, all deep in shadow; then the ocean again, clearly as high as the dike. 'There's where we were staying!' Nick called, pointing.

They banked in a gyre that cut through the bottom layers of the clouds. Dark, light, rain, clear, they flew from one state to the next. Rain skittered across the outside of the glass in sudden streaming deltas. They saw the ferries at the dock on the north side of the island; they were casting off, and Drepung shouted something up to the pilots. He gave the Quiblers a thumbs-up. Then the helo continued its curve, and they saw other outer islands of the Sundarban archipelago, many of them submerged by the flood already and no more than shallow reefs. The channels between these were a pale brown, flecked with dirty white.

They curved back over Khembalung and saw that the dike had been breached on its southwest curve, where it faced the battering of the storm surf. Brown water, heavily flecked with foam, poured whitely down onto the fields below the break, in its rush clearly ripping the gap in the dike wider. Soon Khembalung would look like all the other Sundarbans.

Now Joe crawled onto Charlie's lap and took a death grip on Charlie's neck, moaning or keening, it was hard to hear in all the racket, but somehow the sound of it cut through everything else. Charlie forced the hands on his neck to loosen their grip. 'It's okay!' he said loudly to the boy. 'It'll be okay! They're all okay! They're on the boats. Big boats! The *people* were on the *boats*! All the *people* were on the *boats*.'

'Da, da, da,' Joe moaned, or maybe it was 'Na, da, na.' He put a hand on the window.

'Oh my God,' Charlie said.

Over Joe's head he could see again the gap where the ocean was pouring in; it was already much wider than before. It looked like the whole southwest curve would go. Already most of the interior fields were sheeted with foamy water.

Ahead of them the pilot and co-pilot were shouting into their headsets. The helo tilted, spiraled higher. Clouds interrupted their view below. A loud buffeted ascent, then they caught sight of Khembalung again, from higher than before; through a break in the clouds it looked like a shallow green bowl, submerged in brown water until only an arc of the bowl's rim remained in air.

Charlie said, 'Don't, Joe! I have to breathe.'

'Ah gone! Ah gone!'

Abruptly the helicopter tilted away, and all they could see outside the window was cloud. The Sundarbans were gone, all their mangrove swamps drowned, all their tigers swimming. The helo flew off like a blown leaf. Joe buried his face in Charlie's chest and sobbed.

# FOUR

## *Is There a Technical Solution?*

*No one thinks it will ever happen to them until suddenly they are in the thick of it, thoroughly surprised to be there.*

*A tornado in Halifax Nova Scotia; the third and catastrophic year of drought in Ireland; major floods on the Los Angeles River: these kinds of anomalies kept happening, at a rate of more than one a day around the world. Sooner or later almost everyone got caught up in some event, or lived in the midst of some protracted anomaly, for the weather events were both acute and chronic, a matter of hours or a matter of years.*

*Still it was hard to imagine it would ever happen to you.*

*At the poles the results were particularly profound, because of major and rapid changes in the ice. For reasons poorly understood, both polar regions were warming much faster than the rest of the planet. In the north this had resulted in the break-up of the Arctic Ocean's sea ice, the imminent extinction of many species, including the polar bear, and the subsequent stall of the Gulf Stream. In the south it had resulted in the rapid break-up of the giant ice shelves hugging the Antarctic coast, unblocking the big glaciers falling into the Ross Sea so that they became 'ice rivers,' moving so rapidly down their channels that they were destabilizing the West*

163

Antarctic Ice Sheet, the biggest variable in the whole picture: if this sheet came off its underwater perch on the sea floor, the world would suffer impacts greater by far than what had been witnessed already, most especially a rapid rise in sea level up to as much as seven meters if the whole sheet came off.

Still it was hard to imagine it would ever happen to you.

There were further ramifications. The ocean bottom, where it drops from the continental shelves to the abyssal seafloor, is in many places a steep slope, and these slopes are coated by thick layers of mud that contain methane in the form of clathrates, a chemical form of freezing that cages molecules of the gas in a frozen matrix. As ocean temperatures rose, these chemical cages were being destabilized, and release of the methane could then cause underwater avalanches in which even more methane was released, rising through the water and rejoining the atmosphere, where it was a greenhouse gas much more powerful than carbon dioxide. Warmer atmosphere meant warmer ocean meant released methane meant warmer atmosphere meant –

A complex of cycles, geologic, oceanic, and atmospheric, all blending into each other and affecting the rest. The interactions were so complex, the feedbacks positive and negative so hard to gauge in advance, the unforeseen consequences so potentially vast, that no one could say what would happen next to the global climate with any certainty. Modeling had been attempted to estimate the general rise in temperature, and actually these had been refined to the point that there was some agreement as to the outside parameters of possible change, ranging from about a two to an eleven degree C. rise in temperatures – a very big range, but that's how uncertain any estimates had to be at this point. And even if the estimates could have been tighter, global averages did not reveal much about local or ultimate effects, as people were now learning. There were non-linear tipping points, and now some *of these were beginning to reveal themselves. The stall of the Gulf Stream was expected to chill the temperature in the northern hemisphere, especially on both sides of the Atlantic; further effects were much less certain. The recent two-year failure of the monsoon was not understood, nor its violent return, and the effects of both, having devastated communities all across south Asia and beyond, in Africa and southeast Asia, would create still further effects as yet unforeseen. China's drought was ongoing, as was the longest-ever El Nino, now called the Hypernino. Desertification in the Sahel was moving south at an ever-increasing rate, and South America was suffering the worst floods in recorded history because of the rain brought by the El Nino. It had rained in the Atacama.*

*Wild weather everywhere. The most expensive insurance year ever, for the eighth year in a row, and by more than ever. That was just a number, an amount of money distributed out through the financial systems of the world by insurance of all kinds; but it was also a measure of catastrophe, death, suffering, fear, insecurity, and sheer massive inconvenience.*

*The problem they faced was that everything living depended on conditions staying within certain tight climatic parameters. The atmosphere was only so thick; as Frank put it once, talking to Anna and Kenzo, when you drive by Mount Shasta on US Interstate Five, you can see the height of the livable part of the atmosphere right there before your eyes. No permanent human settlement on Earth was higher than Shasta's summit, at 14,200 feet, so the mountain served to show in a very visible form just how thick the breathable atmosphere was – and the mountain wasn't very tall at all, in comparison to the immense reach of the plateau the highway ran over, or to the height of the sky above. It was just a snowy hill! It was sobering, Frank said; after you saw the matter that way, looking at the mountain and sensing the size of the whole planet, you were changed. Ever afterward you would be aware of an invisible ceiling low overhead containing all the breathable air under it – the atmosphere thus no more than the thinnest wisp of a skin, like cellophane wrapped ever so tightly to the lithosphere. An equally thin layer of water had liquefied in the low basins of this lithosphere, and that was the life zone: cellophane wrapping a planet, a mere faint exhalation, wisping off into space. Frank would shake his head, remembering it.*

*Still, it was hard to imagine.*

Frank's habits were his home now, and so the trip to Khembalung and its aftermath made him feel a bit homeless all over again. What to do with the day; again this became a question he had to answer anew, hour by hour, and it could be hard.

On the other hand, all the Khembali refugees flying into Washington helped him keep things in perspective. He was homeless by choice, they were not; he had his van, his tree, his office, his club – all the rooms of his house-equivalent, scattered around town; they had nothing. Their embassy's house in Arlington gave them temporary shelter, but everything there was in cheek-by-jowl crisis mode, and would be for a long time.

And yet they were cheerful in their manner. Frank found this impressive, though he also wondered how long it would last. Doubly exiled, first from Tibet, then from their island; now, he thought, they would join the many other refugee groups who had come to Washington to plead their case in an attempt to get back to their homes, then failed and never left, adding their children, cuisine, and holidays to the metro region's rich mix.

Because Khembalung was wrecked. There was talk of draining the island and repairing the dike, but there was no ready source of electricity to drive the pumps, no equipment available to rebuild the dike; and though those problems could be dealt with, maybe, their fresh water supply appeared to have been compromised as well; and the island was being thoroughly saturated by seawater; and the longer things were submerged, the worse the damage got.

Above all, Khembalung was simply too low. It had always been too low, the Sundarbans were swampy islands, seasonally wetlands; and now, with the ocean's average level rising, the margin of safety had disappeared. No matter what they did, catastrophic floods were bound to inundate all the Sundarbans again and again. Moon tides, storm surges, even the occasional tsunamis, likely to become more frequent as methane clathrates warmed and triggered underwater landslides – all these would be flooding the coastal lowlands of the world more often.

So the immense expense and effort that would be necessary to pump out and rebuild Khembalung was not worth it. The Khembalis had other options: there were other Tibetan refugee colonies scattered around India, and the Khembalis themselves owned some land in the hills north of Calcutta. And some people at the embassy in D.C. were talking about buying land in the metro area, and settling there. Meanwhile, it could be said that all twelve thousand citizens of Khembalung had for their national territory just one old Arlington house and an office in the NSF building.

So it was a crowded house and office. Frank was always amazed to see just how crowded they were. He dropped by often to say hi, and see if there was anything he could do to help, and every time he was struck anew at how many people could be crammed into a place without breaking anything but zoning codes. Carrying boxes from delivery trucks into the kitchen, talking to Rudra in English, getting the old man to teach him some Tibetan words, Frank was always happy to see them, and always happy to get out of there – to be able to drive over the Potomac to Rock Creek and the refuge of the forest.

*     *     *

The late summer days were still pretty long, and this was good, because Frank needed the light. He hiked into the park checking in on his FOG phone, getting the latest fixes and hoping he could locate the gibbons, whom he had learned were a family, Bert and May and their kids, or the siamangs; but any of the ferals would do. In the last hour before sundown many of them made their way to the watering hole in the gorge for a last drink for the night, and he often had good luck spotting them. Ostrich, tapir, spider monkey, eland, sitatunga, tamarin, red deer, brown bear; his personal list of sightings kept growing.

His Acheulian hand axe came in the mail at work, and he pulled it out of its bubble wrap and held it up to the light. Instantly it was his favorite rock. It had a lovely weight, and fitted his hand perfectly; it was the classic Acheulian oval, with a sharp tip at its smaller end. Chipped on both sides very expertly, so that it seemed as much a work of sculpture as a tool, a little Andy Goldsworthy sculpture; a petroglyph all by itself, speaking in its heft a whole world. The people who made it. Gray quartzite, slightly translucent, the chipped faces almost as smoothed by patination during their four hundred thousand years of exposure as the browned curve of original core. It was beautiful.

He took it to the park and pulled it from his daypack to show to Spencer and Robin and Robert the next time they ran, and they spontaneously fell to their knees to honor it, crying out wordlessly, like the gibbons. 'Ahh! Ahh! Oh my God. Oh God, here it is.' Robin salaamed to it, Spencer inspected every chip and curve, kissing it from time to time. 'Look how perfect it is,' he said.

'Look,' Robin said when he held it, 'it's shaped for a left-hander, see? It fits a lot better when you hold it in your left hand.' Robin was left-handed. 'Do you think maybe *homo erectus* were all left-handed?' he went on. 'Like polar bears? Polar bears are all left-handed, did you know that?'

'Only because you've told us a thousand times,' Spencer

said, taking it from him. 'How old did you say?' he asked Frank.

'Four hundred thousand years.'

'Unbelievable. But look, you know – I really hate to say this – but it doesn't look like it would fly like a frisbee.'

'No, it doesn't.'

'Also, that thing about how it wouldn't make a very good hand axe, because it's sharpened all the way around? Actually it seems to me you could hold it almost anywhere and still hit something without cutting your hand. The edge isn't sharp enough.'

'True.'

'Have you tried throwing it yet?'

'No.'

'Well heck, let's give it a try.'

'Let's throw it at a rabbit!'

'Now come on.'

'Hey we have to test this thing, how else are we going to do it? Throw it at one of those tapirs, it'll bounce right off them.'

'No it won't.'

'You kill it you eat it.'

'Fine by me!'

They ran the course, and when they came to the meadow near picnic site 14, they stopped and Frank pulled out the axe, and they threw it at a tree (it left an impressive gash) and then at trash bottles set up on a log. Yes, you could break a bottle with it, if you could hit it; and it did tend to spin on its axis, though not necessarily horizontally; in fact it tended to rotate through a spiral as it flew forward.

'You could kill a rabbit if you hit it.'

'True with an ordinary rock though.'

'You could spook a big animal by the watering hole.'

'True with an ordinary rock though.'

'All right, okay.'

'It'd work to skin an animal I guess.'

'That's true,' Frank said. 'But they've tried that in South Africa, and they've found that they lose their edge really quick, like after one animal.'

'You're kidding.'

'That's what they found. That's why they think there might be so many of them. They think they used to just knap a new one pretty much any time they needed to do something.'

'Hmm, I don't know. This thing looks pretty perfect for a throwaway. It looks like someone's favorite tool.'

'His Swiss Army knife.'

'That's just patination. It's four hundred thousand years old, man. That's *old*. Older than art and religion, like you said.'

'It *is* art and religion.'

'A fossilized frisbee.'

'Fossil killer frisbee.'

'Except it doesn't look like that's what it was.'

'Well, I'm sticking with it,' Spencer said. 'It's too good a theory to give up on just for the sake of some evidence.'

'Yahhh!'

'This is just anecdotal evidence anyway. Means nothing.'

Frisbee golf in the last hour of light, running through the flickering shadow and light. Working up a sweat, making shots magnificent or stupid. Living entirely in his frisbee mind, nothing else intruding. The blessed no-time of meditation. Sports could do that sometimes, and in that sense, it did become religion. Turning the moment into eternity.


His shelter was completely rain-proofed now, and given the frequent summer showers, this made for a wonderfully satisfying situation: his little room, open-sided under its clear plastic canopy, was frequently walled by sheets of falling water, like a bead curtain perpetually falling. The rain pounded down with its plastic drumming noise, like the shower you hear in the morning when your partner gets up – a susurrus or patter, riding on the liquid roar of the forest and the clatter of the creek below. The air less humid than during those muggy days when the rain held off.

Often it rained just before dawn or just after. Charcoal turning gray in the dimness of a rainy day. Low clouds scudding or lowering overhead. Sometimes he would sleep again for another half hour. The night's sleep would have been broken, no matter where he spent the night; something would bring him up, his heart racing for no reason, then the brain following: thinking about work, or Caroline, or Marta, the Khembalis, the homeless guys, the frisbee players, housing prices in north San Diego county – anything could spark it off, and then it was very difficult to fall back asleep. He would lie there, in van or treehouse or very occasionally his office, aware that he needed more sleep but unable to drop back in.

Rain then would be a blessing, as the sound tended to knock him out. And rain in the morning gave him time to lie there and think about projects, experiments, animals, papers, money, women. Time to remember that many men his age, maybe most men his age, slept with a woman every night of their lives, to the point where they hardly even noticed it, except in their partner's absence.

Better to think about work.

Or to look at the pattern leaves made against the sky, black against the velvet grays. Stiffly shift around, trying to wake up, until he was sitting on the edge of the platform, sleeping bag draped over him like a cape, feet swinging in air, to listen for the gibbons. Insomnia as a kind of a gift, then, from nature, or Gaia, or the animals and birds, or his unquiet unconscious. Of course one woke a little before dawn! How could you not? It was so beautiful. Sometimes he felt like he was sitting on the edge of some great thing that only he could see was about to happen. Some change like morning itself, but different.

Other days he woke and could only struggle to escape the

knot his stomach had been tied into during the night. Then it took the gibbons to free him. If they were within earshot, and he heard them lift their voices, then all was immediately well within him, the knot untied. An aubade: all will be well, and all will be well, and all will be perfectly well. That was what they were singing, as translated by some nuns in medieval Europe. It was another gift. Sometimes he just listened, but usually he sang with them, if singing was the right word. He hooted, whooped, called; but really it was most like singing, even if the word he sang was always 'ooooooooop,' and every ooop was a glissando, sliding up or down. Ooooooop! Oooooooop!

If they sounded like they were nearby, he would descend from his tree and try to spot them. He had to be quiet, and as invisible as possible. But this was true for all his stalking. Light steps, looking down at the still-gray ground, seeking footfalls between the ubiquitous twigs, in the bare black mud.

All the animals in the park were pretty skittish by now, and the gibbons and siamangs were no exception. At the least noise someone in the gibbon gang would shout some kind of warning (often a loud 'Aaack!,' as in the comic strip *Cathy*) and then they would tarzan away with only a few muffled calls to indicate even what direction they had gone. Typically they moved fifty to a hundred yards before resettling; so if they spooked, Frank usually shifted his hunt to some other animal. You couldn't beat brachiation in a forest.

He would work his way down Rock Creek, headed for the waterhole overlook. FOG had put a salt lick on the edge of the water. He was careful in his final approach, because the overlook itself had been marked by big paw prints, feline in appearance but large, huge in fact – like sign of the missing jaguar, still unsighted, or at least unreported. Or maybe the prints were of one of the forest's smaller cats, the snow leopard or lynx or the native bobcat. In any case not a good animal to catch by surprise. Sometimes he even approached the overlook clutching his hand axe, reassured by the heft of it.

Once there he could watch the animals below, drinking warily and taking licks of the salt lick. On this morning he saw two of the tiny tamarins, a gazelle, an okapi, and the rhinoceros, all radio-tagged already. The day before he had seen a trio of red wolves bring down a young eland.

After the waterhole he explored, striking out to get mildly lost, in the process checking out the tributaries in Rock Creek's rippled watershed. Stealthy walking in the hope of spotting animals: again, as with the heft of the hand axe, or the swaying of his tree in the wind, it felt familiar to his body, as if he had often done it before. Used to things he had never done. Stalking – paparazzi following movie stars –

Slink of gray flashing over the creek.

In his memory he reconstructed the glimpse. Silvery fur; something like a fisher or minx. Bounding over the rocks in a hurry.

Around a corner he came on the hapless tapirs, rooting in the mud. This forest floor did not have what they needed, and Frank had heard they were living off care packages provided by the zoo staff and FOG members. Some people argued that this meant they should be recaptured. Only animals that could make their way in the forest on their own should be considered for permanent feral status, these people argued.

Of course many of the feral species were tropical or semitropical. Already there was a lot of debate about what to do when winter came. Possibly the feral project for these creatures would come to an end; although it wasn't clear exactly how some of them could be recaptured.

Well, they would cross that bridge when they came to it. For now, GPS the tapirs, add them to his FOG phone's log. So far his list included forty-three non-native species, from aardvarks to zebras. Then trudge out west to his van, to drive over the river to Optimodal. Often all this would happen and he would still get to the gym before seven.

\*     \*     \*

After that, the day got more complicated. No meetings at eight, so a quick visit to the Optimodal weight room. If he ran into Diane, they worked out together. That was habitual, and it was getting a little complicated, actually. Not that it wasn't fun, because it was. Her hand on his arm: it was interesting. But friendly conversations and shared work-outs with a woman at the gym suggested a certain kind of relationship, and when the woman in question was also one's boss – also single, or at least known to have been widowed several years before – there was no way to avoid certain little implications that seemed to follow, expressed by the ways in which they didn't meet each other's eye or discuss various matters, also little protocols and courtesies, steering clear of what might be more usual behaviors in the gym situation. He often began a workout feeling he was too preoccupied by other concerns to think about this matter; but quickly enough it was unavoidable. Diane's businesslike cheer and quick mind, her industry and amusement, her muscly middle-aged body flexing and pinking before him, sometimes under his care – it was impossible not to be affected by that. She looked good. He wanted Caroline to call him again.

To tell the truth, ever since his encounter with Francesca, all women looked good to him. In the metro, at NSF, in the gym. Some mornings it was better just to shower and shave and get right over to work. Into his office, sit down with coffee, survey the huge list of *Things To Do*. Many of them were very interesting things, like:

1) Quantify the 'estimated maximum takedown' for every carbon capture method suggested in the literature (for next Diane meeting)
2) Talk to Army Corps of Engineers
3) Formalize criteria for Macarthur-style awards to researchers
4) Talk to UCSD about assisting new institute in La Jolla

Pick one and dive in, and then it was a rapid flurry of meetings, phone calls, reading at furious speed, memos, reports, abstracts – God bless abstracts, if only everything were written as an abstract, what would be lost after all – writing at the same furious speed, memos mostly, abstracts no matter what, need to do this, need to do that. All the little steps needed if things were ever going to get done.

Then another meeting with Diane and several members of the National Science Board. Diane seemed a bit grim to Frank this time; not surprising to him, as really she was trying almost by force of will to make NSF a major node in the network of scientific organizations working on climate. So she was doing exactly what Frank had urged her to do in his presentation before the flood, and though no one would ever speak of it in that way, he found himself pleased. Jump into action as soon as they could identify an action. All the board members in attendance seemed on board with that. Potential partners were being identified in the scientific community, also supportive members of Congress, sympathetic committees. As Diane kept saying, they needed legislation, they needed funding. Meanwhile she was working with the Intergovernmental Panel on Climate Change, the International Council for Science, the World Conservation Union, the National Academy of Engineering, NASA and NOAA, the U.S. Global Change Research Program, the World Meteorological Organization, the World Resources Institute, the Pew Charitable Trust, the National Center for Atmospheric Research, the President's Committee of Advisors on Science and Technology, the Office of Science and Technology Policy, the Nature Conservancy, the Ecological Society of America, DIVERSITAS, which was the umbrella program to coordinate global research effort in the biodiversity sciences, and GLOBE, which stood for Global Learning and Observations to Benefit the Environment –

'And so on,' she concluded, looking impassively at the

Power Point slide listing these organizations. 'There are many more. There is no shortage of organizations. Government agencies, UN, scientific societies, NGOs. The situation is in many ways being intensely monitored. Whether all these efforts can be coordinated and lead to any action is another question. It's the question I want to discuss today, after we've gotten through the other items on the agenda. This is the real problem: we know, but we can't act.'

The more Frank watched Diane in these meetings, the more he liked her. She got things done without making a fuss. She was not diverted, she kept to the important points, she made sure everyone knew what she thought was important. She didn't waste time. She worked with people and through people – as she did with Frank – and people worked like maniacs for her, thinking they were pursuing their own projects (and often they were), but enacting Diane's projects too; and she was the one coordinating them, enabling them. Setting the pace and finding the money.

Now she came back to Frank's chief interest. 'We have to consider potential interventions in the biosphere itself,' shaking her head as if she couldn't believe what she was saying. 'If there are ways to tip the global climate back out of this abrupt change, we should identify them and do them. Too much else that we want to do will be hammered if we don't accomplish that. So, can it be done, and if so, how? Which interventions have the best chance, and which can we actually do?'

'It makes sense to try to work on the trigger we've already identified,' Frank said.

Diane nodded. That meant the stalled downwelling of the thermohaline circulation, and she had already begun discussions with the UN and the IPCC broaching the possibility of overcoming the stall. 'We'll get a report on that later. Right now, what about carbon capture methods?'

Frank went down the list he had compiled.

1) freezing carbon dioxide extracted from coal-fired power plants and other industrial sources, and depositing the dry ice on the ocean floor near subduction zones or river deltas, where it would be buried,

2) injecting frozen $CO_2$ into emptied oil wells or underground aquifers (a DOE project, tested by Canada and Norway already),

3) fertilizing oceans with iron to stimulate phytoplankton and absorb more $CO_2$,

4) gathering agricultural wastes and dropping them to the ocean floor in giant weighted torpedoes,

5) gathering ag waste and converting to ethanol for fuel,

6) growing biomass, both to burn in biofuels and to sequester carbon for the life of the plants (corn, poplar trees)

7) altering bacteria or other plant life to speed its carbon uptake, *without* triggering release of nitrous oxides that were more potent greenhouse gases than $CO_2$ itself.

This last point was vexing all plans to stimulate carbon drawdown by biological means. 'It's the law of unintended consequences,' as one ecologist had put it to Frank. Now he explained to Diane and the others: 'Say your iron spurs the growth of marine bacteria, drawing down carbon, but that includes the growth of types of bacteria that release nitrous oxides. And NOs are a much worse greenhouse gas than $CO_2$. Also, a lot of the carbon in the ocean is fixed in dead diatom shells. Some marine bacteria feed on dead diatoms, and when they do, they free up that carbon, which had been fixed in carbonates that would have eventually become limestone. So is fertilizing the ocean with iron necessarily going to result in a net drawdown in greenhouse gases? Even in the short term it isn't sure.'

'We need to be sure,' Diane said.

'That's going to be hard, in this area anyway.'

In another meeting they discussed methods that had been proposed for direct climate alteration, including adding chemicals to jet fuel so that contrails would last longer and reflect more light back into space; seeding clouds; shooting dust into the upper atmosphere in imitation of volcanoes; and flying various sunscreens to high altitude. Again, because of the complexity of the various feedback mechanisms, and the importance of water vapor both in blocking incoming light and holding in outgoing heat, it was hard to predict what the result of any given action would be. No one had a good sense of how clouds might change in any given scenario.

'I don't think we're ready for anything like these projects,' Diane said. 'We can't be sure what effects we'll get.'

At the time she said it, they were all looking at a slide from an NSF polar programs ecologist's presentation. Both poles were heating up fast, but especially the Arctic; and the slide informed them that one-seventh of all the carbon on Earth was cached in biotic material frozen in the Arctic permafrost, which was rapidly melting. Once it was liquid again, bacterial action would start releasing some of that carbon into the atmosphere. 'It could be another positive feedback, like the methane hydrates unfreezing on the continental shelves.'

'It's the law of unintended consequences again.'

'Wouldn't the tundra just turn into peat bogs?' Frank asked.

'Peat bogs are anoxic. Permafrost isn't.'

'Ah.'

In a meeting the next day, a team from NOAA gave a presentation on what they had done to try to get a handle on the numbers involved in any potential scheme to intervene in the North Atlantic. It was a matter of sensitive dependencies, their main speaker claimed, so there was chaos math involved. Frank was interested in the algorithms used in the computer modeling, but he saved that aspect for later; accuracy within orders of magnitude was probably good enough for the questions facing them now. How much water used to sink in the downwelling? What volume of water would have to sink at each particular site to start it again? What kind of thermohaline differentials were they talking about? How much more saline would the sea have to be to sink through the fresh water cap on the ocean now there? How much dry weight of salt would be needed to create that differential?

The NOAA people did their best with these questions. Frank and the others there tried out various back-of-the-envelope calculations, and they talked over what it might take to bring that much salt to bear. It seemed within the industrial and shipping capacities of the advanced nations, at least theoretically – somewhat similar to the numbers involved in oil transport – although there were also questions concerning whether this would be a one-time application, or would have to be an annual thing to offset the Arctic sea ice that would presumably form every winter, break up every spring, and float south every summer.

'We can deal with that issue later,' Diane declared. 'Meanwhile I want all the answers here as constrained as possible, so I can take a plan to Congress and the President. Anything we can do that makes the point we are not helpless will be useful on other fronts. So, as far as I can tell, this is as good a place to start as any.'

At lunch he ran with the NSF runners, when he could get away. It was an indulgence but he couldn't help himself. He justified it by inventing questions he could ask Kenzo about the Arctic climate and so on. That would get Kenzo started on his Master of Disaster shtick, detailing the latest like a curator with an exceptionally good show; but this was likely to happen anyway, for Kenzo never tired of the role, nor seemed to think he was telling the story of the beginning of the end of civilization.

That part was Edgardo's job. 'How are your Khembalis doing, Frank?'

'Well, it's getting pretty crowded at their house.'

'I can see they're sleeping in their office too.'

'Yes. I think Immigration is beginning to get on their case. They're going for some kind of refugee status.'

'They'll never get that,' Edgardo advised. 'They should call themselves Washington's only Buddhist think tank.'

'Maybe so.'

'They should say they are the embassy from Atlantis.'

'That'll really help them with access to Congress.'

Edgardo laughed. 'It would! They would love it! Atlantis, Shambala – your guys have to be from somewhere interesting. Do they have lawyers identifying who to sue for compensation?'

'No.'

'Do they have insurance companies ready to back their suit?'

'No! Be quiet and run, will you?'

But Frank couldn't run fast enough to wind them. They were stronger runners than he was, and so it was talk talk talk, every step of the way. Scientists, bureaucrats – scientific bureaucrats – technocrats – they were all *intellectuals* to one degree or another. Although of course not therefore all equally talkative, or the same in personality. Frank pounded along behind Edgardo and Kenzo contemplating the different characters in even so homogeneous a technocracy as NSF. There were shy types; there were science geeks like Kenzo; then also raving intellectuals like Edgardo; and bluff 'simple folk' like Bob or Clark, who weren't willing to admit to knowing anything or having any opinions except in their areas of expertise, implying that this modesty was the purest form of scientific precision and right action: no opinions, only assert what you think you can prove.

Edgardo was not like that. He had come up with another idea for a popular science best-seller: 'I was reading an enormously long paper on hypergraphia when it came to me that the researcher suffered from the disease and that was why he was interested. I wonder how often that is the case. Anyway this hypergraphia is kind of like epilepsy, it happens in the same part of the brain.'

'Hard to imagine the evolutionary history of that,' Frank noted. 'A tendency to write things down?'

'Presumably it's just a variant of hyperloggia,' Kenzo said, 'which would explain Edgardo's interest too.'

'Ha ha, but no that's a different part of the brain. Talking is in Broca's and Wernicke's, hypergraphia is in the epilepsy region, and it actually creates a kind of style. There is a suite of stylistic habits that can be abstracted and quantified by computer to make the diagnosis. Of course sheer mass of output is still the first clue, and it must have been useful to several very prolific novelists, this is a nice match of problem and solution. But even with the hypergraphic greats like Balzac or Dick it seems to have been as much a pain as a benefit, like a kind of priapism, but what I noticed immediately is that these stylistic tics common to hypergraphics are all evident in both the *Book of Mormon* and the writings of Mary Baker Eddy, and then of course the Koran, and I thought, of course, all these prophets, writing down the truth at great length – and the religious center of the brain is also tightly bound with the epilepsy center! It's all one complex! So these scribbling prophets were all suffering from a form of epilepsy, they wrote under the spell of a convulsion.'

'Mohammed dictated the Koran.'

'Is that right? Well, maybe hyperloggia is also implicated.'

'How many religions do you think you could offend at once with this book?'

'I would think many, but that would not be the point. Explanation of our behavior is the point. Besides humanism too could be included here. Sartre was clearly hypergraphic, especially when he used amphetamines.'

'You're going to have quite a tour promoting this one!' Kenzo said.

\*　　\*　　\*

On other lunchtimes Frank went out and ate with Anna and Drepung at the Food Factory. Drepung would come in with the latest from the embassy, shaking his head as he ate. Every week it seemed clearer that they had lost Khembalung for good. Salvage plans had replaced restoration in his talk.

'Did you have any flood insurance?' Anna asked.

'No. I don't think anyone would underwrite it.'

'So what will you do?'

Drepung shrugged. 'Not sure yet.'

'Ouch,' Anna said.

'I do not mind it. It seems to be good for people. It wakes them up.'

Frank nodded at this, but Anna only looked distressed. She said, 'But you're making arrangements?'

'Yes, of course. Such freedom from habit cannot last, people would go mad.' He glanced at Frank and laughed; Frank felt his face get hot. 'We're talking with the Dalai Lama, of course, and the Indian government. Probably they would give us another island in the Sundarbans.'

'But then it will only happen again,' Frank pointed out.

'Yes, it seems likely.'

'You need to get to higher ground.'

'Yes.'

'Back to the Himalayas,' Anna suggested.

'We will see. For now, Washington D.C.'

'Go higher than that for God's sake!'

Sometimes Drepung would leave on errands and Frank and Anna would order another coffee and talk a few minutes more before taking the coffees back up to work. They shared their news in a desultory fashion. Anna's was usually about Charlie and the boys, Frank's about something he had done or seen around the city. Anna laughed at the discrepancy between their tales: 'Things are still happening to you.'

Frank rolled his eyes at this. For a while they talked in a different way than they usually did, about how things felt;

and they agreed that lives were not easily told to others. Frank speculated that many life stories consisted precisely in a search for a reiterated pattern, for habits. Thus, one's set of habits was somehow unsatisfactory, and you needed to change them, and were thereby thrown into a plot, which was the hunt for new habits, or even, but exceptionally, the story of the giving up of such a hunt in favor of sticking with what you have, or remaining chaotically in the existential moment (not adaptive if reproductive success were the goal, he noted under his breath). Thus Frank was living a plot while Anna was living a life, and when they talked about personal matters he had news while she had the 'same old same old,' which was understood by both to be the desired state, irritating and difficult though it might be to maintain.

Anna merely laughed at this.

One day the *Things To Do* list included a lunch meeting at a Crystal City restaurant with the four-star general who headed the US Army Corps of Engineers, a friendly and unassuming man named Arthur Wracke, 'pronounced *rack*,' he said, 'yes, as in rack and ruin.' White-haired, brown-skinned, grizzled. A strangely pixie grin. Unflappable; this, Frank saw, was what had gotten him his four stars. And along the way he had surely been in any number of political firestorms over major environmental interventions like the ones they were now contemplating at NSF.

When Frank expressed doubt that any major climate mitigation was possible, either physically or politically, Wracke waved a hand. 'The Corps has always done things on a big scale. Huge scale. Sometimes with huge blunders. All with the best intentions of course. That's just the way things happen. We're still gung-ho to try. Lots of things are reversible, in the long run. Hopefully this time around we'll be working with better science. But, you know, it's an iterative process. So, long story short, you get a project approved, and we're good to go. We've got the expertise. The Corps' esprit de corps is always high.'

'What about budget?' Frank asked.

'What about it? We'll spend what we're given.'

'Well, but is there any kind of, you know, discretionary fund that you can tap into?'

'We don't seek funding, usually,' the General admitted.

'But could you?'

'Well, in tandem with a request for action. Say you came to us with a request for action that would cost more than you have available. We could refer it up, and it would have to go to the Joint Chiefs of Staff to get supplementary funding. Do even the Chiefs have much discretionary funding?' He grinned. 'Sure they do. But not as much as you might think. They got into some trouble for what they called reprogrammed funding. Really, it all goes back to Congress. They control the purse-strings. Even more than the President. So if *they* were to allocate funds, the Joint Chiefs would do what they're told to with it, by and large.'

Frank nodded. 'But if it was just the Pentagon . . .'

'We'd have to see. But we could make your case, and if the funding's there, we are good to go.'

'Major climate mitigation.'

'Oh heck yes. We like these kinds of challenges. Who wouldn't?'

Frank had to laugh. The world was their sandbox. Castles and moats, dams and bulwarks . . . they had drained and then rehydrated the Everglades, they kept New Orleans dry, they had rerouted all the major rivers, irrigated the West, moved mountains. You could see all that right there on the general's happy face. Stewardship, sustainability – fine! Rack but not ruin! Working for the long haul just meant no end, ever, to their sandbox games.

'No deep ecologists in the U.S. Army Corps of Engineers, I guess.'

185

'Ha ha.' Wracke's eyes twinkled. 'You give us a chance and we'll *become* deep ecologists. We'll go right down to the *mantle*.'

Driving back to the office Frank considered how interesting it was to see the way some people enjoyed becoming the avatar of the institution they worked for, expressing the organizational personality like an actor in a role they love. Most people played their institution's personality with diligence but no particular flair; sometimes, however, he met good actors in a role well-matched to them. Diana was somewhat like that herself, though as Edgardo had noted, she was pushing the NSF character into realms it had never entered before, so the vibe she gave was not like Wracke's evocation of the Corps, supremely at ease with his role, but rather that of a person in the midst of a great awakening, or coming into one's own. Diane as Science, becoming Self-Aware. Maybe even unbound. Diane the prometheus.

In the last hour of the work day Frank usually sat back in his office chair and glanced through jackets. No matter that you might be inventing a new-but-old world religion, or saving the biosphere itself, you still had to complete NSF's unconscious life-support activity, its heartbeat and breath. How many jackets did you process today?

Sometimes he couldn't stand that, and he scanned submissions to *The Journal of Sociobiology* instead. Maternal sentiment not innate, one paper said; this asserted because women in northern Taiwan, also European women in the medieval and early modern period, gave away their own children on a regular basis, for economic reasons. Maternal sentiment therefore perhaps a learned response. Frank had his doubts, and besides all these conclusions were long since outlined in Hrdy, a source the paper's authors seemed unaware of. That ignorance and the huge generalizations given the evidence probably would doom this paper to rejection.

Abstract, conclusion; abstract, conclusion. Female brown

capuchin monkeys throw things if they see other monkeys getting more than they got from an equivalent exchange. Aversion to inequity therefore probably very deep-rooted, evolutionarily. Sense of fairness evolved. Thus cooperative groups, long before hominids. Monkey ethics; interesting.

First primate found and identified, in China, 55 million years old. Named *Teilhardina*, very nice. One ounce; fit in the palm of your hand. Amazing.

Groups of female baboons could coerce new male members of the troop into more peaceful behaviors. Females of the Japanese quail *Coturnix japonica* tended to choose the losers in male-male confrontations. Maybe that's why Caroline likes me, Frank thought, then grimaced at this traitorous self-judgment. It was postulated that for the female quails, choosing the loser reduced the risk of later injury, the males being rough during sex. Previously-mated females more likely to choose losers than virgins were.

On he read, his face thrust forward into the laptop so eagerly that his nose almost touched the screen. There could not be another person on earth who read these things with more intense interest than he did, for to him these were questions of immediate practice, influencing what he might do later that very day. To him every paper had the unwritten subtitle *How Should I Live Right Now?*

When his wristwatch alarm beeped the question always remained unanswered. Time to get up and invent the evening.

Run a round of frisbee, drop in on the bros, play chess with Chessman, visit the Quiblers, sit in Kramer's or Second Story to read, have an ouzo at Odysseus. For about a month he played chess with Chessman almost every night, becoming a regular mark, as Zeno put it, as Chessman was getting unbeatable. He played more than anyone else, he was a pro, and it might be that he was getting really good; Frank didn't play well enough to be sure. Paradoxically, the youth's style had become less aggressive. He waited for people to extend a little, then beat them. The games took more time, and maybe that was the point; it gave people hope, and thus might create more repeat customers.

In between games they sat by a kerosene lantern, nursing coffees or beers. Chessman read paperbacks under the lamp, books with titles like *One Hundred Best End Games*. Once it had been *The Immortal Games of Paul Morphy*, another time *The Genius of Paul Morphy*. Frank chatted with the others. It was another iteration of a conversation they had had many times before, concerning the inadequacies of the National Park Service. All their various conversations were like performances of long-running plays, alternating in repertory style. Laughs in the usual places. The bros laughed more than anyone Frank knew, but it was seldom happy laughter. They were shouting defiance. Vocalizations were as important to people as to gibbons. The daily hoot, oooooooooop!

So they sat there, telling stories. Awful things from Vietnam, a rare item in their repertory, but sometimes Zeno and Fedpage and Andy got a horrible urge to reminisce. More often they described recent scuffles, re-enacted in full. The bros retained a choreographic memory of every fight they had ever been in. Then also, recent meals; ranger actions of any kind, important or trivial; the weather. Cutter would drop by almost every night, even though he clearly had somewhere else he could go. In that sense he was like Frank, and perhaps as a result he and Frank didn't talk much. The truth was that Frank spoke to few but Chessman and Zeno. Sometimes he would talk to Fedpage about items from the *Post*, or Andy would command that he join one of Andy's stock exchanges. Cutter always brought a six pack or two, and they would fall to and divide the cans and drink until the drink was gone. This usually perked them up.

'Cutter is a tree surgeon,' Zeno clarified to Frank, 'our tree surgeon, currently unemployed.'

'Not city parks?' Frank asked Cutter, gesturing at the patch on the shoulder of his shirt.

'Used to be.'

'But you look like you're still doing it?'

'Oh I am, I am.'

'Cutter is the keeper of the forest. He is the unsung savior of this fucking city.'

'What else am I gonna do.'

'So you cut on your own?'

'Yes I do.'

'He steals gas outta cars to keep his chainsaw going, don't ya, Cutter?'

'Someone's gotta do it. This town'd disappear like *that*.'

'The forest it *wants* this city back, you know it does! *That's* who's winning.'

'– two three years I swear. But city knows some of us'll keep at it, so they keep cutting staff.'

'They cut more people than trees!'

Cutter laughed. 'Yesterday Byron couldn't buckle his harness but in the last hole, you know he's so fat these days, and so it gave loose on him as he finished dropping a big branch, and he fell and popped out of the waist belt but his legs held, so he swung down and the chainsaw smacked him right here on top of his leg. So he's hanging there screaming like a fool, I cut my leg, I cut off my leg oh *God*! But weren't no cut on his leg, just a bruise and a scrape. So we calling up to him, Byron you okay, ain't no cut on your leg, quit your wiggling, you gonna slip out your harness and crack your head like a egg. But he was yelling so loud he never heard us, My leg, my leg, I've cut off my laaig! I can't *feel* it no more! And we telling him, Open your eyes fool and look you're fine, and he won't do it. I can't stand to see it! His eyes all squished shut, No no *no*, I can't *do* it I can't stand to see it, I can't stand to *look* it's too horrible, I can *feel* it's gone, I can *feel* the blood *dripping*!'

The bros loved this. 'I can *feeeel* it!' It was obvious this was something they'd be saying for months to come, a new addition to their clutch of stock phrases.

'How'd you get him down?'

'We had to pinch his eyelids open and *make* him look.'

Bursts of raucous laughter, shouted comments, a mocking re-enactment of how it must have been. Another little climax of hilarity or celebration punctuating the day.

After that they sank slowly into sullen peacefulness or sullen squabbling, same as always. The various aches and complaints. Fedpage went back to his *Post*, the rest to the chessboard or the scraps on the grill topping the flue of the smoky fire. Dry leaves and wet branches and again the meat was both black with smoke and undercooked. Prod the fire to keep it sputtering along. Out into the dark for a round of copious urination. Some slipped off to find another haunt; others slumped in their places, the evening's entertainment over.

Frank walked out into the night. Sound of the creek, the citysurround. Voices in the distance; there were people at site 20, as always, and also at 18, which was a surprise. As he closed on his tree it got quieter and so did he, making his final approach as quietly as possible, covered by the noise of the creek a short distance below. Under his tree he waited, listening carefully. Night goggles, survey the scene; nothing warm upstream or down. When he was convinced no one was nearby, he called down Miss Piggy and clambered up into the night, up into his aerie, like a mountaineer scaling a last overhang to a ledge camp.

He pulled through the gap in the rail and sat on the plywood. Cranking Miss Piggy up, it occurred to him that the rent he was saving these days might eventually enable him to afford a down payment on a house, when he finally returned to San Diego. A quick calculation indicated that to save enough he would have to stay up here some five or six years.

Well – it could be worse. It was not such a bad prospect, really. Up in the night and the wind, swaying slightly north and south; how bad was that?

He lay down on his bed. In the mellow glow of his battery-powered Coleman lantern, he opened a paperback copy of Italo Calvino's *The Baron In the Trees*. He had seen the book in Second Story and bought it, thinking it might teach him something. But so far it had been short on logistical detail, and lacking also the explanatory power he was hoping for. The young baron had barged into the trees one day after a fight with his father, which was believable enough, but un-illuminating. And his decision to stay up there the rest of his life, without ever coming down at all, was simply unreason-able. Cosimo could have done everything he had done and still come down from time to time. Not coming down made it more of a parable than a program. An allegory, perhaps, for staying in nature no matter what. Well, in that sense Cosimo was a hero, his story a good fable.

But Frank was content to be up here when he was, without wanting more. Around him the aging leaves clattered, and in the distance the cry of a loon, or maybe even a coyote – in any case one of those crazies who would not shut up at night. Like certain of the bros. Every animal trait had its echo in some human quality. 'Owwww,' he howled quietly. 'Owwwwwww.' The tree rocked him in its slight syncopa-tion against the wind.

He wanted Caroline to call him. He was tired of waiting for her to call, why didn't she call? Surely she knew he was waiting. Even if she had trouble at home, even if she couldn't get away, surely she could call? Could she be in trouble? Could her husband (an awful phrase) have her under surveillance? Such tight surveillance that she couldn't get away to call? Could he have that same kind of surveillance trained on Frank, making it doubly hard for her to call? Was there some reason why she couldn't get loose like she had before? After all, she had both called and appeared in the Bethesda park. Perhaps it required a stay with her friends. Who were these friends she had stayed with? Whose boat had she been on during the flood? Had she been under surveillance then? Why didn't she . . . but maybe she couldn't – but why didn't she call?

He was getting sleepy. There were so many questions he couldn't answer, couldn't ask. So much he didn't know. There were so many times when he wanted to touch her again. Kiss her. Have his face in her hair. In her absence this specific desire was becoming a general desire, diffusing into the landscape itself. In D.C. that could be quite an experience; the women of Washington were gorgeous. All the exiled goddesses of Earth passed you by on the street. Every woman metamorphosed into the movie star who would have played her on screen; every woman became the avatar of her particular type and yet remained completely herself. Why didn't she call?

Voices below. Frank hung like a spirit above them. No way people would see him in the dark, even infrared wouldn't work through the plywood and the branch-camouflaged insulation tacked to its underside; he had tested that to be sure.

The voices were discussing something, it sounded like plans. He surveiled until they moved off and were lost in the sound of the creek.

She didn't call because of surveillance. Frank had looked into this a little, what this might mean to be under surveillance in this day and age. But he had been using his computer at work to make the search, at first, and that began to seem like it might put out a flag of some kind. He had felt constrained, and started to do his research in the NSF library, a very different resource. Maybe he had already given himself away. Would they become suspicious (if they were watching), concluding that he knew they were watching? And if so, would that increase or otherwise alter the watching?

Frank read and heard all kinds of things about modern

surveillance, and whenever he asked Edgardo about it on their runs, when they would not be overheard, Edgardo would grin and nod and say 'That's right.' He said 'That's right' to everything, until Frank said 'Are you saying you don't really know what's going on and neither does anyone else on Earth?'

'That's right.'

It was an impossible situation. No amount of googling would clarify it, and indeed any very extensive hunt might catch someone's attention and make his situation worse. Better to lay low. Better to investigate by talking only to people who might know, and wouldn't tell anyone else, in places where they wouldn't be overheard. Strange but true; the possibility of electronic surveillance was driving him back to the oldest technology of all, talking out in the open air.

He wondered if Yann knew he was under surveillance, or that he was the reason many people of his acquaintance were also. He was going to have to talk to Yann.

He had discussed with Diane his idea of head-hunting Pierzinski, and she had liked it. Carbon sequestration was in large part a biological problem; the amount of carbon they wanted to shift was beyond any currently affordable and deployable industrial capacity. They needed to involve the bacterial world, if they could. Pierzinski had been working on an algorithm that Frank thought might give them a much finer ability to predict and manipulate genomes, and apparently Yann and Eleanor and Marta were having their best successes at the bacterial level.

So he should go to Atlanta and talk to Yann. Add that to his visit to Francesca and he might even tweak the futures market in a way that Caroline could notice and tell him about when she called. And he needed to get a sense of how Pierzinski's algorithm was coming along, and what Yann might be thinking about how he wanted his work situation to be configured.

But talking to Yann meant he would have to see Marta again. She and Yann lived together, so it seemed that if he flew down to meet with Yann, Marta would have to be part of it one way or another. That might very well be awful. The last time he had seen her had been terrible. However, too bad; he still had to do it. It would end up worse if he went down there and tried to see Yann while avoiding her. That would backfire for sure, although it might not be possible to make her any more angry with him than she already was, so maybe it didn't matter.

But a part of him wanted to see her again anyway. All these women he was thinking about – mainly Caroline, the thought of whom made his heart pulse, and also perhaps spread a certain feeling over thoughts of Diane and her clever calmness, or even Francesca, whom he didn't want to think about at all – all these thoughts often led in the end back to Marta, a woman he had lived with for years, someone he really knew and had had a relationship with, even if it had imploded. She would still be mad at him. But he had to see her.

From Atlanta's airport he took a shuttle to a hotel downtown. The area around Georgia Tech featured wide avenues running up and down waves of low hills, between huge glossy skyscrapers, copper and blue and dragonfly green. The school's football stadium appeared below street level to his right as the shuttle inched along, reminding him with a brief pang of Khembalung.

After checking into the hotel Frank showered, then dressed with more care than usual. Uneasy glances in the mirror. Pierzinski had a little touch of Asperger's, not uncommon in mathematicians; over the phone he had agreed to Frank's request for a meeting with innocent delight, saying, 'I'll bring Marta along, she'll love to see you.'

Frank had recalled his last encounter with Marta in San Diego, and held his tongue. It was enough to make him wonder just how close Yann and Marta were. Maybe she was not in the habit of talking to Yann about her past. Frank hoped not.

Anyway, she would be there. Her unavoidable connection to Yann still surprised Frank a little; Marta and Yann did not seem to him a likely couple; but then again what couple did?

Yann had suggested a restaurant nearby as a place to meet. Frank remained stuck before his hotel bathroom mirror. He found he really didn't want to go. He was almost afraid to go. He looked neon pink in the mirror, somewhat boiled by the shower. He looked like he was wearing a costume signifying 'academic at lunch.' Best give up on appearances. Marta knew what he looked like.

As did whoever was spying on him. And spying on Yann and Marta as well! This would be a red-blink situation, presumably: three of that market's commodities getting together.

He left the hotel and walked to Manuel's, a restaurant Yann had suggested. It was a sultry night, a wet wind pouring like syrup through the streets. Marta had sent him directions in an e-mail that had no personal touches whatsoever. Not a good sign.

Manuel's turned out to be an old-fashioned saloon, thick with the smell of old cigar smoke and machine politics. Wooden beams crossed the ceiling in Tudor style, dividing the space into small rooms. Sports paraphernalia, TVs overhead. A perfect place to spy on someone. The walls of the entryway were covered with black-and-white photos of groups sitting at the biggest tables, men in vests. Campaign buttons surrounded the photos. It was hard for Frank to imagine Marta even entering such a place.

But she was there already, it turned out, seated in a booth at the back with Yann. 'Hi Yann, hi Marta.'

Yann rose and shook his hand; Marta didn't. After one

charged look Frank avoided her gaze and sat down, trying not to cringe. He thought of Caroline, brought her deliberately to mind; the look in her eye; then by accident thought of Diane too. Francesca. Caroline's touch. He knew some powerful women. Too many one might say. He met Marta's eye again, held his ground. Ooooop! Oooooop!

They made small talk of the how-have-you-been variety, ordered drinks. It was early, and Frank and Marta declined food, while Yann ordered French fries. When they arrived Yann downed them like popcorn, bang bang bang.

Silence inevitably fell, Yann being so busy. 'So what brings you here?' Marta said.

'Well, I'm doing another year at NSF.'

Frank knew that Marta thought he had gone to NSF to escape her, back when they were breaking up. So this also might be construed as saying he had had other reasons for going there.

She wasn't buying it. 'Why would you do that?'

'Well, I've gotten interested in things NSF can do that UCSD can't. National policy, and some big new programs. I was offered the chance to help with some of them, so I decided to give it a try.'

'Uh huh,' Marta said. 'So what are you doing?'

'Well, a number of things. But one of them is looking into trying to start up some institutes, like the Max Planck Institutes in Germany, that would focus on particular problems. And, you know, one of the obvious things to look at would be the stuff you guys were doing out in San Diego. You know, trying to do a really robust proteomics, with the idea that if we got that going properly, it might lead to some really important advances. So I came down to see, well, you know – to see if you'd have any interest in joining something like that.'

Well, if spies were listening in, then they knew all. Frank shuddered at the idea that he had ever tried to rig this game with his Thornton-in-the-panel.

Head-hunting, however, was standard practice.

'It's going fine,' Marta said curtly. 'Small Delivery is part of Bizet.' One of the Big Pharms, as Edgardo put it. 'We've got a budget bigger than anything NSF could offer.'

This was not true, and Frank longed to say *I've got two billion dollars to spend, does Bizet have two billion dollars?* He clamped his jaw shut; his jaw muscles would be bunching in a way she knew to notice. She knew him. He tried to relax. 'Well . . . so, you're still working on the same stuff you were in San Diego?'

The french fries were gone, and Yann nodded. 'The algorithm is working better on plant genomes? So some of the algae work is getting really predictable.'

Marta frowned. She didn't like Yann saying even this much.

Frank felt his stomach shrinking. He and Marta had been together for four very intense years, and their break-up had been so terrible . . . the dread and remorse from that time were like a vise inside him still, ready to clamp down any time he thought about it. A lot of what had happened between them had been his fault. He had known that for most of the last year, but now it was all falling on him again. Anger vibed across the table at him in waves, and he couldn't meet her gaze.

Yann appeared oblivious to all this. It was kind of hard to believe. It was also hard to imagine these two together. Yann was describing some of the tweaking he had done to his algorithm, and Frank did his best to follow, and to ask the questions he had come down to ask. How did that work? How would that work? Would more research funds speed the work on it? It was important to concentrate. It was important to get a better fix on how Pierzinski's work was progressing. Frank still had ideas about where it could go, and he wanted to talk about that.

But it became clear Yann had changed emphasis during his time at Small Delivery. At first Frank didn't follow the significance of the changes. 'So you're engineering changes in lichen?'

he asked, feeling that Marta's glare was making him stupid.

Marta answered for Yann. 'It's not about human health anymore,' she said, sharply. 'We're interested in engineering a tree lichen that will incorporate carbon into the host trees much faster than they do naturally.'

Frank sat back. 'So, a kind of carbon sink thing?'

'Yes. A kind of carbon sink thing.'

Frank thought it over. 'Why?' he said finally.

Yann said, 'The problems with gene uptake in humans were getting too complicated, we just couldn't . . .'

'We couldn't make it work,' Marta said flatly. 'No one can. It may be the show stopper for the whole idea of gene therapy. They can't get altered genes into cells without infecting them with a virus, and a lot of times that's a really bad idea. That's what it comes down to.'

'Well, but these nanobits look promising,' Yann said enthusiastically. 'We're making little bits of metal? They hold DNA on one side, and then when the metal bits imbed in cell walls, the DNA leaves the nanobits and crosses inside and is taken up.'

'In vivo?'

'No, in vitro, but they're about ready for phase ones.'

'We,' Marta corrected him.

'Yeah, but the other lab. And we're working on some Venter viruses too, you can build some pretty harmless viruses that alter the bacteria they jump into. The algorithms there are about the same as the lichen augmenters.' Suddenly he looked at his watch. 'Hey, I'm sorry, Frank, but I have to go. I had a previous appointment I can't let down.'

Abruptly he stood and extended a greasy hand to Frank, shook hands briefly, and with a quick wave to Marta was out the door.

Frank stared at the space Yann had vacated. What was Yann thinking, this was an appointment they had made, Frank had flown down for it! And now here he was alone with Marta. It was like the things that tended to happen in his nightmares, and quickly fear began to fill him.

'Well,' he said experimentally.

Marta continued to alternate between staring and glaring. Unbidden, and indeed squirting out with the sudden force characteristic of the return of the repressed, he recalled her on the beach at Cardiff Reef, shouting *leave me alone*.

'Look,' he said abruptly, as if cutting her off in the middle of a rant, 'I'm sorry.'

'What?'

'I'm *sorry*.'

'Hey. You don't *sound* sorry.'

'I *am* sorry.'

'Sorry for *what*?'

Frank pursed his lips, tried to achieve a level tone. It was a fair enough question after all.

'I'm sorry I borrowed money on the house without telling you about it. I owe you some money because of that.'

'You owe me more than that.'

Frank shrugged. 'Maybe so. But I figure I owe you about eighteen thousand four hundred dollars, on the house deal.' He was surprised how readily the figure came to mind. 'I can at least pay you back the money. What you put into the place.'

While they had been together, their financial arrangement had been informal; a mess, in fact. And so when they broke up, which had come as a surprise to Frank, the money situation had caused big trouble. It had not been entirely Frank's fault, or so he told himself. At the time they bought a house together in Cardiff, Marta had been in some sort of bankruptcy snarl with her soon-to-be ex-husband. She had married an ex-professor of hers, very foolishly as it had always seemed to Frank, and after the first year they had lived apart, but Marta had not bothered to get an official divorce until it became necessary. All this should have told Frank something, but it hadn't. Marta was therefore bogged in her ex's financial disasters, which had gone on for years – making her extra-intolerant of any funny business, as Frank only realized later, when his own affairs had gotten snarled in their turn. His had not been as bad as her ex's, but on the other hand, there were aspects that were maybe worse, as her ex had gotten into his trouble mostly after he and Marta had split up, whereas Frank had deliberately concealed from her a third mortgage on their house, a mortgage he had taken to give him money to invest in a biotech start-up coming out of UCSD. This start-up had sparked his interest but unfortunately no one else's, and soon the money from the third mortgage was gone, sucking all the equity they had accrued out of the place with it. So it was a really bad time for Marta to move out and demand that they sell the place and split the proceeds. He had had no time to put back the money, and when he confessed to her that there were no proceeds to split – that the money she had paid into the place, a matter of many thousands, was not there – she had freaked out. First she screamed at him, indeed threw a lamp at him; then she had refused to speak to him, or, later, to negotiate a payment schedule by which he could pay her back. At that point, it seemed to Frank, she actually wanted him to have ripped her off, the better to feel angry at him. Which no doubt helped her to avoid admitting to herself, or anyone else, that it was her wildness – specifically her sexual escapades, always 'a part of the deal' of being with her, as she claimed, but increasingly upsetting – that had caused him to demand a different basis to the relationship, which had then started the whole break-up in the first place. In other words, it had actually been all her fault, but with the money situation she didn't have to admit it.

He could only hope she knew this. She had to know it; and probably she felt some guilt or responsibility, which helped to make her so abrasive and hostile. She had cheated on him, and he had cheated her. Love and money. Ah well. The pointless wars of the heart.

'Why did you do it?' she burst out.

'Do what?'

'Why did you take out a third on *our house* without *telling me*? Why didn't you just *talk* about it? I would have been up for it.'

Well, he owed her an explanation for this. 'I don't know. I didn't think you would be up for it.'

'Well either I would or I wouldn't, but since you lost it all, because it was a bad idea, maybe if I hadn't gone for it, it would have been for a good reason! I'm not *stupid* you know.'

'I know.'

'You *don't* know! You think I'm just a lab tech. You think I'm the surfer slut who kills the mice and makes the coffee –'

'I do not! No way!'

'Fucking right no way.' She glowered viciously. She hated killing lab mice. 'I've got my own lab here, and the stuff we're doing with Yann is really interesting. You'd be amazed.'

'No I wouldn't.'

'Yes you would! You have no idea.'

'You're making a carbon sink organism. You told me. A way to sequester carbon quickly by biotechnical means.'

'Yes.'

'That's great. But you know,' Frank said carefully, 'much as we need a quick carbon capture these days, your customers are going to have to be governments. Corporations aren't going to pay for it, or be able get the permits. It's the US government or the UN or something like that who will.'

She glowered less viciously. 'So?'

'So, you'll need to get government approvals, government funding –'

'It's no different than the drug stuff.'

'Except for the customer. It won't be individuals, if I understand you right. It can't be. So it's not like drugs at all.'

'Not that part. We know that.'

'So, well, you know, you've got to have some government agencies on your side. DOE, EPA, OMB, Congress, the White House – they'll all have to be on board with it.'

She waved all that away. 'We're talking to the Russians.'

This was news to Frank, and interesting, but he ignored it for the moment and said, 'But if you had NSF behind you, you'd be set to get the rest of the US government behind you too.'

'What are you saying?'

'I'm saying I'm working on this stuff. I'm saying there's a committee at NSF that's working with two billion dollars in this year's budget alone.'

There. He had said it.

She was determined not to be impressed. 'So?'

'So, that's two billion dollars more than Small Delivery Systems has.'

She cracked up despite herself. 'You're head-hunting me. Or rather, you're head-hunting Yann.'

'I am. You and Yann and Eleanor, and whoever else is working on this.'

She stared at him.

'You and Yann could stay together,' he heard himself saying. 'Maybe the institute could be paired somehow with UCSD, and you two could move back to San Diego.'

She was frowning. 'What do you mean?'

'Well, you know. You wouldn't end up with job offers in different places. That happens to couples all the time, you know it does. And you guys probably aren't done moving.'

She laughed abruptly. 'We're not a couple either.'

'What?'

'You are so stupid, Frank.'

'What do you mean.'

'Yann is gay. We're just friends. We share a house here. We share a lot more than you and I ever did. We talk instead of fight and fuck. It's very nice. He's a really good guy. But he has his boyfriends, and I have mine.'

'Oh.'

She laughed again, unamused. 'You are such a . . .'

She couldn't think of a word that fit. Frank couldn't either. He waited, staring down at the battered wooden table top. He was such a – a what? A something. Really, there was no word that came to mind. A fool? A mess?

Was he any more of a mess than anyone else, though? Maybe so.

He shrugged. 'Did you . . . know about Yann in San Diego?'

'Yeah sure. We were friends, we went out. It was nice not to have to think about guys. People left us alone, or went for Yann. He's a sweet guy, and this stuff in math – well, you know. He's a kind of genius. He's like Wittgenstein, or Turing.'

'Hopefully happier than them.'

'Were they unhappy?'

'I don't know. I seem to remember reading they were.'

'Well, Yann seems pretty happy to me. He's really smart and really nice and he pays attention to my work.' Unlike you, her expression said. 'And he and Eleanor and I are getting good results.'

'I'm glad. I really am! That's why I came down here. I wanted to tell you about this, this possibility, of federally funded work.'

'Why not talk with the Small Delivery management?'

'I want the new institutes to be in full control of their scientific results. No private trade secrets or patents.'

She thought that over.

'What about with public universities?'

'Like UCSD and a federal lab, you mean?'

'Yeah.'

'I think that would be okay. I wish there was more of it. And there will be. We're trying a bunch of things like that.'

Marta nodded, interested despite herself.

'We've got the go-ahead,' Frank said. 'The go-ahead and the budget.'

Now she was pursing her lips into a little bloodless bloom, her sign of serious thought. 'San Diego.'

'What?'

'You said UCSD.'

'Yes, that's right. I'd have to recuse myself because of my position there, but it makes so much sense, Diane would run it through, I'm sure. Why? Do you want to move back there?'

She gave him another look. 'What do you think?'

'I thought you liked it here.'

'Oh for God's sake, Frank. We're in Atlanta Georgia.'

'I know, I know. I thought it looked pretty nice, actually.'

'My God. You've been out here too long.'

'Probably so.'

'It's warped your mind.'

'That's very true.'

Her stare grew suspicious, then calculating. 'You can't possibly like Washington D.C.'

'Well, I don't know. I'm beginning to think it's okay.'

'It's the East Coast, Frank! Jesus, you've lost your perspective out here. It's a swamp! No beach, no ocean –'

'There's the Atlantic –'

'No *waves*, and it's hours to get to there, even if there were.'

'I know.'

'Frank,' she said, looking at him with new interest. 'You've gone crazy.'

'A little bit, yeah.'

'*That's* why you apologized to me.'

'Well, I meant it. I should have said it before.'

'That's true.'

'So maybe I'm getting *less* crazy.' He laughed, met her eye. She shook her head. 'I don't think so.'

'Ah well.'

She watched him, shrugged. 'Time will tell.'

Again Frank understood that he had lost a relationship with someone he could have gotten along with. But now what

204

had happened in the past had a kind of trajectory or inertia to it, that could not be altered; the relationship was wrecked for good. He caught a quick glimpse of a different life, he and Marta still together in San Diego. But the bad things that had happened could never be undone, and that whole world of possibility was gone, popped like a soap bubble.

What if humanity's relationship to Earth was like that?

A nasty thought.

It occurred to him that he could warn Marta about the surveillance they were living under, Yann too. But as with Francesca, he found he wasn't ready for that – for what he would have to get into to tell her about it. I have this spook girlfriend, we're all under surveillance, we're part of an experiment in which computer programs bet on us, and our stock may now be rising. No.

Instead he said, 'So you would consider an offer to move your lab to a federal institute?'

'Maybe. I'll talk to Yann. But it might really crimp any chance for big compensation for all this.'

'Well, but it won't have much chance of happening at all if it stays in the private sector.'

'That's what you say. I'll talk to Yann about it. And Eleanor. We'll come to a decision together.'

Frank nodded, yeah yeah yeah: point already taken, blade in to the hilt, no call to be twisting it.

Marta, eyeing him, relented. 'Make it so it could get us back to San Diego. That might do it. I need to get back in the water.'

**Anna was convinced that** Joe had caught something in Khembalung, or on the long journey home. He had been more than usually fractious on all the return flights, and worse as they went on, from the confused tears in the helicopter to the exhausted screams on the final LA-to-Dulles leg. What with that and their own exhaustion, and the shock of the flood over-whelming Khembalung, they had reached the moment that some-times happens in a bad trip, when everyone is thinking what a terrible idea it was to begin with and no one can think of anything to say, or even meet their fellow sufferers in the eye. Anna and Charlie had endured a few of these trips before, none quite so bad, but they both knew what the lack of eye contact meant and what the other one was thinking. Dispense with talk and do the necessary, in a kind of grim solidarity. Just get home.

But then, at home, Joe's dis-ease had continued, and to Anna he felt a little hot. She got out the thermometer, ignoring Charlie's heavy look and biting her tongue to avoid yet another ridiculous argument on this topic of medical data gathering. Though he would not usually admit to it, Charlie suffered from a kind of magical thinking that believed that taking a temper-ature might invite an illness to appear which did not exist until it was measured. Anna suspected this came from the Christian Scientists in Charlie's family background, giving him a tendency to see illness as the taint of sin. This was, of course, crazy.

And Anna craved data, as usual. Taking a temperature was just a matter of getting more information. It always helped her to know things more precisely; the more she knew, the less her fears could imagine things worse than what she knew. So she took Joe's temperature without consulting Charlie, and found it registered 99.0.

'That's his *normal* temperature,' Charlie pointed out.

'What do you mean?' Anna said.

'He always charts high.'

'I don't remember that.'

'Well it's true. It happens every time I take him in for a check-up. I don't think they've ever gotten a reading under 99 for him.'

'Hmm.' Anna let that go. She was pretty sure it wasn't true, but she certainly didn't want to get into an argument that could only be resolved by getting into medical records. She knew that Joe felt warmer now than he had before, in her arms and on the nipple. And his face was always flushed. 'Maybe we should take him in to be checked anyway.'

'I don't see why.'

'Well, when is he scheduled for a check-up?'

'I don't know. It hasn't been that long since the last one.'

Anna gave up on it, not wanting to seethe. She would wait and see how things went for a day or two more, then insist if necessary. Take him in herself if she had to.

After a fraught silence went on for quite a while, Charlie said, 'Look, let's see how he goes. If it still seems like there's a problem I'll take him in next week.'

'Okay, good.'


So it went in the world of Charlie and Anna, a world of telepathic negotiations made out of silence and gesture; a world in which the sharp words were usually felt in the air, or, if spoken in a burst of irritation, taken as one part of a mind reproving another, in the way one will easily snap at oneself for doing something foolish, knowing there is no one to misunderstand or get upset.

But of course even an old matrimonial mindmeld is never total, and for his part, Charlie did not articulate, indeed hid in one of the far reaches of his mind, outside the reach of Anna's telepathy, his worries about what might be wrong with Joe. He knew that to Anna he seemed afraid of the idea of illness, ready always to ignore it or condemn it, and that to her this was inappropriate, craven, counter-productive. But first of all, mind-body studies of placebos and positive attitudes gave some support to the idea of not tolerating or ritually opposing the idea of illness; and second, if she knew what he was really worrying about, the whole Joe/Khembalung dynamic, she would have thought him foolish and maybe even a little naive and credulous, even though he respected the Khembalis and knew (he hoped) that they took this kind of thing seriously. How she managed to reconcile that he was not sure, but in regards to their own interaction, better for her to think he was still just in his old curse-the-disease mode. So he kept his thoughts to himself.

Thus there was a dissonance there palpable to both of them, an awareness that they were not as fully known to each other as they usually were. Which also would worry Anna; but Charlie judged that the lesser of two worries, and held his tongue. No way was he going to bring up the possibility of some kind of problem in Joe's spiritual life. What the hell was that, after all? And how would you measure it?

So at work Anna spent her time trying to concentrate, over a persistent underlying turmoil of worry about her younger son. Work was absorbing, as always, and there was more to do than there was time to do it in, as always. And so it provided its partial refuge.

But it was harder to dive in, harder to stay under the surface in the deep sea of bioinformatics. Even the content of the work reminded her, on some subliminal level, that health was a state of dynamic balance almost inconceivably complex, a

208

matter of juggling a thousand balls while unicycling on a tightrope over the abyss – in a gale – at night – such that any life was an astonishing miracle, brief and tenuous. But enough of that kind of thinking! Bear down on the fact, on the moment and the problem of the moment!

Frequently she found herself unable to concentrate no matter her exhortations, and she would spend an hour or two digging around on the internet, to see if she could find anything useful for Diane and Frank. Old things that had worked but been forgotten; new things that hadn't yet been noticed or appreciated. This could be rather depressing, of course. The government sites devoted to climate change were often inadequate; the State Department's page, for instance, began with the administration's ludicrous goal of reducing carbon emissions by eighteen percent over ten years, by voluntary actions – a thumbing-of-the-nose to the Kyoto Treaty that was still the current administration's only tangible proposal for action. Conference proceedings on another page spoke of 'climate change *adaptation*,' actually development agendas, with only a few very revealing admissions that 'adaptation' had no meaning in regard to actual technologies, that the whole concept of 'adaptation' to climate change was a replacement for 'mitigation,' and at this point completely hollow, a word only, a way of saying *Do nothing*. Whole conferences were devoted to that.

After discoveries like this she would give up and search elsewhere, on scientific sites that were more technically oriented, that had real content. More and more it seemed to her that science as it was ordinarily practiced was really the only thing that worked in the world; so that even with abrupt climate change upon them, requiring an emergency response, dispersing science more rapidly was still not only the only thing she could do to help, but the only thing anyone could do.

Edgardo shook his head when she expressed this thought. 'One tends to think only the method one knows will work.'

'Yes I'm sure. But what if it's true?'

Site after site.

Once after one of these hunts, she went into one of Diane and Frank's meetings and said, 'Let me tell you some history.'

In her reading she had run across a description of a 'Scientists For Johnson Campaign' in the presidential election of 1964. A group of prominent scientists, worried by Goldwater's nuclear bravado, had organized into what would later be called a political action committee, and taken out ads urging people to vote for Johnson. Dire warnings were made of what could happen if Goldwater won, and a vote for Johnson was portrayed as a vote for world peace, for the reality principle, for all good things.

All of which had perhaps helped Johnson; but it backfired when Nixon won four years later, because he came into the White House convinced that all scientists hated him.

'But Nixon was paranoid, right?'

'Paranoid or clear-sighted.'

'Both. He thought people hated him, and then he made it come true so he could feel clear-sighted.'

'Maybe.'

But for science this had been a bad thing. Nixon had first shut down the Office of Science and Technology, then demoted the remaining position of presidential science advisor out of the Cabinet, exiling the office to the hinterlands. Then he had kicked NSF itself off the Mall, out to Arlington.

'It's like we're still in some feudal court,' Frank observed, 'where physical proximity to the king actually mattered.'

'You're sounding like Edgardo.'

'Yes, he said that out on the run today, actually.'

In any case, science had been in effect booted out of the policy arena, and it had never come back.

'Meaning?' Diane said.

'Meaning science isn't part of policy making anymore! It doesn't support candidates, and scientists never run for office themselves. They just ask for money and let it go at that.'

'Science is a higher activity,' Edgardo proclaimed. 'What it does is so valuable that you have to give it a lot of money, no strings attached. Pay up or die.'

'Pretty clever.'

'I think so.'

'Too bad it doesn't work better though.'

'Well, that's true. That's what we're working on.'

Frank was shaking his head. 'It seems to me that this story about Johnson and Nixon is just one more indication that science is generally thought of as being liberal in its political orientation.'

No one wanted to think about this, Anna could tell.

'How so?' Diane asked.

'Well, you know. If the Republican Party has been hijacked by the religious right, which most people say it has, then the Democrats begin to look like the party for secular people, including lots of scientists. It's like the debate over evolution all over again. Christianity versus science, now equating to Republican versus Democrat.'

This was a bad thought. Diane said, 'We can't afford to get caught on one side in the so-called culture wars.'

Anna said, 'But what if we *are* on one side? What if we've been put there by others?'

They thought about this.

'Even so,' Diane said. 'Getting tagged as leaning Democrat could be really dangerous for science. We have to stay above that fray.'

'But we may already be tagged. And we are trying to affect policy, right? Isn't that what this committee is about?'

'Yes. But we have to be jumping *on* the fray. Squashing it from above.'

They laughed at this image. Edgardo said, 'Beyond good and evil! Beyond Marx and Jesus! Prometheus unbound! Science über alles!'

Even Anna had to laugh. It was funny even though it wasn't; and less so the more she thought about it; and yet she laughed. As did the others.

Diane shook her head ruefully. 'Oh well,' she said. 'Let's give it a try. Time for science in the capital.'

Afterward the situation did not seem so funny. It did not help of course to come home to Joe's low-grade fever, after which nothing seemed funny. Charlie had already given in and taken him to the doctor; but they hadn't found anything.

It wasn't a matter of energy levels. Joe was as energetic as ever, if not more so. Hectic, irritable, ceaselessly in motion, complaining, interrupting . . . but had he ever been any different, really? This was what Charlie seemed to be implying, that Joe was perhaps just a little hotter now, more flushed and sweaty, but otherwise much the same feisty little guy.

But she wasn't buying it. Something was different. He was not himself.

Sometimes she worried so intensely that she could not talk to Charlie about it at all. What if she convinced him to join her in her worry, what good would that do him or any of them?

The best way to prevent worry was to be so busy by day that there was no time for it. Then, at night, to go to bed so exhausted that sleep hit like a wall falling on her, giving her several hours of oblivion. It was heavy and somehow unrestful sleep; she woke with the gears of her mind already engaged in something – memory, dream, work calculation – on it ran, unstoppable, thoroughly awake at 4:30 in the morning. Miserable.

And no matter where her night thoughts began, they always came back to Joe. When she remembered the situation her pulse would shoot up. Eventually she would get up, with a brief touch to the sleeping Charlie, and go stand in the shower for twenty minutes, trying to relax. What was worry, after all, but a kind of fear? It was fear for the future. And in fact the future was bound to bring its share of bad things, there was no avoiding that. So worry was really a hopeless enterprise, in that it could not do anything. It was an anticipation of grief, a nightmare of the future. A species of fear; and she was determined not to be afraid.

So she would steel herself and turn off the shower, and motor through her preparations for work, thinking about how to sequence the day's activities. But before she left she had to go up and nurse Joe, and so all her plans were overthrown by his hot little body lying cradled in her arms. His mouth was hot. The world was hotter, Joe was hotter, even Charlie was hotter. Everything seemed to have had more energy poured into it than it could handle. All but Anna, and her Nick. She put her sleeping wild man back in his crib and went to Nick's room and kissed her firstborn on his head, inhaling him gratefully, his cool curly hair – her soulmate in this chaos, her fellow stoic, her cool calculator – imperturbable, unflappable, amused by his hectic brother and everything else; amused where others would be enraged. Who could imagine a better older brother, or a better son, a kind of young twin to her. In a sudden blaze of maternal affection she held his shoulder, squeezed it as he slept; then clumped down the stairs and walked up Wisconsin to the re-opened Metro, shaking her wet locks from side to side to feel their cool damp in the cool air.

Then meeting with Diane, wet-haired herself. Session with Alyssa on visiting program directors, their timing and assignments. Lunch at desk while reading papers to *The Journal of Biostatistics*. Calls one through six on her long list of calls to be made. Brief visit downstairs to the Khembali women in the embassy office, to see how they were doing with their resettlement issues. Then hellos to Sucandra and Padma, who were leading an English lesson; they enlisted her briefly to aid them, Anna feeling helpless across the great divide of languages. She resolved once again to learn Tibetan, tried to remember the Tibetan words she heard them explaining. It was a habit of mind, this inhaling of information. Charlie would laugh when he heard about it.

Back to the office, glancing briefly at the Tibetan language cheat-sheet they had given her. 'The tide rises in six hours. The waves are hollow when the tide ebbs.'

In the next meeting with Diane and Frank, Anna brought to the screen another web page she had found. This one was on FCCSET, the Federal Coordinating Council on Science, Engineering and Technology.

'What's this?' Frank said as he read over her shoulder. 'Fuck set?'

'No, they pronounced it *Fix-it*,' laughing.

'Oh right, so very clever these acronyms. I like DICE, Dynamic Integrated Model of Climate and the Economy, where you just skip the M.'

'*Fix-it* was a program that looked at scientific problems and tried to identify already-existing federal programs that could match up with other programs, to work together on particular problems.'

'So what killed it?'

'How do you know it got killed?'

Frank just looked at her.

'Well, it was a matter of money, I guess. Or control. The programs identified as worthy by Fix-it were automatically funded by the Office of Management and Budget. There was an OMB person sitting in on all the Fix-it meetings, and if the program was approved then it was funded.'

'Now that's power!'

'Yes. But too much power, in the end. Because the top people in the agencies being identified didn't like getting funding like that. It took away from their control over the purse strings.'

'Oh for Christ's sake. Is that really why it ended?'

'Apparently. I mean it didn't end, but it had that budgetary power taken away. So, I'm wondering if we could get Congress to bring it back.'

'Worth a try,' Diane judged.

Frank was still shaking his head. 'Territoriality really does run deep. They might as well be peeing around the edges of their building.'

'I guess.'

'You don't sound convinced.'

'I don't know. It's a theory. Anyway, I think we should try to reintroduce this program. You'd be able to get agencies all across the board coordinated. What if they were all doing parts of the same large project?'

Frank's eyebrows were arched. 'Talk about a theory. This is Bob's Manhattan Project idea again.'

'Well, the method is there,' Anna claimed. 'Potentially, anyway. What if you could get a proposal funded through all those agencies, using Fix-it as a coordinating committee?'

Diane liked the idea. 'We need Congress to put it in place, obviously. I'll talk to Sophie.'

After a moment's silence Frank said, 'We could really use a president with that in his platform.'

'Unlikely,' Diane judged.

Frank scowled. 'I don't see why. What century do people think they're living in?'

Anna and Diane shared a look, anticipating a rant, but Frank saw it and said, 'Well, but why? Why why why? We should have a *scientist candidate* for president, some emeritus biggie who can talk, explaining what the scientific approach would be, and *why*. A candidate using ecological theory, systems theory, what-have-you, in-out throughputs, some actual economics . . .'

Diane was shaking her head. 'Who exactly would that be?'

'I don't know, Richard Feynman?'

'Deceased.'

'Stephen Hawking.'

'British, and paralyzed. Besides, you know those emeritus guys. There isn't a single one of them who could go through the whole process without, I don't know . . .'

'Exploding?' Anna suggested.

'Yes.'

'Make up a candidate,' Anna said. 'What science would do if it were in the White House.'

'Like Nick's Swiss council,' Frank said. 'A phantom candidate.'

'Shadow candidate,' Diane corrected. 'Like in Europe.'

'Or,' Anna said, 'just put the platform out there, with a virtual candidate. Dr Science. See which party picks it up.'

'Neither,' Frank and Diane said together.

'We don't know that,' Anna said. 'And it would be safer than endorsing one party over the other, or starting some kind of scientific third party that would only hurt politicians who are on our side. Either way we could get pushed out of policy for years to come. Cast into the wilderness.'

'We're already there,' Frank pointed out.

'So what have we got to lose?'

'Well, that's true enough.' Frank thought it over. 'We could get hammered.'

'Like we aren't already?'

'Hmmm.'

'Maybe we have to take a stand. Maybe that's what it means to get involved in politics. You have to declare. You have to talk about what people should do.'

They sat there, thinking things over. Edgardo walked in and they explained to him what they were thinking.

He laughed hard.

Frank kept scribbling. 'Social Science Experiment in Politics.'

'In *elective* politics,' Anna insisted, frowning at Edgardo. 'Then it's, what, SSEEP. Pronounced "Seep". Like we're *seeping* into policy.'

'Seep!' Diane laughed. 'We'll seep in like a bull in a china

216

shop! Seep in and the whole shop will start screaming.'

'Maybe so. But the china shop is going under. It needs a bull to, what, to pull the whole thing up to higher ground.'

They laughed at this image.

'Well,' Diane said, 'we need to do everything we can. Sort all this out, Frank. Look into all of it.'

Frank nodded. 'Bold and persistent experimentation! I have a list here.'

Diane waved a hand. 'More later. I'm starving.'

'Sure. You want to go get a bite?'

'Sure.'

Anna quickly glanced down. They had just arranged a date, right in front of her eyes. And not the first one, from the sound of it.

She thought, what about Frank's woman from the elevator? Had he given up on her? That didn't seem like him. Anna was obscurely disappointed; she liked that story, that possibility. It had appealed to the romantic in her, which was buried but substantial. And as for Frank and Diane, well, she could not imagine what it meant. Surely she had misread the situation. Diane was nice, certainly; but even in the light of Anna's own puritanical work ethic, she was a bit much. What would she be like socially? It was hard to imagine.

And she herself would never know what Diane was like socially. She was a woman, and married; while Frank was a man, and unmarried; and Diane was now unmarried too, poor thing. And Frank had been plucked out from among the visiting program directors by Diane, to run her climate project committee.

'I've got to get home,' she said, throwing her things together. Home to her boys, who would leap on her and say the same things, all deep in their own worlds, and the dinner only partly made. Although in the same flare of irritation she felt a deep relief and a desire to be there at once.

\*    \*    \*

217

At home her boys did leap on her, as predictable as clock-work, and the house was warm with kitchen smells.

The flood had revolutionized their cooking habits, Charlie trying old recipes and new, based on whatever produce the grocery store had available. Tonight, Mexican. Joe commanded her attention, insisting on *Good-night, Moon* again, read in an up-tempo declamatory sing-song very unsuited to the book's soporific nature, which worked like a charm on her no matter what, but not on him. He was fretful again, and sucked at her desperately, as if seeking a relief beyond food. She spoke in quiet tones to Nick, and he read as he replied, or didn't, mostly off in his own world. She tried not to worry about Joe, although his distemper had now lasted six weeks. Every test had been taken. Nothing had been discovered, except that slightly elevated temperature, which the record showed was real, if ever so slight. Its periodicity reminded her of her own temperatures when she had kept records to find her time of ovulation every month.

The red face, the lack of ease. No matter how hard she tried she was still scared by these changes in him. She knew what he should be like. And she knew this had started after their trip to Khembalung. She watched him, and nursed him, and played with him – tried to feel him, there in his body – tried to think about work, while humming to him as he sucked. She crooned the book in Tibetan, 'Don nom, zla-ba.' Joe started slightly, hit her as he drowsed. Anna went back to the inviolable rhythms of the hypnotic little book; and she did everything she could to make herself stop worrying; but it never really went away. And so the days passed; and almost surreptitiously, while Charlie was doing other things, she took Joe's temperature, and charted it, then went on; and tried to think about work; but she would have given the Nobel Prize in Chemistry and the Gulf Stream itself for just a week of normal temperatures.

# FIVE

## *Autumn In New York*

The most beautiful regatta in the history of the world convened that year on Midsummer Day, at the North Pole.

The sun hung in the same spot all day long, blazing down on open water that appeared more black than blue. A few icebergs floated here and there, most low and white, but including a few dolmens of jade or turquoise, standing in an obsidian sea.

Among these floating extravaganzas sailed or motored some three hundred boats and ships. Sails were of every cut and color, some even prisming through the spectrum as they bent to the shifts of the mild southern breeze. People said the prisming sails allowed one to see every gust's impact in a manner never possible before. That it also looked cool was too obvious to mention. All manner of sail, all possible rigs and hulls; catamarans and schooners, yawls, ketches, trimarans; also square-riggers, from caravels to clipper ships to newfangled experiments obviously not destined to prosper; a quintet of huge Polynesian outriggers; and every manner of motor launch, rumbling unctuously through the sails, each sporting a unique profile in white or cream; and a lot of single-person craft, including many kayakers and wind-surfers in black drysuits.

The larger fleet jockeyed until their navigators linked up and devised a kind of spiral galaxy formation, centered on the pole and rotating clockwise if seen from above. Everyone thus sailed west together, following the two simple rules that birds use when flocking in a gyre: change speeds as little as possible, keep as far apart from everyone else as possible.

Senator Phil Chase smiled happily when the flocking rubric was explained to him. 'That's the Senate for you,' he said. 'Or maybe it's all you need to get by in life.'

By a happy coincidence, the North Pole itself, as determined by GPS, was marked for the day by a tall aquamarine iceberg that had drifted over it. In the immediate vicinity of this newly-identified 'Pole Berg' idled many of the largest ships in the fleet, ranging from small cruise ships to huge private yachts, with a few old icebreakers on hand as well, looking overweight and unwanted.

This was the fifth midsummer festival at the pole. Every year since lanes of water had opened in the summer Arctic ice, a larger and larger group of sea craft had sailed or motored north to party at the pole. The gatherings had a Burning Man festival aspect to them, the sybaritic excess and liberal shooting off of fireworks leading many to call it Drowning Man, or Freezing Your Butt Man.

This year, however, the party had been somewhat taken over by the Inuit nation Nunavut, in conjunction with the Intergovernmental Panel On Climate Change, who had declared this 'The Year of Global Environmental Awareness,' and sent out hundreds of invitations, and provided many ships themselves, in the hope of gathering a floating community that would emphasize to all the world the undeniable changes already wrought by global warming. The organizers were willing to accept the risk of making the gathering look like a party, or even God forbid a celebration of global warming, in order to garner as much publicity as possible. Of course a whole new ocean to sail on was no doubt a cool thing for sailors, but all *that missing winter ice was floating down into the North Atlantic at that very moment, changing everything. IPCC wanted people to see with their own eyes that abrupt climate change was already upon them, and that it could soon cast the entire world into thousands of years of bad weather, as it had during the Younger Dryas just eleven thousand years before.*

*But of course there were many people there who did not regard the polar party in its official light, just as there were many in the world who did not worry overmuch about entering the Youngest Dryas. On the sail up to the festival, some of them had encountered an oil tanker, only slightly smaller than the ULCCs (Ultra-Large Crude Carriers) of the late twentieth century, double-hulled, as was legally required, and making a dry run on a Great Circle route from Japan to Norway that passed near the pole. This voyage was demonstrating that the Northwest Passage was open for business at last; and better late than never. Oil could be shipped directly from the North Sea to Japan, cutting the distance by two-thirds. Even if oil was passé, post-peak, old paradigm and all the rest, Japan and the North Sea oil countries were nevertheless awfully pleased to be able to move it over the pole. They were not ashamed to admit that the world still needed oil, and that while it did, there would be reasons to appreciate certain manifestations of global warming. Shipyards in Glasgow, Norway, and Japan had been revitalized, and were now busy building a new class of Arctic Sea tankers to follow this prototype, boldly going where no tanker had gone before.*

*And here at the pole itself, on Midsummer day, things looked fine. The world was beautiful, the fleet spectacular. In danger or not, human culture seemed to have risen to the occasion. It was noon, summer solstice at the North Pole, with a glorious armada forming a kind of sculpture garden. A new kind of harmonic convergence, Ommmmmmmm.*

\*     \*     \*

On one of the bigger craft, an aluminum-hulled jet-powered catamaran out of Bar Harbor, Maine, a large group of people congregated around Senator Phil Chase. Many of them were bundled in the thick red down jackets provided to guests by the National Science Foundation's Department of Polar Programs, because despite the black water and brilliant sun, the air temperature at the moment was 28 degrees Fahrenheit. People kept their hoods pulled forward, and their massed body warmth comforted them as they watched the group around Chase help him into a small rainbow-colored hot-air balloon, now full over the top deck and straining at its tether.

The World's Senator got in the basket, gave the signal; the balloon master fired the burners, and the balloon ascended into the clear air to the sound of cheers and sirens, Phil Chase waving to the fleet below, looking somewhat like the Wizard of Oz at the moment when that worthy floats away prematurely.

But Phil was on a line, and the line held. From a hundred feet above the crowd, Phil could be seen grinning his beautiful grin. 'Here we are!' he announced over the fleet's combined radio and loudspeaker array; and of course millions more saw and heard him by satellite TV. A big buoy clanged the world to order as Phil raised a hand to still the ships' horns and fireworks.

'Folks,' he said, 'I've been working for the people of California for seventeen years, representing them in the United States Senate, and now I want to take what I've learned in those efforts, and in my travels around the world, and apply all that to the work of serving the people of the United States, and all the world, as its president.'

'President of the world?' Roy Anastopholous said to Charlie, and began to laugh.

'Shh! Shh!' Charlie said to Roy. They were watching it on TVs in different parts of the city, but talking on their phones as they watched.

'It's a crazy thing to want to do,' Phil was conceding. 'I'm the first to admit that, because I've seen what the job does to people. But in for a penny in for a pound, as they say, and we've reached a moment where somebody who can handle it needs to use the position to effect some good.'

Roy was still giggling. 'Be quiet!' Charlie said.

'– there is no alternative to global cooperation. We have to admit and celebrate our interdependence, and work in solidarity with every living thing. All God's creatures are living on this planet in one big complex organism, and we've got to act like that now. That's why I've chosen to announce my candidacy here at the North Pole. Everything meets up here, and everything has changed because of changes that started here. This beautiful ocean, free of ice for the first time in human existence, is sign of a clear and present danger. Recall what it looked like here even five years ago. You can't help but admit that huge changes have already come.

'Now what do those changes mean? Nobody knows. Where will they lead? Nobody knows. This is what everyone has to remember; no one can tell what the future will bring. Anything can happen. Anything at all. We stand at the start of a steep ski run. Black diamond for sure. I see the black diamonds twinkling everywhere down there. Down the slope of the next decade we will ski. The moguls will be on us so fast we won't believe it. There'll be no time for lengthy studies initiated by political administrations that never actually do anything, that hope for business as usual for one more term, after which they will take off for their fortress mansions and leave the rest of us to pick up the pieces. That won't work, not even for them. You can get offshore, but you can't get off planet.'

Cheers and horns and sirens echoed over the water. Phil waited for them to quiet back down, smiling happily and waving. Then he continued:

'It's all one world now. The United States still has its historical role to fulfill, as the country of countries, the mixture *and amalgam of all humanity, trying things out and seeing how they work. The United States is child of the world, you might say, and the world watches with the usual parental fascination and horror, anxiety and pride.*

*'So we have to grow up. If we were to turn into just another imperial bully and idiot, the story of history would be ruined, its best hope dashed. We have to give up the bad, give back the good. Franklin Delano Roosevelt described what was needed from America very aptly, in a time just as dangerous as ours: he called for a course of "bold and persistent experimentation". That's what I plan to do also. No more empire, no more head in the sand pretending things are okay while a few rich guys wreck everything. It's time to join the effort to invent a global civilization that we can hand off to all the children and say, "This will work, keep it going, make it better." That's permaculture, as some people call it, and really now we have no choice; it's either permaculture or catastrophe. Let's choose the good fight, and work so that each generation can hand to the next one the livelihood we are given by this beautiful world.*

*'That's the plan, folks. I intend to convince the Democratic Party to continue its historic work of helping to improve the lot of every man, woman, child, animal and plant on this planet. That's the vision that has been behind all the party's successes so far, and moving away from those core values has been part of the problem and the failure of our time. Together we'll join humanity in making a world that is beautiful and just.'*

*'We'll join humanity?' Roy said. 'What's this, Democrats as aliens?' But Charlie could barely hear him over the ship horns and cheers. On the screen he could see they were beginning to reel Phil in like a big kite.*

**Living outdoors the seasons** were huge, simply huge. Talk about abrupt climate change – housebound people had no idea. Shorter days, cooler air, dimmer light, slanting through the trees at a lower angle: you might as well be moving to another planet.

It was one of the ironies of their time that global warming was about to freeze Europe and North America, particularly on the eastern seaboard down to around Washington, D.C. Kenzo predicted a few weeks at least of severe, record-shattering lows: 'You're not going to believe it,' he kept saying, although it was already beginning in Europe, where a cool drought had prevailed all summer. 'The winter high will park over Greenland and force the jet stream straight south to us from Hudson Bay. Sometimes from the Yukon, but mostly from Hudson Bay.'

'I believe it,' Frank replied. Although, in another irony, the weather at that very moment was rather glorious. The days were still hot, while the cold between two AM and sunrise was sharp and bracing. Here they were only a few weeks past the depths of their Congolese summer, and already there was frost on the leaves at dawn.

For Frank these chill nights meant the deployment of his mountain gear, always a pleasure to him. He basked in that special warmth that hominids have enjoyed ever since they started wearing the furs of other animals. Clothes made the man – and therefore one of the earliest instances of the technological sublime, which was to stay warm in the cold.

Waking up in his treehouse, Frank would wrap his sleeping bag around him like a cape and sit on the plywood edge, arms over the railing, swinging his heels in space, looking at the wall of trees across the gorge. The leaves were beginning to turn, the autumn spectrum invading the green canopy with splashes of yellow and orange and red and bronze. As a Californian Frank had seldom seen it, and had never imagined it properly. He had not understood that the colors would be all mixed together, forming a field of mixed color, like a box of Trix spilled over a green lawn – spelling in its gorgeous alien alphabet the end of summer, the passing of time, the omnipresence of mortality. To all who took heed it was an awesome and melancholy sight.

He let down Miss Piggy, descended into this new world. He walked absorbed in the new colors, the mushroomy smells of decay, the clattering susurrus of leaves in the wind. The next hard frost would knock most of these leaves down, and then his jungle treehouse would be exposed to the gaze of those below. Lances of sunlight already reached parts of the forest floor they hadn't before. The park was still officially closed, but Frank saw more and more people out there, not just the homeless but also the ordinary citizens of the city, the people who had used the park before the flood as a place to run or walk or bike or ride. Luckily the creekside roads and trails were irreparable, and few would venture up the gorge past the giant beaver dam, which had started like a beaver dam and now really was one. You had to bushwhack to get around the pond's unstable shore. Still, the treehouse's exposure would exist.

But that was a problem for another day. Now Frank walked north on the deer's trail by the creek, observing how the variegated colors of the leaves altered the sense of space in the forest, how there seemed to be an increase in sheer spaciousness, as his depth of field now took in a vast number of individual leaves in complete clarity, be they ever so small.

And so when he ran with the frisbee guys, these leaves all functioned as referent points, and he seemed to be engaging a new GPS system that locked him more than ever into the here-and-now. He saw just where he was, moment to moment, and ran without awareness of the ground, free to look about. Joy to be out on days so fresh and sunny, so dappled and yellow. Immersion in the very image and symbol of change; very soon there would come an end to his tenuously established summer routines, he would have to find new ones. He could do that; he was even in a way looking forward to it. But what about the gibbons? They were subtropical creatures, as were many of the other ferals. In the zoo they would have been kept inside heated enclosures when temperatures dropped.

Native species, and the ferals from temperate or polar regions, would probably be all right in that regard. Very often playing frisbee they spotted white-tailed deer; these would generally survive the winter without much trouble. But there were many different feral species out there. Once when they were up in the thickets of the northwest corner of the park, coming back from the ninth hole, Spencer stopped in his tracks and everyone else froze instantly; this was one of the sub-games they had invented, and very useful if they wanted not to spook animals they sighted.

'What in the fuck is that,' Spencer whispered urgently to Frank.

Frank stared. It was a big ox, or a small bull, or . . .

It was huge. Massive, heraldic, thick-haunched, like something out of a vision; one of those sights so unbelievable that if you were dreaming it you would have woken up on the spot.

Frank got out his FOG phone, moving very slowly, and pushed the button for Nancy. How many times had he done this in the past weeks, moving the phone as slowly as he could, whispering, 'Nancy – hi, it's Frank – can you tell me what I'm looking at?'

Pause, while Nancy looked at his phone's GPS position and checked it on her big board.

'Ah ha. You're looking at an auroch.'

'A what?'

'We're pretty sure it's an auroch. North Europe, ice age –'

Suddenly it looked familiar to Frank.

'– some Polish researchers took frozen DNA from one and cloned it a few years ago. Birthed from a sheep or something. They had an enclosure in their southern forest with a herd running around it. We don't know how these we're seeing got here, actually. They're mostly up in Maryland. Some kind of private act of dispersion, I think, like that guy who decided to transplant all the bird species mentioned in Shakespeare to North America, and gave us the starling infestation among other problems . . .'

Frank took the phone from his ear, as Spencer's face was contorting grotesquely to convey to him the question WHAT WHAT WHAT.

'Auroch,' Frank whispered loudly.

Spencer's face shifted again, into the mask for The Great AH HA of Comprehension, then Delight, his blue eyes blazing like Paul Newman's. He looked at the beast, foursquare on the ridge, and in slow motion crumpled to his knees, hands clasping his frisbee before him in prayer. Robin and Robert held their frisbees before them as well, grinning as they always did. Robin stretched his hands palm out over his head to indicate homage, or express the bigness of the animal.

Its proportions were strange, Frank saw, the rear legs and haunches big and rounded. A creature from the cave paintings, sprung live into their world.

Spencer stood back up. He held his frisbee out to the other guys, waggled his eyebrows, mimed a throw at the auroch: make it a target? Eyes ablaze, on the edge of a shout: never before had Frank seen the shaman in Spencer so clearly. Of course they had already discussed throwing at animals many times before. It would be the greatest thing in the world to make targets of the ubiquitous white-tailed deer, for instance. The stalk, the throw, the strike – exhilarating. Like catch and release fishing, only better. No one disputed this. The animals would not be hurt. It would be hunting without killing.

But really, as Spencer himself had argued when they discussed it, they were hunting without killing already. And sometimes, if they threw at them, animals would get hurt. If they wanted the animals to prosper in the park, which after all was not so big – if they wanted animals to inhabit the world with them, which also was not so big – then they oughtn't harass them by whacking them out of the blue with hard plastic disks. Best dharma practice was compassion for all sentient beings, thus using them for targets contra-indi-cated. So they had refused the temptation.

Now, Spencer's point seemed to be that this was a magical occasion, outside all everyday agreements. There stood an icon from the ice age – a living fossil, in effect, sprung to life from out of the cave paintings of Lascaux and Altamira – so that really they *had* to abandon their ordinary protocols to do justice to the beast, to enter the sacred space of the paleolithic mind. Make this magnificent creature their target as a sort of religious ritual, even a religious obligation one might say.

All this Spencer conveyed by mime, alternating the hands-in-prayer position with the throwing motion, making faces as contorted and clear as any demon mask. Holy activity; tribute to *homo erectus*; form of nature worship.

'All at once,' Frank whispered. The others nodded.

Frank aimed and threw with the rest of them, and four disks flashed through the forest. One hit a tree and startled the auroch a step forward, then another struck him on the flank, causing him to bolt up the ridge and away, out of sight before they were even done screaming. They high-fived each other and ran to collect their frisbees and play on.

So each blustery afternoon changed his life. That was autumn, that was how it should feel, Frank saw, the landscape suffused with the ache of everything fleeting by. A new world every heartbeat. He had to incorporate this feeling of perpetual change, make it an aspect of optimodality. Of course everything always changed! How beautiful that the landscape sang that truth so clearly! Ooooooooop!

More than ever he loved being in his treehouse. He would have to find a way to continue doing it as the winter came on, even in the midst of storms, yes of course. John Muir had climbed trees during storms to get a better view of them, and Frank knew from his mountaineering days that storms were a beautiful time to be out, if one were properly geared. He could pitch his tent on the plywood floor; and his heaviest sleeping bag would keep him warm in anything. Would he bounce around like a sailor at the top of a mast? He wanted to find out. John Muir had found out.

He would not move indoors. He did not want to, and he would not have to. The paleolithics had lived through ice ages, faced cold and storms for thousands of years. A new theory postulated that populations islanded by abrupt climate change had been forced to invent cooperative behaviors in bad weather time and time again, ultimately changing the gene and bringing about the last stages of human evolution. Good snowshoes, clothing as warm as Frank's mountain gear, fire carriers, bow and arrow. The appearance in the archeological record of bone sewing needles and trap nets correlated with a huge extension northward, some forty thousand years ago. They had not only coped, but expanded their range.

Maybe they were going to have to do that again.

Clothing and shelter. At work Frank could see that civilized people did not really think about these things, they took

them for granted. Most wore clothing suited to 'room temperature' all the year round, thus sweltering in the summer and
shivering in winter anytime they stepped out of their rooms
– which however they rarely did. So they thought they were
temperature tough-guys, but really they were just indoors all
the time. They used their buildings as clothing, in effect, and
heated or cooled these spaces to imitate what clothing did,
no matter how crazy this was in energy terms. But they did
it without thinking of it like that, without making that calculation. In the summer they wore blue jeans because of what
people three generations before had seen in Marlboro ads.
Blue jeans were the SUVs of pants, part of a fantasy outdoor
life; Frank himself had long since changed to the Khembali
ultralite cotton pants in summer, noting with admiration how
the slight crinkle in the material kept most of the cloth off
the skin.

Now as it got colder people still wore blue jeans, which
were just as useless in the cold as they were in the heat. Frank
meanwhile shifted piece by piece into his mountaineering gear.
Some items needed cleaning, but were too delicate to run
through a washing machine, so he had to find a dry cleaners
on Connecticut, but then was pleasantly surprised to discover
that they would take all his other clothes too; he had disliked
going to the laundromat up the street from Van Ness.

So, autumn weather, cool and windy: therefore, Patagonia's
capilene shirts, their wicking material fuzzy and light against
the skin; a down vest with a down hood ready to pull onto
his head; nylon wind-jacket; Patagonia's capilene long underwear; wool pants; nylon wind-pants if windy. Thick Thurlo
socks inside light Salomon hiking shoes. As an ensemble it
actually looked pretty good, in an *Outside Magazine* techno-
geek way – a style which actually fit in pretty unobtrusively
at NSF. Scientists signaled with their clothes just like anyone
else, and their signal often proclaimed, 'I am a scientist, I do
things because they Make Sense, and so I Dress Sensibly,'

which could resemble Frank's mountaineering gear, as it meant recreational jackets with hoods, hiking boots, ski pants, wool shirts. So Frank could dress as a high-tech paleolithic and still look like any other NSF jock.

Work itself was becoming bogged down in the bureaucratic swamps that had replaced the physical ones. The actual bogs had been drained but somehow remained as ghosts, dragging down each generation of trespassers in turn; the federal capital thus retained the psychic nature of the original swamp, and its function too, as all the toxins of the national life were dumped there to be stirred together and broken down in its burbling pits.

Trying to hack her way through this wilderness was beginning to get Diane both results and resistance. She spent about fourteen hours a day, Frank reckoned, in meetings up on the eleventh floor at NSF and elsewhere in the area. Many of these meetings he did not attend and only heard about, usually from Edgardo, who as director of the math division and a long-time colleague of Diane's took part in quite a few. Some agencies were interested in joining the cause, Edgardo reported, and others resented the suggestion that things be done differently, considering it an attack on turf. In general the farther removed from making policy, the more interested they were to help. A fair number of agencies with regulatory power were fully turned by the industries they were supposed to regulate, and thus usually agents of the enemies of change; among these were the Department of Energy (nuclear and oil industry), the FDA (food and drug), the US Forest Service and other parts of the Department of Agriculture (timber and ag), and the EPA (a curious mix, depending on division, but some of them bound to the pesticide industry and all under the thumb of the President). Republican administrations had regularly staffed these agencies with people chosen from the industries being regulated, and these people had then written regulations with the industries' profits in mind. Now these agencies were not just toothless but actively dangerous, no matter how good their people were at the technocrat level. They were turned at the top and their potential good suborned.

Thus it was that Diane had to work around and against several of these agencies, particularly Energy. Not that nuclear wasn't arguably a valid part of some mid-range clean energy solution, as Edgardo often argued; but the Energy leadership took this to mean also trying to cripple other, less dangerous alternatives. It was becoming clear that part of NSF's project had to include making efforts to get leadership of the captive agencies changed, for the good of the environment and the long-term health of the country; but that implied involvement in presidential politics. For the turned agencies were now out to do the same to NSF, working on the administration to remove the director and upper management and replace them with people more sympathetic to the economy.

So, on top of everything else: war of the agencies.

The first manifestation of this new realm of conflict was the appointment of a new NSF Inspector General, who turned out to be a man who had most recently been Inspector General in the Department of Energy; before that he had worked for Southern California Edison, and had been a major contributor to the President's campaign.

No accident, of course, Edgardo said. It was a first shot, aimed by OMB itself. That was bad, very bad. Edgardo went on a long paranoid aria during one of their runs, detailing just how bad it could be, and all the ways Diane was going to have to be on guard in the months to come; and her past had better be spotless. 'I said to her I hope you have a very honest tax man, and she just laughed. "Two can play at that game," she said, "and I'm cleaner than they are." So off we go, off to the mattresses.'

Frank sang, 'Territoriality, ooooop! Does that mean we're screwed then?'

'No, not necessarily. There are too many funding sources with a really serious interest in mitigating climate damage. The science agencies, emergency services, even NIH, even the Pentagon. It's up to Diane to build an alliance that can get things done. They'll have to fight for everything they get. It would help a lot if they could turn the other side right at the head, and convince the President's team that this stuff has to be done, and that it could be taken as an opportunity for new technologies and businesses that the rest of the world is going to have to use. Whether that could work, I don't know the White House well enough to say. They seem like idiots, but they can't be as stupid as they seem or they wouldn't be there. Anyway Diane says she's going to give it a try. Senate first, but White House too.'

In Frank's meetings with her, Diane did not refer to this part of the struggle, preferring to discuss the technical aspects of their work. The North Atlantic project was still being researched, and Diane still liked it very much, but she was very concerned that they also pursue a vigorous hunt for some biologically-based carbon capture method. Frank wondered if the legal and political problems inherent in releasing a genetically modified organism into the environment could ever be overcome; but he knew exactly who to call about the technical aspects of it, of course.

He had been thinking of calling Marta and Yann again anyway. So, after a meeting with Diane, he steeled himself to the task. Thinking of the surveillance issue, he wondered if he should call them from a public phone, but realized both ends had to be unsurveilled for that to work. No, best to do this work in the open and let the chips fall where they may, the stocks rise as they might. So he called them at their Small Delivery numbers, from his office.

'Hi Marta, it's Frank. I wanted to talk to you and Yann about the carbon capture work you described to me. Can you tell me how that study is coming along, I mean just in general terms?'

'It's going okay.'

'So, you know – in the absence of long-term field studies, have you gotten any back-of-the-envelopes on how quickly it might work, or how much it might draw down?'

'We can only extrapolate from lab results.'

'And what does that indicate, if anything?'

'It could be considerable.'

'I see.'

Marta said, 'How's the San Diego project coming along?'

'Oh good, good. I mean, I'm recused from any direct action on that front, but I'm following the process, and people at UCSD and in the biotech community there are really excited about it. So I think something will happen.'

'And we'll have a place in it?'

'Yes, well, they're working on an offer. There's going to be a kind of Macarthur award committee disbursing some research money, it won't be quite as unconstrained as Macarthur money, but there will be a lot of it, and it will be awarded without applications to people judged deserving.'

'I see.' Marta's voice was still heavy with skepticism, but Frank noted that she was not being actively hostile either. 'Well, I look forward to seeing how that goes.'

'It would surely help you if you're ever going to try to deploy anything like this lichen you've described.'

'We've got an array of options,' she said shortly, and would not elaborate.

Next morning at NSF he found out from Edgardo that Diane had been in a fight with the President's science advisor, Dr Zacharius Strengloft. Strengloft had suggested to her in a meeting at the Capitol with the Senate Natural Resources Committee that NSF should keep to what it was good at, which meant disbursing grant money. Diane had given him her Look of Stone and then told him in no uncertain terms that NSF was run by her and the National Science Board and no one else. Senate and staff who had witnessed the confrontation would of course take differing meanings from it.

Soon after that Diane convened a full meeting of the National Science Board, which was NSF's board of directors, in effect. The twenty-four members of the board had all been appointed by the President, from a list which, though vetted by Strengloft, had been created by the National Academy of Sciences and other sources. This meant they were a mixed-ideology group, and clearly Diane wanted to make sure they were behind her for the coming battles. She made it a closed meeting, and when she came out of it Frank couldn't tell if she had gotten what she wanted or not. But later she told him they had been almost unanimous in their support for NSF trying to coordinate a national response, even an international response. Then he saw again the little smile that crossed her face sometimes when she had gotten her way in these struggles. She seemed unflustered, even content. She shook her head wonderingly as she told Frank about it, put a hand to his arm, as in the gym, smiled her little smile. What a strange game they were caught in, she seemed to say. But clearly no one was going to intimidate her. Frank certainly wouldn't want to be the one to try it.

Meanwhile, to implement anything in the North Atlantic, they would have to coordinate plans with the IPCC, and the rest of the UN, and really the whole world; get approvals, get funding, get the actual materials manufactured or gathered, whatever they might be.

Eventually this need to liaise with international agencies impelled them to arrange a day's meetings in the UN building in New York. Diane asked Frank to join her for a few of these, and he was happy to agree.

'Easy travel to other planets,' he said.

'What?'

236

'Manhattan.'
'Oh, yes.'

When hanging with the bros in the evenings, Frank some-times became curious about their plans. The picnic tables and fireplace were not going to hack it as winter furniture. The fireplace was such a misbegotten thing, like a pizza oven placed on the ground, that it was useless for heating, cooking, or fire-gazing. Perhaps that was the point; surely the men of the CCC, or whoever had built the thing, had to have known better. Some of the other picnic sites had open fire rings; but the bros had chosen to hang here by the oven.

One night Frank arrived to find they had tried to solve this problem by commandeering a steel trash barrel and starting a fire inside it, a fire that only just flickered over its rim. Possibly the entire barrel gave off some radiant heat, and the fire would not be visible from a distance, of course, if that was a concern. But it was a miserable excuse for a campfire.

'Hey Perfesser!' Zeno bellowed. 'How's it hanging, man? We haven't seen you for a while.'

The others chimed in with their habitual welcomes. 'He's been too *busy*!' 'Those co-eds *wanted* him.'

They were all bulked up, thick with thrift shop sweaters and coats, and also, Frank was pleased to see, greasy down jackets. Old down jackets were probably cheap, being unfash-ionable; and there was nothing better in the cold.

'Hey,' he said. 'Super long time. What was it, yesterday?'

'Yarrr. Ha ha ha.'

'I know you've done so much you want to tell me about.'

'HA!!!' They crowed their approval of this jape. 'We ain't done a fucking thing! Why should we?'

And yet it soon transpired that they had all experienced an extraordinary number of traumas since Frank last came around. They interrupted each other ceaselessly as they related them, making a mish-mash that no one could have followed, but Frank knew from the start not to try. 'Yeah *right*,' was all he had to say from time to time. Again it struck him how well they recalled scrapes, scuffles, or fights; they could re-enact every move in slow motion, and did so when telling their tale – it was part of the tale, maybe the most interesting part: 'I twisted like this, and he missed over my *shoulder*, like this, and then I ducked,' ducking and weaving against the absent but well-remembered opponent.

'We had to pull him right *off* the guy, yeah! I had to peel his fingers right off of his *neck*! He was pounding his head right against the *concrete*.'

Finally they were done. Frank said, 'Hey, your fire? It sucks.'

A shout of agreement and dissent. Zeno said, 'Hey whaddya mean, dude? It's perfect for shoving yer head in the can!'

'YARRR.'

'That's the only way you could see it,' Frank countered. 'Why don't you go where one of the good firepits are?'

They laughed at his naiveté. 'That'd be too *good* for us!'

'Might have us a *fire* if we did that!'

One of them mimed a karate kick at the stone oven. 'Piece of shit.'

'You need fire,' Frank said.

'We GOT a fire.'

'Can't you knock the top of this thing off, or make a fire-ring next to it or something? Aren't there any demolition sites or construction sites around here where you could get some cinder blocks?'

'Don't be bringing the man down on us any more than he already is,' Fedpage said.

'Whatever,' Frank said. 'You're gonna freeze your asses off.'

'It's a half-assed fire.'

'You have to put your hands right on the metal, it's ridiculous.'

'No fucking way, it's warm from here!'

'Yeah right.'

They settled in. The topic shifted to winter and winterizing in general, so Frank sat back and listened. No way were they going to respond to his words by jumping out into the night and putting together a decent fire ring. If that had been their style they wouldn't be out here in the first place. Maybe later it would sink in.

A few of them discussed the prospects of sleeping at the Metro stops just coming back on line; the regulars for these spots had dispersed, so that good grates were going unclaimed. You could nest on a good site all day. But that risked a poorly-timed rousting by the cops. But if you didn't take the risk, you weren't likely to find a good spot.

Zeno declared he was going to build a hut and sleep right there by their site. Others agreed immediately that good shelters could be made. It all sounded hypothetical to Frank, he thought they were just covering for the fact that they didn't want to talk about where they really slept.

That made sense to Frank; he wasn't telling people where he slept either. The bros were under a different kind of surveillance than he was, more erratic but potentially much more immediate, with consequences much worse than Frank's (one hoped). They had police records, many of them extensive. Technically much of what they were doing was illegal, including being in Rock Creek Park at all. Luckily a lot of people were doing the same thing. It was the herd defense; predators would pick off the weak, but the bulk of the herd would be okay. The more the better, therefore, up to a point – a point they had not yet reached, even though many little squatter settlements and even what could be called shanty towns were now visible in flood-damaged parts of town, especially in the parks. Ultimately this might trigger some large-scale crackdown, and Rock Creek Park was high profile. But the gorge's new ravine walls were steep and unstable, impossible to patrol at night. To clear the gorge they would have to do it by day and call out the National Guard – both of them, as Zeno always added. If they did that the bros could slip away into the city, or north into the forest across the Maryland border.

Meanwhile, out of sight, out of mind. They were off the grid, they had slung their hooks, they had lit out for the territory. The firelight bounced on their worn faces, etching each knock and crease. Little more of them could be seen, making it seem like a circle of disembodied faces, masks again, or a Rockwell Kent woodblock.

'There was this guy living on the streets in San Francisco who turned out was like totally rich, he was heir to a fortune but he just liked living outdoors.'

'But he was a drunk too, right?'

'Fucking George Carlin is so funny.'

'They said I was grade ten but they wouldn't give me dental.'

Blah blah blah. Frank recalled a fire from his youth: two climber gals slightly buzzed had come bombing into Camp Four around midnight and hauled him away from a dying fire, insisting that he join them in a midnight swim in the Merced River, and who could say no to that. Though it was shocking cold water and pitch black to boot, more a good idea than a comfortable reality, swimming with two naked California women in the Yosemite night. But then when they got out and staggered back to the fire, near dead from hypothermia, it had been necessary to pile on wood until it was a leaping yellow blaze and dance before it to catch every pulse of lifesaving heat. Even at the time Frank had understood that he would never see anything more beautiful.

Now he sat with a bunch of red-faced homeless guys bundled in their greasy down jackets, around a fire hidden at the bottom of a trashcan. The contrast with the night at Camp Four was so complete that it made him laugh. It made the two nights part of the same thing somehow.

'We should build a real fire,' he said.

No one moved. Ashes rose on the smoke from the trashcan.

Frank reached in with a two-by-four and tried to stir it up enough to give them some flame over the rim. 'If you have a fire but you can't see it,' he said as he jabbed, 'then you go out of your mind.'

Fedpage snorted. 'Central heating, right?'

'So everyone's crazy, yarr. Of course they are.'

'*We* certainly are.'

'Is that what did it hey?'

'Where there's smoke there's fire.'

'When did someone first say that, a million years ago? Oooop! Ooop! Oooop!'

'Hey there monkey man, quit that now! You sound like Meg Ryan in that movie.'

'Ha ha haaaa! That was so fucking funny.'

'She was faking it! She was *faking it.*'

'I'll take it fake or not.'

'As if you could tell!'

'– greatest human vocalization ever recorded.'

'Yeah right, you obviously don't know your porn.'

Things that would warm a body: laughter; reenacting fights; playing air guitar; playing with the fire; talking about sex; thinking about climber gals.

Knocking a stone oven apart would definitely warm the body. Frank got up. What he needed was a sledgehammer and a crowbar; what they had were some lengths of two-by-four and an old aluminum baseball bat, already much dented.

One stone in the little opening at the top was loose in its cement. Frank moved to what looked like the right angle and smashed the stone with a two-by-four. The bros were pleased at the diversion, they guffawed and urged him on. He knocked the first stone down into the firepit, reached into the ashes and rolled it out. After that it was a matter of knocking loose one stone at a time. He used the longest two-by-four and pounded away. The cement was old, and stone by stone the firepit came down.

When he had gotten it down to knee height it made a sensible firepit, with a gap in one side where the old doorway had been. He filled the gap with stones. There were enough left over to make another firepit if they wanted one. Or maybe bench supports, if they found some planks.

'Okay, let's move the trashcan fire into the pit,' he said.

'How you gonna pick it up? That can is red hot down there at the bottom, don't you pick that up!'

'You'll burn your fucking hands off, man!'

'It's not red hot,' Frank pointed out. 'Lets a couple of us grab it around the top. Wear gloves and tilt it, and we'll lift the bottom with the studs here.'

'Roll and burn your fucking leg off!'

'Yeah right!'

But Zeno was willing to do it, and so the rest gathered round. The ones who had gloves grasped the rim, lifted and tilted. Frank and Andy wedged studs under the bottom from opposite sides and lifted it up. With a whoosh the whole fiery mass sparked into the new ring and blasted up into the night. Howls chased the uprush of smoke and sparks.

They sat around the cheery blaze, suddenly much more visible to each other.

'Now we need a pizza!'

'Who'll get a pizza?'

They all looked at Frank. 'Ah shit,' he said. 'Where's Cutter.'

'Get some beer too!' Zeno said, with the same fake laugh as before.

Kicking through piles of fallen leaves, the cold air struck him like a splash of water in the face. It felt good. He had to laugh: all his life he had traveled to the mountains and the polar regions to breathe air this bracing and heady, and here it was, right here in the middle of this ridiculous city. Maybe the seasons would become his terrain now, and winter be like high altitude or high latitude. It could be good.

\* \* \*

The afternoon before he and Diane were going to leave for New York, he phoned Spencer to see when they were playing, because he wanted to get one more game in before he left town.

It was a perfect October day, Indian summer, and in the amber horizontal light of sunset they threw across a stiff western breeze that brought a continuous rain of yellow and brown leaves spinnerdrifting down on them. Frank slung his disk through the forest's ticker-tape parade, hooting with all the rest, and he was deep in the game when they ran into the bros' little clearing.

Spencer stopped so abruptly that Frank almost rammed into him, thinking *auroch*, but then he saw half a dozen men wearing flak jackets, aiming big assault rifles at the astonished bros.

'Get down on the ground!' one of the men shouted. 'Get down right now! GET DOWN.'

The guys dropped awkwardly, faces on the ground, arms out to the side.

The frisbee players stayed frozen in place. One of the men turned and said to them, 'We'll be just a minute more here. Why don't you be on your way.'

Frank and the frisbee guys nodded and took off down Ross, jogging until they were around the corner, then stopping and looking back.

'What the fuck was that?'

'A bust.'

'Yeah but who?'

'We'll find out on the way back.'

They played on, distracted, missing shot after shot. On the way back they hurried the pace, and came into site 21 huffing.

The guys were still there, sitting around – all but Jory.

'Hey guys what was that all about?' Spencer cried as they ran in. 'That looked horrible!'

'They rousted us,' Zeno said.

Redbeard shook his head resentfully. 'They made us lie down on the ground like we were criminals.'

'They didn't want any trouble,' said Zeno. 'They thought Jory might be carrying.'

Ah ha. Jory, the only one who had ever made Frank feel seriously uncomfortable. So it had not been a misreading.

'They were ready to shoot us,' Redbeard complained.

'Sure they were. They probably heard Jory was armed.'

'So it was Jory they were after?' Spencer said. 'What did he do?'

'Jory's the one who beat up on Ralph! Don't you know?'

'No.'

'Yes you do, it was in the papers. Ralph got pounded by Jory and a guy, down at Eighteen.'

'We had to pull him right *off* the guy, yeah! I had to peel his fingers right off of his *neck*! He was pounding his head right against the *concrete*.'

'Yeah, so Ralph was in the hospital after that, but then a couple weeks later Jory showed up again and started hanging out with us like nothing had happened.'

'Jesus,' Frank said. 'Why didn't you go to the police and get rid of this guy?'

They shouted 'YEAH RIGHT' at him in unison. Then, interrupting each other in their eagerness:

'What do you think *they're* going to do?'

'They'll call in and find out about my outstandings and get my parole officer –'

'Fuck that, they'll *beat* on you –'

'You could end up put away for fucking *years*.'

Zeno's grin was sharklike. 'Some things you just gotta live with, Doctor. The police are not there for us. Assholes come to hang with us, that's just the way it is.'

'Hard to believe,' Frank said.

On they ran, and after they had finished their frisbee, Frank asked Spencer about it. 'So they can't get help from the police if they need it?'

Spencer shook his head. 'We can't either, for that matter. People without a legal place of residence are kind of outside the legal system. It's very property-based.'

'Don't you guys have places to live?'

Spencer, Robin and Robert laughed.

'We do have places to live,' Spencer said, 'but we don't pay for them.'

'What do you do then?'

'We wander a bit. Just like you, right? We hunt and gather in the technosurround.'

'A godly state,' Robin said.

'Come to dinner and see,' Spencer offered. 'The fregans in Klingle Valley are having a potluck.'

'I don't have anything to bring.'

'Don't worry. There'll be enough. Maybe you can buy a bottle of wine on the way over.'

On the walk through the park to Klingle Valley, one of the park tributaries of Rock Creek, Spencer and the others explained to Frank that they were ferals.

'You use that word?'

Yes, that's what they usually called their mode these days, but also squatters, scavengers, fregans. There were ferals living in every city. It was a kind of urban wilderness thing.

'Fregan, what's that?'

'It's like vegan, only they'll only eat food that they've gotten for free.'

'Say what?'

'They eat out of dumpsters and such. Scavenge food that is going to waste.'

'Whoah.'

'Think about how many restaurants there are in DC,' said Spencer. So many fine restaurants, so much wonderful food, and a certain percentage of it thrown away every night. Perfectly good fresh food. That was just the way the restaurant business had to run. So, if you knew the routine at these dumpsters, and you resolved never to spend money on food, but always either to grow it or scavenge it – or kill it, in the case of the many white-tailed deer being culled and eaten – then you were a fregan. They were going to a fregan potluck that very night. There would be lots of venison.

The house hosting the potluck was boarded up, having been badly damaged in a fire. They slipped in the back to find a party going on, a whole bunch of people, young and not so young, some tattooed and pierced, others tie-died and rastafied. There was a fire in the fireplace, but the flue wasn't drawing well; added to this smokiness was a funky mix of wet dog, patchouli, potluck food and whatever was burning in a hookah in the corner: a mix of hash, cigars and clove cigarettes, judging by the cloud Frank walked through.

The frisbee players were greeted warmly, and Spencer was acclaimed as some kind of local celebrity, a gypsy king. He introduced Frank very informally, and hustled him through to the food table – 'always wisest to get it while you can' – and they feasted on a selection of Washington restauranteering's finest, slightly reconstituted for the occasion: steaks, quiche, salad, bread. Spencer ate like a wolf, and by the time they were done Frank was stuffed as well.

'See?' Spencer said as they sat on the floor watching the crowd flow by. 'There are lots of empty buildings in this city. If you work as a team and spend your time taking care of business, then you can find shelter and food for free. Scavenge clothes or buy in thrift shops, talk with people or play frisbee for fun, walk wherever you go – you can step outside the money economy almost entirely. Live off the excess, so you don't add to the waste. You reduce waste, you pour energy back into the grid. Do a little street theater down in the lawyer district to gather some change, even do day labor or take a job in one of the shops. You don't actually need money at all, although a little bit helps.'

246

'Wow,' Frank said. 'And about how many people are doing this?'

'It's hard to tell. It's best to stay under the radar, because of just the sort of police issues you were asking the bros about. I think there's several hundred people at least, maybe a thousand, who think of themselves as fregans or ferals. Obviously there are a lot more homeless people than that, but I'm talking about the people going at it like we are.'

'Wow.'

'It makes a huge difference how you think about what you're doing.'

'That's true.'

A group in the corner was preparing to play some music: two guitars, mandolin, fiddle, wooden flute, a Bombay harmonium. Two young women came over to haul Spencer to his feet; a command performance, he was needed on percussion.

Frank said, 'Thanks, Spencer, I'm going to have to go soon.'

'That's all right, man, there'll be more of these. Frisbee tomorrow?'

'No, I've got to go to New York. I'll check in when I get back.'

'See you then.'

**Frank and Diane took** the train to New York. They sat facing each other over a table on the morning express from Union Station to Penn Station, rocking slightly as they worked on their laptops, stopping from time to time to sip their coffees and look out the window and talk. Sometimes this lasted half an hour, then they returned to work. It was companionable.

Out the window flashed the backs of long row houses, tawdry unkempt yards. Old industrial buildings of the Mid-Atlantic states, rusty and broken-windowed, flying by click-click-click, sway sway, gone. Over one of the great rivers, then by the gray Atlantic, mumbling its dirty whitecaps onshore.

Then descending underground, to go under the Hudson and enter Metropolis, just like Fritz Lang pictured it. Dark ancient brick walls, unmarked by any graffiti.

The train stopped in mid-tunnel.

'Did you ever live in New York?' Diane asked.

'No. I've hardly even visited.'

'Wow.'

'You lived here?'

'Yes, I went to Columbia.'

'What for?'

'Med school.'

'Really.'

'Yes, a long time ago.'

'Did you practice medicine?'

'Sure. Five years, but then I got into research, and the administration, and that just kept going, I guess you'd say.'

'Yes, I would,' peering at her laptop screensaver, which cycled a succession of Asian American faces. 'I mean, director of NSF – that's administration all right.'

She sighed. 'It's true. Things just kept on happening.'

She tapped a button and made the faces go away. Replacing them was her calendar, every hour and half hour obviously accounted for. Under it was a spreadsheet of projects, a kind of Things To Do list, but with events categorized and broken down by background reading, pre-meetings, biographies of participants, and so on.

'You must have a system too,' she noted, seeing him looking at it.

'Sure,' Frank said. 'A Things To Do list.'

'That sounds healthier than this. So, are you enjoying yourself?'

'Well, I suppose I am.'

She laughed. 'More than last year anyway, I hope?'

He felt himself blushing. 'Yeah, sure. It's more of a challenge, of course. But I asked for it.' He gulped at that topic, and said quickly, 'I'll be a lot happier if the UN goes for one of these projects.'

'Sure. But the work itself, in the building?'

'Yeah, sure. More variety.'

'It still isn't research.'

'I know. But I'm trying. Maybe it's a different kind. I don't know. I've never been too sure what we're up to at NSF.'

'I know.'

His face was fully hot now. He thought: Come on, don't be chicken here; if ever there was a chance to talk about this, it's here and now. Only a few short months before, Diane had taken Frank's angry critique of NSF and

1) pretended she had never seen it,

2) asked him to give a presentation on its contents to the NSF Science Board, and

3) asked him publicly to stay at NSF another year and chair a committee to study his suggestions, and all other possible methods for increasing NSF's impact on the global warming situation – thus, in front of his ostensible peer group, making him prove that he was not a blowhard by taking on a hard thankless job for the good of all.

And he had agreed to do it.

So he took a deep breath, and said, 'Why didn't you say anything when I gave you that letter?'

She pursed her lips. 'I thought I did.'

'Yes,' he tried not to be irritated, 'but you know what I mean.'

She nodded, looked down and tapped a note into her schedule. 'It read to me like someone who was burnt out on doing jackets, and wanted to be doing something else. NSF itself didn't really seem to be what you were talking about, not to me.'

'Well, maybe not entirely, but I did want to talk about it too.'

'Sure. I thought you made some good points. I thought you might be interested in trying them out. So, here you are.'

'So you let the other stuff go.'

'It has to stay in your file, I can't change people's files. But there's no sense looking for trouble. I find letting trouble stay in a file often works pretty well. And in your case, it was all going to work out one way or another. Either you'd go back to San Diego, or you'd help us here. In that sense you did good to give it to me in person like you did, I mean just the hard copy.'

'I tried to take it back,' Frank confessed.

'You did? How?'

'I came back and looked for it. But Laveta had already given it to you.'

'I see. I'm glad she did. I think it's worked out for the best.'

Frank thought about it.

'Don't you?'

'Well, yes. I don't know. I guess I'm still finding out.'

She smiled her little smile again, and he discovered he liked to see it. He liked to cause it.

The train moved again, and soon pulled into Penn Station. Up on the streets of Manhattan they walked through the immense slots created by the skyscrapers, across midtown to the UN building, Frank goggling at the views with an ex-window washer's awe.

The day's work at the UN was interesting. Frank got to see another side of Diane, perhaps a glimpse of her true métier, as some kind of international diplomat or technocrat. She knew all these people already, and in the meetings she got up from her seat from time to time to look over their shoulders at their screens, putting a hand to a shoulder while pointing and asking a question. They all had met many times before, clearly; there was even a pause wherein the Secretary General himself dropped by to say hi to her, thanking her lavishly for 'all she was doing.' Back in the discussions, she was always driving the issue, always pushing for action, occasionally joking about the fact that she was a representative of the United States and yet still promoting a vigorous array of environmental actions. She didn't overplay this, but her message seemed to be that although the US historically had been part of the problem in global warming, from rejecting Kyoto to pumping more carbon than any other country into the atmosphere, that was all about to change. As for the past, Diane and her allies had nothing to be ashamed of just because they had not prevailed politically. In one conversation she made the point that polls showed that a majority of American citizens were interested in protecting the environment, and wanted

251

their government to do something about climate change, so that it was not a matter of being outnumbered so much as denied, as part of a more general breakdown of democratic systems in the US. Diane shrugged as she said this; no cause for outrage – the fight against greed was never going to end – meanwhile, she served as an ambassador for all the elements of American society who wanted to engage the climate problem. Now they might be in a position to prevail.

Mostly all this was implicit in her manner: cheerful, unapologetic, intent on the present, and on future results. She pushed relentlessly all day, discussing plan after plan, typing memos into her laptop and then without further ado moving on to the next matter, sometimes with a changed cast facing her, other times abruptly with the same people, with nothing more than an: 'Okay, what about this?'

Late in the day they met with representatives of the European carbon emissions trading group and futures market; there was a futures market in carbon credits, as there was for everything else, and Diane felt its calculations could be tweaked to make it more accurate and useful. The carbon treaty talks scheduled for the following year were almost certain to make emissions much more expensive, and this was the kind of prospect that often gave a huge push to a futures market, as people tried to buy while the commodity was still cheap. (Frank followed this discussion very closely, thinking about his own commodity status.) That kind of investment could generate a big fund in advance of the need for it in pay-outs, and that could be used to prime the pump for various mitigation projects. Calculations using the Dynamic Integrated Model of Climate and the Economy, DICE-99, showed that a carbon tax as low as ten cents a gallon of gas at the pump could have built up a hedge fund large enough to fund almost any mitigation they could conceive, if they had pegged the tax to inflation and started it some years before; they had missed that precautionary opportunity as they had so many others, but in many ways it still existed, and most nations were instituting some version of a carbon exchange and a carbon tax.

After that they met with delegations from China, then India, then the European Union and the African Union. Usually representatives from the Intergovernmental Panel on Climate Change were on hand, and the discussions had a curiously suspended or hypothetical air; if Diane were the American president or a representative of his, they would have been more intent perhaps to press their positions; as it was they knew they were dealing with a kind of shadow government figure, or with the amorphous scientific community out there beyond the government, which Diane might be said to represent. She understood this and dealt with it using a kind of tightrope-walking tact, diplomatic and attractive; there were things NSF could do, and things it might do, were the political climate to change; and the physical climate changes might drive the political ones.

After these meetings, it was the IPCC crowd itself who stayed on in the meeting rooms. The IPCC was one of the oldest and most influential global warming study groups; their list of suggested amelioration projects was huge, and they had already performed or commissioned preliminary studies of most of them, so that they had them sorted by cost, size, type, area, time needed, potential carbon drawdown, estimated time of sequestration, secondary effects, and many other determinants. They went over this list item by item in the late afternoon and early evening, and by the time they were done it certainly seemed like a robust carbon capture campaign could be constructed, if the funding were there and political obstructions did not exist.

Diane and Frank's questions to them about an intervention in the North Atlantic broached new territory, however, and though they were interested, the discussion could only outline the parameters of the problem. The International

Maritime Treaty was administered through the UN, so there were experts available to answer some of Diane's questions, but it would take them some time.

Then they were done, and it was dark outside, the windows reflecting them in the room. Workday over, in Manhattan in the cocktail hour, on a clear chill November evening.

'Dinner,' Diane announced, looking down at the East River and its bridges.

'Right,' said Frank. He was hungry.

'Shall we try this place I know?'

They were on a date.

They were on a date in the big city, the world's great city, paradigmatic and incomparable. Manhattan always boggled Frank; he had spent very little time in it, and that spread out over the years. Here the primate mind had to be stunned by the verticality of the cliffs and canyons and towers. Add to those unnatural landforms the rivers of cars and taxis, and the omnipresence of people, hundreds in view at every moment, and the cumulative effect was staggering – literally so for Frank, as he had no inhibitions about spinning down the sidewalks, head swiveling like an owl's to see more. Diane had to grab his arm and pull him out of traffic when he tried to get a better view of the Chrysler building. Yes, there they were, arm in arm on the streets of Manhattan, laughing at Frank's hick amazement, his window-washer's euphoria. West through mid-town, then up toward Central Park, where Diane knew of a good restaurant. In the crowd at the next red light she slipped her arm out of his, which released him from an awkward position, in which his forearm had hung as if from an invisible sling to give her forearm something to rest on. These old postures. And yet the touch had coursed through him as he walked, like a light charge of electricity, or a new idea. Oooooooop.

The restaurant proved to be run by Chinese or east Asians

254

of some other kind, Frank didn't inquire because in every other respect the restaurant was pure Provençal. It was jammed into an archetypal Manhattan restaurant space, two stories of narrow rooms with a patio in the airshaft out back, a deep brick-walled enclosure, home to a hardy old tree; the whole burnished to a mysterious black-brick and battered-wood perfection.

Two faces in candlelight over a restaurant table: an old situation, and they both knew it. Although probably only Frank was also helplessly theorizing the event in terms of its million-year-old tradition. Two faces in the light of a fire, one male one female: eat, drink, man, woman. Big parts of the brain were no doubt ignited by the candlelight alone, not to mention the smells and tastes. A million years.

They talked about the day, the work in hand. Frank admitted to being impressed by the IPCC group and the work they had done. 'Still, I'd like to do something faster, if we could. I think we'll need it.'

'You think so?'

He told her about seeing Khembalung go under. Then his notions for dealing with the changing ocean, for clean energy, for really serious carbon drawdown from the atmosphere.

'So,' Diane said, 'really you're talking about global cooling.'

'Well, if we can warm it, maybe we can cool it too.'

'But the warming took a lot. The whole world's economy, two hundred years.'

'Well, but just by accident though. The economy wasn't dedicated to warming. It was just a byproduct.'

'Making things cooler might be harder than warming.'

'But if we actually direct part of the economy to that project. Like as if paying for a war or something.'

'Maybe.' She thought about it, shook her head as if freeing herself from the subject.

Then they talked about their pasts, in brief disconnected anecdotes. She described her children, Frank his parents. This

255

seemed odd, but then she described her parents too; quite like his in some ways, it sounded. Her mother had been born in China, and Diane could do a funny imitation of her primitive English, 'You go in street car squish you like bug!' After that Frank could hear better the Chinese accent in Diane's own speech, which was perfectly grammatical and idiomatic, California Standard in fact, but with a lilt to it that he now understood better.

Then world events; problems in the Middle East; travels, New York; other meals in New York. They tried each other's dishes, refilled each other's wine glasses. They each drank half the bottle; then, over creme brulee, sipped samples of cognac from a tray of ancient bottles offered for their inspection by the waiter.

Complex sensations, coursing through the sensorium. Some part of the parcellated mind watched all the parts coming together. Nice to be so here in the moment. Frank watched Diane's face and felt something like the glow he had felt when she took his arm on the street. She too was enjoying herself. Seeing that was part of the glow. Reciprocity: this kind of mutual enjoyment, he thought, only works if it *is* mutual. We live for this, we crave this. He felt a little vertiginous, as if climbing a hard pitch or maybe the Chrysler Building up the street. Aware of a risk.

He saw again how beautiful her arms were. This was an Optimodal thing; not just biceps but the whole upper arm, amazingly thick front to back, from shoulder to elbow; unlike anyone else's arms. Gorgeous. It was different for everybody, what looked good to them. The argument that beauty corresponded to adaptive function was obviously stupid. Deviance from the norm was what drew the eye. Francesca Taolini had a crooked nose and various other asymmetries typical of narrow sharp-edged faces, and yet she was gorgeous; Diane had a blunt pentagonal face, perfectly symmetrical, and she too, while not as glamorous as Francesca, was yet still very attractive, one might even say charismatic. Yes, a true star that day at the UN. She drew the eye.

At a table near the door to the kitchen, another couple was having a similar sort of dinner, except they were much more demonstrative, more romantic; from time to time they even leaned together and kissed, in that New York way of pretending they were alone when they weren't. Frank thought they were showing off, and turned his head away; Diane saw them and his response too, and smiled her slight smile.

She leaned over and whispered, 'They have wedding bands.'

'Ah?'

'No way they are married to each other.'

'Ahhh,' Frank said.

She nodded, pleased by her deduction.

'The big city,' Frank said awkwardly.

'It's true. I waited table here for a while when I was going to school. I liked to guess the stories, like with these two, though this was easy. Usually it was harder. You only see an hour. But sometimes you can tell it's an important hour. People forget to eat, or they cry, or argue. You could see the story. The other girls thought I was crazy, but it was just to be doing something.'

'Recreational anthropology.'

She laughed. 'Yes, or Nancy Drew. Passing the time.'

Then they were done, the bill divided and paid. Out on the sidewalk she said, 'Where are you staying?'

'The Metropolitan.'

'Me too. Okay. We can walk through the park and see if the ice skating is going yet.'

'It's certainly been cold enough for it.'

As they walked into it, Central Park's similarity to Rock Creek Park struck Frank. Flat terrain instead of a ravine, but they were still in a piece of the great eastern hardwood forest. It was very familiar.

'I've been spending time around the National Zoo,' Frank said impulsively. 'It's kind of like this.'

'What do you do there?'

'I've joined a group trying to keep track of the animals they haven't yet recaptured.'

'That must be interesting.'

'Yes, it is.'

'And are you recapturing these animals?'

'Eventually I suppose they will. We're mostly watching them now. It would be hard to trap some of them. The gibbons are my favorite, and they can get away from people very easily, but they'll need some help with this cold.'

'I like their singing.'

'So do I!' Frank glanced down at her, suppressing several inane comments as they arose; in the end saying nothing. She walked beside him, relaxed and easy, short and solid, her dark hair gleaming where it reflected a distant streetlight or park light, seeming unaware of his gaze.

'Ah look, it is going. How nice.' She led him onto the bridge overlooking the northern bank of the ice rink. They leaned against it, watching New Yorkers expert and inexpert gliding over the illuminated white ice.

'Come on,' Diane said, tugging his arm. 'I haven't skated in years.'

'Ah God,' Frank said. 'I'm terrible at it.'

'I'll teach you.'

She took his rental boots from him, demanded a stiffer and tighter pair from the help, then laced them up for him. 'Nice and stiff, that's the secret. Now just stand straight and set a line. Glide forward. Shift quickly back and forth.'

He tried it and it worked. Sort of. Anyway it went better than he remembered earlier times having done. He staggered around and tried not to fall, or run into anybody. Diane glided past from time to time, undemonstrative but deft, throwing him off balance every time he caught sight of her.

She skated with him, held him up, helped him up, then took off and skated by, red-cheeked and grinning.

'Okay,' she said after a while. 'I'm losing it here, my ankles are tired.'

'Mine are broken.'

'Ah.'

Back into shoes, back walking on the ground – stumping along, it felt, after the skating. Frank felt a little tense, and they drew apart as they walked. Frank searched for something to talk about.

They walked more slowly, as if to prolong the evening, or stave off an awkward moment. Two single adults, out on a date in Manhattan, with empty hotel rooms waiting, in the same hotel; and no one on Earth knew where they were at that moment, except them. The theoretical possibilities were obvious.

But she was his boss, and about a decade older than him. Not that that mattered – though it did – but it was the professional relationship that was the main thing, standing like the bottom half of a Dutch door between them. So much could go wrong. So much could be misinterpreted. They were going to be working together for the coming year, maybe more. And then there was Caroline too, the existence of Caroline which had changed everything in his life; except not, it seemed, the content of this parcel of it.

The incorrigible scientist inside him was trying to analyze the situation. Every street they came to had a red light, and there was time to think, perhaps too much time. Alpha females often led their troop in all the most fundamental ways, particularly matters of sexual access, meaning reproductive success. The alpha males (and really, in this situation Frank almost might be considered a beta male) – they were almost ceremonial in their powers. They got what they wanted, but did not control the troop.

Well, whatever; at this moment that wasn't really the point.

He needed to know what to do. It was like being in high school. He had hated high school for this very reason.

Diane sighed. He glanced at her; she was smiling her little smile. 'That was fun,' she said. 'I never take time like this anymore.'

She was keeping a good distance between them.

'We'll have to do it in DC,' Frank suggested. 'Take a break.'

'That would be nice. We might even have outdoor ice skating this winter, if the forecasts come true.'

'Yes, that's right. Out on the Potomac for that matter.'

Another block.

Frank said, 'You do work long hours.'

'No more than anyone else.'

'I hear it's a lot more.'

'Well, there's a lot to do. Anyway, it won't last much longer.'

She pointed down a crossing street this time, rather than nudging him along. 'Down that way. The hotel's at Fifty-first and Lex.'

'Ah yeah. What do you mean, not much longer?'

'Well, my term is almost up.'

'It's a term?'

'Yes, didn't you know?' She looked up at him, laughed at his expression. 'Heading NSF is a presidential appointment, it lasts for six years. I have just over a year to go.'

They stopped in front of their hotel.

'I didn't know that,' Frank said stupidly.

'They must have told you when you did the orientation.'

'Oh,' said Frank. 'I missed some of that.'

'You blew it off.'

'Well, yes, a little bit, not all of it . . .'

She watched him, seeming amused but guarded. He had thought she was going to be his boss indefinitely. Now he had suddenly learned she was not as powerful as he had thought. And power is attractive. On the other hand, this meant she was not going to be his boss indefinitely, which meant that particular strangeness would go away, leaving them unconstrained by work issues – by the past in any manifestation – free to examine whatever was between them. So, less powerful in the pure sense, but less constrained in her relation to him; and how did these factors affect his feelings?

She was watching his face to see!

He didn't know himself, so there was no way his face could show anything. But then that too must have been visible. And the unconscious mind –

He shivered at his own confusion, tried to smile. 'So there's light at the end of your tunnel,' he said.

'But I like the job.'

'Ah. Yes. Well . . . that's too bad, then.'

She shrugged. 'I'll do something else.'

'Dang.'

She shrugged again. She was still watching him; interested in him. He wondered how much longer they could stand outside the hotel talking before it began to look strange.

'I want to hear more about this down in D.C.,' he said. 'What you're thinking of doing, and all.'

'Okay.'

'Good. Well, six o'clock train – shall we meet in the lobby and walk over to the station?'

'Sure. Five AM sharp.'

They turned together into the hotel and walked to the elevator. Up it went, opened at the third floor:

'Good night.'

'Good night.'

'That was fun.'

'Yes it was.'

**When Charlie cleaned house** he worked in a burst of maniacal effort powered by very loud music, making the event into a kind of indoor extreme sport, a domestic pentathlon performed in a last-minute attempt to stave off utter shabbiness. The ancient insane and incontinent cats, the ineradicable musk that the swimming tiger had left in the basement (perhaps contributing to the cats' paranoia), Joe's depredations and accidents, Nick's absent-minded tendency to use the furniture as a napkin, for instance to clean his fork so as to keep his food pure; all these left marks. Even the divinely slovenly Anna left marks, dropping her clothing wherever she happened to take it off, depositing books and papers and mail wherever she finished with them – all behaviors in stark contrast to the extreme order of her abstract thinking – all these had an impact. And Charlie himself was disorganized in both the abstract and the concrete; so that eventually their house's interior came to consist of narrow passageways through immense tottering middens of household detritus.

Charlie would therefore occasionally knock something over and block the way, notice the chaos and freak out. He would leap into action, trying to rectify everything in a single morning. He had to begin by putting things away, to the extent possible, as all closets and drawers remained mysteriously full, middens of their own despite all that was strewn at large. However, he at least got things off the floors, into stacks on tables and dressers near where they were supposed to go. Then he cleaned the bathrooms and the kitchen, scrubbing madly; then it was time for vacuuming.

All this was Charlie's version of the zen meditation practice called 'chop wood carry water,' and he enjoyed it as such; but it had to be fueled by music or it was no good. Vacuum cleaning in particular needed music, fast intricate surging music that sounded good at high volume. The buzzsaw solos of Charlie Parker made an excellent vacuuming soundtrack, allowing Charlie to shout 'Salt – PEEEEnuts!' over and over as he crashed about. Certain rock guitarists could of course push a vacuum as well; when Steve Howe was soloing the world practically vacuumed itself.

But the apotheosis of vacuum cleaning, Charlie had found over the years, was that part of Beethoven's late work that expressed the composer's sense of 'the mad blind energy of the universe,' which was just what vacuuming needed. These movements as defined by Beethoven's biographer Walter Sullivan, who had identified and named the mode, were those characterized by tunes repetitive and staccato, woven into fugues so that different lines perpetually overlapped in dense interference patterns, relentless, machinelike, interminable. Possibly only a deaf man could have composed such music. The famous second movement of the Ninth Symphony was a good example of this mode, but to Charlie the two very best examples were the finale of the 'Hammerklavier' sonata, opus 106, and the 'Grosse Fugue,' originally the finale of string quartet opus 130, later detached and designated opus 133. The finale of the Hammerklavier was so difficult to play that concert pianists often gave up performing it years ahead of their full retirement; while the Grosse Fugue had caused the first quartet that attempted it to beg Beethoven to write a replacement finale more within human capacities – a request which Beethoven had granted with a laugh, no doubt foreseeing that quartet players in the future would end up having to perform both finales, compounding their problem.

In any case, the cosmic inexorability of these two huge fugues made perfect music to propel a vacuum cleaner around the house. And long ago Charlie had discovered by accident that it worked even better to *play them both at once*, one on the stereo upstairs, the other downstairs, with the volumes on both stereos turned up to eleven.

Joe of course loved this unholy racket, real big truck music, and he insisted on lending a hand with the vacuuming itself, causing Charlie to dodge and leap about to avoid trampling him, and to catch the machine if it got loose and began to drag the undetachable toddler down some lane of open space toward furniture or walls. After a few such mishaps Joe would usually hand it back over and follow Charlie around, slinging dinosaurs into the vacuum's path to see if they would survive.

So, now a day came when Charlie was flying around the dining room, smashing chairs aside with the vacuum cleaner to make room under the table, lots of odd rattles and clunks under there as usual, glorying in the criss-cross of the two monster fugues, the way they almost seemed to match each other, the piano rippling up and down within the massed chaos of the strings, everything sounding wrong but right, insane but perfect – and then came that magic moment when both the hammering on the klavier and the grossness of the fugue quieted *at the same time*, as if Beethoven had somehow foreseen that the two pieces would be played together someday, or as if there was some underlying method in both, introducing a little eye to the storm before the exhilarating assault on all meaning and sense started to chomp away again – when Charlie looked around and saw that Joe was sitting on the floor of the living room, red-faced and open-mouthed, bawling his eyes out, unheard in the cacophony.

Charlie killed the vacuum cleaner, rushed over to turn off Charles Rosen, then slid across the hardwood floor to snatch the boy up in his arms.

'Oh Joe! Joe! What's wrong, buddy? What's wrong?'

Joe stuck out his lower lip. 'Loud.'

'Oh God, Joe, I'm sorry. I'm sorry. But, you know – we're vacuuming! It's always loud when we vacuum the house.'

'Too loud,' Joe said, and whimpered pathetically.

Charlie hugged him, held him. 'Sorry, guy,' he said. 'I'm really sorry. I didn't know. This is the way we've always done it before.'

And also, it seemed to him, in the past, if Joe had wanted something like the sound turned down, he would have let Charlie know by beating on his kneecap or launching a dinosaur at his head. Charlie was used to a very frank and open exchange of views with Joe, so that they would bicker with each other, sure, tussle, whack, yell – but cry? To have Joe Quibler whimpering in his arms pathetically, content to snuggle up against his chest . . . it was not right. And though it felt good to be able to comfort him, to rock him side to side in his arms, as he had many years before when trying to get Nick to fall asleep – humming gently the main theme of the Grosse Fugue until the Arditti Quartet finished with it upstairs, then continuing to hum it, until it became something like a lullaby for infant robots – it was still extremely disturbing. It just wasn't like Joe.

He sat down and for a long time hugged the child, communing. Then Joe looked up at the big front window, and his eyes grew round.

'Snow,' he said.

'Yes, that's right, that's snow! Very good, Joe! I didn't know you knew how to say that. It must be last winter since you saw snow, and you were just a baby then.'

Joe conducted the snow with outstretched arms, looking rapt, or maybe just stunned. 'Snow go down.'

'It sure does. Wow, that's pretty heavy for a first storm. It looks like it's going to bury the house. I thought this was supposed to be global warming we were having.'

'Berry house?'

'No not really, I was joking there. It might come up to the

windows though, see? I don't think it will get any higher than that.'

'No?'

'Oh, well, no reason really. It just never does. At least so far. And cold dry winters are supposed to be the thing now. The great paradox. I guess it's been kind of dry this fall. But now it's snowing. When it snows it snows.' Charlie was used to babbling meaninglessly at Joe; they were privileged conversations, as between lawyer and client. It was actually a little bit disconcerting to have Joe be starting to understand him.

Joe kept conducting the snow, his hands making evocative little flutters downward.

Impulsively Charlie gave him another hug. The boy was hot as usual. Not by much, but Charlie could feel it. Anna was keeping a chart on him now, and she had established that he was hotter by day, just under a hundred, and a bit cooler at night, right over 98.6; average 98.9, she concluded after going through one of her statistical fits. It was a way of not thinking, Charlie thought. Quantification as coping. Charlie just felt the heat with his fingertips, as now. Joe shrugged him aside. He was more sensitive these days. Was that true? Well, there was this sudden aversion to Beethoven squared. But one of the weird things about living with a toddler was how fast they changed, and how hard it then became to remember what they had been like before the change, overwhelmed as that memory was by the present state, now so vivid to the eye. Probably Joe *was* different, because of course, he had to be different. He was growing up. He was adding several million brain cells an hour, and several hundred experiences.

And occasionally he burst out with a newly angry version of his old vehemence; so it wasn't as if he were mellowing out. No one who knew him would put it that way. But before, he had been permanently and so to speak impersonally irritated, at the slowness of everything, perhaps; now when he got upset it appeared more deeply felt, and often directed at

Charlie. It almost seemed as if he were *unhappy*. This had never been true before; Joe had been furious often, unhappy never. Even the thought of him unhappy cut Charlie to the quick. And fearful, needy, even affectionate . . . all these were strange things for Charlie to witness.

Now he watched Joe stare out the window at the falling snow: not writhing in his arms, not trying to throw anything, not bouncing around absorbed in solitary play, not babbling. Of course the snow was a startling sight, so fair enough. But Charlie was scared by the way Joe felt in his arms.

'Maybe we should go out there and play in the snow!'

'Okay.'

'Come on, it'll be fun! We can dress warm and make a snowman. Throw snowballs.'

'Okay Da.'

Charlie sighed. No leap up, no marching to the door shouting GO GO GO with finger imperiously extended . . .

He got up and started to get them dressed. It was a long operation. It was eighteen degrees outside. Already he was thinking Fire in the fireplace, Thomas the Train on the carpet, snow drifting down outside the window. 'We won't be able to stay out long.'

The phone rang. 'Oh, wait just a second here.'

Joe's eyes bugged out in their old style. 'Daaa! Wanna GO! GO!'

'Ha! I bet you do! Good for you! Just a second, ha ha. Hello?'

'Charlie it's Roy.'

'Roy! how are you?'

'I'm fine you? Is this a good time?'

'No worse than usual.'

'Still suffering the slings and arrows of outrageous children?'

'Yes. Joe and I are about to go outside in the snow, but I can talk to you out there. Let me get my earplug in.'

'I won't keep you long, you guys just keep doing what you're doing. We've been talking about what Phil can say to counter the President's people's attacks. Now that he's declared he's running, they're clearly concerned, and they keep saying that he'll gut the economy in a futile attempt to reverse climate change.'

'As opposed to letting it continue on its merry way?'

'Yes. Adaptation opportunities are a big thing in certain think tanks now. There are regions due to see more productive climates, they say.'

'I'll bet they do. Well, let's hold them to that. Phil has to keep saying that getting right with the planet has become an industrial activity, and getting there first could be a spur to any nation's economy. It'll be like the dot com boom, only real.'

'Uh huh, uh huh, I'm writing all this down –'

'Yeah right.'

'– but why shouldn't we just let private enterprise take care of it, like they say it will?'

'The free market is not good at disaster recovery. Catastrophe is not profitable.'

'But they say it is.'

'We'll have to point out that it isn't true.'

'Maybe that's why we keep losing.'

'Think positive, Roy. Here, put your legs in first, it works better that way. It's warmer. No way are we going outside unless you agree to put that on. You're so funny!'

'Charlie, do you need to go?'

'No no. Hey, come on! No, not at all. Here we go. Now, what were we saying, that we're doomed to lose this election?'

'No, it's not that, I'm just trying to refine the message.'

'Job creation! Helping people get through the bad weather by stimulating these two new industries, adaptation, then mitigation.'

'The time for a Work Projects Administration may have passed.'

'Roy –'

'I'm just trying to see their next move!'

'You're bumming me out. I'm out in the beautiful white snow, whee!'

'Ooh! Ooh!'

'Okay, Charlie. Call me back, I don't think my ear can handle you guys besporting yourselves like that.'

'Right, think it over and I'll call you back. We won't be out long. Oh but wait just a sec – when I do call back, remind me we should talk about insurance, they might be interested hey Joe! Bye.'

'Bye.'

Charlie hustled after Joe, out into the street. Their street dead-ended right in front of their house, and there was a blanket of snow covering it. Joe kicked around in an ecstasy, his cheeks red, his eyes a brilliant blue. Charlie kicked around behind him, calling, 'Go! Ha! Take that!'

Snow drifted down on them. It was cold but almost windless. Beautiful, really. Maybe they could adapt to any climate.

Well, but that was thinking about individuals, the body in its clothing. The support system more generally might not fare as well: food production, energy . . .

As he danced in the snow, Charlie considered what could be said to the American public to convince them they needed to elect Phil Chase as their next president, rather than the current happy occupant. Incumbents had an advantage; but the Republican party had stood firm, so far, on a policy of denying the existence of climate change. Surely the time was coming when they could be held to account for that heedlessness?

Maybe, maybe not.

The snow lofted down. Looking up it was strange to see so many tiny white missiles plunging down out of the gray cloud that covered the sky, flocking down in waves.

Individual flakes caught in Joe's hair. His mittens were too big; he looked displeased and shook his hands. Angrily he tried to pluck the mittens off, one hand then the other, but both hands were equally impeded.

'DAAAA!'

'No, Joe, wait, don't do that, Joe, your hands will freeze. Cold! Cold!'

'Wanna! Wanna!' Joe flung his arms wildly around him, and off the mittens flew.

'Ah shit, Joe. Come on. We'll have to go back inside if you do that.'

'Wanna snow.'

Happily Joe scooped up loose snow and smooshed it into snowballs to throw at his dad. Quickly his hands turned pink and wet, but he didn't seem to mind. Charlie helped him build a little snowman. Base, torso, head. The new snow cohered very nicely. Seed cones from a low branch for eyes. 'Very cool.'

Joe stood facing it. He put his red wet hands together. 'Namaste,' he said.

Charlie jerked upright. 'What did you say?'

'No ma stay.'

'Oh! You want to go back inside?'

'Owee.' Holding out a red-and-white hand for Charlie's inspection.

'I bet! That looks cold! That's what I was telling you, about the mittens.'

'Too big.'

'Sorry. We'll look for some smaller ones.'

Joe began kicking the snowman. Charlie watched him fondly. This was his Joe, kicking his creation to pieces. Like a sand mandala poured into the river. Huge gusto when wiping a slate clean. His snowsuit looked like it was covered with wet diamonds.

'Come on, let's go back inside. He's all gone now. People won't even know what we did. They'll think that two big tigers have been out here wrestling in the snow.'

'Coo Da.'

Back inside they went to the kitchen and made hot chocolate. They took their cups out by the fire and put them on the coffee table, then wrestled casually, taking breaks to sip chocolate. Joe charged Charlie, slammed into him, then rolled away on the carpet, squealing happily; there was little he liked more, particularly when he knocked Charlie over. He growled like a dog, grunted like a martial artist, shrieked like a banshee; did not cry when he fell down.

Except this time he did; he bonked his head on the radiator and wailed. He just wasn't as tough these days. It took quite a bit of hot chocolate to make it okay. Then it was back to rolling, growling, shouting 'Ha!' or 'Gotcha,' until they were content to lie there in a heap on the carpet. Charlie was exhausted; Joe faked exhaustion for a second, to show what a mighty ordeal it had been to defeat the monster, then sat playing with his trains, shaking his head and proclaiming 'Po Da.'

The fire crackled. Outside the snow fell. Looking up at it from the floor, Charlie had the impression that it was aiming at him and just missing. Maybe this was just the way it was going to be now. Maybe that's the way it had always been. People had lived cocooned in oil for a few generations, but beyond that the world remained the same, waiting for them to re-emerge into it.

Joe was staring into the fire. He whimpered, as in the last gulp of a cry. Charlie leaned over and hugged him, held him; the boy felt hot again, slightly sweaty. He twisted a little, trying to get comfortable, and Charlie resisted an urge to squeeze him tightly; he put his nose into the boy's fine hair, breathed in the faint smell of infancy. All that was going away. He was filled suddenly with a fearful joy, beautiful but frightening, like the snow outside. Snow inside him. They leaned against each other. They sighed one of their synchronized sighs, the same breath filling them, then leaving in a prolonged exhalation. Joe and Da by the fire.

# SIX

# *Optimodal*

***Social Science Experiment in Elective Politics (SSEEP)***

*(notes by Edgardo Alfonso, for Diane Chang, the Vanderwal committee, and the National Science Board)*

*The experiment is designed to ask, if the scientific community were to propose a platform of political goals based on scientific principles, how would it be formulated, and what would the platform say?*
*In other words, what goals for improvement in society and government might follow logically from the aggregate of scientific findings and the application of the scientific method?*

*The platform could conceivably take the form of the 'Contract With America' adopted by the Republican Party before the 1994 election (a kind of list of Things To Do):*

*'Contract with Humanity'*
*'Contract with the Children'*
*'Contract with the Generations to Come'*
*commitment to inventing a sustainable culture*

*(Permaculture, first iteration*
*   – what science is for)*

Some kind of underlying macro-goal or foundational axiom set might have to be synthesized from the particulars of scientific practice and the composite standard model of physical reality expressed by the various disciplines.

1) One axiom or goal might be some form of the 'Greatest good for the greatest number' rubric.

Without implying in any way that this 'greatest good' could include or justify any planned or accepted structural or permanent disadvantaging of any minority of any size. As should be clear in the wording of the rubric, the greatest number is of course one hundred percent, including also the generations to come.

2) Even in the context of any religious or humanistic anthropocentrism, the life of our species depends on the rest of Earth's biosphere. Even the utilitarian view of nature as something distinct and subservient to humanity must grant the biosphere the status of a diffused expression and aspect of our bodies. Interdependence of all the components of biosphere (including humanity) is undeniable. An observable, confirmable fact (breathing).

Given some version of these foundational axioms, the scientific community suggests these platform particulars for government:
    *(preliminary partial list, please add to as you see fit)*

'Contract with Our Children'

1. protection of the biosphere:

*sustainable uses; clean technologies; carbon balance; climate homeostasis.*

2. *protection of human welfare:*
*universal housing, clothing, shelter, clean water, health care, education, reproductive rights*

3. *full employment:*
*Current economy defines 5.4% unemployment as optimum for desired 'wage-pressure balance,' treating labor (people) as a commodity and using a supply/demand pricing model. Five percent in USA = approx. fifteen million people. At the same time there is important work not being done.*

*If government-insured full employment reduced 'wage pressure' (fear), forcing a rise in minimum wages from the private sector, this would help pull millions out of poverty, decrease their government dependence and social service costs, and inject and cycle their larger incomes back into the economy.*

4. *Individual ownership of the majority of the surplus value of one's labor.*

*People create by their work an economic value beyond what it costs to pay them and provide their means of production. This averages $66,000 per year for American workers, a surplus legally belonging to owners/stockholders.*

*American workers therefore receive between a tenth and a fourth of the actual value of their work. The rest goes to owners.*

*A minimum share of 51% of the value of one's work should be returned to one as surplus value beyond salary, this value to be measured by objective and transparent accounting as defined by law.*

*3. and 4. combined would tend to promote the greatest good for the greatest number, by distributing the wealth more equitably among those who have created it.*

## 5. Reduction of military spending

*Match US military expenditures to the average of other nations; this would halve the military budget, freeing over two hundred billion dollars a year.*

*More generally, all national militaries should be integrated in an international agreement upholding non-violent conflict resolution. (Using black helicopters of course.)*

*Disproportionate size of US military and arms industry a waste of resources. Doubling since September 11, 2001 resembles panic response or attempt at global hegemony. Results undermine goals outlined in the foundational axioms.*

## 6. Population stabilization

*Human population stabilized at some level to be determined by carrying capacity studies and foundational axioms. Best results here so far have resulted from increase in women's rights and education; also a goal in itself, thus a powerful positive feedback loop with chance for results within a single generation.*

*Context/ultimate goal: Permaculture*

*A scientifically informed government should lead the way in the invention of a culture which is sustainable perpetually. This is the only normative bequest to the generations to come. It is not adaptive to heavily damage the biosphere when our own offspring and all the generations to follow will need it, like we do, in order to survive. If reproductive success is defined as life's goal, as it is in evolutionary theory, then stealing from descendants is maladaptive.*

*Protection of the environment, therefore, along with restoration of landscapes and biodiversity, should become one of the principal goals of the economy. Government must lead the way in investigating potential climate-altering strategies to mitigate current problems and eventually establish a balance that can be maintained in perpetuity.*

*Process Notes: how to enact platform.*

*Broader outreach. Public discussion. Performance evaluation methodologies. Scientific organizations and universities as information transmitters. Individuals in these organizations as catalysts in information cascade; also, candidates for elections and appointments. Advocacy.*

*Study governing methods in other countries to suggest possible reforms to our system where currently function (democracy) is impaired. Some candidates for study:*

*Swiss presidential model (executive council)*

*Australian ballot (preferential voting)*

*transparency in government (freedom of information, watchdog groups)*

*Diane and the Vanderwal committee sat around the table in the meeting room next to Diane's office. Some shook their heads as they read Edgardo's draft; others just gave up and held their heads in their hands.*

*'Okay,' said Diane. 'Anyone want to add anything else?'*

**The first big windstorm** tore the last leaves off the trees in a rush. It was an amazing thing, and when Frank got out of his van the wind cut into him and he reached back for a windbreaker. The wind was loud in the branches, hooting and keening and whooshing like the roar of distant jets. He ran to the park and stopped on the overlook. Leaves tumbled down into the gorge, the stream was running with them; it looked like a million yellow paper boats had been launched and were now bouncing down the rapids together, covering the water entirely. Frank hooted loudly, 'Ooooooooop!' into the blanketing roar of the wind. Nothing would hear him. It was colder than it had yet been this year.

At his tree he called down Miss Piggy. He had to catch her on an inswing, and the climb was tough, up into piercing cold wind, swinging a little; then over the lip and onto the plywood, in his treehouse.

Only now it was like a crow's nest, swaying back and forth on the top of the mast. 'Wow!' He sat down, belayed himself to the railing. Was it going to be possible to get used to this? He watched the wind toss the forest about. The canopy was a network of black branches and twigs bouncing vigorously in place, a few stubborn leaves flapping like prayer flags. Strong gusts caused the network to course and flow like seaweed in a current, then rebound to their usual violent fluttering in place.

His own tree moved gently back and forth. Rock a bye

baby. It seemed like it would be okay. He was liking it already. 'Ooooop!'

He crawled over to his duffel, opened it and pulled out his largest tent, a North Face South Col. It was very strong and stable, therefore quiet, as tents went. It was meant for two people and a lot of gear.

He screwed ringbolt screws into the plywood, measuring carefully and staking down the tent as he went to make certain it was stretched out tautly.

He pulled the tent poles into their sleeves and posted them into their grommets, leaning into the windswept fabric of the tent until they were secure and all was well. He stepped in; it was really big for a two-person tent, expedition scale for sure, with room to stand right at the high point, sloping quickly down to the four corners. Nylon blue, and in the lantern's glow the color of twilight. It smelled like the mountains.

He moved his duffel and the rest of his stuff inside. Zip the door shut, zooop! and he was in a nylon-walled room. Like a kind of yurt. People had lived in yurts through entire ice ages. This one swayed, but that still seemed okay. It reminded him of waterbeds, back in the day. Rock a bye baby!

He pulled out his sleeping bag, sat on his groundpad, draped the bag over his legs. Arranged his pillows. Everything was slightly blue, including his laptop screen. He regarded all of it with pleasure; this was the bedroom he loved most in all the world, the only constant in all his years of wandering. Nothing lacking, everything at hand, the taut walls curving up aerodynamically.

He got comfortable and tapped around on the laptop. A little reading to help him to sleep. An article in *Nature*, linking paleoclimate and human evolution in a manner similar to the killer frisbee guy's argument: many rapid and severe fluctuations in climate had islanded small human numbers in various refugia, where gene pool and behavioral pockets survived in isolation. When the weather improved, these were the only people left. Thus ice ages as repeated selectors for flexibility, innovation and cooperation.

Another altruism-as-adaptation argument, in other words. Frank wasn't sure it made the case that cooperation had been key. It was a group selection argument, and evolutionary theory was still struggling with the concept of group selection, as opposed to the solid case for kin selection, which one tended to see everywhere in nature. Living things would clearly sacrifice for their kin; whether they would for their group was less sure.

Still, it was interesting to think about. And it combined in a very interesting way with another article in *Nature*, describing the latest in game theory studies of altruism. Prisoner's dilemma was part of it, of course; this simple game had been studied for decades. Two prisoners, kept separately, were asked to testify against the other, to benefit themselves. Rewards were quantified for easy computer trials: if both refused to defect, each earned three points; if they both defected, they earned one point; if one defected and the other didn't, the defector got five points while the sap got zero. A simple game, with a simple if depressing result: in most scenarios one accumulated points fastest by always defecting.

But there were other strategies that sometimes outperformed always-defect, expressed for the computer trials as algorithmic formulas, but given names like tit-for-tat, or firm-but-fair, or irregular firm-but-fair, or even always-generous, which under certain circumstances (climate fluctuation?) could create an upward spiral of maximizing points for both players.

This *Nature* article described some new experiments. Researchers had first tried the game using only always-defect and always-generous strategies – in essence, parasites and hosts. As predicted by previous results, the defectors took over the system; but the average fitness of the population then dropped.

A variant of the game was then introduced, called Snowdrift, in which players were supposedly stuck in cars in the snow, and could either get out and shovel, or not. The generous got points even if the other defected, because eventually their car would be clear. Here cooperators and defectors coexisted stably, in a mix determined by the details of the game rules.

The researchers then mapped the Snowdrift results onto a graph program, finding long tendrils of association between clusters of cooperators. When the tendrils were cut by rule changes, the clusters were destroyed by defectors. The implication was that islanding was dangerous, and that some rules allowed cooperation to prosper while others didn't. It was also interesting to consider what the analog of tendrils would be in real world situations. Extending help to people from other groups, perhaps – as Anna had, for instance, when welcoming the Khembalis into her family's life after they appeared in the NSF building. This kind of generosity could be explained as group selection, but only if the definition of the group was enlarged, perhaps even by some leap of the imagination. Empathy. Someone in the *Journal* recently had suggested this was the story of human history so far, successive enlargement of the sense of the group.

The authors of this *Nature* article went on to tentatively suggest that generosity which held no advantage at all to the giver might be structurally sounder in the long run than generosity that brought some kind of return to the cooperator. The paper concluded with the reminder that at the beginning of life, RNA had had to cooperate with proteins and other molecules to band together and form cells. So clearly cooperation was a necessary component of evolution, and a strong adaptive strategy. The authors of the paper admitted that the reasons for the success of cooperation were not well understood. But certain proteins now ubiquitous in cells must have gotten there by being always generous.

Falling asleep in his tent, swaying gently, Frank thought: Now that is interesting ... suggestive ... something to be tried. I will be like that protein ... or like Anna at work ... I will be

always generous.


Winter came.

His treehouse was now visible from the ground, if one knew what to look for. But who was looking? And if anyone saw it, what could they do about it? Theoretically someone could lie in wait nearby, then arrest him or ambush him. But as he hiked in the park under the bare-limbed skeletal trees, over ground thick with rime-frosted and snow-drifted leaves, he could see sometimes half a mile in all directions, and in truth the park was nearly depopulate. He was much more likely to see deer than people. The only humans out in the area near his treehouse tended to be park staff or other FOG volunteers; and many of these were acquaintances by now. Even strangers did not represent a danger, during the day anyway. People out there in winter were often interested in being alone. You could tell when you spotted them whether this was true or not, in another of those unconscious calculations that the savannah brain was so good at. But mostly he just saw deer. He hiked the empty forest, looking for the auroch and seeing only deer; although once he spotted what looked to him like an ibex, and Nancy ID'ed as a chamois.

The other ferals he spotted were often suffering from the cold, and the sudden absence of leaves. Many of these animals were tropical or subtropical, and even if they could have withstood the cold, the disappearance of the leaves meant their food was gone. Seeing an eland snuffling in a pile of leaves packed into a windrow gave one a new respect for the native animals, who could survive such drastic changes in the environment. It was a tough biome, and the natives were tough customers. The coyotes were even getting kind of brash.

The zoo staff and FOG were now recapturing every endangered feral they could. The ones that remained elusive, or seemed to be doing okay, were aided by heated feeding stations. These were mostly simple two-walled shelters, Ls with their open sides facing south. Frank helped build some, lifting panels and beams of playground plastic to be screwed into place. A few shelters were three-walled, and had trap doors suspended over their open sides, so that the zoo staff could capture animals inside them. None of the FOG members liked it, but it beat a mass die-off.

So now there were parts of the park that seemed like an open-air or unwalled zoo, with animals of many different species hanging out near the shelters and visiting when their kind of food was put out. It looked to Frank like these creatures felt they had returned to the zoo already, and were content to be there.

But not all the ferals came in from the cold. And some of the stubbornnest animals were among those least capable of surviving. The gibbons and siamangs were only going to the shelters that did not have trap doors, and leaving them as soon as they had eaten. The gibbons continued to brachiate through the leafless trees. The siamangs had been seen walking around on the ground, their long arms raised over their heads to keep them from dragging on the ground; it looked like they were trying to surrender and not succeeding, but if they saw people approaching they tarzanned away at high speed.

Both species were also now joining the ferals who were venturing out of the park into the residential neighborhoods nearby, finding sources of heat and food on their own; one siamang had been electrocuted while sleeping on a transformer, but now the rest didn't do that any more. The gibbons Bert and May and their sons had been reported sleeping in a kid's backyard treehouse.

'If they obviously don't want to be recaptured,' Frank said to Nancy, 'then we should help them from the shelters and let them stay feral.' He knew most of the FOG membership felt the same.

But Nancy only said, 'I'm afraid that unless we bring them in, we'll lose a lot of them.'

December days were too short. He tried to get in a brief animal walk at dawn; then it was over to work, where things were hectic as always. Along with the Gulf Stream project, Frank's committee was involved with organizing a series of trials of various clean energy sources, especially solar; they were trying to determine which were closest to ready for mass production, the latest photovoltaics, or flexible mirrors that redirected sunlight to elements that transformed the heat to electricity. Both showed some promise, and trials of the Stirling transformer were making the mirrors look unexpectedly competitive, although the various photovoltaics were always gaining in efficiency, and getting cheaper too. It seemed that one system or other might soon be ready for mass deployment, which would greatly reduce the amount of carbon still being tossed into the atmosphere.

Into these and other matters Frank threw himself, and the work days passed in their usual rush; and then in the dusk, or in full dark, he hiked down into the park and climbed his hanging ladder.

Recline on his groundpad, then, in the open doorway of his tent. Only when it was windy did he retreat fully inside. As long as the air remained still, his heavy sleeping bag had kept him warm on climbs in Alaska and the Canadian Arctic; it would do the same here. And the nights were too beautiful to miss. The highest branches spiked around him like a forest of giant thorns, the stars brilliant through their black calligraphy. He watched the stars, and read his laptop, or a paperback set under the lantern, until sleep came on him; then snuggled into the bag; slept well; woke serene, to the sight of the treetops bobbing and rustling on the dawn breeze.

Lines of blackbirds flew out of town to look for food, under a flat sky of pewter and lead. Really the important thing was to be out in the world, to feel the wind and see the full spaciousness of being on a planet whirling through space. A feeling of beatitude; was that the right word? Sit up, click on the laptop, Google 'beatitude;' then there on the screen:

'**beatitude** dips from on high down on us and we *see*. It is not in us so much as we are in it. If the air come to our lungs, we breathe and live; if not, we die. If the light come to our eyes, we see; else not. And if truth come to our mind we suddenly expand to its dimensions, as if we grew to worlds.'

My. Ralph Waldo Emerson, from a website called Emersonfortheday.net. Frank read a little more: quite amazing stuff. He bookmarked the site, which apparently featured a new thought from the philosopher's writings every few days. Earlier samples read like some miraculously profound horoscope or fortune cookie. Reading them, Frank suddenly realized that the people who had lived before him in this immense hardwood forest had had epiphanies much like his. Emerson, the great Transcendentalist, had already sketched the parameters or the route to a new kind of nature-worshipping religion. His journal entries in particular suited Frank's late night go-to-sleep reading, for the feel they had of someone thinking on the page. This was a good person to know about.

One night after he fell asleep skimming the site, his cell phone jolted him awake. 'Hello?'

'Frank, it's Caroline.'

'Oh good.' He was already sitting up.

'Can you come see me, in the same place?'

'Yes. When will you be there?'

'Half an hour.'

\*       \*       \*

She was sitting on the same bench, under the bronze dancer. When she saw him approaching she stood, and they embraced. He felt her against him. For a long time they breathed in and out, their bodies pressed together. A lot was conveyed, somehow. He could feel that she had been having a hard time – that she was lonely – that she needed him, in the same way he needed her.

They sat on the bench, holding hands.

'So,' she said. 'You've been traveling.'

'Yes?'

'Boston, Atlanta – Khembalung, even?'

'Yes, that's right.'

'But – I mean – I told you this Pierzinski was probably the reason you were listed, right? And Franccsca Taolini is on the list too?'

'Yes, you did.' Frank shrugged. 'I needed to talk to them. I couldn't do my job without talking to them. So I thought I'd go ahead, and see if you noticed any, I don't know – change in my status or whatever.'

'Yes. I did.'

'So, were we taped?'

'No. You mean beyond your office phones? No. Not yet.'

'Interesting.'

She gazed at him curiously. 'You know, this could be serious. It's not a game.'

'I know that, believe me. I'm not thinking of it as a game. More like an experiment.'

'But you don't want to draw any more attention to yourself.'

'I suppose not, but why? What could they do to me?'

'Oh I don't know. Every agency has its inspector general. You could suddenly find your travel expenses questioned, or your outside consulting. You could lose your job, if they really wanted to make it happen.'

'Then I'd just go back to UCSD.'

'I hope you don't do that.'

He squeezed her hand. 'Okay, but tell me more. How did my status change exactly?'

'You went up a level.'

'So my stock rose?'

'It did. But that's a different issue. Your stock rose, fine, but that means it hit an amount that triggered your level of surveillance to go up. At that level, you'll have more intrusive methods applied to you. It's all set in the programs.'

'But why, what for?'

'I'm sure it's something to do with Pierzinski, like you said last time. Taolini was really Googling him after your trip to Boston, him and you both.'

'She was?'

'Yeah. She called up pretty much everything you've ever published. And lots of Pierzinski too. What did you two talk about?'

'She was on the panel I ran that reviewed Pierzinski's proposal.'

'Yes, I know.'

'So, we talked about the work he's doing, stuff like that.'

'She looks like she's cute.'

'Yes.'

He didn't know what to say. She laughed at him, squeezed his hand. Now that he was with her he understood that the others were all just displacements of his real desire. 'So my calls are being recorded?'

'Your office calls, yes. I told you that last time.'

'I guess you did. And my cell phone?'

'They're being recorded now too, but so far no one's actually checking them. They're just saved in your file. If you went up another level or two, they'd be there, and they'd get reviewed.'

'And what about my FOG phone?'

'No, not that one. Isn't that just a walkie-talkie system?'

'Yeah.'

'Those only work off one tower. I have to call your cell, but I don't like doing that anymore. I'm calling you from public phones, so someone would have to make a complete search of your file to find me, but I'm in there if they look hard enough. If someone knows my voice . . . Meanwhile, they can tell where you were when you got calls because of the towers involved.'

'So you know where I am?'

'To an extent. Your van is tagged too. I can see you're spending time over near Rock Creek Park. Have you got a place over there?'

'Yes.'

'You must be renting a room? There aren't any home arrangements showing. No water or electric or home phone or sewage.'

'No.'

'So you're renting a room?'

'Like that, yes.'

She considered him. She squeezed his hand again. 'I . . . well. I hope you trust me.'

'Oh I do. It's just that I'm, I don't know. Embarrassed.'

'Embarrassed?'

'Yes. Only not really.' He met her gaze. 'I live in a treehouse. I'm out in Rock Creek Park, living up in a little treehouse I built.'

She laughed. Then she leaned in and gave him a peck on the cheek. 'Good for you! Will you take me up to it sometime?'

'Oh yes,' he said, warming. 'I'd like that very much.'

She was still leaning into him. They leaned, wordlessly feeling the pressure of arm against arm. Then they shifted, and suddenly were kissing.

It all came instantly back to him, how it felt. He fell headlong back into the space they had occupied when they were trapped in the elevator, as though the intervening months had vanished and they were back there again in an eternal now, passionately making out. Nowhere but in their little bubble universe.

After some indeterminate time, they paused for breath. Such intensity could not be maintained; it had to lead somewhere else, either forward to orgasm or backward to talk. And since they were out on a park bench; since there were still so many questions pricking at other parts of his mind; he fell back toward talk. He wanted to know more –

But then she pulled him back to her to kiss again, and obviously that was a much better idea. Passion blew through him again, sexual passion, my God who could explain it? Who could even remember what it was like?

Again it went on for some time, he couldn't have said how long. The night was cold, her fingers were cool. The city rumbled around them. Distant siren. He liked the feel of her body under her clothes: ribby ribs, soft breasts. The iron solidity of her quads. She squeezed him, gasped and murmured a little, all through their kisses.

Again they came up for air.

'Oh my,' she said. She shifted on the bench, conformed herself to him like a cat.

'Yes.'

His questions slowly resurfaced. He looked down at her face, tucked against his shoulder.

'Are you staying with your friends again?'

'Yes.' She looked at her watch. 'Uh oh.'

'What time is it?'

'Four.'

'Wow. The witching hour.'

'Yes.'

'When do you have to be back?'

'Soon.'

'And . . . look, is there some way I can call you? Is *your* phone tapped?'

290

'Maybe.' She hesitated. 'I don't want to use it for anything important.'

'Ah.' He thought about it. 'There must be some protocols you guys use . . .'

She shook her head quickly. 'It really isn't like that in my department. Although sure, there are methods. We could use phone cards and public phones.'

'We'd have to synchronize.'

'Right, but that's part of the method.'

'Fridays at nine kind of thing.'

'Right. Let's do that. Let's find pay phones we think will work, maybe get a few numbers from a few in a row, so there would be alternates. We'll share them next time I get a chance to call you, and after that we won't be putting anything on your phone. You might get bumped up again any time, the way things are going in the market. You guys are really impressing the investors.' She looked at her watch. 'Ah hell.'

She twisted into him, kissed him again. 'Hmmm,' she said after a while. 'I've gotta go . . .'

'That's okay.'

'Sorry.'

'I understand. You'll call?'

'Yes. When I can. Get those pay phone numbers ready.'

'I will.'

One last kiss and she was off into the night.

**Ooop oop!**

Now Frank went fully optimodal. For a few days he even experienced the 'walking on air' phenomenon, which was surely a physiological effect caused by an incomplete integration of happiness into sense data. Life in his tree, in the winter forest, at the gym, at work, in the restaurants he frequented, out in the brief hour of pale winter evening sun, running or throwing the disks or stalking animals – every day parcellated but full, every night a forest adventure, always alive, always generous. Ooop!

How big the world became in a wind. Everything expanded, inside and out. Hike in the dreamlike black forest, huge and blustery. Evening sky over the black branches, violet in the east shading to aquamarine in the west, all luminous, a Maxfield Parrish sky, only now it was obvious that Parrish had never exaggerated at all, but only done his best to suggest a reality that was so much more vivid and intense than any art.

One evening he tromped into 21 not long after sunset and found only Zeno and Redbeard and Fedpage and a couple more. 'Where is everybody?'

'Over on Connecticut.'

'Seeking the heat, man.'

'What about Chessman, where's he?'

Shrugs all around.

'Haven't seen him for a while.'

'I bet he found a place to stay for the winter. He's smart.'

'Come and go, Doctor Checkmate, come and go.'

Frank couldn't read their attitude. He wondered if the chess hustlers at Dupont Circle might know where Chessman was, and resolved to visit and see. There was nothing more to be learned here.

Snow began to fall, small flakes ticking down. After the first heavy snowfall there had been little more of it; and it was usually this kind of frozen frost, swirling on the wind. The bros noted it gloomily, then wandered off. They had actually built the little shelters Zeno had proposed, Frank saw, in the dip they now called Sleepy Hollow, just to the west of the site. Some of them were already tucked into their low shelters, staring out red-eyed at the fire and the snowflakes. Cardboard, trashbags, branches, sheets of plywood, drop cloths, two-by-fours, cinder blocks: under that, dirty nylon or even cotton sleeping bags, toeing into snowbanks. You needed a groundpad under a sleeping bag for it to work.

Frank found himself annoyed. Living like rats when they didn't have to; it was incompetent. Even if it was all they could find to build with.

It was hard to judge what was happening with them. One time Frank was running with the frisbee guys, completely absorbed in it, when they came into 21 and there was a quartet of young black men, wearing multiple cotton hooded sweatshirts, hands deep in their pockets. Spencer pulled up sharply and turned to the tables. 'Hey how's it going?'

'Oh good!' Zeno said sarcastically. 'Real good! These brothers are wondering if we have any *drugs* to sell.'

'*You* guys?' Spencer laughed, and Robert and Robin echoed him as they flanked him on both sides, their golf disks held before them like Oddjob's hat. Frank was just comprehending the situation when the young men joined the laughter, smiles flashing in the gloom, and headed down Ross without a farewell.

293

'Catch you guys,' Spencer said as he moved on to the next tee.

'Yeah, catch you,' Zeno growled. 'Fucking drop by any time.'

At work that week, a group from NOAA came over to share their analysis of the Gulf Stream stall. They had done the calculations and modeling necessary to say something quantitative about the idea of restarting the far north downwelling, and Diane had asked General Wracke and several members of the Science Board to attend. The NOAA PI ran them through a quick recap of the problem: fresh water cap introduced onto the surface of the far north Atlantic, reducing salinity and raising the water temperature both; normal temperatures for this month averaged −1.2 C, so melted ice actually warmed it. Density was a function of salinity and temperature combined, which was why the movement of sea water was called the thermohaline cycle. Before the fleet of Arctic icebergs had arrived, the surface in the downwelling regions had had a salinity of 31.0 p.s.u. (practical salinity units; these were measured in various ways, but a p.s.u. was still roughly equivalent to how many grams of salt per kilogram of water). Now the surface salinity was 29.8, the temperature −1.0 C. Following the PI's red laser dot down the isopycnals on her graph, they could see just how much salinity would have to be bumped to make the cap dense enough to sink down into the water underneath it.

The biggest downwelling region had been north of Iceland and east of Greenland, but the PI explained that all that region was not equally involved. Currents branching from the great current had flowed north and east almost to the coast of Norway, then turned left toward Greenland in very predictable currents, slowing and then swirling down in giant whirlpools that were thirty or fifty kilometers wide, but only three or four centimeters deep. These whirlpools were visible only to satellite laser altimetry, where false color graphing could make them psychedelically obvious. They had been relatively stable in location, presumably constrained by the sea bottom, the nearest coastline configurations, the force of the currents, and the Coriolis force.

They were small areas compared to the total surface of the ocean, so that the idea of restarting the current did not seem immediately impossible; but as the PI pointed out, one could not restart the circulation merely by increasing density at the old downwelling sites in isolation, separated from the thrust of the Gulf Stream by some hundreds of kilometers of stalled and unusually fresh water. It would be necessary to draw the full momentum of the Gulf Stream back up to the old sites again, by causing surface water to sink just north of the current downwelling sites, then continue the process, in Pied Piper fashion, until they had drawn the Gulf Stream up behind them and could dump as much as needed in the old down-welling locations. This was the only method that the NOAA team could think of to renew the flow; but it added greatly to the amount of water that they had to make sink. To 'isopy-cnalate,' as Edgardo called it.

Extensive computer modeling of various scenarios had led them to believe that in order to create the masses of sinking water necessary, they would have to alter its salinity about two p.s.u., from 29.8 to 31.6 – meaning the addition of about two grams of salt for every kilogram of water they had to alter. The necessary volume of water was a much less certain thing, depending as it did on various assumptions plugged into the model, but the minimal volume they had gotten to get good results totaled approximately five thousand cubic kilometers of water. About a thousand kilograms per cubic meter of water, depending on temperature; two grams of salt per kilogram of water . . . thus, about ten billion kilograms of salt.

Five hundred million tons.

Someone whistled.

'Just how much salt is that?' Frank asked.

Edgardo and General Wracke laughed. Diane smiled but said to the NOAA people, 'Can you give us a sense of what that means in terms of volumes, availability, shipping capacities and so on?'

'Yes, I'm sure we can. We would have done that already but we just finished the analysis this morning. But I have to say, you know, before we get to that part, that we're still very uncertain about the wisdom of trying this at all. I mean we don't really know what effect it will have, and just going by the law of unintended consequences –'

'Please!' Edgardo said, raising a hand. 'No more of this law of unintended consequences! There is no such law. You hear this said and then you look for the equation that expresses this law, or even the principle, and there is no equation or principle. There is just the observation that actions have unintended consequences, though sometimes they matter and other times they don't. It's like saying "Shit happens."'

'Okay, maybe you're right. Although shit does happen.'

'Just look into the practicalities of gathering and moving that quantity of salt,' Diane said with her little smile. 'It may be completely impossible, in which case no consequences will follow.'

At night the trees of the forest were bare black statues, fractal and huge. There were points from which one could see down great lengths of the gorge. The snow was still rather thin on the ground, drifted into banks against the flood windrows and then icing over, leaving uneven layers of slimy black leaves underfoot. The resulting black-and-white patchwork made the topography of the park almost impossible to read, a kind of Rorschach space in which the tossing branches of the canopy were the best way to stay oriented to the ravine's forms. The wind hooted and roared like the air choir of the world, gibbons had nothing on the winter forest as far as vocalizations were concerned. Ooooooooooooooooooo!

Bouncing patterns, shifting whether he walked or not, and yet somehow the brain made the picture cohere. But sometimes it didn't, and briefly he would be in an abstract world, all pattern, shifting shifting – ah, that was Military Road bridge – and then a sudden understanding of what he was seeing would snap back into place with its customary 'YOU ARE HERE' function. It was remarkable just how much understanding one lost when the visual field went haywire like that – not just what one saw, but where one was, who one was; a glitch in which everything blanked for a moment, pure consciousness caught in a mystery – then bang, all the explanations falling back in at once, leaving only a faint memory of absence.

He was the paleolithic in the park. A recent article in *The Journal of Sociobiology* had reminded him of the man in the ice, a man who had died crossing a Tyrolean pass some five thousand years before. He had lain there frozen in a glacier until something, perhaps global warming, had caused him to emerge and be discovered, in 1991. All his personal possessions had been preserved along with his body, giving archeologists a unique look at the technology of his time. Reading the inventory of his possessions, Frank had noticed how many correlations there were between his gear and the man in the ice's. Probably both kits were pretty much what people had carried in the cold for the last fifty thousand years.

The Alpine man had worn a coat made of sewn furs, the stitching very fine, all similar in design and effect to the down jacket Frank was wearing at that very moment. The Alpine man had worn a fanny pack like Frank's, filled with several small tools that added up to the equivalent of Frank's Swiss Army knife. The Alpine man's unfinished bow stave and copper-headed axe (a marvel) had no ready equivalent in Frank's equipment, though the axe resembled the ice axe he kept in his treehouse; and he had taken to carrying his Acheulian hand axe around with him, in his fanny pack or even sometimes in his hand, just for the pleasure of the heft of it. It might even do a little good, in terms of personal defense; there were more and more people in the park, including some little gangs that did not look good to Frank. Not to mention the jaguar.

The Alpine man had worn a backpack made of wood and fur, quite similar in design to Frank's nylon backpack; inside it were stuff sacks. A birch bark container had been designed to carry live embers, and there was also a little stone bowl in which to place flammable stuff to light by striking flints; all that equivalent to Frank's handy cigarette lighter. Frank also had a little Primus stove up in the treehouse, a primitive-looking steel thing that roared like a blowtorch and was almost as hot. How the Alpine man would have loved that! In effect Frank had a little bottle of fire he could light anywhere. The technological sublime indeed, when he had a little pot of coffee or soup on the boil.

The Alpine man had also carried a flat circular piece of white marble, holed through its middle. A loop of leather ran through the central hole, and a number of smaller leather loops were tied around through the main loop: this 'tassel' as the archeologists called it, looked to Frank like a sling of carabiners. It was the one possibly non-utilitarian piece on the man (though his skin had also displayed tattoos). The birch fungus in his fanny pack had perhaps been medicinal, like the aspirin in Frank's bathroom bag.

All down the list, familiar stuff. People still carried around things to do the same things. Frank's kit had a provenance of thousands of years. It was a beautiful thought, and made him happy. He was Alpine man!

And so when he hiked into site 21 and saw again the bros' ramshackle shelters, he said, 'Come on, guys. Let's try to get up to paleolithic code, eh? I brought along a roll of ripstop nylon this time, check it out. First class army-navy surplus, it'll match your camo flak jacket color scheme.'

'Yarrrr, fuck you!'

'Come on, I'm going to cut you all a tarp off the roll. Everyone in the park is under this stuff but you.'

'How you know?'

'You Santa Claus?'

'He knows because he give it to them all is how.'

'Yeah that's right. Just call me Johnny Appletent.'

'Har har har! Perfesser Appletent!'

They cackled as he measured out rectangles of about ten by six, then cut them off with the scissors on his Swiss army knife. He showed them how the nylon could be secured, in many cases right on top of their already existing shelters. 'Dry means warm, bros, you know that.' A well-set tarp was a complete home in itself, he told them. Sides down to the ground, suspend the middle on a line, high enough to sit up in at one end, don't worry about how low the rest of it was. The lower the warmer, except don't let it come down on bottom of sleeping bag. Get plastic to put under the bags for God's sake.

It was the kind of camp work that Frank enjoyed. He wandered around among them as they fiddled, evaluating their obstacles and the solutions they were concocting to circumvent them. They were inept, but it was a learned skill. Winter camping. Maybe they had only stayed out in the summertime before, and in previous winters sought conventional shelter. Winter backpacking was a very technical matter – well, ultimately simple; but it took attention to detail, it was a meticulous thing if you wanted to stay comfortable. A technique. The Alpine man would have been superb at it. And now they were all being carried up to the heights.

The bros lay there watching him or not, Andy calling 'Watch out, will ya.' Some lit cigarettes and blew plumes of smoke onto the new insides of their tarps, frosting them grayly.

'The first wind'll knock that down on you,' Frank warned Andy. 'Tie that far corner out to that tree.'

'Yeah yeah.'

'Here, I am going to save your lazy ass.'

They all laughed at this.

'He's saving us now! Look out!'

'Preacher Pastor Perfesser.'

'Yeah right!' Frank objected. 'The Church of Dry Toes.'

They liked this.

By the time all the tarps were set Frank's hands were white and red. He swung them around for a while, feeling them throb back to life, looking around at the scene. You could see another fire down toward the zoo.

He bid them good-night. They mumbled things. Zeno said, 'Nyah, get your ass outta here, quit bothering us with your crap, goddamn Peace Corps bleeding heart charity pervert think you know what you're doing out here fuck that shit, get out a here.'

'You're welcome.'


Another night, through the snowy forest under a full moon: a solid snowfall had come down at last, and now surreal whiteness blanketed everything, every bump and declivity suddenly defined by the snow's infinitely shaded luminosity. Low cloud, noctilucent on the western half of the sky, every black stroke of branch and twig distinct against it, wind and even a bit of snow whirling down, the flakes catching the moonlight and sparking like bits of mica among the stars. The world all alive. 'The great day in the man is the birth of perception.' (Emersonfortheday, February 22nd.)

Frank had taken his snowshoes and ski poles out of the storage unit in Arlington, and now he cruised over the drifts. In many places the snowshoes were not needed, but they saved him from postholing into taller drifts, so they were worth it.

No need to turn on his miner's headlamp tonight! It was light you could read by.

He came on a black thing half-buried in snow. He stopped, fearing some child had died of exposure, thinking of Chessman. But when he knelt by the form he saw that it was a wombat. 'Ah shit.'

Two, actually. Mother and infant, it looked like. Frank called in the GPS location on his FOG phone, cursing sadly as he did. 'God damn it. You poor guys.'

It looked like Nancy was right. They needed to recover the warm weather ferals. 'Yeah,' she confirmed when he called her next day, 'a lot of them aren't making it. The shelters are helping, but we really have to bring them back in.'

'I hope we can,' Frank said.

At work Frank continued to hack away at his list of Things To Do, which nevertheless continued to grow at the bottom faster than he removed things at the top. Settling in after a session at Optimodal, his days for a while were mostly concerned with:

1) arranging small business exploratory grants for the photovoltaic programs with the most robust results. These were getting rather exciting, actually. Progress in this field was measured by efficiency and cost. Efficiency as the percentage of photonic energy striking the cell transferred to electrical energy, now reaching well above forty percent; and cost, now down to six cents per kilowatt-hour, very competitive with any other form of energy generation. Switching over to solar would be a major expense, but after that the possibilities were rather staggering. One of the grantees calculated that it would soon be possible, theoretically, to power the entire country from a ten-mile by ten-mile photovoltaic array located in some sunny desert location in the Southwest.

2) keeping in touch with the people establishing the Max Planck equivalent in San Diego. This was proceeding nicely, and the Scripps Institution of Oceanography had pitched in to help, seeing that a federal research center in climate issues would very often require their help, and send funding their way, becoming another component of the already powerful UCSD research complex. The old Torrey Pines Generique facility was being remodeled and equipped, and a lot of hires about to be made. The people involved were already aware of Yann, Marta and their colleague Eleanor, and were preparing a salary and research funding offer for all three, a really impressive package deal.

3) consulting with the various people in-house trying to deal with the SSEEP melodrama, already a mess. The platform had been released as a National Academy of Sciences study, but the connection to NSF was well-known. Scientific organizations and op-ed pages had weighed in on the matter of a 'scientific political platform' – whether it was possible, whether it was a good idea, whether it was dangerous, either to science or society. Some of the usual suspects in the science world had quickly disavowed any knowledge of such a program, attacking it as unscientific and inappropriate; while others had surprised Frank by welcoming the move and suggesting additions and modifications to the platform. Attacks in Congress and the press were common, and sometimes exhibited the kind of spluttering rage indicative of a fear-based response. Phil Chase had immediately embraced the platform as a scientifically backed version of what he had been advocating for many years. As he was emerging as the clear frontrunner in the race for the Democratic nomination, outraising a tired and undistinguished pack of competitors two-to-one even when all their contributions were combined, this looked to Frank to be an interesting convergence of political forces.

4) looking into a new analysis of the Sekercioglu study which

had claimed that the bird extinctions they were now seeing on every continent, up to two thousand species in the coming century, were going to leave gaps in ecological function so serious that whole biomes might crash. Things like pollination and dispersal of seed, predation and fertilization, the list went on. At first it seemed odd to think of birds as so crucial, but of course they were very ancient elements of the system. So Frank got to think about the algorithms in biodiversity theory, a welcome dip into math and theory – and damned if the corridors in habitat network theory didn't look just like the tendrils in Snowdrift, in the version of the game in which always generous prospered.

5) investigating amorphous or glassy metals, in particular amorphous steel, made by a new method that scrambled the atomic structures of the metal by yttrium, chromium and boron, making the resulting 'glassy steel' stronger, non-magnetic, and less corrosive. The Navy was interested in making ship hulls of this stuff, and it seemed to the materials team working with Frank that all kinds of ocean-proofed machinery could perhaps be improved, enough so that practical methods of tapping into the ocean's energy might be built.

6) talking to General Wracke over the phone about the salt-mining and transport capabilities of modern civilization. Wracke was upbeat; the quantities being discussed were not completely off the charts when compared to the amount of oil shipped around the globe, and the oil tanker fleet included a significant percentage of single-hulled ships due to be replaced, or rather overdue. As for salt availability, they were still looking into it, but as the general said, 'There's a lot of salt in this world.'

Money was a different matter. The Pentagon had recently gotten in trouble with Congress, Wracke said, for its practice of hiding money left over at the ends of budget years, then using these savings for its own purposes, calling them 'reprogrammed funds.' Congress did not approve, and any high-profile project was likely to have to get conventional funding.

'Does it look like it will be expensive?' Frank asked.

'Depends what you call expensive. Billions for sure.'

'Can you be more specific?'

'I'll get back to you on that.'

'Thanks. Oh – different subject – does the Pentagon have an intelligence service of its own?'

Wracke laughed. 'Is that a trick question?'

'No, how could it be?'

'You'll have to ask the CIA about that. But yes, sure. After the other intelligence agencies in this town let us down so bad, we almost had to have one, to get good data. We were the ones getting killed you know. So there's the Strategic Support Branch, and they're an intelligence-gathering unit publicly acknowledged. They're sometimes a bit more hands-on than the other agencies, but gathering intelligence is their job. Why, is there some secret climate group you're having trouble with? Clandestine cloud seeding?'

'No no. I was just curious. Thanks. See you at the next meeting.'

'I look forward to it. You guys are doing great.'

In that same couple of weeks, along with everything else, Frank made an effort to locate Chessman. He centered the search on Dupont Circle, because that was the city's outdoor chess epicenter. So much so, he found, that chesshounds converged on it from everywhere, and of course dispersed back out, using all eleven of the streets that converged there. To ask about a young black kid was to ask about more than half the chess-playing population, and no one appreciated an inquiry framed that broadly. His motives also appeared to be questioned. So after a while, rather than ask, Frank simply

304

walked and watched, played and lost and walked again, checking out the games, noting also the new little semi-winterized shelters popping up here and there all over town.

Cleveland Park sported many of these camps, especially in the fringe of buildings damaged by the flood and abandoned. Spencer's crowd, clearly, as well as others less organized and competent. It seemed from his observations that the homeless population of Northwest alone must be in the thousands. The formal shelters and newspaper reports gave similar numbers. Between the Klingle Valley Park and Melvin Hazen Park, both small tributary ravines dropping into Rock Creek, there were many abandoned houses. If they had not been burned out, or even if they had, squatters were likely to be occupying them.

This made for a very quiet neighborhood. No one wanted to attract the attention of the police. Any lit windows Frank gave a wide berth on principle, and so apparently did everyone else. Good avoidance protocols make good neighbors. Chessman might be tucked away in one of these hulks, but if so Frank wasn't going to find out by knocking on doors or looking in windows.

And he doubted the youth would be in any of them anyway. Chessman had had a healthy propensity for staying outdoors.

That being the case, where was he?

Then Frank ran into Cutter out on Connecticut, and a tendril connected two parcels in his mind. 'Cutter, do you know what happened to Chessman?'

'No, I ain't seen him lately. Don't know what happened to him.'

'Do you know anyone who might?'

'I don't know. Maybe Byron, he used to play chess with him. I'll ask.'

'Thanks, I'd appreciate that. Do you know what his real name was, by chance?'

'No, only thing I heard him called was Chessman.'

\* \* \*

305

Out in the park proper the forest now seemed wilderness, with most human sign snowed over or overgrown or flooded away. It was a whole world. Firelight in the distance the only touch of humanity. A kind of Mirkwood or primeval forest, every tree Yggdrasil, and Frank the Green Man. Encountering a structure now was like stumbling on ruins. The Carter Barron amphitheater and the huge bridges south of the zoo looked like the work of Incans or Atlanteans.

The campfires in the park, unlike the squatter houses, could be investigated. It was possible to approach them surreptitiously, to put them under surveillance, to see if any of the little firelit faces were known to him. Stalking, pure and simple. Peering around trees, over flood snags, now flanked by snowdrifts. Rain had hardened the snow. Stepping through the crust made a distinct crunchy noise. One had to float on top with one's weight on the back foot until the next step was pressed home. Time for the tiger mind to come to the fore. Someone had reported seeing the jaguar, east of the park.

Once he came on a single old man shivering before a smoky little blaze, obviously sick, and he roused him and asked him if he could get himself out to one of the homeless shelters on Connecticut, or the ER at the UDC hospital; but stubbornly the old man turned away from him, not quite coherent, maybe drunk, but maybe sick. All Frank could do was call 911 and give GPS coordinates, and wait for an EMS team to hike in and take over. Even if you were healthy, living out here was a tenuous thing, but for a sick person it was miserable. The paramedics ended up talking him onto a stretcher and carrying him out. The next night Frank passed by again, as part of his rounds, to see if the man had returned and if he was okay. No one there, fire out.

And never a sign of Chessman. The longer it went on the less likely it seemed Frank would ever find him. He must have moved to a different part of the city, or out of the metro area entirely.

One evening before climbing into his treehouse Frank hiked under the moon, in a stiff north wind that tossed the branches up and down and side to side, a glorious skitter-skatter of black lines against gray sky. When he headed north the wind shoved his breath right into his lungs. How big the world seemed with the moonlight on the snow.

Then he came over the rise next to site 21 and saw around its fire shouting figures, fighting furiously. 'Hey!' he cried, rushing down in a wild glissade. Something hit the fire and sparks exploded out of it; Frank saw a figure swing something to hit one of the prone bros, and as Frank plunged through the last trees toward him, shouting and pulling the hand axe from his fanny pack, the man looked up and Frank saw suddenly that it was the crazy guy who had chased him off Highway 66 in his pick-up truck. Frank screamed and leaped forward feet first, kicking the man right above the knees. The man went down like a bowling pin and Frank jumped up over him with the hand axe ready to strike, then the man rolled to the side and Frank saw that he was not in fact the driver of the pick-up, he had only looked like him. Then Frank was down.

He was on his knees and elbows and his hands were at his face, trying uselessly to catch the rush of blood from his nose. He didn't know what had hit him. Blood was shooting out both nostrils and he was also swallowing it as fast as he could so that he wouldn't choke on it. He felt nothing, but blood shot out in a black flood, he saw it pool on the ground under him. He heard voices but they sounded distant. Don't, he thought. Don't die.

Charlie was startled out of a dream in which he was protesting, 'I can't do it, I can't –' and so his first words into the phone no doubt sounded like an objection: 'Ha, what, what?'

'Charlie, this is Diane Chang.'

Charlie saw his bedside clock's red 4:30 AM and his heart pounded. 'What is it?'

'I just got a call from the UDC Hospital. They told me that Frank Vanderwal was admitted to their ER about three hours ago with a head injury.'

'How bad is it? Is he all right?'

'Yes, but he has a concussion, and a broken nose, and he lost a lot of blood. Anyway, I'm going there now, I was just leaving for work anyway, but it'll take me a while to get to the hospital, and I realized it's near you and Anna and that you know Frank. You guys were the second number on his who-to-call form. So I thought you might be able to go over.'

'Sure,' Charlie said. 'I can be there in fifteen minutes.'

Anna was sitting up beside him, saying 'What, what is it?'

'Frank Vanderwal's been injured. He'll be all right, but he's over at UDC Hospital. Diane thought – well here.' He handed her the phone and got up to dress. When he was ready to go Anna was still on the phone with Diane. Charlie kissed the top of her head and left.

He drove fast through the nearly empty streets. In the hospital ER receiving room the fluorescent lights hummed loudly. The nurses were matter-of-fact, pacing themselves for the long haul.

They treated Charlie casually; people came in like this all the time. Finally one of them led him down the concrete-floored hallway to a curtained-off enclosure on the right.

There Frank lay, pale in his hospital whites, wired up and IVed. Two black eyes flanking a swollen red nose, and a bandage under his nose covered much of his upper lip.

'Hey, Frank.'

'Hey, Charlie.' He did not look surprised to see him. Behind his black eyes he did not look like anything could surprise him.

'They said your nose is broken and you've been concussed.'

'Yes, I think that's right.'

'What happened?'

'I tried to break up a fight.'

'Jesus. Where was this?'

'In Rock Creek Park.'

'Wow. You were out there tracking the zoo animals?'

Frank frowned.

'Never mind, it doesn't matter.'

'No, I was out there. Yes. I've been out there a lot lately. They've been trying to recapture the ferals, and they don't all have radio collars.'

'So you were out there at night?'

'Yeah. A lot of animals are out then.'

'I see. Wow. So what hit you?'

'I don't know.'

'What's the last thing you remember?'

'Well, let's see . . . I saw a fight. I ran down to help. Some people I know were being attacked. Then something hit me.'

'Never mind,' Charlie said. Thinking seemed to pain Frank. 'Don't worry about it. Obviously you got hit by something.'

'Yes.'

'Does your face hurt bad? It looks terrible.'

'I can't feel it at all. Can't breathe through it. It bled for a long time. It's still bleeding a little inside.'

'Wow.' Charlie pulled a chair over and sat by the bed.

After a while a different nurse came by and checked the monitor. 'How are you feeling?' she asked.

'Strange. Am I concussed?'

'Yes, like I told you.'

'Anything else?'

'Broken nose. Maxillary bone, cracked in place. Some cuts and bruises. The doctor sewed you up a little inside your mouth – there, inside your upper lip, yes. When the anesthetic wears off it will probably hurt more. Sorry. We put some blood back in you, and your blood pressure is looking, let's see . . . good. You took quite a whack there.'

'Yes.'

The nurse left. The two men sat under the fluorescent lights, among the blinking machinery. Charlie watched Frank's heartbeat on the monitor. It was fast.

'So you've been going into Rock Creek Park at night?'

'Sometimes.'

'Isn't that dangerous?'

Frank shrugged. 'I didn't think so. A lot of the animals are nocturnal.'

'Yes.' Charlie didn't know what to say. He realized he didn't know Frank all that well; had met him only in party contexts really, except for the trip to Khembalung, but that had been a busy time. Anna collected odd people, somehow. She liked Frank, always with an undercurrent of exasperation, but he amused her. And Nick really enjoyed doing the zoo thing with him.

Now he fell asleep. Charlie watched him breathe through his mouth. Strange to see such a distant and even self-contained person in such a vulnerable state.

Diane arrived, then Anna called as she was getting Nick up for school, wanting to know how Frank was. Frank woke up and Charlie handed his phone to him; he now looked slightly embarrassed, and definitely more alert. 'Conked in the nose,' he was saying to Anna as Diane pulled Charlie out into the hall. 'I don't remember very much.'

'Listen,' Diane said, 'Frank only had a driver's license and NSF card on him, and both had his address from last year. Do you know where he's living now?'

Charlie shook his head.

Diane said, 'He told me he had found a place over near you.'

'Yes – he's been joining us for dinner sometimes, and I think he said he had a place over near Cleveland Park, I'm not sure.' Frank seldom talked about himself, now that Charlie thought of it. He looked at Diane, shrugged; she frowned and led him back to Frank's bedside.

Frank handed Charlie his cell phone. Anna wanted Charlie to come home and watch Joe, so she could visit the hospital.

'Sure. Although I think they're going to release him soon.'

'That's good! Well, maybe I can drive him home.'

Charlie said, 'Anna says she'll come over and be able to give you a ride home when you're released.'

Frank nodded. 'I'll have to get my van. She can drive me to it.' He frowned suddenly.

'That's fine, we'll take care of that. But I wonder if you should drive, actually.'

'Oh sure. It's just a broken nose. I have to get my van.'

Charlie and Diane exchanged a glance.

Charlie said hesitantly, 'You know, we live near here, maybe we could help you get your van to our place, and you could rest up there until you felt well enough to drive home.'

'It doesn't actually hurt.' Frank thought it over. 'Okay,' he said at last. 'Thanks. That would be good.'

Frank was discharged that afternoon, by which time Anna had visited and gone on to work, and Charlie had returned with Joe. Before going out to get his car, Charlie checked at the desk. 'I'm driving him home. Did he give you a home address?'

'4201 Wilson.' That was the NSF building.

Charlie thought about that as he drove Frank back to their house. He said, 'I can take you home instead if you want.'

'No that's okay. I need to be taken back to my van so I can pick it up.'

'There's no rush with that. You need some food in you.'

'I guess,' Frank said. 'But I need to get my van before it gets towed. Tonight is the night that street has to be cleared for the street-cleaners.'

'I see.' How come you know that, Charlie didn't say. 'Okay, we'll get it first thing after dinner. It shouldn't be that late.'

The other Quiblers had welcomed Frank in with a great fanfare, marveling at his bulbous red nose and his colorful black eyes. Anna got take-out from the Iranian deli across the street, and after a while Drepung dropped by, having heard the news. He too marveled as he scooped clean the take-out boxes; Frank had had little appetite.

In the kitchen Charlie told Drepung about Frank's mystery housing. 'Even Diane Chang didn't know where he lives. I'm wondering now if he isn't living out of the back of his van. He bought it right after he left his apartment in Virginia. And he knows which night of the week the street he's parked on gets cleaned.'

'Hmmm,' Drepung said. 'No, I don't know what his situation is.'

Out at the dining room table Drepung said to Frank, 'I know you are from San Diego, and I don't suppose you have family in this area. I was wondering if, while you are convalescing, you would move in with us at the embassy house.'

'But you have all those refugees from the island.'

'Yes, well, but we have an extra bed in Rudra Cakrin's room, you see. No one wants to take it. And he is studying English now, as you know, so . . .'

'I thought he had a tutor.'

'Yes, but now he needs a new one.'

312

Frank cracked a little smile. 'Fired another one, eh?'

'Yes, he is not a good student. But with you it will be different. And you once told me you had an interest in learning Tibetan, remember? So you could teach each other. It would help us. We can use help right now.'

'Thanks. That's very kind of you.' Frank looked down, nodded without expression. It seemed to Charlie that the concussion was still having its way with him. And no doubt a monster headache. Drepung went to the kitchen to boil water for tea. 'Not Tibetan tea, I promise! But a good herb tea for headache.'

'Okay,' Frank said. 'Thanks. Although I don't really have a headache. I'm not sure why. I can't feel my nose at all.'

# SEVEN

## *The Cold Snap*

*The weather got worse. The new year's January saw:*

*High temperature in London for the week of Jan 10, –26 F. In Lisbon, a 60 degree drop in 7 minutes. Snow in San Diego, snow in Miami. New York Harbor froze over, trucks drove across. Reunion Island: 235 inches of rain in ten days. In Montana, temp dropped 100 F in 24 hours, to –56 F. In South Dakota the temperature rose 60 degrees in 2 minutes. On Hawaii's big island, 12 inches rain in an hour. In Buffalo, New York, 30 foot snowdrifts, all from snow blown in from frozen Lake Erie, on 60 mph winds. Reindeer walked over fences from the zoo and went feral. On the Olympic peninsula in Washington, a single down-draft knocked over forest trees estimated at 8 million board feet of lumber.*

*In a North Sea storm similar to that of 1953, Holland suffered four hundred dead and flooding up to 27 miles inland.*

*February was worse. That February saw:*

*A storm in New England with 92 mph winds. Waterloo, Iowa, had 16 days straight below 0 F. 7 inches snow in San Francisco. Great Lakes totally frozen over. Snow in LA stopped traffic. Ice in New Orleans blocked the Mississippi river. –66 F in Montana. 100 mph winds in Sydney, Australia.*

*Feb 4, 180 tornadoes reported, 1,200 killed; named the 'Enigma Outbreak.'*

*A low-pressure system experiencing extremely rapid intensification of the kind called 'bombogenesis' brought 77 inches of snow in one day, Maine. Storm surge was 12 foot high. Reunion Island, 73 inches rain in 24 hours. Winds 113 mph in Utah. Rhine floods caused 60 billion dollars damage. An Alberta hailstorm killed 36,000 ducks.*

*A thunderstorm complex with winds of hurricane force, called a derecho, struck Paris and surrounding region, 20 billion in damage. 150 mph wind storm in Oslo. Two Bengal tigers escaped a Madison Wisconsin zoo in a tornado. Thousands of fish fell in a storm on Yarmouth, England.*

*165 mph winds make a category 5 storm; there had been three in US history; two struck Europe that February, in Scotland and Portugal.*

*At that point they were only halfway through February. Soon it would be Washington's turn.*

*During 1815's 'year without summer,' after the Tambora volcano exploded, temperatures worldwide lowered by 37 F average.*

**As soon as he** felt he could make an adequate display of normality to the Quiblers, Frank thanked them for their hospitality and excused himself. They regarded him oddly, he thought, and he had to admit it was a bit of a stretch to claim nothing was wrong. Actually he felt quite bizarre.

But he didn't want to tell them that. And he didn't want to tell them that he had no place to go. So he stood in their doorway insisting he was fine. He could see Anna and Charlie glance at each other. But it was his business in the end. So Charlie drove him down to his van, and after a final burst of cheerful assurances he was left alone.

He found himself driving around Washington D.C. It was like the night he lost his apartment; again he wasn't sure what to do. He drove aimlessly, and without deciding anything, found himself back on the streets west of Rock Creek Park.

His nose and the area behind it were still numb, as if shot with Novocain. He had to breathe through his mouth. The world tasted like blood. Things out the windshield were slightly fogged, slightly distant, as if at the wrong end of a telescope.

He wasn't sure what to do. He could think of any number of options, but none of them seemed quite right. Go back to his tree? Drive to the NSF basement? Try to find a room? Return to the ER?

He had no feeling for which course to pursue. Like the area behind his nose, his sense of inclination was numb.

It occurred to him that he might have been hit hard enough to damage his thinking. He clutched the steering wheel as his pulse rose.

His heartbeat slowed to something more normal. Do anything. Just do anything. Do the easiest thing. Do the most adaptive thing.

He sat there until he got too cold. To stay warm on a night like this one he would have to either drive with the heater on, or walk vigorously, or lie in the sleeping bag in the back of the van, or climb his tree and get in the even heavier sleeping bag there. Well, he could do any of those, so . . .

More time had passed. Too cold to stay still any longer, he threw open the driver's door and climbed out.

Instant shock of frigid air. Reach back in and put on windpants, gaiters, ski gloves. Snowshoes and ski poles under one arm. Off into the night.

No one out on nights like these. At the park's edge he stepped into his snowshoes, tightened the straps. Crunch crunch over hard snow, then sinking in; he would have posted through if he had been in boots. So the snowshoes had been a good idea. Note to self: when in doubt, just do it. Try something and observe the results. Good-enough decision algorithm. Most often the first choice, made by the unconscious mind, would be best anyway. Tests had shown this.

Out and about, under the stars. The north wind was more obvious in the Rock Creek watershed, gusting down the big funnel and cracking frozen branches here and there. Snaps like gunshots amidst the usual roar of the gale.

No one was out. No fires; no black figures in the distance against the snow; no animals. He poled over the snow as if he were the last man on Earth. Left behind on some forest planet that everyone else had abandoned. Like a dream. When the dream becomes so strange that you know you're going to wake up, but then you discover that you're already awake – what then?

Then you know you're alive. You find yourself on the cold hill's side.

Back at site 21. He had come right back to the spot where he had gotten hurt, maybe it wasn't wise. He circled it from above for a while, checking to be certain it was empty. No one out. What if you had a world and then one night you came home to it and it was gone? This sometimes happened to people.

He clattered down to the picnic tables, sat on one, unbuckled his snowshoes. He looked around. Sleepy Hollow was empty, a very unappetizing snowy trench with black mud sidewalls, the sorry little shelters all knocked apart. Tables bare. The fire out. Ashes and charcoal, all dusted with snow.

Strange to see.

So . . . He had run in from the direction of the zoo. Knocked one of the assailants down; funny how that skinny face and moustache had fooled him, taken him back to an earlier trauma; but only for a second. Facial recognition was another quick and powerful unconscious ability.

So. He had to have been about . . . about *here* when he was struck.

He stood on the spot. It did not seem to be true that the memory held nothing after such impacts; he actually recalled a lot of it. The moment of recognition; then something swinging in from his left. A quick blur. Baseball bat, branch, maybe a two-by-four . . . Ouch. He touched his numb nose in sympathy.

After that moment there were at least a few seconds he did not recall at all. He didn't recall the impact (although he did, in his nose, kind of; the feel of it) nor falling to the ground. He must have gotten his hands out to catch himself; his left wrist was sore, and the first thing he remembered for sure was kneeling and seeing his nose shoot out blood like a fountain. Trying to catch black blood in his hands; not

319

staunch it, just catch it; finding it hard to believe just how much blood was pouring through his hands onto the ground, also down his throat and the back of his mouth. Swallowing convulsively. Then touching his nose, fearing to know what shape his fingers might find; finding it had no feeling, but that it seemed to be occupying much the same space as before. Peculiar to feel his own nose as if someone else's. It was the same now. His fingers told him the flesh was being manipulated, but his face didn't confirm it.

Very strange. And here he was. Back on the spot, some days later . . . let's see; must be . . . two days.

He crouched, looked around. He got on his hands and knees, in the same position he had been in while watching the blood fountain out of him. It was still seeping a little bit. Taste of blood. For a second during the prodigious flow he had wondered if he would bleed to death. And indeed there was a large black stain on the ground.

Now he twisted slowly this way and that, as if to prick more memories to life. He took off a glove and got his little keychain flashlight out of his pocket. He aimed the beam of light; frail though it was, it made the night seem darker.

There. Off to his right, up the slope of snow, half embedded. He leaped over with a shout, snatched it up and shook it at the wind. His hand axe.

He stared at it there in his hand. A perfect fit and heft. Superficially it looked like the other gray quartzite cobbles that littered Rock Creek. It was possible no one would ever have known it was different. But when he clutched it the shaping was obvious. Knapped biface. Frank whacked it into the nearest tree trunk, a solid blow. *Thunk thunk thunk thunk*. Quite a weapon.

He put it back in his jacket pocket, where it jostled nicely against his side.

He hiked through the trees under bouncing black branches, their flailing visible as patterns in the occlusion of stars. The north wind poured into him. Clatter and squeak of snow-shoes. He slept in his van.

Inevitably, he had to explain what had happened to a lot of people. Diane of course had seen him at the hospital. 'How are you feeling?' she asked when he went into Optimodal the next morning.

'I think a nerve must have been crushed.'

She nodded. 'I can see where the skin was split. Broken nose, right?'

'Yes. Maxillary bone. I just have to wait it out.'

She touched his arm. 'My boy broke his nose. The problem is the cartilage heals at new angles, so your breathing could be impaired.'

'Oh great. I hate having to breathe through my mouth when I have a cold.'

'They can ream you out if you want. Anyway it could have been worse. If you had been hit a little higher, or lower –'

'Or to either side.'

'True. You could have been killed. So, I guess your nose was like the air bag in a car.'

'Ha ha. Don't make me laugh or I'll bleed on you.' He held his upper lip between thumb and forefinger as he chuckled, squeezing it to keep from re-opening the vertical cut. Everything had cracked vertically.

'Your poor lip. It sticks out almost as far as your nose. You look like the spies in Spy Vs. Spy.'

'Don't make me laugh!'

She smiled up at him. 'Okay I won't.'

In his office about twenty minutes later, he smiled to think of her; he had to press his upper lip together.

His appreciation for Diane grew as he saw more of the responses he got to the injury. Over-solicitous, amused, uninterested, grossed out – they were bad in different ways. So

Frank kept discussions limited. The lunch runners were okay, and Frank told them a bit more about what had happened. Same with the frisbee guys, who all nodded rather grimly as they listened to him. There had been quite a few incidents like the fight Frank had joined, Spencer said: robbery, assaults, site stealing. For a while it had been really bad. Now, as the news of these attacks spread, and the cold got worse, the park had lost a lot of people, and the fights were fewer. But they hadn't ended, and the frisbee guys were now telling everybody to move around in packs.

Frank did not do this, but when he strapped on his snow-shoes and went for walks, he kept away from the trails and did his best never to be seen.

Work was more problematic. When he sat down in his office, the list of Things To Do sometimes looked like a document in another language. He had to look up acronyms that suddenly seemed new and non-intuitive. OSTP? PITAC? Oh yeah. Office of Science and Technology Policy. Executive branch, a turned agency, an impediment to them. There were so many of those. PITAC: President's Information Technology Advisory Council. Another advisory body. Anna had a list of over two hundred of them, followed by a list of NGOs (non-governmental organizations) just as long. All calling for some kind of action – from the sidelines. Unfunded. Anna had waved a whole sheaf of lists in her hand, not appalled or angry like Frank had been, more astonished than anything. 'There's so much information out there. And so many organizations!'

'What does it all mean?' Frank had said. 'Is it a form of paralysis, a way of pretending?'

Anna nodded. 'We know, but we can't act.'

The phrase, something Diane had once said, haunted him as he tried to get back to work. He knew what should come next for most of the items on his list of Things To Do, but there was no obvious mechanism for action in any case; nor any way to decide which to do first. Call the science and technology center coordinator's office, and see if the leasing of Torrey Pines Generique's empty facility was complete. Call Yann, and therefore Marta; put them directly in touch with the carbon drawdown and sequestration team. Talk to Diane and General Wracke about the Gulf Stream project. Check in with the carbon emissions team, see if photovoltaics clearly outperformed mirrors before dropping the mirror funding. Okay but which first?

He decided to talk to Diane. She could not only update him, but advise him on how to prioritize. Tell him what to do.

Again Diane was easier to talk to than anyone else. But after she told him what she had heard from Wracke and the Coast Guard and the International Maritime Organization, all of which seemed to indicate that assembling a transport fleet, loading it and sailing it to the Greenland Sea would be at least physically possible, she shifted to something else with a quick grimace. Their new Inspector General appeared to be on the hunt, and the pattern of his interviews and requests seemed to indicate that Diane herself was his quarry, along with several of the most active members of the National Science Board, including its best contact to National Academy of Science, and the one with the strongest links to the Senate. 'I've got to meet with OMB and have it out with them,' she said darkly. 'Maybe call in the GAO for a cross-check to this guy.'

'Is there any chance he'll . . .'

'No. I am clean. They are looking at my son's affairs too. All the program directors; you too, I assume. We will hope for the best. They can twist things that are real, and suddenly you're in trouble.'

'Oh dear.'

'It's all right. I can get some help. And the colder it gets this winter, the better for us. People are getting motivated to try something. If it comes out that the Department of Energy is trying to stop us from helping the situation here, they will catch hell. So, the colder the better!'

'Up to a point,' Frank warned.

'True.' She looked over his list. 'Talk to your carbon drawdown people, we need to get them to commit to the new institute in San Diego.'

'Okay.' That meant a call to Yann and Marta.

Back in his office, Anna was waiting to discuss their alliances program. She was pleased with a search program that was identifying groups tightly allied to NSF's current goals. Also, FCCSET had been funded and given back its budgetary power, and should be able to coordinate climate spending from the federal government, including the Corps of Engineers. It looked like even if the President and Congress refused all funding for climate work, still engaged in their head-in-the-sand exercise, they could be bypassed by a more diffuse economic network, now interested in taking action.

So that was nice; but Frank still had to call Marta. It was amazing how his pulse rose at the prospect. His lip throbbed with each heartbeat. Every other item on the list seemed suddenly more pressing. Nevertheless, he took a deep breath and punched the number, wondering briefly how much this would bump his stock in the futures market. Why, if only he could get some shares, he could do things to raise their value, and then sell! Maybe this was what was meant by the ownership society. Maybe this was capitalism; you owned stock in yourself, and then by your actions the price per share rose. Except that you didn't own a majority share. You might not even own any shares, and have no way to buy in; as with Frank and the spooks' virtual market.

But there were other markets.

Marta picked up, and Frank said, 'Hi Marta it's Frank,'

all in a rush. Forging on through her cold greeting and lack of conversation, he asked her how it was going with the lichen project.

She told him that it was going pretty well. 'Do you have a cold?'

'No.'

They had engineered one of their tree lichen's algae to a much more efficient photosynthesis, and altered the fungus component of the lichen so that it exported its sugar to the tree faster than the original lichen had. This lichen had always taken hormonal control of its trees, so now the sugar production from photosynthesis was merely being packed into the lignin of the trees faster than before; meaning extra carbon, added to the trees' trunk girth and root size. So far the alterations had been simple, Marta said, and the trees would live for centuries, and had millions of years' experience in not getting eaten by bacteria. The sequestration would therefore last for the lifetime of the tree – not long on geological scales, but Diane had declared early on in this discussion that the length of sequestration time was not to be a heavily weighted factor in judging the various proposals; any port in a storm, as she put it.

'That all sounds great,' Frank said. 'And which trees do these tree lichen live on?'

They were pretty much omniarboreal, Marta said. Indigenous to the great world-wrapping forest of the north sixties latitudes, crossing Europe, Siberia, Kamchatka and Canada.

'I see,' Frank said.

'Yeah,' Marta replied, suddenly chilling. 'So what's up?'

'Well, I wanted to let you know that the new center is ongoing out in San Diego. You aren't going to believe this, but they're going to lease the old Torrey Pines Generique facility.'

'Ha! You're kidding.'

'No.'

'Well. You ought to hire Leo Mulhouse too while you're at it. He'd get a cell lab working better than anyone.'

'That's a good idea, I'll pass that along. I liked him.'

Frank described the input from UCSD, Scripps, Salk, the San Diego bio-tech council. Then he told her about the progress with NSF's unsolicited grants program. 'There's already a Small Grants for Exploratory Research program that's been under-utilized, and Diane has upped the maximum award. So the possibility is there for grants without external review.'

He couldn't say any more; indeed, even saying this much might be dangerous: surveillance, recorded phone line, conflict of interest, hostile inspector general . . . shit. He had to leave the rest unsaid, but the implications seemed pretty damned obvious. And head-hunting was still legal, he assumed.

'Yeah it sounds good,' Marta said sullenly, clearly in no mood to be grateful, or to hope. 'So what?'

Frank had to let it go. He didn't say, You're going to have to be part of a government to get permission to release a genetically modified organism designed to alter the composition of the atmosphere. He didn't say, I've arranged things so that you and Yann can both go back to San Diego and work on your projects with more power and funding. She could figure it out, and no doubt already had, which was what was making her grumpy. She didn't like anything that might impede her being mad at him.

He stifled a sigh and got off as best he could.

One windless night he snowshoed out and saw that some of the fires were back. Sparks in the darkness, at picnic sites and squatter camps. People out and about. Perhaps it was the lack of wind.

Under the luminous cloud the snow was a brilliant white. The forest looked like the park of some enormous estate, everything groomed perfectly for a demanding squire. Far to the north a movement in the trees suggested to him the auroch, or something else very big. The jaguar wouldn't be that big.

The bros were back home, he was happy to see, several of them sitting at the picnic tables, a few standing by a good fire in the ring.

'Hey Perfesser! Perfesser Nosebleed! How ya doing, man?'

They did not gather around him, but for the moment he was the center of attention. 'I'm okay,' he said.

'Good for you!'

'You look terrible!'

'Now's when you should pop him on the nose if you were ever gonna!'

Frank said, 'Oh come on.'

'I don't have to ask who's winning now! The other guy's winning!

Frank said, 'Don't make me laugh or I'll bleed on you.'

This pleased them very much. They went on ragging him. He threw a branch on the fire and sat down next to the woman, who nodded her approval as she counted stitches.

'You did good,' she told him.

'What do you mean?'

'The bozos here say you came blasting in like the cavalry.'

'So who were those guys?' Frank asked the group.

'Who knows.'

'Fucking little motherfuckers.'

'It's one of them Georgia Avenue gangs, man, those guys just live off the streets like us, or worse.'

'But they were white,' Frank observed.

The fire crackled as they considered this.

'It's getting kind of dangerous out here,' Frank said.

'It always was, Nosebleed.'

'Just got to keep out of the way,' the woman murmured as she began needling again, bringing the work up close to her eyes.

'How you doing?' Frank asked her as the others returned to their riffs and arias.

'Day hundred and forty-two,' she said with a decisive nod.

'Congratulations, that's great. Are you keeping warm?'

'Hell no.' She guffawed. 'How would I do that?'

'Did you get one of my tarps?'

'No, what's that?'

'I'll bring them out again. Just a tarp, like a tent fly, you know.'

'Oh.' She was dismissive; possibly she had a place to sleep. 'How'd you do up at the hospital?'

'What? Oh fine, fine.'

She nodded. 'They've got a good ER.'

'Did you – I mean, I don't remember going there.'

'I'm not surprised.'

Frank was. He could recall the blow, the moments immediately afterward. It hadn't occurred to him that the next thing he recalled after that was sitting in the ER waiting room, bleeding into paper towels waiting to be seen. 'How'd I get up there?'

'We walked you up. You were okay, just bleeding a lot.'

'I don't remember that part.'

'Concussion, I'm sure. You got hammered.'

'Did you see what hit me?'

'No, I was tucked down in a lay-by during the fight. Zeno and Andy found you afterward and we took you on up. You don't remember?'

'No.'

'That's concussion for you.'

One day at NSF he worked on the photovoltaic cell trials. Department of Energy was now squawking that this was their bailiwick. Then his alarm went off and he went down and sat in his van.

He couldn't figure out what to do next.

He could taste blood at the back of his throat.

What did that mean? Was something not healing right, some ruptured blood vessel still leaking? Was there pressure on his brain?

Blood was leaking, that was for sure. But of course there must still be swelling inside; he still had a fat lip, after all, and why should swelling inside go away any faster? His black eyes were still visible, though they were turning purple and brown. Who knew? And what now?

He could go to the doctor's. He could visit the Quiblers, or the Khembalis. He could go to his treehouse. He could go back up to work. He could go out to dinner. He could sleep right there in the NSF basement, in the back of his van.

The sense of indecision hadn't been like this for a while. He was pretty sure of that. Recalling the past week, it seemed to him it had been getting better. Now worse. The stab of elevated heart rate galvanized him again. Maybe this was what they meant by the word terror.

He felt chilled. And in fact it was freezing in his van. Should he put on his down jacket, or – but stop. He grabbed the down jacket and wrestled his way into it, muttering 'Do the obvious things, Vanderwal, just do the first fucking thing that pops into your head. Worry about it later. Leap before you look.'

Indecision. Before his accident he had been much more decisive. Wait, was that right? No. That could not be quite true. Maybe it was before he came to Washington that he had been sure of himself. But had he been? Had he ever been?

For a second he wasn't sure of anything. He thought back over the years, reviewing his actions, and wondered suddenly if he had ever been quite sane. He had made any number of bad decisions, especially in the past few years, but also long before that. All his life, but getting worse, as in a progressive disease. Why would he have risked Marta's part of their equity without asking her? Why would he ever have gotten involved with Marta in the first place? How could he have thought it was okay to sabotage Pierzinski's grant proposal? What had he been thinking, how had he justified it?

He hadn't. He hadn't thought about it; one might even say that he had managed to avoid thinking about it. It was a kind of mental skill, a negative capability. Agile in avoiding the basic questions. He had considered himself a rational, and, yes, a good person, and ignored all signs to the contrary. He had made up internal excuses, apparently. All at the unconscious level; in a world of internal divisions. A parcellated mind indeed. But brain functions *were* parcellated, and often unconscious. Then they got correlated at higher levels – that was consciousness, that was choice. Maybe that higher system could be damaged even when most of the parts were okay.

He twisted the rear-view mirror around, stared at himself in it. For a while there in his youth he would stare into his eyes in a mirror and feel that he was meeting some Other. After returning from a climb where a falling rock had missed him by a foot – those kinds of moments.

But after Marta left he had stopped looking at himself in the mirror.

Now he saw a frightened person. Well, he had seen that before. It was not so very unfamiliar. He had never been so sure of himself when he was young. When had certainty arrived? Was it not a kind of hardening of the imagination, a dulling? Had he fallen asleep as the years passed?

Nothing was clear. A worried stranger looked at him, the kind of face you saw glancing up at the clock in a train station. What had he been feeling these last several months before his accident? Hadn't he been better in that time? Had he not, from the moment Rudra Cakrin spoke to him, tried to change his life?

Surely he had. He had made decisions. He had wanted his treehouse. And he had wanted Caroline. These sprang to mind. He had his desires. They might not be entirely conventional, but they were strong.

Maybe it was a little convoluted to be relieved by the notion that having been a fuck-up all his life, there did not have to be a theory of brain trauma to explain his current problems. To think that he was uninjured and merely congenitally deformed, so that was okay. Maybe it would be better to be injured.

He fell asleep at the wheel, thinking I'll go back to the treehouse. Or out to San Diego. Or out to Great Falls. Or call the Khembalis . . .

The next morning he did not have to decide what to do, as the conference room next to Diane's office filled with European insurance executives, come to discuss the situation. They politely ignored Frank's face as Diane made the introductions. They were all people from the four biggest re-insurance companies, Munich Re, Swiss Re, GE Insurance Solutions, and General Re. Two CEOs were there, also Chief Risk Officers, Heads for Sustainability Management, and some men who were 'nat cat' guys, as they called it, scientists expert in natural catastrophes, and the mathematical modeling used to develop scenarios and assign risk values.

'We four handle well over half of the total premium volume in re-insurance,' the Swiss Re CEO told Diane and the rest. 'Ours is a specialized function, and so we are going to need help. Already we are stretched to the limit, and this winter is going very badly in Europe, as you know. And here too of course. The destruction is really severe. Food shortages will come very quickly if winters become like this regularly. We are having to raise premiums immediately, just to make this first round of payouts. Re-insurance is just one part of a distributed load, but in a situation like this, essentially unprecedented, re-insurance is caught at the end of the stick. This may be the last payout that re-insurance will be able to afford to make. After that the system will be overwhelmed, and then there will have to be a bailout by governments.'

So naturally they were interested in mitigation possibilities; and they had heard at the UN that the most advanced work in the US was being done here at NSF. Diane agreed that this was so, and told them about the North Atlantic project they were evaluating. It turned out they had been discussing the same idea among themselves; all over Europe people hoped it might be possible to 'restart the Gulf Stream,' because otherwise European food self-sufficiency was in danger.

The GenRe nat cat expert suggested that surfactants might be spread on the ocean surface to increase evaporation, which would thereby increase the salinity on the surface.

'Take away water instead of just adding salt,' Diane said, looking over at Frank. 'That's good. We've been coming up with some pretty high values for the amount of salt likely to be needed.'

They punched up the Power Point slides and ran through the isopycnal tables, each curve on the graph suggestive of the slide of cold salty water, down the isopycnal surface to the sea floor.

The cold winter they were now experiencing might also help this plan to restart the circulation, the nat cat expert pointed out. The Arctic sea ice might bulk up to a thickness that wouldn't break up and drift south when spring came. Surface temperatures would then drop in the fall as they always did, and if they had gotten a fleet loaded with salt, and into position . . . clouds might also be seeded to the west, to keep precipitation out of the region as much as possible . . .

Everyone seemed to agree they were onto something. Diane explained that the UN was aware of the plan, and approved it in principle; the remaining problems were likely to be financial and logistical, and perhaps political within the United States.

But maybe the United States was not a make-or-break participant, the Europeans seemed to be suggesting. Neither Diane nor Frank had ever entertained that notion before, but as the Europeans talked about finances, it became an implication too clear to miss, and Frank and Diane exchanged the blank glance that had replaced raised eyebrows between them to express discreet surprise. 'We insure each other,' one of them said. 'We keep a kind of emergency fund available.'

'This is not actually very expensive, compared to some projects we have been contemplating.'

Wow, Frank said to Diane with another blank look.

**He was reading in** his sleeping bag when his cell phone rang and he snatched it up.

'Frank, it's Caroline.'

'Oh good.'

'Are you all right?'

'I'm all right. I broke my nose, it's all stuffed up.'

'Oh no, what happened?'

'I'll tell you about it when we meet.'

'Okay good. Can you meet?'

'Of course. I have two black eyes.'

'That's okay. Listen, can we meet at your place in Rock Creek Park?'

He swallowed. 'Are you sure?'

'Yes.'

'Do they – is it known where it is?'

'Yes. But I think I can help with that.'

'Oh, well. Sure. I wanted to show it to you anyway.'

'Tell me where to meet you.'

He descended and crossed the park. His heart was beating hard, his lip throbbing. Everything seemed transparent at the edges, the branches tossing and crashing in slow motion. What a slow pace time had when you paid attention to it. At the corner of Broad Branch and Grant he stood in a shadow, listening to the city and the roar of the wind, watching the luminous cloud pour south overhead. He shivered convulsively, started to hop and dance in place to regenerate some heat.

She turned the corner and he stepped out into the light of a streetlamp. She saw him and quickly crossed the street, banged into him with a hug, started to kiss him but drew back. 'Oh my God sorry! Your poor face.'

'It doesn't feel that bad.'

'Let's go to your place,' she said.

'Sure.' He turned and led her into the park. Under the trees he took her by the hand. He followed the cross trail; even if she couldn't see it, the footing would be better.

'Wow, you're really in here.'

'Yes. So now your surveillance knows I'm here? How did that happen?'

She tugged at his hand. 'You know your stuff is chipped, right?'

'No, what's that?'

'Microchips.'

He stopped, and she stood beside him, squeezing his hand, holding his arm with her other hand. This was how the gibbons often touched.

'You know how everything now is sold with an electronic chip in it? They're really small, but they bounce a microwave back to a reader, with their ID and location. Businesses use them for inventory. All kinds of stuff.'

'How do they know what stuff is mine?'

'Because you bought most of it with credit cards. It's easy.' She sounded almost exasperated; she wanted him up to speed on this stuff.

'So they always know where I am?'

'If you're within the range of a source beam. Which you are most places in DC.'

'Shit.'

She squeezed his arm. 'But not out here.'

Frank started walking again. For a second he did not

remember where they were, and he had to stop and think about it before he could go on.

'No one will be able to track us up in my tree?'

'No. The usual chips don't have much range. Someone would have to be out here with a scanner nearby.'

'Is my stock still rising?'

'Yes.'

'But why?'

'Not sure. Whatever you're up to at NSF, I guess.'

He looked over his shoulder. 'Maybe it was meeting you that did it.'

'Ha ha.' He could tell by the drag from her hand that she wasn't amused by this.

'But we'll be okay now,' he repeated.

'Yes. Well, in terms of being tracked tonight. But if someone came out here it might be different. I brought a reader wand with me, and I think we can clean you out. Maybe even move all the chips somewhere else, so it will look like you've moved. I don't know. I've never dechipped anyone before.'

Frank thought about this as they crossed Ross and made the final drop to the edge of the gorge. Under his tree he took out his remote and called down Miss Piggy. He looked at the remote.

'I bought this with a credit card,' he said.

'Radio Shack?'

'Jesus.'

She laughed. 'I just guessed that. But it's in your records, I'm sure.'

'Shit.'

Miss Piggy hummed down out of the night, looking like the ladder you climbed to get into the flying saucer hovering overhead. Frank showed her where to grab, where to step. 'You go first and I'll hold it steady. That'll be better.'

Up she went, quick and lithe, soon a black mass in the stars overhead, like a bole on the trunk. It took her a while at the top, and he shook his head, thinking she must think he was nuts. When she was off he climbed swiftly, pulled through the entry hole. 'Sorry, the last part can be the trickiest.'

'No problem. This is so cool!'

'Ah. Thanks.' He sat down beside her. 'I'm glad you like it.'

'I love it. We used to have a treehouse in our backyard.'

'Really! Where was this?'

'Outside Boston. My dad built it in a big old tree, I don't know what kind it was, but it was wider than it was tall. We had several platforms, and a big staircase running down to the ground.'

'Nice.'

'This is smaller,' she noted, and pulled closer to him. They sat side by side, cold hands entwined on top of her legs. The wind was tossing the tree gently north and south. 'It's like a nest.'

'Yes. We can get out of the wind if we need to,' he said, indicating the tent behind them.

'I like it out here, if it doesn't get too cold.'

'Let's use it as a wind-block, then.'

They shifted into the lee of the tent, bumping against each other as the tree swayed.

'It's like being on a train.'

'Or a ship.'

'Yes, I suppose so.'

They huddled together. Frank felt too strange to kiss; he was distracted, and it was hard to get used to the presence of someone else in his treehouse. 'Um – do you think you could show me what you mean about the chips?'

She dug in her jacket pocket, took out a short metal wand, like the devices used by airport security. 'Do you have some light?'

'Sure,' he said, and clicked on the Coleman lamp. The lit circle on the plywood floor gleamed under them, ruining their night vision. The wind hooted and moaned.

She had him bring his belongings to her one by one. Sometimes she would get a beep as she passed the wand over them, and these she put to one side. Clock, lightweight sleeping bag, some of the clothes, even the little stove.

'Damn,' he said.

'Yeah. That's the way it is. You're not as bad as some. A lot of your gear must be pretty old.'

'It definitely is.'

'That's the way to do it. If you want to get out from under surveillance, you have to go back in time.'

'You mean only use old stuff?'

'That's right. But really you don't want to get yourself entirely clear, that would trigger interest you don't want. But there are levels and levels. You could make it so that nothing on you tells where you are at any given moment. That might not even be noticed. The program would just use the stuff you do have, like your phone. It would assume you are where your phone is.'

'I see. Damn.'

'I know.' She had finished with his things. Now she leaned away from him, sweeping the foot of the platform methodically, right to left, coming back to them by a foot or so per sweep, then past them and to the wide part at his head, and around the corner. Then inside the tent. It was a small platform, but she was being thorough. 'I don't think it's known that you're up in a tree. Before you told me, I thought you were just camped out in the woods, on the ground. I wonder if anyone's come out to ground-check you.'

She waved the wand over him, and it beeped.

'Shit,' she said.

She moved him. It wasn't where he was sitting. It was him.

'Maybe my clothes?'

She grinned. 'We'll have to check. Get into the tent.'

They brought the Coleman lamp inside with them, zipped down the tent door. Frank turned on his little battery heater, and they watched its element turn orange and begin radiating.

The wind was still noisy, and they could feel the tree swaying, but the warm air cocooned them.

She helped him unbutton his shirt, pull it off. The air was still cold. 'Your poor face.' She ran the wand over him. It beeped when she held it over the middle of his back.

'Interesting. That's the same spot it was on me.'

'You were chipped too?'

'That's right.'

'By who?'

She didn't answer. 'Here, turn your back to the lamp. Have you got an extra flashlight? Yes? Good. Here, let me.' She inspected him. He could feel her fingers on his back, poking and then squeezing. 'Ah ha. There it is.'

'You sure it isn't just a blackhead?'

'Actually it looks more like a tick, you know how when you pull off a tick and part of it breaks in you?'

'Yuck. You're grooming me.'

'That's right. Then it'll be your turn to groom me.' She kissed the nape of his neck. 'Hold steady now. I brought some tweezers.'

'How did you get yours out?'

'I had a hell of a time. I had to use a barbeque tong. Like a back scratcher. I watched in the mirror and gouged it out.'

'Back stabber.'

'Yes. I stabbed myself in the back, but I'll never do it to you. Except for now.'

'Don't make me laugh or I'll bleed on you.'

'You're going to bleed anyway.' She poked gently at his back.

'How the hell did they get it in me?'

'Don't know. When you hurt your nose did you go to a hospital?'

'Yes. I was there for a few hours.'

'Maybe that was when. Okay, here it is. Hold steady.'

Then a quick cut. Frank held himself immobile. Now she was wiping off his back with her fingers, and kissing his spine

339

at the base of his neck. She ripped open a little square band-aid and applied it to the spot.

'You thought of everything,' he said.

'I hope so.'

'What about you?'

'What do you mean?'

He picked up the wand.

'Oh that. I think I'm okay.'

But he ran it over her anyway, and it beeped over her back. Her mouth tightened to a hard line. 'Shit.'

'It wasn't there before?'

'No.' She ripped off her jacket, took the wand and ran it over it. No beep. She pulled her shirt off over her head; shocking lovely curve of freckled white skin, spine deep in a furrow of muscles, ribs, shoulder blades, the curve of her right breast in its bra cup as she faced away from him. He ran the wand over her back, listened for the beep, watched for the green lights on its black face. Like finding the stud in a wall; but nothing. He ran it over her crumpled shirt and it beeped. 'Ah ha.'

'Okay,' she said, spreading the shirt out and inspecting it. 'That's good. Here. It'll just be a few millimeters long.' She ran the wand closely over the shirt, inspected the part under the beeping. 'In a seam . . . yep. Here it is.' She cut with a pair of keychain scissors, held up a tiny black cylinder, like a tiny bike pump valve stopper.

'Maybe there's another one in your bra,' Frank suggested, and she laughed and leaned forward to kiss him; and then they were hugging hard, kissing lightly, she only brushing her lips against his, murmuring, 'Oh, oh, it must hurt – watch out, I'm going to hurt you,' and him replying, 'It's all right, it's all right, kiss me.'

They got off the rest of their clothes and onto his ground-pad, under his unzipped sleeping bag. All warm and cozy and yet still bobbing on the wind. Finally completing the dive

340

that they had launched in their stuck elevator, so many months before; they finally fell in and were both seized up in it together. This was Frank's overriding impression, to the extent he had any thoughts at all; the togetherness of it. She kissed him gingerly, squeezed him hard, as sure with her caresses as she had been with her little surgery. Frank began to bleed again down the back of his throat, he tasted blood and was afraid she could too.

'I'm going to bleed on you I'm afraid.'

'Here – let's turn over.'

She straightened her left leg under his right, and they rolled to that side together as if they had done it a thousand times before; then crabbed back onto the mattress pad. Frank swallowed blood, held her as she moved on him. Off they went again.

Afterward she lay beside him, her head on his chest. He could feel that she could hear his heartbeat. He ran his fingers through the tight curls of her hair. 'Wow.'

'I know.'

'I needed that.'

'Me too.' She shifted her head to look at him. 'How long has it been for you?'

Frank calculated. Marta, the last time . . . quite some time before she moved out. Some of those last times had been very strange: sex as hatred, sex as despair. Usually he managed not to know that a nearly eidetic memory of those encounters had been seared into him, but now he glimpsed them, quickly shoved them away again in his mind. 'About a year and a half? Jesus.'

'It's been four years for me.'

'*What?*'

'That's right.' She made a face. 'I told you. We don't get along.'

'But . . .'

'I know. That's just the way it is. He has other interests.'

'Someone else, you mean?'

'I don't know.'

'But that chip in your shirt?'

'That was him.'

'So – he keeps tabs on you?'

'Yes.'

'But why?'

She shrugged. 'Just to do it. I don't know really. He started working with another agency, and it seems to have gotten worse since then. He's always been kind of obsessive. It's a control thing.'

'So this new job is with another security agency?'

'Oh yes. I think it's linked to Homeland Security, maybe just a blackblack inside it.'

'So, these chips. Will he know you've been here?'

'No, he would have to be following me. The chips ping back a radio signal with their information and location, but the range isn't very big. It's getting bigger though, and they've been installing a network of transmitters that will give comprehensive coverage in the capital area. But it hasn't been activated yet, as far as I know. I think you still need to be tracking to get a bounce from a chip. Not that he wouldn't do that too. But he's out of town.'

Frank didn't know what to say.

Long silence. They let it go. There they were, after all, just the two of them. Rocking back and forth. She lay her head on his chest. Back and forth, back and forth.

'This feels so good. It's like being in a cradle.'

'Yes,' Frank said. 'You can tell which direction the wind is coming from. See, it's coming from the north, from behind our head. When it swings toward our feet, there's a little pause at the end, while the wind holds it out there. Then it springs back with an extra little push, like it's been released. Whereas behind our heads we're going into the wind, so it slows sooner and makes the turn-around quicker, with no extra acceleration from the release. See, feel that?'

'No.' She giggled.

'Feel it again. Downwind, upwind, downwind, upwind. They're different.'

'Hmm. So they are. Like a little hitch.'

'Yes.'

'It's like clocks going tick tock. Supposedly there's hardly any difference between the two sounds.'

'True.' Frank felt a deep breath fill him, lifting her head. 'I'm glad you don't think I'm crazy.'

'Me? I'm in no position to think anyone else is crazy. I am fully out there myself.'

'Maybe we all are now.'

'Maybe so.'

They lay there, swaying back and forth. Please time stop now. The wind strummed the forest; they could hear individual gusts sweep across the watershed. Creaking branches, the occasional snap and crash, all within a huge airy whoosh, keening and hooting, filling everything with its continuo.

They talked quietly about treehouses. She told him all about the one in her backyard, her nights out, her tea parties, her cats, a neighborhood raccoon, a possum. 'I thought it was a big rat. It scared me to death.'

Frank told her about his love for the Swiss Family treehouse at Disneyland. 'I had a plan to hide when the park closed. Tom Sawyer Island was divided by a fence, with a maintenance area north of the public part. I was sure I could swing around the fence and hide, but then I would be stuck on the island. I decided in the summer that would be okay, I could swim over to Frontierland and sneak through New Orleans to the tree. Clothes on my head, towel, the whole bit. I practiced swimming without my arms.'

She laughed. 'Why didn't you do it?'

'I couldn't think of anything to tell my parents. I didn't want them to worry.'

'Good boy.'

'Well, I would have gotten in such trouble.'

'True.'

Later she said, 'Do you think we could open the tent and look at the stars? Would we get blasted by wind?'

'Somewhat. We can move halfway out and zip down the tent door. I do that a lot.'

'Okay let's try it.'

He zipped open the tent. The cold poured in on them, and they bundled into the sleeping bag. Frank zipped it up until only their faces emerged from the hood of the bag. Set properly on the groundpad they started to warm up against each other. They kissed as much as Frank's face could handle, which was not much. When they started to make love they fell into it more languorously. They moved with the sway of the tree in the wind, a slow back and forth, like being on a train or truly huge waterbed. But this was too perfect and they started to laugh, they had to break rhythm with the tree and they did.

Afterward he said, 'What should I do about these chips?'

'I'll leave you this wand. You can get completely clear, and they might not have this spot GPSed. Could you move to another tree, with stuff you're sure is clean?'

'I guess so. It's all pretty modular, sure.' Frank realized he had grown fond of his tree, even though there were ten thousand others just like it all around him.

'That way, if you kept it a clean site, they wouldn't know where you were. When you were away from your van, anyway.'

'I'd have to leave a lot of stuff in the van.'

'They would think you were living in it. You'd have to wand yourself when you came up here, and see if you'd picked anything up. If you wanted to be serious about it, you'd get rid of the van and cell phone, and only use public stuff, and buy everything with cash. We call it devolving.'

Frank laughed. 'I've been trying to do that anyway.'

'I can see that. But you'd have to do it in this other area.'

He nodded. He put his face into the hair on the top of her head. Tight curls, a kind of lemon and cypress shampoo; he felt her body on his, and another jolt of desire ran through him. She was helping him. She was strong, bold, interested. She liked him, she wanted him. After four years she would probably want anybody, but now it was him.

'What about you?' he said.

She shrugged.

'So does your, does he know that you know he's spying on you?'

'He must.' Her grimace as underlit by Frank's floor lamp gave her the look of one of the Khembali demon masks: fear, despair, anger. Seeing it Frank felt a wave of deep dislike for her husband pour through him. He wanted to get rid of him. Remove him like a chip. Protect her, make her happy –

'– but we don't talk about it,' she was saying.

'That sounds bad.'

'It is bad. I need to get out of there. But there are some complications having to do with his new job. Some things I need to do first.' She fell silent, and her body, though still on top of his, was not melted into him as before. This was another new sensation, her otherness, naked and on top of him. He shivered and pulled the down bag back over their heads.

'So you got your pay phone numbers.'

'Yes.' He had remembered despite the injury.

'And when will we talk?'

'Nine p.m. every Friday?'

'Sure. And if we have to miss for some reason, the next week for sure, and if we miss again, I'll call your cell phone.'

'Okay. Good.'

Her warmth coursed into him. Up in the tree they hugged each other. This moment of the storm.

'Oh good,' he said.

**Leap before you look.**

Now winter was here in earnest. A series of brutal storms fell on the city, like the ones that had struck London only drier, all of them windy and cold, not very much snow, but that only made them seem colder. Kenzo said there hadn't been a winter like this since the Younger Dryas; it was worse than the Little Ice Age of the fourteenth century, a true North Atlantic stall event. Average temperatures in eastern North America and western Europe down by a full thirty degrees Fahrenheit.

Frank spent as much time as he could out in these storms. He loved being in them. He loved the way he felt after the night with Caroline. The walking-on-air sensation returned, obviously a specific body awareness in response to certain emotional states, giving birth to the cliché. Lightness of being.

Then also the intense winter was like moving into ever higher altitudes, or ever higher latitudes. He was in the wilderness and he was in love, and the combination was a kind of ecstatic state, a new realm of joy –

'the **joy** which will not let me sit in my chair, which brings me bolt upright to my feet, and sends me striding around my room, like a tiger in his cage – and I cannot have composure and concentration enough even to set down in English words the thought which thrills me, what if I never write a book or a line? – for a moment, the eyes of my eyes were opened.'

Emersonfortheday indeed. A man who knew how joy could loft you. No wonder they named schools after him! You could learn a lot just by reading him alone.

He snowshoed the park regularly, but also began to range more broadly in the city, taking long walks on each side of the park. This was where the homeless guys were finding refuge, and where the fregans and ferals made their homes. Frank decided that whenever he did not know what to do, he was to go out and visit as many of the bros and the other homeless of Northwest as he could, and make sure their gear kit was up to the ferocity of the elements. Even if he found total strangers huddled on the metro vents and in the other little heat sinks of the city, he talked to them too; and if they were at all responsive he got them under another layer of nylon, at the very least. Most had some down or wool on them, but a surprising number were still shivering under cotton, cardboard, plastic, foam rubber, newspaper. Frank could only shake his head. Don't wear cotton! he would insist to perfect strangers. Some of them even recognized him as Johnny Appletent.

He started visiting thrift stores and sporting goods stores too, buying overlooked or sale items, particularly synthetic clothes, and cheap but effective down bags. Once he bought a whole rack of capilene long underwear and matching long-sleeved shirts. These were really nice, similar to one of the inner layers he wore himself, and the next time he was out in the park and saw some of the bros were back in Sleepy Hollow, their shelters more knockabout than ever, he threw a top-bottom pair knotted together in to each one of them. 'Here, wear this against your skin. Nothing but this stuff against your skin. *No cotton!* Throw all that cotton crap away. You're going to freeze in that cotton shit.'

'It's fucking cold.'

'Yeah it's cold. Get this gear on and stay out of the wind when it blows.'

'No shit.'

Andy said, 'It's not the cold, it's the wind.' The wee-und.

'Yeah yeah yeah. That's right.'

'That's what everybody says.'

Frank snorted. 'That's for sure.'

It was the new truism, and already Frank was sick of it. Just as in summer people said, 'It's not the heat, it's the humidity,' until you wanted to scream, in the winter they said, 'It's not the cold, it's the wind.' So tedious to hear over and over! But Andy's default mode was repetition of the obvious, so this new mantra was unavoidable.

Certainly it was true. On windless nights Frank snowshoed through the forest completely removed from the cold; his exertion warmed him, and his heat was trapped in his layers of clothing, under jacket and windpants. The only problem was not to break a sweat. He might as well have been in a spacesuit.

But in a wind everything changed. How big the world became, yes, but how cold too! His outer layer was as wind-proofed as you could get, but the wind still rattled through it and sucked at every move he made. On the very worst nights, if he wanted to walk into the wind he had to turn his back to it and crab backwards to keep his face from frost-bite. During the days he had taken to wearing sunglasses with a nose-piece, because with his nose numb all the time he couldn't be sure if it was getting frostbitten or not. More than once it had been white in the mirror when he got back in his van. The nose-piece helped with that, as well as giving him a medieval look, like a burgher out of Brueghel. Icicles of snot would hang from the tip of it at the end of a walk, but his nose would stay warm.

Fine for his poor nose, but then he discovered there were other protrusions that also needed extra protection; he finished one long tramp on a windy Saturday afternoon, stopped in the forest to pee, and discovered to his dismay that his penis was as numb as his nose! Numb with cold, meaning, oh my . . . yes; it was thawing out in his hand, as painful a needling effect as he had ever felt, a burning *agony* lasting some ten minutes. He cried and his nose ran and it all froze on his face. An unusual demonstration of the density of nerve endings in that area, as in that old illustration of the human body in which the parts were sized in proportion to how many nerves they had, making a nightmare figure with giant mouth, hands, and genitalia.

The lunch runners already knew all about this problem. Penile frostbite was a serious concern, and extra precautions simply had to be taken; at the least, a sock or glove jammed into one's shorts, but also windproof nylon shorts, longer jackets, all that kind of thing.

'What you need is a rabbit fur jock strap, the fur side in of course. You could make a fortune selling those.'

So, Frank never again forgot to pay attention to this matter, and not just for himself. A couple weeks later, when he clattered into Sleepy Hollow:

'Hey, Nosebleed.'

'Hello, gentlemen. How are your penises?'

'Yarrrr!' Cackles, laughter: 'Now the truth comes out! Now we know what he's here for!'

'You wish. Are you managing to stay un-frostbitten?'

'NO.'

Various grumbles and moans.

'Look, there's a shelter open over by UDC, it's the closed high school's gym and some classrooms too, it's pretty nice.'

'We know. Fuck you.'

'Mr Nose. Mr Nosey Noser.'

'Mr Nosey Nose That Knows It All.'

'Yeah well it beats freezing to death.'

'Yarrr, fuck off. We have our ways.'

'It is our fate to stay out here, but we will survive.'

'I hope so.'

\*    \*    \*

Friday came and he went out to eat at a Mexican restaurant on Wisconsin near the Metro. He could tell already this would become his Friday night routine. It was an unpretentious little place where Frank could sit at the bar reading his laptop. Go to Emersonfortheday.net, search 'fate':

'Mountains are great poets, and one glance at this cliff undoes a great deal of prose. All life, all society begins to get illuminated and transparent, and we generalize boldly and well. **Space is felt as a great thing.** There is some pinch and narrowness to us, and we laugh and leap to see forest, and sea, which yet are but lanes and crevices to the great Space in which the world swims like a cockboat in the sea.'

*So* true. But that turned out to be from the essay 'Fate,' not about fate per se. Try again, word search in texts:

'The right use of **Fate** is to bring up our conduct to the loftiness of nature. A man ought to compare advantageously with a river, an oak, or a mountain. He shall have not less the flow, the expansion, and the resistance of these.'

Oh my yes. So well put. What a perceptive and eloquent worshipper of nature old Waldo was. And why not. New England had heroic weather, often casting its prosaic forest right up to the heights of the Himalaya or the shores of the Arctic.

But it was almost nine. He hopped up and paid his bill, using cash, which he did as often as he could now.

The payphone he had chosen was in the Bethesda Metro complex itself, down by the bus stop. There were several phones in a row, and he went to the one on the end and pulled out a phone card, ran it through the slot, dialed her number.

No answer. He let it ring a long time, then hung up.

He stood by the phone, thinking things over. Was this bad? She had said it might not work every week. He had no idea what her daily routine was. How did that work, with a husband you hadn't slept with for four years?

When the phone rang he jumped a foot and snatched it up. 'Hello?'

'Hi Frank it's Caroline. Did you call before?'

'Yes.'

'Sorry, this was as early as I could make it. I was hoping you'd still be there.'

'Sure. We should have a kind of window anyway.'

'True.'

'So . . . how's it going?'

'Oh, crazy. All over the place.'

'Everything's okay?'

'Yes.'

Gingerly they re-established the intimacy they had inhabited the week before. It was hard over the phone, but that voice in his ear brought back a lot of it, and he took chances: How are things going at home? I thought of you . . . Then she was telling him about her relationship, a bit, and the link between them was there again, that sense of closeness she could establish with a look or a touch, or, now, with her voice, clear and low. The distance between her and her husband had existed for years, she said; maybe since the beginning. They had met at work, he was older, he had been one of her bosses, now in a different agency, 'blacker than black.' They had not had any huge fights, ever, but for some years now he had not been home much, or showed any interest in her sexually ('Incredible,' Frank said). But before they had met he had worked for a while in Afghanistan, so who knew where he was at.

That gave him a chill. 'How did you two ever hook up?' he couldn't help saying.

'I don't know. My sister says I like to fix messed-up guys not that I mean you!' she added in a rush.

351

Frank only laughed. 'That's all right. Maybe your sister was right. I am certainly messed up, but you *are* fixing me.'

'And you me, believe me.'

But then, she went on, she had discovered by accident that he had chipped her, why she could not be sure; and a cold war, silent and strange, had gone on since then.

Frank shivered at the thought of this. They talked about other things, then. Their work-outs, the weather: 'I thought about you the other night when it got windy.'

'Me you too.'

Their windy night, oh my –

'I want to see you again,' she said.

'When can we?'

'I don't know. I'll look for a chance. There's some stuff happening I may have to deal with. Maybe I'll have something set up by next week.'

'Okay, next week then. Which one of us should call, by the way?'

'I'll call you. I'll start with this same number.'

'Okay good.'

He walked back to his van, passing first their elevator box on Wisconsin Avenue, then the little park where they had met the first two times. His Caroline places. This would be a new addition to his set of habits, he could tell, and all the rest would be transformed by it. He had gone feral, he had gone optimodal, he had become the Alpine man; and on Friday evenings he would get to talk to his Caroline on the phone, and those talks would lift and carry everything else, including the next time they met in person.

**But faster than Frank** could follow, winter went from the sublime to the ridiculous, and then to the catastrophic. He was enjoying it right up to the moment it started killing people.

That night, for instance, it was cold but not terribly so; there wasn't much wind, and its bite was invigorating. It made so much difference *how* you were experiencing it – not just what you wore, but how you felt about it. If you thought of it as an Emersonian transcendental expedition, ascending further in psychic altitude or latitude the colder it got, then it was just now getting really interesting – they were up to like the Canadian Arctic or the High Sierra, and that was beautiful. A destination devoutly to be wished.

But temperatures the following week plummeted from that already low point, an astonishing development no matter what they had been reading in the newspapers about other places. And that drop took them out to the equivalent of Antarctica or the Himalayas, both very dangerous places to be.

The first big drop was like a cold snap in a cold front, barreling in from Edmonton. It arrived at midnight, and by two AM he could not get warm even in his sleeping bag – a rare experience for him, and frightening as such. He fired up the space heater and cooked the air in the tent for a while, and that helped. But the heat sucked out of the tent the moment he killed the heater, and after a couple of burns he decided he had to go for a walk, maybe even a drive, to soak in some of the van's warmth.

Climbing down Miss Piggy was a nasty surprise. He started to swing in the wind, and then his hands got too cold to hold onto the rungs properly, so that he had to hook his elbows over and hang on for dear life, waiting for the wind to calm; but it didn't calm. He had to continue one rung at a time, setting his feet as securely as possible and then reaching down for another elbow hook. One rung at a time.

Finally he dropped onto the snow. He pushed the remote, but the ladder did not swing up into the night. Battery too cold.

Really very cold. You could only survive exposure in this kind of cold with the appropriate gear. Even ensconced in his spacesuit, Frank was struggling to stay warm. This was a temperature equivalent to being in the death zones of Everest or the Antarctic plateau.

And yet people were still out there in cotton. Out there in blue jeans and black leather jackets, for God's sake. Newspaper insulation for the most hapless. And the animals, all but the polar ones – they would be dying if they weren't in one of the shelters. The wind cut him in a way he had felt only a few times before, most of those in the Yukon's Cirque of the Unclimbables, on multi-day wall climbs. For it to happen in this semitropical city was bizarre, and an immediate emergency. And indeed it sounded like people were calling 911. He could hear sirens from every direction.

He could take care of himself, of course. Ceaseless motion was the key. So he hiked hard; but even so he got cold. He had forgotten what a furious assault cold made on you, he had to bury his face in the windward side of his hood, and had no idea how his nose was faring. For a while he even got lost, and worried that he had turned somehow and was headed south on the ridge trail. Narrow as it was, the park that night was too wide to cross.

He headed uphill, hoping it was west but knowing he would emerge eventually if he kept going up. He kicked right up the sides of snow drifts, noticing again what a huge difference his snowshoes made. It would have been horrible to post up a slope like that in deep snow. And yet he was one of the few people using snowshoes in the city. Only the FOG people used them, as far as he had seen. Surely the ferals must be into it, if they weren't skiing.

He came out on Broad Branch Road, almost exactly where he had hoped to be. God bless the unconscious mind.

He was very happy to hear his van start when he turned the key. After revving the engine for a while, he drove off with the heater on high. The van rocked on the gusts. The few other vehicles on the streets were weaving like drunks. SUVs finally looked at home, as if they had all moved to Fairbanks.

After driving around for a while he warmed up. The day arrived on a broad red sky. He snowshoed back out into the park, went first to 21 to check on the bros.

'Hey, Noseman! You should have a fucking barrel of brandy under your chin.'

'I'm amazed you guys are alive. How did you do it?'

'The fire.' Zeno gestured at it, pale in its giant mound of ashes. 'We sat right next to it all night long.'

'We kept it real big, we had to keep running out for more branches, shit. It was so fucking cold. I stood like six inches from this mother bonfire and even so my backside was freezing. One side of me was frying and the other was freezing.'

'It was cold all right. Do you have enough firewood, or what are you burning?'

'We have all the flood wood.'

'Isn't it green still?'

'Fuck yeah, but we've got a can of gas, and Cutter keeps siphoning cars to fill it up. Car gas burns like a motherfucker, it *explodes* in that fire, you've got to be really careful.'

'Okay, well don't burn yourself up. There's that shelter up at UDC –'

'Yeah yeah gowan! Gowan witcha! Go help some of them poor fools out there who probably need it.'

This was a valid point, and so Frank snowshoed off. Out of the park, into the paralyzed city.

In Starbucks they said it had been fifty below zero Fahrenheit at dawn. Almost a hundred degrees below the average daytime temperature for the day – now that was climate change. Sirens were still howling all over the city.

Frank called Diane. She was already at work, of course, but only because she had spent the night there. Forget about coming in, she told him. 'No one should even try. I mean, can you believe this?'

'I believe it,' said Frank.

FEMA had already declared it a disaster area, Diane said. Federal employees were now being told to stay home, along with everyone else but emergency personnel. Lines were down, and power outages had been reported; all those areas were in crisis mode. Water mains had frozen and burst, there were fires going unfought, and no doubt thousands were in danger of freezing to death in their own homes. Six AM and already it was a huge emergency.

'Okay, Diane, I'll stay in touch today and I'll keep my phone on.'

'What are you going to do?'

'I'm going to see how I can help at the zoo, I think. There are still a lot of animals at large.'

'You be careful! It's dangerous when it's this cold.'

'Yeah I will. I've got polar gear, I'll be okay.'

'Good. Okay, let's talk.'

So Frank was free to do what he had wanted to anyway. 'Ooooop!'

All the streets in Northwest were empty, or very close to it. No more blue jeans and windbreakers; the only people out and about were dressed as for polar exploration, or at the very least, a day of very cold skiing. These people greeted each other with the cheeriness of people who have survived a rapture and inherited the world. They were mostly men at first, out to see if they could help somehow, out for the hell of it really; and then there were quite a few women out too, more and more as the day wore on, often in bright ski colors. Esprit de corps was high. People waved to each other as they passed, stopped to talk on the street. Everyone agreed that anybody out in this without good gear would quickly go hypothermic, while on the other hand, good gear and constant exertion meant one could thrive. It was a stunning experience of the technological sublime, an evident natural religion. Space was indeed felt as a great thing. And some of the coffee shops were still open, so Frank ducked in them from time to time, like everyone else, for a break from the penetrating chill. Heated caves, there to take shelter in any time it got to be too much – as long as the area still had electricity, of course. The areas without power would be in trouble, perhaps need of evacuation.

'I'm from Ohio,' one man said to Frank outside a Starbucks. 'This is nothing!'

'Well, it's pretty cold,' Frank said.

'True! But it's not windy. Thank God for that. Because it's not the cold, it's the . . .'

Having toured Connecticut Avenue, Frank began a comprehensive hunt through Rock Creek Park, walking the Western Ridge Trail and venturing down every side trail. He was relieved to find that the park was basically empty. The deer were tucked into their brakes and hollows; he wondered whether these would be enough, this could be a major die-off. But you never knew. Snow was a tremendous insulator and windguard, and these deer had gone through winters before.

And the truth was, they could use some culling. It was the ferals he was really worried about.

357

Then he found three people, still huddled together in a wood-and-cardboard shelter, down by site 9. At first he thought they were dead; then they stirred. He called 911 and waited, getting colder and colder as he tried unsuccessfully to rouse them, until some firemen got there. He helped them get the three up to the road and the truck, two on stretchers; the one who had been in the middle had done a bit better.

He went back to look for more. Rock Creek itself was frozen to its bottom, of course. The whole park was quiet, the city beyond it unusually quiet too, except for the ongoing wail of sirens, criss-crossing like tortured coyotes or the gibbons with megaphones.

The firemen had said the power grid might go comprehensively when the demand for juice was so high. The power companies had instituted pre-emptive brown-outs to keep from blowing the system. Fire trucks were some of the only vehicles that would still start reliably, because they were kept in heated garages. Battery heaters were crucial at temps like these, but of course no one had any.

'My van started this morning,' Frank had told them.

'You get one, usually, but don't be sure it'll happen again, they're done for at these temps. It's fifty below!'

'I know.'

Lucky no wind! they said.

Frank checked the hot boxes left out for the ferals. If there was a loss of power to these the result would be catastrophic. Every box was crowded with a menagerie of miserable animals, like little shipwrecked bits of Noah's Ark, every single creature subdued and huddled into itself. The gibbons hung from the corners of the roof near the heating elements, their little faces frowning like Laurel and Hardy after a reversal.

Frank called in to Nancy and reported what he saw. Zoo staff were doing what they could to collect any creatures they could, but the hold-outs were skittish and determined to stay out; if the zoo folks tried for them now they stood a very good chance of driving them away and killing them. Best to let them take to the shelters, and hope it would be enough.

'Is the power to the heaters on generator stand-by?'

'No way. Cross your fingers.'

He continued with his survey. The low sun turned everything blinding silver. By now the temperature had risen to about twenty below, which in combination with the midday sunlight made a huge difference in how it felt to walk around. It came back to his body's memory how major distinctions could be made between cold and super-cold, so that eventually ten below became comfortable, because thirty below was so miserable; and ten above became shirtsleeve weather, while fifty below was always on the edge of sudden death.

The power went out west of Connecticut Avenue, and Frank went over there and helped for a while with a crew going door to door to make sure people were all right, occasionally carrying the hypothermic out to fire trucks and ambulances and off to shelters or hospitals. Eventually his hands got too cold to carry on. He had to retreat into a UDC coffee shop and drink a coffee with the other adventurers sardined into the place. Painful buzz of his fingers regaining their feeling, though it was nothing to the way his penis had felt. Then the coffee shop had to stop serving, as their pipes had frozen and their water supplies on hand were all used up. They stayed open just to provide shelter. The damage to pipes alone was sure to cost millions, someone said, and take weeks or months to fix. They might be in for a water crisis as bad as the one after the flood, when for several days potable water and functioning toilets had been very hard to find. People didn't think about these kinds of things until they happened, and then it was like discovering yet another Achilles heel, because it had ruptured.

The sounds of sirens seemed to be converging on them. Frank went out and looked around, saw black smoke rising in a thick plume over the neighborhood between Connecticut and the park, just south of where his van was parked. He hustled over there, slapping his tingling hands together as he walked.

It looked as if squatters might have accidentally set an abandoned house on fire. Already the blaze was out of hand, several houses burning, a whole knot of trees, all roaring in pale flames. The radiant heat beat on Frank's face. When the fire trucks arrived they found that the water had frozen in the fire hydrants. They had to work on that instead of the fire. A helicopter chattered in and dropped its load of chemicals, to no great effect as far as Frank could tell. It had to be dangerous to fly helicopters in this kind of cold; they did it in Antarctica, but those helos were specially prepped. No doubt the Antarctic guys at NSF were extremely busy right now, helping in any way they could. No lunch run today. Corps of Engineers likewise. It was essential they keep power flowing. If there was any kind of significant power outage throughout the city, many people would freeze.

Talking to some of the firemen around the hydrant, Frank learned that there were already as many as two dozen fires in the metro area. All emergency response people were out: firemen, police, paramedics, the power company repair crews; the National Guard had been called up, yes both of them. Everyone else was being urged to stay home. Nevertheless the number of people walking the streets increased as the day wore on, all of them bundled and ski-masked and walking out in the empty streets. It looked as if bank robbers had pulled off a major revolution.

Another fire started in Georgetown, which then lost power, and it also had frozen water mains. Frank drove down there, as his van kept starting for him, and he served as a taxi for a couple of hours, shuttling people from frigid houses and apartments onto the Georgetown University campus, where generators were keeping most of the buildings warm. George Washington University hospital was also working on generators, and for a while it was clear that taxiing people was the best thing Frank could do to help; but then the streets began to jam up with traffic, amazingly – it was still twenty below and yet stop-and-go had returned to Foggy Bottom. So he parked in Georgetown again and joined a group of volunteers going door-to-door in the outage area, making sure everyone was out who wanted to be out.

The residential streets of Georgetown were a surprise to Frank. He had never walked around, or even driven in, this part of town, and it was like being transported to some quaint and comfortable old quarter of a northern European town. Colorful, neat, handmade, human scale – the streets were like what Main Street in Disneyland had always hoped to suggest, much more real of course, but still, toylike. Like the village in a snow-filled paperweight. He would have to return and check it out under more normal circumstances.

The sky overhead was unlike that in any paperweight, dark with smoke that streamed in fat bands all across the sky. A huge population lived hidden in the forest around the city, and nearly every single fireplace must have had a blaze in it; and a certain percentage had gone wrong and burned down their houses and added their greater smokes to the chimney fires, so that now the sky was streaked with black, and flakes of ash drifted down, lighter than snowflakes. Frank's nose kept him from smelling the smoke, but he could taste it as grit on his tongue, a little acrid. He wondered if he would ever be able to smell again.

A fire truck wailed down Wisconsin, and the firemen in it jumped out and ran a pump and hose line down to the Potomac. It took some awkward work with chainsaws to break through the ice covering the river, which was now a big white sheet from bank to bank. A crowd gathered to watch and cheer, their breath frosting over them in a small cloud. Sputter and roar of a big Honda generator powering up, downshift as the pump motor was engaged, a moment of suspense while nothing happened; then the flattened hose bulked like a snake swallowing a mouse, and water shot out of the big nozzle held by two firemen, who quickly secured it to a stand and aimed the white flow at the leading edge of their blaze. The crowd cheered again. Spray flying upward from the jet of water had time to freeze in the air, flocking the nearby rooftops with the kind of snow one saw at ski resorts. A tall black man grinned hugely at Frank: 'They froze that fire.'

Late in the day Frank went back down to the Potomac to walk out on the ice. Scores of people had had the same idea. It had happened the same way in London two weeks before, and all over the world people had seen images of the grand festival the Londoners had spontaneously thrown, celebrating the freeze in the Elizabethan style. Now on the Potomac people were mostly standing around or skiing, playing football or soccer or ad hoc versions of curling. One or two wore ice skates and glided through the crowd, but most were slipping around in boots or their ordinary shoes. A hot dog cartman was busy selling out his entire stock. The ice on the river was usually white but here and there was as clear as glass, the moving black water visible below. It was freaky at first to walk on these clear sections, but even big groups and giant leaps into the air did not cause a shudder in the ice, which looked from the occasional hole chopped in it to be about two foot thick, maybe more.

When sunset slanted redly across the Potomac the light struck Frank like another vision out of Brueghel. One of his Flemish winter canal scenes, except most of Washington D.C.'s population was black. Out here on the river you could finally see that in a way that Northwest and Arlington never revealed. It was like Carnavale on ice, the celebrants improvising clothing that was warm enough to keep them out there, which then became costumes too. A giant steel drum band added to the Caribbean flavor. Snowfights and slip-and-slides, break dancing and curling that was more like bowling, touch football, tackle football, it all was happening out there between Virginia and the District, on this sudden new terrain. In the fading light the whole world took on a smoky red cast, the river ice both white and red, and the contrast between the snow and the dark faces finally diminished to the point where Frank could see people properly. It seemed to him to be an extraordinarily beautiful populace, every race and ethnicity on Earth represented – the many black faces vivid and handsome, cheerful to the point of euphoria, laughing as they took in the scene – the white folk flushed as red as the sunset snow, dressed like L.L. Bean or gypsies or Russians or anything they had at hand – all partying together on the frozen Potomac, until with the dark it got too cold to stay out any longer.

The fires burned all night and into the next day, but on the other hand, the temperatures never dropped lower than ten below. Some in the coffee shops next morning thought all the smoke had created a smudge pot effect, the ultimate urban heat-island insulator; but even out in the country the temperatures had not dropped as low as they had gotten the night before. The low had been a freak thing, an all-time record for the city, and even the *Post* the next morning had a headline like a London tabloid: FIFTY DEGREES BELOW.

Though it never got that cold again in the days that followed, it always remained well below zero, keeping the city somewhat in crisis mode. First the great flood, now the great freeze, with widespread fires as well – what next? 'There's an excellent chance of drought next summer,' Kenzo cackled when Frank talked to him on the phone. 'We could hit for the cycle. And it's going to get windy tomorrow.'

NSF stayed closed, along with the rest of the federal government. Frank called Diane every morning, and once when he lamented the lost work time she said 'Don't you worry about that, I'm working Congress every day, I take them out until they look like they are frostbit, and every one of them will vote for what we ask next time. It couldn't be better.'

So Frank would wish her good luck, and spend that day cruising up and down Connecticut, hiking into the park, and helping out wherever he could, mostly with FOG work. Repair a hot box, keep them supplied with food, help lift out a tranquilized camel; always keeping an eye out for Chessman or the bros. Down to Dupont Circle, up to Adams Morgan, crossing the frozen creekbed to get to Georgia Avenue, marveling at the stream's white arabesques, the frolic architecture of ice and snow.

On the third night of the snap he ran into the bros, hunkered in a concrete embayment surrounding a Dupont metro station grating. They had walled off the indentation from the sidewalk with refrigerator boxes, and cantilevered a roof of flattened boxes as well. The interior was even frosting up like an old refrigerator.

'Come on you guys,' Frank said. 'You should get to one of the shelters, the wind is supposed to hit soon. This is serious.'

'It's always been serious, Bleeder.'

'Hey who's winning! Where's that barrel of brandy?'

'The UDC gym is open as a shelter.'

'Fuck that.'

'This is warmer here.'

'Yeah yeah. Whatever.'

He went up into the UDC shelter himself, and spent an hour or two walking down the rows of cots, handing out paper cups of hot chocolate to the kids. The homeless or the heatless, it was hard to tell the difference in here. He ran across the knitting woman, sitting on her cot knitting away, and greeted her with pleasure. He sat and they talked for a while.

'Why won't the guys come in?'

'They're stubborn. What about you, have you come in?'

'Well, no. But I don't need to.'

She smiled her gap-toothed smile. 'You're all the same.'

'Hey what about Chessman? Do you know what happened to him?'

'I don't. He just stopped showing up. It don't mean nothing. I think he probably moved.'

'I hope.'

She knitted on imperturbably. She had knitted herself pale yellow gloves that left her fingertips free, poking out of the fabric like tree roots. 'He lived over in Northeast somewhere. His people may have moved.'

'You don't think something bad happened to him?'

She shook her head, counting under her breath. 'I don't think so. I've been living out for twelve years. Hardly anything bad ever happens. It's not so much dangerous as it is unhealthy.'

'I suppose so. Don't you want a place?'

'Sure. But, you know. Wherever you are is a place.'

'If you see Chessman will you tell me?'

'Sure I will. I was gonna do that anyway. I'm curious myself.'

Frank wandered on up Connecticut, looking into the coffee shops and student cafes. He was not reassured by the woman's words. Thinking about it, he started making calls to people whose whereabouts he did know. The Quiblers were fine, Charlie and Anna working from home, school cancelled, fire in the fireplace. Anna noted that hoarding had begun at the grocery stores and that this was a breakdown in social trust that could be very debilitating to normal supply dynamics. It was starting to happen at gas stations already, lines to tank up, people freezing as they waited, all on their cell phones out stamping their feet. Frank promised to drop by and say hi. Same with the Khembalis, who again offered him a place to stay, despite the crowd. He promised to drop by.

He gave Spencer a call, and the shaman picked up after the first ring. 'Hello?'

'Hey why no frisbee, what the hell?'

Spencer laughed appreciatively. 'We tried, believe me! But if the disks hit a tree they shatter! We broke a whole bunch of them Monday, although we did establish the low temperature record, of course. Maybe we should try again.'

'That would be fun. Where are you guys staying, are you keeping warm?'

'Oh yeah, we're squatting around like always, it's fine. There's a place on McKinley just off Nebraska that's got good insulation and a big fireplace, you should join us, have a meal.'

'Still doing the fregan thing?'

'Sure, it works even better in this cold, the dumpsters are like big freezers.'

'Well maybe I'll just look for you in the park.'

'Ha ha ha, you chicken. We'll give you a call next time we go out, give me your cell phone number again.'

Then it was back on the street.

The cold snap had been going on for so long that it had somehow stabilized. Search and rescue had been turned over to the professionals, and Frank didn't quite know what to do. He could go back in the park, he could drive into the office and do some work, he could go to Optimodal and take a hot shower . . . he stopped himself from thinking about plans. There was a lot to do still in Northwest, surely.

And just as he thought that he saw Cutter, out in the street working on a tree that had split and fallen across three of the four lanes. Frank joined him and offered help that Cutter gladly accepted. As they worked Cutter said that a column of water had evidently filled a crack in the trunk, then frozen and split the tree apart. Frank picked up cut branches and carried them to the pile they had established on the sidewalk. Cutter thanked him without taking an eye off his work. 'You seen the park guys?'

'Yeah I ran into them, they appear to be okay.'

Cutter shook his head. 'They ought to get a place.'

'No lie. You've got a lot of new work like this, I take it?'

'Oh Lordie! We should cut down every tree in this city. They all gonna fall on something they not spose to.'

'I'm sure. When it's this cold, will it kill them?'

'Not necessarily. Not except they split open like this.'

'So how do you choose which ones to work on?'

'I drive till I see one in the street.'

'Ha. Is it okay if I help you some more?'

'Of course.'

It was good work, absorbing and warm. Dodge around the work and the cars, never stop moving, get the wood off the street. The chainsaw was loud. It took four people lifting together to get the biggest section of trunk over into the gutter.

Frank stayed with them through the rest of that afternoon. The days were getting a little longer. After a while he felt comfortable enough to say, 'You guys shouldn't wear cotton against the skin, it's the worst possible stuff for cold.'

'What, are you a vapor barrier man? I hate that shit.'

They were all black. They lived over in Northeast but had worked mostly Northwest when they had worked for city Parks. One of them went on about being from Africa and not capable of handling this kind of cold.

'We're all from Africa,' Frank said.

'Very true but your people obviously left there before mine did. Your people look to have gone directly to the North Pole.'

'I do like the cold,' Frank admitted.

'Like to die in it.'

That night Frank slept in his van, and rejoined Cutter's tree crew for the morning, after a dawn walk up and down the park. Deer nibbled unhappily among the snowdrifts; the rest of the animals stuck near the hot boxes. The gibbons looked more and more unhappy, but Nancy said an attempt to capture them had only caused them to swing away through the trees, hooting angrily. The zoo zoologists were thinking of trying to dart them with tranquilizers.

The air temperature remained well below zero, but now there was an almost full load of traffic back on the streets, and a great number of trees and branches to be cleared. More people walked the sidewalks, some bundled up like the Michelin Man. The tree crew put out orange plastic stripping to keep crowds away from their work, especially when things were falling. Frank carried wood. No way did he want to go up in a tree and end up like poor Byron, hollering My leg my leg . . . Chop wood, carry water; chop water, carry wood.

When they took a break for lunch he left them and walked down to see how people were doing in the UDC shelter, and at the Dupont metro vent. Then back up to the zoo, where many people from FOG and FONZ were still working to capture the ferals. In the zoo enclosures they were reduced to supplementing the regular heating system with weird combinations of battery-powered space heaters to try to keep the enclosures a bit warmer. The animals looked miserable anyway, and quite a few had died.

It was such a busy week that Frank almost forgot when Friday rolled around, until that morning, when it became all he thought about. He ate Friday evening at the Rio Grande, then stood stamping his feet and blowing into his gloved hands at his pay phone in Bethesda.

But no call; and when it was ten after nine, he called Caroline's number, and let it ring and ring, with never an answer.

What did that mean?

He would find out next Friday, at best. So it seemed. Suddenly their system looked very inadequate. He wanted to talk to her!

Nothing to be done. He tried one last time, listened to the

ring. No answer. He had to do something else. He could go to work, or he could . . . no. Just leap. Deflated or not, indecisive or not.

Walking back to his van, he called Diane on his cell phone, as he had every day of the cold snap. She always answered, and her cheery voice held no huge aura of meaning or possibility. She considered that it had been a very good week for the cause. 'Everybody knows now that the problem is real. This isn't like the flood; this could happen three or four times every winter. Abrupt climate change is real, no one can deny it, and it's a big problem. Things are a mess! So, come on in as soon as they call off the shutdown. There are things we can do.'

'Oh I will,' Frank promised.

But the cold snap went on. The jet stream was running straight south from Hudson Bay. The wind strengthened, and added to every already-existing problem – fire, frostbite, trees down, power lines down. It began to seem like street work and polar emergency services were what he had always done. Get up in the frigid van and drive to get warm. Hike out to the treehouse, climb the trunk to pull Miss Piggy up a ways and tack her there on a piton; downclimb, most awkwardly. Scrounge, like a real homeless person, for cold weather clothing he could give away at the UDC shelter. His own gear at fullest deployment was more than adequate: an old knit hat, a windbreaker shell with a hood, an old Nike ACG (All Conditions Gear, well maybe), a windstopped fleece jacket made of Dupont's Drylete material, very warm stuff; capilene long underwear and long-sleeved shirt, Insport briefs that had a windstop panel in front, which would also hold a mitten to give his privates extra protection, until the rabbit fur arrived; then some bike shorts with the padding ripped out, some fleece knickerbockers, and then Koch pants, which covered the feet and went up to the waist, though they should have gone higher; Frank couldn't imagine what Koch had been thinking. Then his low-topped Salomon walking boots and Thorlo synthetic socks, seamless and perfect; he even started putting one of them down the front of his pants instead of a mitten. Very rabbit furlike. And low-topped gaiters to keep the snow out of his boots, stylish, like black spats. Over all that, on windy days, a jacket that went down to the thighs, and covered the hands and stuck out far beyond the face; a baseball hat to keep snow off the face, help with sun in eyes. Ski gloves, snowshoes and ski poles.

Frank could not be more set; he was probably the best-dressed man in the city. He was the Alpine man, come back to life! And his goal, Johnny Appletentlike, was to get everybody else living out-of-doors into gear that was at least adequate. Into shelters at night if the cold was too much. It was no easy task, because it called not only for acquisition of gear that was disappearing fast from all the thrift shops (though people didn't recognize wool, apparently), but the money to fund it. He used a grant from the zoo's feral fund, among other things, considering that with that name it was not even a case of reprogrammed funds. But the distribution of the gear could be tricky. No one liked gratitude, but many people were cold enough to take what he gave them. Cotton and cardboard were no longer hacking it. The stubborn ones were likely to die. The newspapers reported that a few hundred already had. Frank could scarcely believe some of the stories in the *Post* about the dumb things people had done and were still doing. They could be six inches from safety and not recognize it. It was as John Muir had said of the Donner Party; a perfectly fine winter base camp, botched by ineptitude. But they didn't know. It was a technique, and if you didn't have it you died. It wasn't rocket science but it was mandatory.

Frank had to be careful not to get careless himself. He stayed out all day every day, and part of him was beginning to think he had it wired, so that he spent longer sessions out. Sometimes he discovered he was so ravenous or thirsty that he was going to keel over; he blew into the coffee shops shivering hard, only to discover white patches on his chin, and fiendishly pinpricking fingers and ears. God knew what was happening to his poor nose. Emergency infusions of hot chocolate, then, blowing across the top and burning his mouth to gulp some down, burning his esophagus, feeling his insides burning while his extremities fizzed with cold. Hot chocolate was the perfect start on a return to proper heat and energy. Cinnamon rolls too; he was coming to believe that cinnamon was a powerful stimulant and that it also allowed him to see better in the black-and-white of his dawn and dusk patrols. Shifting dapple under cloudy moonlight, it didn't matter to him now, he saw the structure of Washington D.C. and Rock Creek Park underneath all that chiaroscuro, high on the magic spice.

One night he found the bros back in the park, around a very hospitable bonfire. Just outside the light the body of a deer lay partly skinned, steaks hacked out of its flank.

'– so fucking cold it made me stupid.'

'Like that's what did it.'

'– I couldn't even talk for a couple days. Like my tongue was froze. Then I could talk, but I only knew like ten words.'

'That happened to me,' Fedpage put in. 'I started talking in old English, and then German. You know, "Esh var *kalt*." The Germans really know how to say it. And then it was just grunts and moans for a while. For esh var kallllt.'

'You're funny, Fedpage. You were wasted in Vietnam.'

'I was indeed wasted in Vietnam.'

Fluctuating radiant pulses of heat washed over their faces.

Frank sat by the fire and watched it burn. 'So you guys really were in Vietnam.'

'Of course.'

'You must be pretty old then.'

'We are pretty old then! Fuck you. How the fuck old are you?'

'Forty-three.'

'What a kid.'

'We're twice as old as that, kid. No wonder your nose bleeds.'

'In point of fact I'm fifty-five,' said Fedpage.

'Boomer scum.'

'Yeah, he went to the University of Vietnam.'

'So what was it like?'

'It was fucked! What do you think?'

'At least it wasn't cold,' Zeno said dourly. 'It might have been fucked but at least you didn't freeze your dick off.'

'I told you to put a sock down there.'

'Put a sock on it! Good idea!'

Fedpage, solemn, calculating: 'I would need one of them knee socks.'

General mirth. Discussion of burning needle sensation during penile thawing. Listing of exceptional cases of genital trauma. Frank watched Zeno brood. Zeno noticed and snapped, 'It was fucked, man.'

'It was everything,' Fedpage said.

'That's true. It was every kind of thing. There were some guys over there who joined up specifically to kill people. Some people were like that. But most of them weren't, and for them it was hell. They didn't know what hit them. We just did what we were told and tried to stay alive.'

'Which we did.'

'But we were lucky! It was sheer dumb luck. When we were in Danang we could just as easily been overrun.'

'What happened there?' Frank said.

'We got caught by the Tet offensive –'

'He don't know about any of that. We were cut off, okay? We were surrounded in a town and we got hammered. They killed a lot of us and they would have killed all of us except the Air Force made some passes. Bombed the shit out of those NVA.'

'Dropped us food too.'

'That's right, we were going to starve as well as get massacred. It was a race to see which. Incompetent bastards.'

'We shared the last food, remember that?'

'Of course. A fucking spoonful. Didn't do any of us a bit of good.'

'It was a team thing. You should have seen Zeno the time we heloed down into a minefield and the medic wouldn't get out to help some wounded. Zeno just jumped out and ran right across that minefield, he led those brothers back in just like there weren't no mines out there. Even after one of them went off and dee-exed a guy who didn't follow right in his footsteps.'

'You did that?' Frank said.

'Yeah well,' Zeno said. He looked away, shrugged. 'That was my Zeno's paradox moment I guess. I mean if you're always only halfway there, then you can't ever step on no mine, right?'

Frank laughed.

'It was great,' Fedpage insisted.

'No it wasn't. It was just what it was. Then you get back to the States and it's all like some bad movie. Some stupid fucking sit-com. That's America, man. It's all such bullshit. People act like they're such big deals, they act like all their rules are real when really they're just bullshit so they can keep you down and take everything for themselves.'

'True,' Fedpage said.

'Ha ha. Well, here we are. Looks like the fire is about halfway down. Who's going to go get more wood for this fire, I ain't gonna do it.'

'So did you ever go up to the shelter?'

'Sure.'

*  *  *

The hard wind finally struck as forecast, and it got bad again for a couple days, as bad as in the beginning. 'It ain't the cold, it's the –'

'Shut the fuck up!'

Frozen branches snapped and fell all over town, on people, cars, power lines, rooftops. Frank went out every day and helped Cutter and his crew. Then one day, clearing a fallen tree from a downed power line, a branch swung his way and thwacked him on the face.

'Oh sorry I couldn't get that! Hey Frank! Hey are you okay?'

'I'm okay,' Frank said, hands at his face. He still couldn't feel his nose. He tasted blood at the back of his throat, swallowed. It was nothing new. It happened from time to time. It even tasted like old blood, left over from the original injury. He shook it off, kept on carrying wood.

The next morning, however, he got out of his van and walked up and down Connecticut, and – he couldn't decide what to do. Time for a leap before you look, therefore; do whatever came to hand. But where to start?

He never got started. He walked up Connecticut to Chevy Chase Circle, then back down to the zoo. How big the world became when it tasted like blood.

He stopped at a stoplight to think it over. He could help at the zoo, or he could help Cutter, or he could look for Chessman (maybe in Brooklyn), or he could help at the shelter, or he could go to work, or he could go for a run, or a hike, or a climb. Or he could read a book. His current reading was *The Long Winter* by Laura Ingalls Wilder, a real beauty, the story of a small Dakota town surviving the extreme winter of 1880. The town had lost all contact with the rest of humanity, cut off by huge snowpacks from October to May. Talk about island refugia! He had gotten to the part where they were almost starving.

So he could read. He could sit in a coffee shop and read

his book, and no one would have any reason to object. Or he could go work out at the club. Or . . .

He was still standing aimlessly at the corner of Connecticut and Tilden when his cell phone rang.

It was Nick Quibler. School had been cancelled for the day, and he was wondering if Frank was available to go on a FOG hunt.

'I sure am,' Frank croaked. 'Thanks for thinking of it.'

**When Charlie got home** from the grocery store, where the shelves had been largely empty, Anna and Joe were out, but Nick was already back, playing his gameboy.

'Hey Nick, how was your FOG trip with Frank?'

'Oh. Well, it wasn't a big accident.'

'Uh oh.' This phrase was a family joke, recalling a time when a much younger Nick had tried to delay telling his parents about something bad he had caused to happen at pre-school; but this time Nick wasn't smiling. Curiously focused on his gameboy, in fact. 'What do you mean it wasn't a big accident?'

'Well, you know. No *people* got hurt.'

'That's good, but what did happen?'

'Well. You know. It wasn't so good for one of the gibbons.'

'Uh oh, how so?'

'One died.'

'Oh no! How did it happen?' Hand to Nick's shoulder; Nick stayed focused on the game. 'What happened, bud?'

'Well you see, it's too cold for them now.'

'I bet! That's true for a lot of the animals, right?'

'Right. And so they have these heated shelters out in the park, and all the animals are using them now, but some of the animals are hard to catch even when they do use them. The gibbons and siamangs are like that, they sit on the roofs and run away if you try to get close, and some of them have died. They found two of them frozen. So they decided they better try to capture the ones still out there, before they died too.'

'That makes sense.'

'Yeah, but they're really hard to get near. They swing through the trees? It's really cool. So you have to kind of hunt them down if you want to, you know.'

'Uh oh.'

'Yeah. You have to shoot them with a tranquilizer dart.'

'Oh yeah. I used to see that on *Wild Kingdom*.'

'They do it on *Animal Planet* all the time.'

'Do they. That's good to know. That's continuity. But I remember one time when I was a kid, this hippo got out of Lion Country Safari, and they shot it with too much.'

'No, not that.'

'What then?'

'Well, they're always up in the trees. And Frank is the only one who can really get very close to them.'

'Ha. Our Frank is something.'

'Yeah, he can sound just like them. And he can walk without making any noise. It's really cool.'

'How the heck does he do that?'

'He looks where he's going! I mean he walks along and his face is pointed right down at the ground most of the time.'

'Like a dog?'

'No, more like a bird. He's always looking around, zip zip, you know.'

'Ah yeah. And so?'

'So we were up by Military Road and we got a call that someone had spotted a gibbon pair near the Nature Center going down toward the creek, so we went down the creekbed, you can walk right on the ice, and we got in those rocks down by the creek?'

'Which?'

'The Nook and Cranny rocks, you can see through the cranny upstream, and so we laid in wait for a while and –'

'What do you do when you're lying in wait?'

'We just stand there real quiet. You can be careful about how you breathe, it's pretty cool.'

'Ah yeah. And so then?'

'So then three gibbons came past us, and they weren't up very high and Frank had the gun balanced on the Nook and was ready for them. He shot one right in the butt, but then some people yelled.'

'Other FOG people?'

'No, just we didn't know who, and the gibbons took off and Frank took off running after them.'

'Didn't you too?'

'Yeah I did, but he was fast. I couldn't keep up. So but neither could he, not with the gibbons, they just fly along, but the one he shot fell. From way up there.'

'Oh no.'

'Yeah.'

'Oh no. So Frank couldn't . . .'

'No, he tried but he couldn't keep up. He wasn't there to catch it.'

'So it died?'

'Yeah. Frank picked it up. He checked it out.'

'He was hoping it was still alive.'

'Yeah. But it wasn't. It got killed by the fall. I mean it looked okay, but it was . . . loose. It wasn't there.'

'Oh no. How awful. What did Frank do?'

'He was kind of upset.'

**The bare branches overhead** were like black lightning bolts striking out of the Earth into the clouds. Like decision maps, first choose this, then that. He was cold, cold in his head somehow. All his thoughts congealed. Maybe if he weren't injured. Maybe next winter. Maybe if it wasn't a long winter. Maybe they all had to find their cave. Fur es war kalt.

Wind ripped through the branches with a sound like tearing cloth. A big sound. Under it the city hummed almost inaudibly. Snow cracked as he stepped on it. There was no way to walk quietly now. The branches overhead were like black fireworks, flailing the sky. He moved under them toward the gorge, shifting his weight one pound at a time.

Eventually he came to one of the heated shelters. Little square hut, its open side facing south. Hot box; all interior surfaces emanated heat. Like a big toaster oven left open. A bad thought, given the way toaster ovens worked.

Inside, and scattered around the opening, they stood or sat or lay. Rabbits, raccoons, deer, elands, tapirs, even foxes, even a bobcat. Two ibex. None meeting the eye of any other; all pretending they were each alone, or with only their own kind. As on an island created in a flood, it was a case of stay there or die. Truce. Time out.

Very slowly he approached. He kept his head down, his eyes to the side. He sidled. He crabbed. Shoulders hunched lower and lower. He turned his back to them entirely as he closed on them, and sat down in the lee of the shelter, about fifteen feet out from it, in a little hollow floored with snow. He shifted back toward them to get off the snow, onto a decomposed black log. Fairly dry, fairly comfortable. The heat from the shelter was palpable, it rushed over him intermittently on the wind, like a stream. He rested his head on his chest, arms around his knees. A long time passed; he wasn't sleepy, but long intervals passed during which no thoughts came to him. A gust of chill air roused him, and he shifted so he could see more of the shelter out of the corner of his eye. At the very edge of his peripheral vision lay what could have been the jaguar.

The animals were not happy. They all stared at him, wary, affronted. He was messing up a good situation. The lion had lain down with the lamb, but the man was not welcome. He wanted to reassure them, to explain to them that he meant no harm, that he was one of them. But there were no words.

Much later there was a crack, a branch breaking. In a sudden flurry many animals slipped away.

Frank looked up. It was Drepung, and Charlie Quibler. They approached him, crouched by his side. 'Come with us, Frank,' Drepung said.

# EIGHT

## *Always Generous*

*The scientific literature on the effects of damage to the prefrontal cortex was vast. Its existence bespoke a variety and quantity of human suffering that was horrible to contemplate, but never mind; it was rehearsed here in the course of attempting to reduce that suffering. Among the cases discussed were traumas so much worse than what Frank had suffered that he felt chastened, abashed, lucky, frightened. He wasn't even sure his brain had been injured. He wasn't sure it wasn't just a broken nose and the taste of blood at the back of his throat. Not much compared to an iron spike through the skull.*

*Nevertheless it was his injury, and how he felt about it was now also part of the symptomology, because emotions were generated or coordinated or felt in the prefrontal cortex, and so the precise kind of emotional change experienced was an indication of what trauma might have occurred. The dysfunction could be very precise and limited: some subjects were rendered incapable of compassion or embarrassment but could still feel happiness or fear, others felt no dismay or even laughed at crippling disabilities they were quite aware of, and so on. Trauma victims thus became in effect experiments, testing what happened if you removed parts of a very complex system.*

*Frank clicked and read apprehensively, reminding himself that knowledge was power. 'Fear and Anxiety: possible roles of the amygdala and bed nucleus of the stria terminalis.' 'Impaired recognition of emotion in facial expressions following bilateral damage to the human amygdala.' The amygdala was behind the nose, a little distance in. A famous case of short-term amnesia had been nicked in the amygdala when a fencing foil went in through his nose.*

*'Emotion: an evolutionary byproduct of the neural regulation of the autonomic nervous system.' The sociobiological view, for once of less interest to Frank. He would come back to that later. 'Reciprocal limbic-cortical functioning and decision-making: converging PET findings in lack of affect and indecision.' 'Neuroanatomical corrrelates of happiness, sadness, and decisiveness.' Both studies of the emotion/decision connection. 'Subgenual prefrontal cortex abnormalities in mood disorders.' Study of a case who was unusually wild and incompetent in life decisions, unlike anyone else in her family, and then they remembered that when she was an infant a car had run over her head.*

*'From the nose to the brain.' Oh my; there were synapses that ran from one end of the head to the other. They went from the nose to everywhere. Scent, memory, behaviors associated with pleasure. These tapped in to dopamine that was made available in the nucleus accumbens in the basal forebrain, behind the back of the mouth. This availability depended on a long biochemical sequence functioning well at every point.*

*The right frontal cortices were more associated with negative emotions than the left; the right somatosensory cortices were active in integrating body management, which might be why it was the apparent seat of empathy. Blocking oxytocin in a female prairie vole did not interfere with its sex drive, but with the attachment to its partner that would usually correlate to sex. Suppressing vasopressin had the same effect on male voles, who would normally be faithful for life, voles being monogamous. You needed both the insula and the anterior cingulate working well to be able to experience joy. Fluency of ideation increased with joy, decreased with sorrow. The brain was often flooded with endogenous opioid peptides such as endomorphines, enkephalin, dynorphin, endorphins – all pain killers. You needed those. Brain systems responsible for ethical thinking were probably not dedicated to ethics exclusively, but rather also to biological regulation, memory, decision making, and creativity. In other words, to everything. You needed joy to function well. In fact, it appeared that competent or successful decision-making depended on full capability in all the emotions; and these in turn depended on a healthy prefrontal cortex.*

*It looked to Frank like all the new research was adding up to a new understanding of the roles played by the various elements of human thought, consciousness, behavior; a new model or paradigm, in which emotion and feeling were finally understood to be indispensable in the process of proper reasoning. Decision-making in particular was a reasoning process in which the outcomes of various possible solutions were judged in terms of how they might feel. Without that, the ability to decide well was crippled. This was Damasio's main point: the definition of reason as a process that needed to abjure all emotion had been wrong. Descartes and most of Western philosophy since the Greeks had been wrong. It was the feel one was looking for.*

*Judging from the evolutionary history of the brain, it seemed clear that feelings had entered the picture in pre-human species, as part of social behaviors. Sympathy, attachment, embarrassment, pride, submission, censure and recompense, disgust (at cheaters), altruism, compassion; these were social feelings, and arrived early on, perhaps before language and the 'string of sentences' that often seemed to constitute conscious thought. And they were perhaps more*

*important, as overall cognitive strategy was formed by uncon-
scious mentation in regions such as the ventromedial frontal
lobe (right behind the nose). Life was feeling one's way toward
a goal which ultimately equated to achieving and maintaining
certain feelings.*

*So an excess of reason was indeed a form of madness! Just
as Rudra Cakrin had said in his lecture. It was something
the Buddhist tradition had discovered early on, by way of
introspection and analysis alone. A kind of science, a natural
history.*

*Which was impressive, but Frank found himself comforted
to have the assertion backed by scientific research and a neuro-
logical explanation. Or some first hypotheses concerning
explanations. For one thing it was a chance to come at the
problem in a fresh way, with new data. Buddhist thinkers,
and those in Western philosophical tradition who used introspection and logic alone to postulate 'how the mind works,'
had been mulling over the same data for five thousand years,
and now seemed caught up in preconceptions, distinctions
and semantic hairsplitting of all kinds. Introspection did not
give them the means to investigate unconscious thought; and
unconscious thought was proving to be crucial. Even
consciousness, standing there in the mirror to be looked at
(maybe) – even what could be introspected or deduced was
so extremely complex, and distributed through so many
different parts of the parcellated brain, that you could not
think your way through it. It needed a group effort, working
on the physical action inside the object itself. It needed science.*

*And now science was using new tools to move beyond its
first achievements in taxonomy and basic function; it was
getting into analysis of evidence collected from living minds,
from brains both healthy and damaged. It was a huge effort,
involving many labs and scientists, and still involved in the
process of paradigm construction. Some academic philosophers cast scorn on the simplicity of these researchers' early*

models, but to Frank it was better than continuing to elaborate theories generated by the evidence of introspection alone. Obviously there was still far to go, but until you took the first steps you would never be on the way.

It was noticeable that the Dalai Lama always welcomed the new results from brain science. It would help Buddhists to refine their own beliefs, he said; it was the obvious thing to do. And it was true that many academic philosophers interested in consciousness also welcomed the new findings.

Welcomed or not, all the papers from the new body of work were accumulating on the net. And so Frank lay there in bed, reading them on his laptop, unable to figure out what he felt, or what he should do next, or if he might have a physical problem. Damasio, a leader in this new research: 'The system is so complex and multilayered that it operates with some degree of freedom.' Oh yes, he was free, no doubt of that – but was he damaged? What did he feel? What was this feeling, like oceans of clouds in his chest? And what should he do next?

**The Khembali house in** Arlington was just as crowded as Frank had thought it would be, maybe even more so. It was a big house, perhaps built to be a boarding house from the start, with a ground floor of big public rooms and three floors of bedrooms above, many of them off long central hallways, and an extensive basement. But as a good percentage of the Khembali populace was being housed in these rooms, all of them were overflowing.

Clearly it would be best if he continued to live out of his van, using the bathrooms at NSF and Optimodal. But his Khembali friends were adamant in their invitation.

Sucandra said, 'Please, Frank. Join Rudra Cakrin in his room. No one else will move in there, and yet he needs someone. And he likes you.'

'Doesn't he like everybody?'

Sucandra and Padma regarded each other.

'Rudra was the oracle,' Padma told Frank.

'So?'

Sucandra said, 'It seems one old Bön spirit that used to visit him comes back from time to time.'

'Also,' Padma added, 'he seems to feel we have lost Tibet. Or failed to recover it. He doesn't think he will see it again in this life. It makes him . . .'

'Irritable.'

'Angry.'

'Perhaps a little mad.'

'He does not blame you for any of this, however.'

'To him you represent another chance for Tibet.'

'No, he just likes you. He knows the situation with Tibet is hopeless, at least for some time to come.'

An exile. Frank had never been an exile in the formal sense, and never would be; but living on the east coast had given him a profound sense of not being at home. Bioregional displacement, one might say; and for a long time he had hated this place. Only in the last year had the forest begun to teach him how it could be loved. And if the great eastern hardwood forest had repelled him, how much more might it repel a man from the treeless roof of the world? Who could never go home?

So Frank felt he understood that part of Rudra's moodiness. The visiting demon, however . . . Well, these were religious people. They weren't the only religious people Frank knew. It should resemble talking to Baptists, and he had gotten used to that. It was just another worldview in which the cosmos was filled with invisible agents, intervening in human affairs.

He could always focus on the shared pain of displacement. Besides, Sucandra and Padma were asking for his help.

So that night Drepung took him in to see Rudra Cakrin, in a tiny room off the stair landing before the flight to Tibet the attic, a space that might once have been a closet. There was only room for a single bed and a slot between it and the wall.

Rudra was sitting up in bed. He had been ill, and looked much older than Frank had ever seen him. 'Please to see you,' he said, peering up at him as they shook hands. 'You are my new English teacher, Drepung say. You teach me English, I teach you Tibetan.'

'That would be good,' Frank said.

'Very good. My English better than your Tibetan.' He smiled, his face folding into its map of laugh wrinkles. 'I don't know how we fit two beds in here.'

'I can unroll a groundpad down here,' Frank suggested. 'Take it up by day.'

'Good idea. You don't mind sleep on floor?'

'I've been sleeping in a tree.'

Startled, Rudra refocused on Frank. Again the strange intensity of his gaze; he looked right into you. And who else had Frank told about his treehouse? No one but Caroline.

'Good idea!' Rudra said. 'One thing right away – I cannot be, what say – guru for you.'

'That's okay, I already have a guru. He teaches me frisbee.'

'Good idea.'

Afterward Frank said to Drepung, 'He seems fine to me.'

'So you will share a room with him?'

'Whatever you like. I'm your guest. You decide.'

'Thank you. I think it will be good for both of you.'


There was no denying that Frank felt deeply uneasy about moving indoors, as if he were breaking a promise to someone. A kind of guilt, but more importantly, a profound physical unease, a tightness in the chest, a numbness in the head. But it was more all-encompassing than that.

On waking in the mornings he would get up from his groundpad in Rudra's room, roll it up, stick it under Rudra's bed, go downstairs and out the door, almost sick to his stomach with anxiety. Shivering in the driver's seat of his van, he would wake up the rest of the way, then drive over to Optimodal, getting there just as they unlocked the doors. Diane was often already there waiting, slapping her mittened hands together. She always had a cheery smile to greet him. He found her consistency impressive. Sometimes his smile in response must have looked wan indeed. And in fact she sometimes put a hand to his arm and asked if he were all right. He always nodded. Yes; all right. Not good not bad. Not anything he could define. Nose still stuffed up, yes, but otherwise okay. Ready to go.

And in they would go, for a workout that now had the two of them wandering semi-autonomously; they had got past feeling they needed to team up to be friendly, and merely did their own things in such an order that they were often in the same room, and could sometimes talk, or help out with weights or holding ankles. Then it was off to the showers and the daily blessing of hot water running over him. Presumably on the other side of the wall Diane was doing the same under a shower of her own. By now Frank could visualize pretty well what Diane would look like. She would look good. Probably this didn't matter. It only made him worry about Caroline and what might have happened to her.

But he worked every day with Diane, and he couldn't help but admire how skillful she was, and determined. They were entering the final stage of arrangements for the North Atlantic intervention, and Diane now devoted a good part of every day talking to the people running the various parts of it. The International Maritime Organization was in charge of shipping; UNEP was making arrangements for salt; the big four re-insurance companies were providing or raising most of the funding. Wracke and the Corps were providing engineering and logistics.

There were some 3,500 oil tankers in operation around the world, they had learned, and about thirty percent of those were still the older single-hulled kind that were legally required to be replaced. Five hundred Very Large Crude Carriers were identified by the IMO as being past due for retirement and potentially available for sale or lease, and as the alternative to a deal would be either the breaker's yard or legal complications, the ship owners were being very accommodating. These old single-hulled VLCCs had an average capacity of ten million tons, small compared to the Ultra Large Crude Carriers now replacing them, but taken altogether, enough to do the job. The real problem here would be maintaining oil supplies at an adequate level with so much shipping taken out of transport all at once, but plans were being made to build up reserves, speed the construction of new double-hulled ULCCs, and return some of the superannuated fleet to oil transport once the salt operation was done.

So shipping capacity was not proving to be the choke point on the operation. More difficult was coming up with enough salt. Five hundred million metric tons turned out to be equal to about two years of total world production. When the working group first learned this they wondered if the project was impossible, at least in the time frame Diane was calling for. But Diane ordered the group to find out how quickly supplementary salt production could be ramped up. It soon became clear that the 225 million tons a year was more a matter of demand than supply; the salt industry in the Caribbean alone had years of salt dried in the pans ready to go, and the hardrock mines of New Brunswick and the rest of Canada also had a huge inventory, although it was more difficult to speed up extraction there than in the salt pans. In general there was a much greater productive capacity than was needed. Annual supply of highway rock salt in the US only amounted to thirty million tons a year. So there was excess salt, ready at hand in almost every drying pan and hardrock mine on the planet.

So the plan was physically possible, and the winter's unprecedented harshness meant it was now greeted with cries of hope and anticipation, rather than the raised eyebrows and shaking heads that had met it the previous summer. Indeed the futures market in salt had already jumped, Frank was interested to learn; prices had shot up five hundred percent. Fortunately enough futures had been bought by Swiss Re to bypass this inflation. Already production had been amped up, and the full complement of salt would be ready later that year, at about the same time the fleet of tankers was ready to be filled. As far as Diane could tell, the project was on course for a rendezvous of the fleet in the north Atlantic that fall. The unlikely-sounding idea first broached in Diane's office was going to happen, at a total cost of what looked to be about a hundred billion dollars. Swiss Re reported that they were on schedule in their fund-raising, and anticipated no problems.

'That's how desperate this winter has made people,' Edgardo observed.

'I told you the cold snap was a good thing,' Diane replied.

Frank found it interesting, but beyond that felt little. It was hard to connect all the activity to the brainstorming of last summer, when it had been only one of many ideas, and not the most likely at that. Now it had the look of something obvious and inevitable, what Edgardo called a silver bullet solution; a grand exercise in planetary engineering that was exciting worldwide attention, funding, and controversy.

Very interesting indeed; but now it was out of their hands, and Frank's daily work centered on other things. The Carbon Capture Campaign legislation was about to be introduced by one of Phil Chase's allies on the House Resources Committee, and Frank was involved with the graphs and tables evaluating various options and scenarios. Then also the test result evaluations on three different heat-to-electricity transformers had to be finished; and the SSEEP project was still generating huge amounts of trouble for NSF, as many accused them of illegally entering into presidential politics, and in a most crassly unfashionable old-left way at that. Diane occasionally thought she would get fired over it, although there was no mechanism or precedent. The heat was coming from all directions – even the Phil Chase campaign, which now appeared to regard the SSEEP platform as some kind of third party competition. Judging by the results so far, it had possibly been a bad idea to suggest a scientific approach to political problems, but on most days Frank was still glad they had tried it. Something had to be done. Although choosing which something remained a problem. One morning, walking from

Optimodal to work, Diane said to him, 'So what are you going to work on this morning?'

And Frank, distracted, said, 'I don't know. I could meet with Kenzo, or talk to George in Engineering, or call Yann. Or I could work on the Stirling calculations, or check into those flexible mirrors. Or call up the photovoltaics group. Or I could call Wracke, or the people at NASA to see if their heavy-duty booster is going to be ready this decade. Or there are these glassy metals I could –'

The light changed and they crossed Wilson. Diane, laughing at him, said, 'You sound like I feel.' But she didn't know how he felt; and he truly didn't know what to do. But then going into the building, the way she looked up at him, he saw that she knew that.

Edgardo and Kenzo dropped by to ask him if he wanted to join them for a run, as he hadn't for a while. He agreed to it, and they got dressed and took off.

It was crisp but sunny, perfect for running. It turned out Edgardo and Kenzo had run all winter long, except for during the cold snap. They were the most faithful of the faithful, also the most talkative of the talkative, which no doubt explained it. Only on a long run could you hold the floor for ten or fifteen minutes straight, discoursing on some subject or other while your audience pounded along, happy to listen because it distracted from their effort.

Edgardo was still the main talker, perhaps only because he was in the best running shape, and could natter on while the others were having to huff and puff. 'Yes,' he was explaining to Bob, 'the series is called the Alexandria Quartet.'

'Someone wrote four books about *Alexandria*?'

'That would be Alexandria, Egypt.'

'Oh!'

'Good books, really. Heavily dependent on Proust, of course, but how bad is that?'

'I don't know.'

'I read a good book,' Frank offered, having contributed nothing to the conversation. '*The Long Winter*, by Laura Ingalls Wilder.'

'Some kind of children's writer?' Edgardo guessed.

'Yes, she wrote *Little House on the Prairie*, and a whole bunch of others. You'd call her a girl's writer I guess, but this book was as good as anything I've ever read. Better, really. I mean really. I can't remember reading a better novel.'

Edgardo laughed delightedly: 'The great American novel! Here is all this debate about which is the Great American Novel, and meanwhile the real thing is a girl's book hiding right under our noses.'

'I think so.'

'That would be so wonderful. But I have to suspect your judgment has perhaps been influenced by the winter we have just lived through. Content of a work of art tends to influence people's aesthetic judgment to an unfortunate extent.'

'Like Anna's husband Charlie, thinking *Mr Mom* is Hollywood's greatest movie.'

'Ha. Exactly! We love the art that tells our story. Maybe that's why I love the Quartet so much. Expatriate angst in a steamy exotic city, full of sin and craziness. Maybe it's the same Alexandria after all.'

'And is that why *The Triplets of Belleville* is your favorite movie?'

'Yes! Story of my life, every single detail of it, right down to the frogs. Right down to the *dog*.'

On they ran, laughing at Edgardo.

In the evenings Frank returned to the Khembali house. He learned that it had an 'entertaining kitchen,' occupying the back half of the house's ground floor. It had been big to begin with, and was now equipped as if for a restaurant and bakery. Its exquisite heat always enveloped a dozen women and half a dozen men, shouting over the steamy clangor in Tibetan, and also a guttural English that was like Indian English but not. Frank now understood why they sometimes put subtitles under the Dalai Lama on film when he was speaking English.

Early on Drepung introduced Frank to two men and three women, all of whom spoke this English Frank could barely understand.

'So good to have you,' one said.

'Welcome to Khembalung,' said another.

'Can I help?' Frank asked.

'Yes. The bread will soon be ready to take out, and there are many potatoes to peel for dinner.'

'How many do you feed per meal?' Frank asked later, surveying the bustle as he scraped the skin off a potato.

'Hundred. First hundred eat here, the rest have to eat out. Or leftovers. Makes people timely.'

'Wow.'

Sucandra came by when he was finished and led him out back past a frozen compost heap to show him the back yard, now a frozen garden patch and a small greenhouse, the steamy clear plastic walls gleaming greenly, like a shower stall for vegetable people. 'Best to join garden duty now,' Sucandra suggested. 'It will be very nice in the spring.'

Frank nodded, inspecting the trees in the yard. Possibly one at the back could support a platform. Something to bring up later, obviously.

Sucandra and Padma's room was a half-flight below Frank and Rudra's. This meant Frank had other acquaintances to talk to, even when Rudra was asleep or Drepung was gone. Sometimes one of them came up to translate something Rudra had failed to communicate in English but still wanted to say. Mostly the two new roommates were left to hash it out on their own. In practice this meant a few exchanges a day, combining with a formal lesson in the last hour before the old man fell asleep. Rudra would nod out over *Richard Scarry's Best Word Book Ever*, muttering in his gravelly low voice, 'chalk, pencil sharpener, milk, cookies, paper clip, thumbtacks, lost clothing drawer,' chuckling as his finger tapped on the latest appearance of the pig man with the wind-blown hat. He would tell Frank the Tibetan words for these items, sometimes, but the main focus of their sessions was on English; Frank could learn Tibetan or not, Rudra did not care, he even appeared to scoff at the idea. 'What's the use?' he would growl. 'Tibet gone, ha.' Many odd things appeared to strike him funny, and he laughed with an abrupt low '*Ha*,' as if laughter were a surprise attack against invisible demons.

Frank was content to lie there on his groundpad in the evening, listening to the old man read and occasionally correcting his pronunciation. Usually Frank worked on his laptop.

'Pumpkin, ghost, what say? What say?' This was something the Khembalis often said as a kind of 'um' or 'er' as they searched for the right word or expression, so Frank had to be prompted to treat it as a real question.

'Oh sorry. That's a witch on a broom, but he's made the witch an owl in this case.'

'Ghost festival?'

'Yes, I suppose so.'

'That is very danger.' Tibetan was made of syllable roots that stayed the same in different word forms, and Frank noticed that a lot of the Khembalis used English nouns the same way, letting them do the work of verbs and modifiers: 'You will learn to meditation.' 'He became enlightenment.'

As they drifted off to sleep the two of them would hold strange conversations, involving both languages and a lot of confusion. Companionship without comprehension; it was just the kind of company that suited Frank. It reminded him of the bros in the park. In fact he told Rudra about his acquaintances in the park, and the winter they had had.

'Wandering tramps are often spirits in disguise.'
'I'm sure.'

The whole situation in the household was proving more congenial to Frank than he had expected it to be. Not knowing the language excused him from many conversations, but there were always people around; a crowd, faces gradually known, amazing faces, but few of them named or spoken to. That too was somewhat like being in the park with the bros. But it was warmer; and easier. He didn't have to decide where to be so often, where to go. What to do next – it was as simple as that. He didn't have to decide what to do every hour or so. That was hard even without damage to the prefrontal cortex.

One decision remained easy; on Friday after work, he drove over to Bethesda and ate at Rio Grande, and then at quarter to nine he was standing before his telephone at the metro bus stop. He waited through nine, and at 9:05 called Caroline's number. No answer.

He wondered if he could find out the location of her number. But would knowing it help him in any way, given that she didn't appear to be going there? What could have happened? What should he do? What might keep her from calling? Deep uneasiness was almost indistinguishable from fear.

He was walking sightlessly down Wisconsin toward his van, deep in his uneasiness, when his cell phone rang. He snatched it out of his pocket, while at the same time seeing that he was standing right before the elevator box that he and Caroline had emerged from last year. His heart leaped – 'Hello?'

'Frank it's me.'

'Oh good. What's happening?'

'– really sorry, I couldn't get there last week and I thought I'd be able to make it this week but I couldn't. I can't talk long I just slipped out.'

'Is something wrong?'

'Well yeah, but look I need to just set up another call here and get off. He's suddenly asking me to do things on Fridays and I don't know if it means anything, but can you be there at that number next Monday at nine?'

'Sure but hey listen, can you make a call to the Khembali embassy house in Arlington? They're not under his surveillance are they?'

'I don't think so. Who are they?'

'Embassy of Khembalung, their house is in Arlington. I'm staying there now and so you can call me there whenever you get free. In the evenings I'll likely be around.'

'Okay I'll look for a chance and call soon. I'm so sorry about this. He's changed jobs again and it's getting really complicated.'

'That's okay I'm just glad to hear from you!'

'Yeah I bet, I mean I would be too. I'll call real soon okay?'

'Okay.'

'Love you bye.'


It was amazing how much better he felt. Lack of affect was clearly not his problem; on the contrary, he had to avoid being overwhelmed by feelings. Giddy with relief, happy, worried, pleased, in love, frightened: but what did all those feelings combined add up to? This was what the studies never seemed to discuss, that you could feel so many different things at the same time. He felt *Caroline*. The uncanny presence of their elevator box, standing there before him throughout their conversation, had given him a palpable sense of her, an instant connection from the moment she spoke. Some quality in her voice drew his affections out. He wanted her to be happy. He wanted to be with her.

Leap before you look, stop trying to decide, just act on the spur of the moment. On Saturday he went over to Rock

Creek, first to move most of his stuff from his treehouse to his van, then to play a round with Spencer and Robert and Robin. The frisbees still tended to shatter if they hit a tree straight on, but other than that the frisbee guys seemed fine with the hard winter. Spencer said it was the same with all the fregans. They were Ice Age people, running with the aurochs and the wolves.

And the bros were back by their fire, stubbornly waiting out the cold. The pile of ashes in their fireplace was huge, and the area beyond Sleepy Hollow where the deer carcasses lay was beginning to look like a real shambles. Fedpage handed Frank a paper plate with a scorched venison steak when he sat down at the picnic table.

'Thanks.'

'You're welcome. It's a little bloody, but –'

'Blood for the hemophiliac! Just what he needs!'

'Uh huh. Hey, Fedpage, how many spy agencies are there in the federal government?'

'Sixteen.'

'Jesus.'

'That's how many they admit to. Actually there's more. It's like those Russian nested dolls, with blacks and superblacks inside.'

'Spy versus spy.'

'That's right. They fight like dogs. They guard their turf by getting blacker.' This statement made Cutter laugh. 'Nobody even knows everything that's out there, I judge. Not the President nor anyone else.'

'How can that happen?'

'There's no enemy, that's why. They pretend there's terror-ists, but that's just to scare people. Actually they like terrorists. That's why they went into Iraq, they got oil and a bunch of terrorists, it was a two-for-one. Much smarter than Vietnam. Because it's all about funding. The spooks' job is to spy on each other and keep their funding.'

'Shit,' Frank said. He prodded his steak, which suddenly tasted off. 'I think you guys need to kill another deer maybe.'

'Ha nothing wrong with that deer! It's Fedpage making you sick!'

On some afternoons Frank walked around Arlington. He had never spent much time there, and this was an odd time to get acquainted with it, its big streets were so wintry. Broad avenues ran for miles westward, past knots of tall buildings erupting out of the forest in every kind of mediocre urban conglomeration. It was possible to walk to the Khembali house from NSF in half an hour, so some days he did that, and got in a winter hike through the snow's bizarre masonry, with cars belching past like steam-powered vehicles.

At night after dinner he usually went up to his room and read on his mattress, chatting with Rudra every half hour or so. Otherwise he drifted around on the internet, looking things up under the long list of sites that came when he googled Khembalung. What he read in these rambles often caused him to shake his head.

*before the great guru Milarepa left Tibet for the Glorious Copper-Colored Mountain, he made a tour of Tibet, among other tasks finding hidden valleys, or beyuls*

'Guru Rudra, what is a beyul?'

'Hidden valley.'

'Like Khembalung?'

'Yes.'

'But you were on an island?'

'Hidden valley moves from time to time. This seems to be what Rikdzin Godem says. He was the guru who knew about the hidden valley. From Tsang. Fourteenth century. He talked about the Eight Great Hidden Valleys, but Khembalung seems to be the only one that ever appeared. A refuge from the kaliyuga, fourth of the four ages. Iron age of degradation and despair.'

'Is that what we're in?'

'Can't you tell?'

'Ha ha. What else did he say about them?'

'He say many things. Many books. He told location and described how to get in. When it would be good to enter, what would be the omens. What say, the power places in Khembalung. The magic.'

'Oh my. And what was that?'

'Like Khembalung as you saw it. A place for good. A buddhafield.'

'Buddhafield?'

'A space where Buddhism is working.'

'I see.'

'Compassion increase, wisdom.'

'And Khembalung was like that.'

'Yes.'

'And where was it, before your island?'

'At head of Arun valley. Phumchu, we call it in Tibetan. And over Tsibri La, into Tibet. That was the trouble.'

'China?'

'Yes.'

'Why is China so much trouble, do you think?'

'China is big. Like America.'

'Ah. So you left there.'

'Yes. South gate in a cave, opens way down Phumchu. Then downvalley to Darjeeling.'

'Does anyone go through that hidden valley any more?'

'They go through without seeing. Too busy!' A gravelly chuckle. 'Buddhafield not always visible. In this case, Dorje Phakmo, the Adamantine Sow, lies along that valley.'

'A pig?'

'Subtle body, hard to find.'

Another time, because of that:

401

'So animals are kind of magical too?'

'Of course. Obvious when you see them, right?'

'True,' Frank said. He told Rudra about his activities with FOG, including the arrival in Rock Creek park of the aurochs.

'Very good!' Rudra exclaimed. 'I liked them.'

'Uh huhn. What about tigers?'

'Oh, I like them too. Very good animal. Scary, but good. They have scary masks, but really they are friendly helpers. At power places they are tame.'

'Tame?'

'Tame. Friendly, helpful, courteous.'

'Kind, obedient, cheerful, brave, clean, and reverent?'

'Yes. All those.'

'Hmm.'

Another time, Frank read a passage on his screen and said, 'Rudra, are you *the* Rudra Cakrin, the one people write about?'

'No.'

'You're not? There's more than one?'

'Yes. He is very old.'

'Sixteen thousand years before the birth of Christ, it says here.'

'Yes, very old. I am not that old.' Gurgle. 'Almost, but not.'

'So are you some kind of boddhisatva?'

'No no. Not so good as that, no.'

'But you are a lama, or what say, a tulku or what have you?'

'What have you, I guess you say. I am a voice.'

'A voice?'

'You know. Vehicle for voice. Spirits seem to speak through me.'

'Like in those ceremonies, you get taken over and say things?'

'Yes.'

'That looks like it must hurt.'

'Yes, it seems so. I don't remember what happens then. But afterward I often seem to be sore.'

'Does it still happen?'

'Sometimes.'

'Are you scheduled for a ceremony anytime soon?'

'No. You know – retired.'

'Retired?'

'Is that not word? What say, get old, give up work?'

'Yes, that's retirement. I just didn't know that your kind of job allowed for retirement.'

'Of course. Very hard job.'

'I imagine so.'

Frank googled 'oracle, Tibetan Buddhist,' and read randomly for a while. It was pretty alarming stuff. What always got him was how elaborated everything was in Tibetan Buddhism; it was not a simple thing, like he imagined American Protestant churches being, with their simple creeds: I believe in God, an abstract or maybe a human image, with some vague tripartite divisions and a relatively straightforward story about a single visit to Earth. Not at all; instead, a vastly articulated system of gods and spirits, with complicated histories and interactions, and ongoing appearances in this world. The oracles when possessed would grow taller, lift enormously heavy costumes, cause medallions on their chest to bounce outward under the force of their elevated heartbeat. If certain powerful spirits entered the oracle, he had less than five minutes to live. Blood would gush from nose and mouth, bodies go completely rigid.

Maybe this was all a matter of adrenalin and endorphins. Maybe this was what the body was capable of when the mind was convinced of something. Oxytocined by the cosmic spirit. But in any case they were quite serious about it; to them it was real. 'The system is so complex and multilayered that it operates with some degree of freedom.' The mind, ordering the incoming data one way or another; different realities, perhaps. And what if they were evaluated on the basis of how they made one feel? On that basis there was certainly no justification to condescend to these people, no matter what strange things they said. They were in far better control of their feelings than Frank was.

Through all of March the winter stayed as cold and windy as ever. Twelve days in a row record lows were set, and on March 23rd it was twenty below at noon. Frank worried that any trees that had survived the worst of the winter would have their blooms killed in the frigid spring; and then where would they be? What would the east coast be like if its great hardwood forest died? Would whole biomes collapse as a result, would agriculture itself be substantially destroyed? How would Europe feed itself? What might happen to Asia's already shaky food security? It seemed to him sometimes that a winter this severe might change things for good.

In this context the campaign for the Presidential election coming up in the fall looked more trivial than ever. Phil Chase wrapped up the Democratic nomination, the President's team upped the firepower of their attacks on him; the SSEEP virtual candidate caused trouble for everybody who came in contact with it. Frank couldn't be bothered, and it seemed there were others like him out there. The long winter came first in the news and in people's thoughts.

Halfway through April the increasing length of the days became impossible to miss. Spring was here, snow or not. Daylight savings time came, and even though the mornings were darker at first, that did not last long. By the first of May there was so much more light that there simply had to be more heat; and then one day without warning it hit eighty degrees, and everyone and everything sweltered. The whole world steamed, thawed branches drooped and hung, thawed pipes leaked, wires shorted, mold grew. It was like a permafrost melt in the tundra, with pingoes and polygonal cracking and fields of new mud, and the air stifling. Mosquitoes came back, and everyone began to wonder if the hard winter had really been that bad after all.

When Frank visited Rock Creek he found Cutter on Connecticut again, using his old orange cones and orange tape to clear space around a tree canted at a forty-five degree angle.

'How's it going?'

'Pretty good! Spring has sprung!'

'Did the trees live?'

'Most of them yeah. Lot of dead branches. It'll make for a busy summer. I swear the forest gonna take over this city.'

'I bet. Can I join you some time?'

'Sure you can. Do you own a chainsaw?'

'No, can't say I do.'

'That's all right. There's other help you can do.'

'I can always drag wood away.'

'Exactly.'

'So where do you take the wood if you're doing something like this on your own?'

'Oh all kinds of places. I take it to a friend's and we cut it up for firewood.'

'And that's okay?'

'Oh sure. There's an awful lot of trees need trimming. Lot of it being done by freelancers. The city need help, and the wood can be the pay.'

'It sounds like it works pretty well.'

'Well . . .' Cutter laughed.

'Hey, did you ever find out anything more about Chessman?'

'No, not really. I asked Byron but he didn't know. He said he thought maybe he moved. There was a chess tournament up in New York he said Chessman talked about.'

'He said something about playing in it?'

'I don't know.'

'Did Byron know his name?'

'He said he thought his name was Clifford.'

All the branches sprouted green buds. Tiny buds of a vivid light green, a color Frank had never seen before, a color that glowed on cloudy days, and sparked in his peripheral vision like fireflies. Green buds on a wet black bough, life coming back to the forest. It could not have been more beautiful. No moment in the Mediterranean climate could ever match this moment of impossible green.

He started going over to the park again, while at the same time he felt less anxious about living at the embassy house.

And yet he never returned to feeling quite himself. His face was still numb, inside his nose and right below it, and behind it. When he was shaving he saw that the numb part of his upper lip looked inert, and thus to himself he seemed deformed. He could not smile properly. He didn't know how he felt about that. He supposed that the effect for others was slight, and that if noticed at all people did not talk about it, out of politeness.

The bros did not worry about that kind of thing. 'Hey Jimmy! Jimmy Durante! How's it hanging, did your dick survive its frostbite? That scared ya didn't it! Did your nose heal straight? Can you breathe through it any more?'

'No.'

'HA ha ha. Hey mouthbreather! I knew you wouldn't be able to the first time I saw it.'

'So who were those guys anyway?' Frank asked again.

'Who the fuck knows? We never saw them again.'

'Lucky for you.'

'No lie.'

'You guys could use a phone. Whip it out and 911 in situations like that.

'Yeah right!'

'So that being the case, I brought you all application cards so you can get into FOG, the zoo group.'

'No way.'

'They tell me the park is going to be regulated this summer, so you'll need to be a member to be able to stay in the park.'

'You think the cops will act any different just because we got some card on us?'

'Yes, I do. Plus, they give you a cell phone if you're a member. It's a little party line, but it works.'

'Oh good I always wanted one of those!'

'Shut up and fill out the form here. Come on – I bet you can put down any name you want. Besides, it can't possibly break any parole agreements. They're not going to throw you in jail for joining the Friends of the National Zoo for God's sake.'

'Ha ha! Who you saying is on parole?'

'Yeah who you saying is on parole? At least we got *noses*.'

'Ha ha. Just fill out the form.'

\* \* \*

Coming up to their little closet, Frank heard someone in there talking to Rudra, and came up to the door curious to see who it was, as the old man seemed somewhat neglected in the house. But no one else was in there. Rudra started at the sight of Frank, stared up at him with an addled look, as if he had forgotten who Frank was.

'Sorry,' Frank said. 'I didn't mean to startle you.'

'I am happy you did.'

'Talking to yourself, were you?'

'Don't think so.'

'I thought I heard somebody.'

'Interesting. Sometimes I, what say . . . I sing to myself. One kind of Tibetan singing makes two sounds from one voice. Head note? Overtone?' He opened his mouth and emitted a bass note lower than Frank would have expected from such a slight body; and at the same time there was a scratchy harmonic floating in the room.

'Very nice,' Frank said. 'It reminds me of Louis Armstrong.'

Rudra nodded. 'Very fine singer.' He opened his mouth again, sang deeply, 'The odds, were a hundred to one against us,' like Louis played at two-thirds normal speed, slower and deeper.

'That's right, very good! So you like him?'

'Very fine singer. Head tone undeveloped, but very strong.'

'Interesting.' Frank unrolled his groundpad, laid himself out with a small groan.

'Go to park?'

'Yes.'

'Find your friends?'

'Some of them.' Frank began to describe them and the situation out there – the bros, the fregans, his own project. He lay down on his back and left the laptop off, and talked about the paleolithic, and how the brain had evolved to feel good because of certain stimuli caused by behaviors performed

408

repeatedly in the two million year run-up to humanity; and how they should be able to feel good now by living a life that conformed as closely to these early behaviors as possible. Which was what he had been trying to do, in his life out in the park.

'Good idea!' Rudra said. 'Original mind. This is Buddhism also.'

'Yes? Well, I guess I'm not surprised. It seemed to me that you were talking about something like that when you spoke at NSF last year.'

Rudra didn't appear to remember this talk, which had been such a shattering experience for Frank – a real paradigm buster, as Edgardo would say. Frank did not press the matter, feeling shy at admitting to the old man what a profound effect he had created, with what had apparently been an offhand comment. Instead he described to Rudra the ways in which he felt that prisoner's dilemma and Snowdrift modeled ethics in a scientific way, how the games were scored and the strategies judged, and how, at the start of the winter, he had come to the tentative conclusion that it made best adaptive sense to pursue the strategy called always generous.

'Good idea,' Rudra said. 'But what are these *points*? Why play for *points*?'

Frank was still pondering this when Sucandra and Padma clomped upstairs to see how the old man was doing. 'Cookies,' Sucandra said, holding out a plate. 'Fresh out of the oven.'

He and Padma sat on the floor in the doorway, and the four of them ate sugar cookies like kids at a sleepover.

'These are good,' Frank said. 'I've been getting so hungry this winter.'

'Oh yes,' Sucandra said. 'You get much hungrier in the cold.'

'And much colder when you're hungry,' Padma added.

'Yes,' Sucandra said. 'We learned that both ways, didn't we?'

'Yes.'

Frank looked at them. 'The Chinese?'

'Yes,' Sucandra said. 'In their prison.'

'How long?'

'Ten years.'

Frank shook his head, trying to imagine this and failing. 'How much did you get to eat?'

'A bowl of rice a day.'

'Did people starve?' Frank said, looking at the remaining cookies on the plate.

'Yes,' Sucandra said. 'Died from hunger, died from cold.'

Padma nodded. 'Others survived, but lost their wits.'

'Maybe we all did.'

'Yes, no doubt.'

'But I know who you mean when you say that. We had this old monk, you see, who was shitting some kind of tapeworm. Long red thing, segmented. Like millipede without legs. We knew this because he cleaned them up when it happened, and brought them to the group to offer them to the rest of us as food.'

'He claimed Bon spirit was inside him making food for us.'

Frank said, 'So what did you do?'

'We chopped the worms up very fine and added them to the rice.'

'No doubt it added some protein to our diet.'

'Not much, it was more a gesture.'

'But anything helped at that point.'

'It's true. I kind of got to looking forward to it.'

They grinned at each other, looked shyly at Frank.

'Yes. It helped us feel like we were together. People need to be part of a group.'

410

'And to help the old monk. He would get very distraught.'

'But then he died.'

'Yes, that's right. But then the rice seemed to be missing something!'

One morning when it was spring and all, cool and green and sweet, like some May day remembered from a distant past that they had assumed would never come again, Charlie drove out to Great Falls and met Frank and Drepung. Frank was going to teach them the basics of rock climbing.

Anna did not thoroughly approve, but Frank assured her he would make it safe, and her risk assessment realism impelled her to concede it was probably all right. Charlie, only momentarily disappointed that he had lost this best excuse to back out of it, now parked next to the other two, and they walked out the short trail to the gorge, carrying two backpacks of Frank's gear and a few tight loops of nylon rope. After coming to an overlook, the trail paralleled the clifftop, and they followed it to a spot under a prominent tree, which Frank declared was the top of a good teaching route.

It was a new route, he said, for the great flood had greatly rearranged Great Falls, tearing new routes all up and down the south wall. When that much water ran over rock it tore at it not only by direct friction but also by a process called cavitation, in which the water broke into bubbles that were in effect vacuums that sucked violently at the cracks in the rocks, cracking them further, so that big blocks were plucked out rather than worn away. The walls of Mather Gorge had been plucked pretty hard.

Frank uncoiled one length of rope and tied it off around the trunk of the tree. He pointed down the cliff. 'See the flat spot down at the bottom? On the right here, you can basi-cally walk down to it, like on stairs. Then you can climb the wall over here, or there. It's like a climbing wall in a gym.'

The knobby black rock was schist, he said. The gorge was an unusual feature in this region; there was another smaller one on the Susquehanna, but mostly the eastern piedmont lacked this kind of rocky outcropping. It had been cut in discrete bursts, the geologists had found, perhaps in the big floods that punctuated the end of ice ages. Their recent flood was a minor scouring compared to those.

Now they stood on the rim of the cliff, looking down at the river's white roil and rumble. 'There's almost every kind of hold represented on this wall,' Frank continued. 'Conveniently identified for the beginning climber by the fresh new chalk marks you see on them. There's been lots of action here already. I'll have you top-belayed the whole time today from this tree here, so even if you slip and come off, you'll only bounce in place a little. The rope has some flex, so you won't be brought up short if it happens. I'll have you jump off on purpose so you know what it feels like.'

Charlie and Drepung exchanged a reassured glance. It was going to be okay. Neither would die as the result of being a bad student, something they both had been a few times in the past.

That being established they became happier, and put on their harnesses cheerfully, indeed prone to sudden bursts of muffled hilarity ostensibly caused by the difficulties of getting their legs in the proper holes. It was pretty lame, and Frank shook his head. Then they were solemnly studying Frank's knots, and learning the simple but effective suspension belaying systems used by climbers, techniques that held without fail when needed, but also would run freely when desired. Frank was very clear and businesslike in his expla-nations, and patient with their fumbling and misunder-standing. He had done this before.

When he seemed to feel they had absorbed the necessary minimum, he retied all their knots himself, then ran Charlie's rope through a carabiner tied to their tree and wrapped it around his waist. Charlie then carefully descended the staircase analog that ran down to a floor just above the river. Standing at the bottom Charlie turned to look up at Frank.

'Okay,' Frank said, pulling the rope between them taut through the carabiner. 'On belay.'

'On belay,' Charlie repeated. Then he started climbing, focusing on the wall and seeing it hold by hold. The chalk marks did indeed help. Monkey up, using the knobs and nicks they indicated. He heard Frank's suggestions as if from a distance. Don't look down. Don't try to pull yourself up by the arms. Use the legs as much as possible. Keep three points attached at all times. Move smoothly, never lunge.

His toe slipped and he fell. *Boing*, fend off wall; bounce gently; he was okay. Relocate holds, get back to climbing. Was that all? Why, it wasn't anywhere near as bad as he had thought it would be! With such a system there wasn't the slightest danger!

The way Frank failed to agree with this served to refocus Charlie's attention on the wall.

Some of what Charlie was doing was familiar to him already, as it resembled the scrambling he had done on backpacking trips in the Sierra. The steps, grabs and motions were the same, but here he was performing them on a surface drastically more vertical than any he and his backpacking friends would have attempted. Indeed if he had ever wandered onto such a face during a scramble in the Sierra, he would have been paralyzed with fear.

But being top-roped really did remove the source of that fear, and with it gone, there was room to notice other feelings. The action felt like a kind of acrobatics, unrehearsed and in slow motion. Charlie became absorbed in it for a long time, slowing down as the holds seemed scarcer, until his fingers began to hurt. For a while nothing existed except for the rock face and his search for holds. Once or twice Frank spoke, but mostly he watched. The tug of his belay, while reassuring, did not actually pull Charlie up; and now he began to struggle, with only a final awkward lunge getting him up to the rim.

Very absorbing stuff! And now a surge of some kind of I'M STILL ALIVE glow was flowing through his whole body. He saw how it was that people might get hooked.

Then it was Drepung's turn. Charlie sat with his feet swinging over the edge, watching happily. From above Drepung looked bulky, and his expression as he searched the rock face was uncomfortable. Charlie had his years of scrambling experience; Drepung did not. After hauling himself up the first few holds he looked down once between his feet, and after that he seemed a bit glued to the rock. He muttered something about a traditional Tibetan fear of falling, but Frank would have none of it. 'That's a tradition everywhere, I assure you. Just focus on where you're at, and feel the belay. Jump off if you want to see how it'll feel.'

'It seems I will get to find out soon enough anyway.'

He was slow, but he kept trying. His moves were pretty sure when they happened. His small mouth pursed in a perfect little O of concentration. In a few minutes more he made it up and hauled himself around to sit beside Charlie, uttering a happy 'Ha.'

Frank had them do it again, trying other routes on the face; then they belayed each other, nervously, with Frank standing beside the belayer making sure all was well. Lastly he had them rappel down, in a simple but scary operation like the old Batman, but for real. They practiced until their hands got too tired and sore to hold on to anything.

After that (it had taken a couple of hours) Frank changed his belay to another tree on the cliff top. 'It looks like both Juliet's Balcony and Romeo's Ladder survived. I'm going to do one of those, or Gorky Park.' He dropped away, leaving Charlie and Drepung sitting happily on the cliff's edge, kicking their heels against the rock and taking in the view. To their left the rearranged falls roared down its drops, every step along the way boiling whitely. Below them Frank was climbing slowly.

Suddenly Charlie leaped to his feet shouting: 'Where's Joe!' and looking around them desperately.

'Not here,' Drepung reminded him. 'With Anna today, remember?'

'Oh yeah.' Charlie sank back down. 'Sorry. For a second there I forgot.'

'That's okay. You must be used to watching him all the time.'

'Yes.'

He sat back on the cliff's edge, shaking his head. Slowly Frank ascended toward them. As he looked up for his next hold his face reminded Charlie of Buster Keaton; he had that same wary and slightly baffled look, ready for anything – unflappable, although *not* imperturbable, as his eyes revealed just as clearly as Keaton's that in fact he was perturbed most of the time.

Charlie had always had a lot of sympathy for Buster Keaton. Life as a string of astonishing crises to be dealt with; it seemed right to him. He said, 'Drepung?'

'Yes?'

Charlie inspected his torn hand. Drepung held his own hand next to it; both were chewed up by the day's action.

'Speaking of Joe.'

'Yes?'

Charlie heaved a sigh. He could feel the worry that had built up in him. 'I don't want him to be any kind of special person for you guys.'

'What?'

'I don't want him to be a reincarnated soul.'

416

'. . . Buddhism says we are all such.'

'I don't want him to be any kind of reincarnated lama. Not a tulku, or a boddhisatva, or whatever else you call it. Not someone your people would have any religious interest in at all.'

Drepung inspected his palm. The skin was about the same color as Charlie's, maybe more opaque. Let that stand for us, Charlie thought. At least as far as Charlie's sight was concerned. He couldn't tell what Drepung was thinking. Except it did seem that the young man didn't know what to say.

This tended to confirm Charlie's suspicions. He said, 'You know what happened to the new Panchen Lama.'

'Yes. I mean no, not really.'

'Because nobody does! Because they picked a little boy and the Chinese took him and he has never been seen again. Two little boys, in fact.'

Drepung nodded, looking upset. 'That was a mess.'

'Tell me. Tell me what happened.'

Drepung grimaced. 'The Panchen Lama is the reincarnation of the Buddha Amitabha. He is the second most important spiritual leader in Tibetan Buddhism, and his relationship with the Dalai Lama has always been complicated. The two were often at odds, but they also helped to choose each other's successors. Then in the last couple of centuries the Panchen Lama has often been associated with Chinese interests, so it got even more complicated.'

'Sure,' Charlie said.

'So, when the tenth Panchen Lama died, in 1989, the identification of his next reincarnation was obviously a problem. Who would make the determination? The Chinese government told the Panchen Lama's monastery, Tashilhunpo, to find the new reincarnation. So, that was proper, but they also made it clear they would have final approval of the choice made.'

'On what basis?'

'Well, you know. To control the situation.'

'Ah yes. Of course.'

'So Chadrel Rimpoche, the head of the Tashilhunpo Monastery, contacted the Dalai Lama in secret, to get his help in making the choice, as was proper in the tradition. His group had already identified several children in north Tibet as possibilities. So the Dalai Lama performed divinations to discover which of them was the new Panchen Lama. He found that it was a boy living near Tashilhunpo. The signs were clear. But now the question was, how were they going to get that candidate approved by the Chinese, while also hiding the involvement of the Dalai Lama.'

'Couldn't Chadrel Rimpoche just tell the Chinese that's who it was?'

'Well, but the Chinese had introduced a system of their own. It involves a thing called the Goldern Urn. When there are any uncertainties, and those are easy to create, then the three top names are put into this urn. The name drawn from the urn is destined to be the correct one.'

'What?' Charlie cried. 'They draw the name out of a hat?'

'Out of an urn. Yes.'

'But that's crazy! I mean presumably if there is a reincarnated lama in one of these kids, he is who he is! You can't be drawing a name from a hat.'

'One would suppose. But the Chinese have never been averse to harming Tibetan traditions, as you know. Anyway, in this case the Dalai Lama's divination was a boy in a region under Chinese control, so it seemed as if chances for his confirmation were fairly good. But there was concern that the Chinese would use the urn to deliberately choose someone other than the one Chadrel Rimpoche recommended, just to show they were in control, and to deny the Dalai Lama any possible influence.'

'Sure. And so?'

'And so, the Dalai Lama eventually decided to announce the identity of the boy, thinking that the Chinese would then be pressured to conform to Tibetan wishes, but satisfied that it was a boy living under their control.'

'Oh no,' Charlie said. 'I'm surprised anyone could have thought that, knowing the Chinese.'

Drepung sighed. 'It was a gamble. The Dalai Lama must have felt that it was the best chance they had.'

'But it didn't work.'

'No.'

'So what happened to the boy?'

'He and his parents were taken into custody. Chadrel Rimpoche also.'

'Where are they now?'

'No one knows. They have not been seen since that time.'

'Now see? I don't want Joe to be any part of that sort of thing!'

Drepung sighed. Finally he said, 'The Panchen Lama is a special case, very highly politicized, because of the Chinese. Many returned lamas are identified without any such problems.'

'I don't care! Besides, you can't be sure whether it will get complicated or not.'

'No Chinese are involved.'

'I don't care!'

Drepung hunched forward a little, as if to say, What can I do, I can't do anything.

'Look,' Charlie said. 'It's upsetting Anna. She doesn't believe in anything you can't see or quantify, you know that. It upsets her even to try. You make this kind of stuff be about Joe and it will just freak her out. She's trying not to think about it right now, I can tell, but even that is freaking her out. She's not good at not thinking about things. She thinks about things.'

'I'm sorry.'

'You should be. I mean, think of it this way. If she hadn't befriended you guys like she did when you first came here, then you would never even have known Joe existed. So in effect you are punishing Anna for her kindness to you.'

Drepung pursed his lips, hummed unhappily. He looked like he had while climbing: unhappy, faced with a problem.

'Besides,' Charlie pressed, 'the whole idea that your kid is somehow not just, you know, your kid – that he's someone else somehow – that in itself is upsetting. Offensive, one might even say. I mean he is a reincarnation already, of me and Anna.'

'And your ancestors.'

'Right, true. But anyone else, no.'

'Hmmm.'

'But you see what I mean? How it feels?'

'Yes.' Drepung nodded, rocking his whole body forward and back. 'Yes, I do.'

They sat there, looking down at the river. A lone kayaker was working her way upstream against the white flow. Below them Frank, who was standing by the shore again, was staring out at her.

Charlie gestured down at Frank. 'He seems interested.'

'Indeed he does.'

They watched Frank watch her.

'So,' Charlie persevered, 'maybe you could talk to Rudra Cakrin about this matter for me. See if he can do something, see if there is some kind of, I don't know, exorcism he can do. Not that I mean to imply anything, just some kind of I don't know. Reindividuation ceremony. To clear him out, and well – leave him alone. Are there such ceremonies?'

'Well . . . in a manner of speaking, yes. I suppose.'

'So will you talk to Rudra about doing it? Maybe just without much fanfare, so Anna doesn't know about it?'

Drepung was frowning. 'If she doesn't know, then . . .'

'Then it would be for me. Yes. For me and Joe. And then

it would get to Anna, by way of us. Why, does it have to be public?'

'No no. It's not that.'

'What – you don't want to talk to Rudra about it?'

'Well . . . Rudra would not actually be the one to decide about such a matter.'

'No?' Charlie was surprised. 'Who then? Someone back in Khembalung, or Tibet?'

Drepung shook his head.

'Well, who then?'

Drepung lifted his hand as if to inspect it again. He pointed the bloodied thumb at himself. Looked at Charlie.

Charlie shifted on the ground to get a better look back at him. 'What, you?'

Drepung nodded with his body again.

Charlie laughed shortly. All of a sudden many things were becoming clear. 'Why you rascal you!' He gave the young man a light shove. 'You guys have been running a scam on us the whole time.'

'No no. Not a scam.'

'So what is Rudra then, some kind of servant, some old retainer you're doing a prince-and-pauper switch with?'

'No, not at all. He is a tulku too. But not so, that is to say, in the Khembali order there are also relationships between tulkus, like the ones between the Dalai Lama and the Panchen Lama.'

'So you're the boss, you're saying.'

Drepung winced. 'Well. I am the one the others regard as their, you know. Leader.'

'Spiritual leader? Political leader?'

Drepung wiggled a hand.

'What about Padma and Sucandra?'

'They are in effect like regents, or they were. Like brothers now, advisors. They tell me so much, they are like my teachers. Brothers really.'

'I see. And so you stay behind the scenes here.'

'Or, in front of the scenes really. The greeter.'

'Both in front and behind.'

'Yes.'

'Very clever. It's just what I thought all along.'

'Really?'

'No. I thought Rudra spoke English.'

Drepung nodded. 'His English is not so bad. He has been studying. Though he does not like to admit it.'

'But listen, Drepung – you do these kinds of switches and cover stories and all, because you know it's a little dangerous out there, right? Because of the Chinese and all?'

Drepung pursed his lips. 'Well, not so much for that –'

'And think about it like this – *you* know what it means to suddenly be called someone else! You must.'

At this Drepung blinked. 'Yes. It's true. I remember my parents . . . My father was really happy for me. For all of us, really proud. But my mother was never really reconciled. She would put my hand on her and say, "You came from here. You came from here."'

'What do they think now?'

'They are no longer in those bodies.'

'Ah.' He seemed young to have lost both parents. But who knows what they had lived through. Charlie said, 'Anyway, you know what I'm talking about.'

'Yes.'

For a long time they sat in the misty rumble of the great falls, looking down at Frank, who had now unclipped from his rope, and was walking over the jumbled rocks by the water, attempting, it appeared, to keep the kayaker in sight as she approached the foot of the falls proper.

Charlie pressed on. 'Will you do something about this then?'

Drepung rocked again. Charlie was beginning to wonder if it signaled assent or not. 'I'll see what I can do.'

'Now don't you be giving me that!'

'What? Oh! Oh, no, no, I meant it for real!'

They both laughed, thinking about Phil Chase and his *I'll see what I can dos*. 'They all say it,' Charlie complained.

'Now, now. They *are* seeing what they can do. You must give them that.'

'I don't give them that. They're seeing what they *can't* do.'

Drepung waggled a hand, smiling. He too had had to put people off, Charlie saw.

They leaned out to try and spot Frank.

As they peered down, Charlie found that he felt better. Talking with someone else about this matter had eased the sense of isolation that had been oppressing him. He wasn't used to having something he couldn't talk to Anna about, and without her, he had been at a loss.

And the news that Drepung was the true power in Khembali affairs, once he got over it, was actually quite reassuring. Rudra Cakrin, when all was said and done, was a strange old man. It was far better to have someone he knew and trusted in charge of this business.

'I'll talk to Rudra Cakrin about it,' Drepung said.

'I thought you said he was a front man.'

'No no. A . . . a colleague. I need to consult with him, for sure. For one thing he would probably conduct the ceremony. He is the oracle. But that also means he will know what ceremonies I refer to. There are some precedents. Certain accidents, mistakes rectified . . . there are some things I can look into.'

Charlie nodded. 'Good. You remember what I said about Anna welcoming you to NSF.'

'Yes.' Drepung grimaced. 'Actually, it was the oracle who told us to take that office.'

'Come on, what, he said "Move to 4201 Wilson Boulevard?"'

'Not exactly.'

'No I guess not! Well, whatever. Just remember how Anna

feels about it. It's probably very much like your mom felt.'

Charlie was surprised to hear himself going for the jugular like that. Then he thought of Joe clutching at him, frightened and pitiful, and his mouth clenched. He wanted all this business cleared away. The fever would follow.

They watched the river roil by. White patches on black water.

'Look – it looks like Frank is trying to catch that kayaker's attention.'

'It sure does.'

The woman was now resting, paddle flat across the kayak in front of her, gliding downstream. Frank was hurrying downstream to stay abreast of her, stumbling once or twice on the rocky bank, hands to his mouth to cup shouts out to her. He started waving his arms up and down. He came to a flatter patch and ran to get ahead of her. He semaphored with his arms, megaphoned with his hands, jumped up and down.

'He must know that person?'

'Or something. But she must be hearing him, don't you think?'

'It seems like it. Seeing him too, for that matter. She must not want to be interrupted.'

'I guess.'

It was hard to see how she couldn't be noticing him; which meant she must be ignoring him on purpose. She floated on, and he continued to chase her, scrambling over boulders now, shouting still.

She never turned her head. A big boulder blocked Frank's way and he slipped, went to his knees, held out his arms; but now she was past him, and did not look back.

Finally his arms fell. Head bowed, shoulders slumped – the very figure of a man whose hopes have been dashed.

Charlie and Drepung looked at each other.

'Do you think that Frank is seeming kind of . . .'

'Yes.'

# NINE

## *Leap Before You Look*

*Frank dropped by the Quiblers' on a Saturday morning to pick up Nick and go to the zoo. He got there early and stood in the living room while they finished their breakfast. Charlie, Anna and Nick were all reading as they ate, and so Joe stared at the back of his cereal box with a look of fierce determination, as if to crack the code of this staring business by sheer force of will. Seeing this Frank's heart went out to him, and he circled the table and crouched by him to chat.*

*Soon Nick went to get ready, but before they left he wanted to show Frank a new computer game. Frank stood behind him, doing his best to comprehend the action on the screen. 'How come he exploded like that?'*

*'It takes like weird mutant bad scientist stuff.'*

*'I see. And whoah, how come that one blew up?'*

*'I'm attacking him with an invisible character.'*

*'Is he good?'*

*'Well, he's hard to see.'*

*Charlie cackled at this. Nick glanced over and said, 'Dad, quit drinking my hot chocolate.'*

*'I thought you were done with it. I only took three sips.'*

*'You took four sips.'*

*'Don't keep Frank waiting around, go get ready.'*

At the zoo they first attended a workshop devoted to learning how to knap rocks into blades and arrowheads. Frank had noticed this on the FONZ website and of course been very interested, and Nick was up for anything. So they sat on the ground with a ranger of about twenty-five, who reminded Frank of Robin. This young man wandered around the group, crouching to show each cluster how to hit the cores with the breaker stones so that they would flake properly. With every good knap he yelled 'Yeah!' or 'Good one!'

It was clearly the same process that had created Frank's Acheulian hand axe, although their modern results were less shapely, and of course the newly cracked stone looked raw compared to the patina that burnished the old axe's broken surfaces. No matter – it was a joy to try it, satisfying in the same way that looking into a fire was. It was one of those things you knew how to do the first time you tried it.

Frank was happily knapping away a protrusion on the end of a core, enjoying the clacks and chinks and the smell of sparks and rock dust in sunlight, when he and Nick both smashed their hands at the same time. Nick's chin trembled and Frank growled as he clutched his throbbing thumb. 'Oh man. My nail is going to be purple, dang it! What about yours?'

'Forefinger,' Nick said. 'Middle knuckle.'

'Big owee. Kun chok sum!'

'Kun chok sum? Is that Khembali?'

'Yes, it's a Tibetan curse.'

'What's it mean?'

Frank grinned. 'Means, three jewels!'

'Three jewels?'

'Heavy eh? They have worse ones of course.'

'Kun chok sum!'

The ranger came over grinning. 'That, gentlemen, is what we call the granite kiss. Anyone in need of a bandaid?'

Frank and Nick declined.

'You can see how old the expression "caught between a rock and a hard place" must be. They've found knapped tools like these a million and a half years old.'

'I hope it doesn't hurt that long,' Nick said.

After they were done they put their new stone tools in their daypacks and went over to look at the gibbons and siamangs.

All the feral primates had either died or been returned to the zoo. This morning Bert and May and their surviving kids were the family out in the triangular gibbon enclosure. They only let out one family at a time, to avoid fights. Frank and Nick joined the small crowd at the railing to observe. The people around them were mostly young parents with toddlers. 'Mon-key! Mon-key!'

Bert and May were relaxing in the sun as they had so many times before, on a small platform just outside the tunnel to their inside room – a kind of porch, in effect, with a metal basket hanging over it where food was placed. Nothing in the sight of them suggested that they had spent much of the previous year running wild in Rock Creek Park. May was grooming Bert's back, intent, absorbed, dexterous. Bert seemed zoned out. Never did they meet the gaze of their human observers. Bert shifted to get the back of his head under her fingers, and she immediately obliged, parting his hair and closely inspecting his scalp. Then something caused him to give her a light slap, and she caught his hand and tugged at it. She let go and climbed the fence to intercept one of their kids, and suddenly those two were playing tag. When they passed Bert he cuffed at them, so they turned around and gang-tackled him. When he had disentangled himself from the fray he swung up the fence to the south corner of the enclosure, where it was possible to reach through and pull leaves from a tree. He munched a leaf, fended off one of the passing kids with an expert backhand.

It seemed to Frank that they were restless. It wasn't obvious;

*at first glance they appeared languid, because any time they were not moving they tended to melt into their positions, even if they were hanging from the fence. So they looked mellow – especially when sprawled on the ground, arm flung overhead, idly grooming partner or kid – a life of leisure!*

*But after watching for a while it became evident that every ten minutes they were doing something else. Racing around the fence, eating, grooming, rocking; eventually it became apparent that they never did anything for more than a few minutes at a time.*

*Now the younger son caught fire and raced around the top of the fence, then cast himself into space in a seemingly suicidal leap; but he crashed into the canvas loop that crossed the cage just above the tops of the ground shrubs, hitting it with both arms and thus breaking his fall sufficiently to avoid broken bones. Clearly it was a leap he had made hundreds of times before, after which it was his habit to run over and bushwhack his dad.*

*Wrestling on the grass. Did Bert remember wrestling his elder son on that same spot? Did the younger son remember his brother? Their faces, even as they tussled, were thoughtful and grave. They seemed lost in their thoughts. They looked like animals who had seen a lot. This may have just been an accident of physiognomy. The look of the species.*

*Some teenagers came by and hooted inexpertly, hoping to set the animals off. 'They only do that at dawn,' Nick reminded Frank; despite that, they joined the youths' effort. The gibbons did not. The teenagers looked a bit surprised at Frank's expertise. Ooooooooooooop! Oop oop ooooop!*

*Now Bert and May rested on their porch in the sun. Bert sat looking at the empty food basket, one long-fingered thumbless hand idly grooming May's stomach. She lay flat on her back, looking bored. From time to time she batted Bert's hand. It looked like the stereotypical dynamic, male groping female who can't be bothered. But when May got up she suddenly bent and shoved her butt at Bert's face. He looked for a second, leaned in and licked her; pulled back; smacked his lips like a wine taster. No doubt he could tell exactly where she was in her cycle.*

*The humans above watched without comment. After a while Nick suggested checking out their tigers, and Frank agreed.*

*Walking down the path to the big cat island, the image of May grooming Bert stuck in Frank's mind. White-cheeked gibbons were monogamous. Several primate species were, though far more were not. Bert and May had been a couple for over twenty years, more than half their lives; Bert was thirty-six, May thirty-two. They knew each other.*

*When a human couple first met, they presented a facade of themselves to the other, a performance of the part of themselves they thought made the best impression. If both fell in love, they entered into a space of mutual regard, affection, lust; they fell in love; it swept them off their feet, yes, so that they walked on air, yes.*

*But if the couple then moved in together, they quickly saw more than just the performance that up to that point was all they knew. At this point they either both stayed in love, or one did while one didn't, or they both fell out of love. Because reciprocity was so integral to the feeling, mostly one could say that they either stayed in love or they fell out of it. In fact, Frank wondered, could it even be called love if it were one-sided, or was that just some kind of need, or a fear of being alone, so that the one 'still in love' had actually fallen out of love also, into denial of one sort or another. Frank had done that himself. No, true love was a reciprocal thing; one-way love, if it existed at all, was some other emotion, like saintliness or generosity or devotion or goodness or pity or ostentation or virtue or need or fear. Reciprocal love was different from those. So when you fell in love with someone else's presentation, it was a huge risk, because it was a matter of chance whether on getting to know one another you both would stay in love with the more various characters who now emerged from behind the mask.*

*Bert and May didn't have that problem.*

*The swimming tigers were flaked out in their enclosure, lying like any other cats in the sun. Tigers were not monogamous. They were in effect solitaries, who went their own way and crossed paths only to mate. Moms kicked out their cubs after a couple of years, and all went off on their own.*

*These two, however, had been thrown together, as if by fate. Swept out to sea in the same flood, rescued by the same ship, kept in the same enclosures. Now the male rested his big head on the female's back. He licked her fur from time to time, then plopped his chin on her spine again.*

*Maybe there was a different way of coming to love. Spend a lot of time with a fellow traveler; get to know them across a large range of behaviors; then have that knowledge ripen into love.*

*The swimming tigers looked content. At peace. No primate ever looked that peaceful. Nick and Frank went to get snow cones. Frank always got lime; Nick got a mix of root beer, cherry and banana.*

**The Khembali house stayed** very busy. With a significant percentage of Khembalung's population cycling through it, occupying every closet and stairwell while waiting for openings in other refugia being established, the place jumped with a sense of crammed life that to Frank often felt surreal. Sometimes it was so obvious that a whole town had moved into a single house, as in some reality TV show. Sometimes as he sat in the corner of the big kitchen, peeling potatoes or drying dishes, he would look at all the industrious faces, cheerful or harried as they might be, and think: This is almost entertaining. Other times the tumult would get to him and his train of thought would leave the room and return to the forest in his mind. It was dark in that particular parcellation, dark and quiet, no, not quiet – the sound of the wind in the trees was always there – but solitary. The leaves and the stars and the creek were peaceful company.

'People are so crazy,' he would say to Rudra Cakrin at the end of the night as he sprawled on his mattress.

'Ha ha.'

Some nights he stayed late at work, working on the list or talking on the phone to a contact Diane had in Moscow, a Dmitri, who worked in the Kremlin's environmental resources ministry. Late at night in DC it was mid-day in Moscow, and Frank could call and try to find out more about the Russians' carbon capture plans. Dmitri's English was excellent. He claimed that no decisions had been made about interventions of any kind. They were very happy to see the North Atlantic project under way.

After these conversations Frank sometimes just slept there on his couch, as he had planned to back at the beginning. It was entirely comfortable, but Frank found he missed his conversations with Rudra Cakrin. There was no other part of the day that held as many surprises for him. Even talking to Diane or Dmitri wasn't as surprising, and the two Ds were getting pretty surprising. Sometimes Frank found himself a little bit jealous; she and Dmitri were old friends, and Frank could hear Diane's voice take on the quality it had when she was talking to someone close to her; also the tone of one great power speaking to another. Dmitri had carte blanche to experiment with one-sixth of the land surface of the Earth. That was power; there were bound to be surprises there.

Even so, Rudra was more surprising. One night Frank was lying on his groundpad in the light of the dimmed laptop, trying to tell Rudra about the impact the old man's lecture at NSF had had on him. When he asked about the particular sentence that had acted on him like a sort of catalyst – 'An excess of reason is itself a form of madness' – Rudra snorted.

'Milarepa say that because his guru beat him all the time, and always a good reason for it. So Milarepa never think much of reason. But that is an easy thing to notice. And hardly anyone ever reason anyway.'

'Yes, I've noticed that.' Frank described to the old man what had happened to him subsequent to the lecture containing that remark, explaining what he could of his ideas about zen koans or paradigm busters, and how they caused actual physical changes in the brain, leading to new systems of parcellation that reorganized both unconscious thought and the way consciousness perceived the world. 'Then on the way to the Quiblers' I got stuck with a woman in an elevator, I'll tell you about that some other time . . .'

'Dakini!' Rudra said, eyes gleaming.

'Maybe,' Frank said, googling the word, some kind of female Tantric spirit, 'anyway it convinced me that I had to stay in D.C. another year, and yet I had put a resignation letter in Diane's in-box that was kind of harsh. So I decided I had to get it out, and the only way to do it was to break into the building through the skylight and go into her office through the window.'

'Good idea,' Rudra said. For the first time it occurred to Frank that when Rudra said this he might not always mean it. An ironic oracle: another surprise.

Another time Rudra knocked his water glass over and said 'Karmapa!' shortly.

'Karmapa, what's that, like three jewels?'

'Yes. Name of founder of Karma Kagyu sect.'

'So, like saying Christ or something.'

'Yes.'

'You Buddhists are pretty mellow with the curses, I guess that makes sense. It's all like Heavens to Betsy!'

Rudra grinned. 'Gyakpa zo!'

'What's that one.'

'Eat shit.'

'Whoah, okay then! Pretty good.'

'What about you, what you say?'

'Oh, we say eat shit also, although it's pretty harsh. Then, like "God damn you" or whatever . . .'

'Means maker of universe? Condemn to hellworld?'

'Yeah, I guess that's right.'

'Pretty harsh!'

'Yes,' laughing, 'and that's one of the mild ones.'

Another night, shockingly warm, the house stuffy and murmurous, creaking under the weight of its load, Frank complained, 'Couldn't we move out to the garden shed or something?'

'Garden shed?' Rudra said, holding up his hands to make a box.

'Yes, the little building out back. Maybe we could move out there.'

'I like that.'

Frank was surprised again. 'It would be cold.'

'Cold,' Rudra said scornfully. 'No *cold*.'

'Well. Maybe not for you. Or else you haven't been outside lately at night. It was as cold as I've ever felt it, back in February.'

'Cold,' Rudra said, dismissing the idea. 'Test for oracle, to see if Dorje truly visits him, one spends night naked by river with many wet sheets. Wear sheets through the night, see how many one can dry.'

'Your body heat would dry out a wet sheet?'

'Seven in one night.'

'Okay, well, let's ask about the shed then. Spring is here, and I need to move outdoors.'

'Good idea.'

Frank added that to his list of things to do, and when the house mother, a kind of sirdari in the Sherpa style, got time to look at the shed with him, she was quick to approve and make the arrangements. She wanted their closet to house two elderly nuns who had just arrived, the oldest one looking frail.

The shed was dilapidated in the extreme. It stood in the back corner of the lot under a big tree, and the leaf fall had destroyed the shingles. Frank swept off some of the mulch and tarped over the roof, with a promise to it to make proper repairs in the summer. Inside its one room they moved two old single beds, a bridge table with a lamp, two chairs, and a space heater.

Immediately Frank felt better.

'Nice to lose things,' Rudra commented.

Frank quoted the Emerson for the day: 'One is rich in proportion to the things one doesn't need.'

'We seem to be getting very rich.'

The Khembali's vegetable garden lay outside their door in the back yard. It was obsessively tended, even in winter, and now that spring was here the black soil mounding up in long rows from the pale mulch was dotted everywhere by new greens. Immaculately espaliered branches of dwarf fruit trees were dotted with lime green points and no longer looked dead. If there was any sun at all during the day the garden would be filled with elderly Khembalis sitting on the ground, weeding and gossiping. Frank joined Rudra and this group for a couple of hours on Sunday mornings, puttering about in the usual gardening way. Rudra spoke to the others in quick Tibetan, not trying to keep Frank in the conversation. Frank had his Tibetan primer, and was still trying to learn, but the language's origins were not Indo-European, and it seemed to Frank a very alien system, hard to pronounce, and employing endings that sounded alike in the same way the letters of the alphabet looked alike. To compound his difficulties, Khembali was an eastern dialect of Tibetan, with some important differences in pronunciation that had never been written down. It made for slow going. Mostly they reverted to English.

The lengthening days got fuller, impossible though that seemed. In the mornings Frank went to Optimodal, then to work; ran with the lunch runners when he could get away, then back to work; in the evenings over to the park for a frisbee run, passing the bros and catching a brief burst of their rambunctious assholery; then to a restaurant, often an impulse stop; and back to the house, to help where he could, usually the final clean-up in the kitchen. By the time he went out to the shed and Rudra, he was almost asleep.

Rudra was usually sitting up in bed, back against the headboard. Sometimes he seemed to be daydreaming, others observant, even if only looking at the candle. He seemed attentive to the quality of Frank's silences. Sometimes he watched

Frank without actually listening to him. Frank found that unnerving – although sometimes, when he quit talking and sat on his bed, reading or tapping away at his laptop, he became aware of a feeling that seemed in the room rather than in himself, of peacefulness and calm. It emanated from the old man. Rudra would watch him, or space out, perhaps humming to himself, perhaps emit a few bass notes with their head tones buzzing in a harmonic fifth. Meditation, Rudra said once when asked about them. What might meditation be said to be doing? Could one disengage awareness, or rather the active train of consciousness, always spinning out its string of sentences? Leaving only awareness? Without falling asleep? And what then was the mind doing? Was the deep thinking in the unconscious actually continuing to cogitate in its own hidden way, or did it too calm? Memories, dreams, reflections? Was there someone in there below the radar, walking the halls of the parcellated mind and choosing which room to enter, going in and considering the contents of that parcellation, and its relation to all the rest?

God he hoped so. It was either that or else he was zoning through his days in a haze of indecision. It could be that too.

He was almost asleep one night when his cell phone beeped, and he roused to answer it, knowing it was her.

'Frank it's me.'

'Hi.' His heart was pounding. The sound of her voice had the effect of cardiac paddles slapped to his chest. The sensation was actually kind of frightening.

'Can you meet?'

'Yeah sure.'

'I know you're in Arlington now. How about the Lincoln Memorial, in an hour?'

'Sure.'

'Not on the front steps. Around the back, between it and the river.'

'Isn't that still fenced off?'

'South of that, then. South of the bridge then, on the new levee path.'

'Okay.'

'Okay see you.'

Rudra turned out to have been sitting up in the gloom. Now he was looking at Frank as if he'd understood every word, as why not; it had not been a complicated conversation.

Frank said, 'I'm going out.'

'Yes.'

'I'll be back later.'

'Back later.' Then, as Frank was leaving: 'Good luck!'

The banks of the Potomac between the Watergate and the Tidal Basin had been rebuilt with a broad levee just in from the river, topped by a path running under a double row of cherry trees. The Corps of Engineers had displayed their usual bravura style, and the new cherry trees were enormous. Under them at night Frank felt dwarfed, and the entire scene took on a kind of pharaonic monumentalism, as if he had been transported to some vast religious site on the banks of the Nile.

He stopped to look over the water to Theodore Roosevelt Island, where during the great flood he had seen Caroline in a boat, motoring upstream. That vision stood like a watermark in his mind, overlaying all his memories of the inundated city. He had never remembered to ask her what she had been doing that afternoon. She had stood alone at the wheel, looking straight ahead. Sometimes life became so dreamlike, things felt heraldic or archetypal, etched since the beginning of time so that one could only perform actions that already existed. Ah God, these meetings with Caroline made him feel so strange, so alive and somehow more-than-alive. He would have to ask Rudra about the nature of that feeling, if he could find some way to convey it. See if there was a Buddhist mental realm it corresponded to.

There in the trees below stood the Korean War Memorial. Caroline emerged from these trees, saw him on the levee and waved. She hurried up the next set of broad shallow steps, and there under the cherry trees they embraced. She hugged him hard. Her body felt tense, and out here in the open he felt apprehensive himself. 'Let's go back to my van,' he suggested. 'It's too open here.'

'No,' she said, 'your van chip is on active record now.'

'So they know I'm here?'

'It's being recorded, is a better way to put it. There's comprehensive coverage in DC now. So they know where you drive. But they don't know I'm here.'

'Are you sure?'

'Yes. As sure as I can be.' She shivered.

He held her by the arm. 'You're not chipped?'

'No. I don't think so. Neither of us are.'

She took a wand from her pocket, checked them both. No clicks. They walked under the cherry trees, dark overhead against the city's night cloud. There were a few solitaries out, mostly runners, then another couple, possibly trysting like Frank and Caroline.

'How can you stand it?' Frank said.

'How does anybody stand it? We're all chipped.'

'But most people no one wants to trace.'

'I don't know. The banks want to know. That means most people.' She shrugged; it happened to everyone, that's just the way things were now. Best not to want privacy.

But now, under the cherry trees, they were alone. No cars, no chips, phones left in their cars. They were off the net. No one else in the world knew where they were at that moment. It was somewhat like being in their little bubble universe of passion. A walking version of that union. Frank felt her upper arm press against his, felt the flushing in all his skin, the quickened pulse. It must be love, he thought. Even with Marta it had never been like this. Or was it perhaps just the element of danger that seemed to envelop her? Or the mysterious nature of that danger?

They sat on one of the benches overlooking the Tidal Basin. For a while they kissed. The feeling that poured through Frank then had less to do with their caresses, ravishing as they were, than with the sense of sharing a feeling; the opening up to one another, the vulnerability of giving and receiving. Very possibly, Frank thought in one of their hard silent hugs, their histories had caused them both to want this feeling of commitment more than anything else. After all the bad that had happened, a way to be with someone, to let down one's guard, to inhabit a shared space . . . Them against the world. Or outside the world. Maybe she was like him in this: that she needed a partner. He could not be certain. But it felt like it.

She curled against him. Frank warmed to her manner, her physical grace, her affection. It was different with her, it just was.

But she wasn't free. Her situation was compromised, even scary. She was breaking promises both personal and professional. That in itself didn't bother Frank as perhaps it should have, because she was doing it for him, and because of him; so how could he fault her for it? Especially since she also made him feel that somehow he deserved these moves, that she liked him for real reasons. That she was right to do what she was doing, because of the way he was to her. Reciprocity: hard to believe; but there she was, in his arms.

The world seeped back. A distant streetlight winked on the breeze.

'You're staying with those friends again?'

She nodded into his shoulder. Her body felt like she was falling asleep. He found this very moving; he could not remember the last time a woman had fallen asleep in his arms. He thought: maybe this is what it would be like. You would only ever know by doing it.

'Hey gal. What if one of your friends wakes up in the night?'

'I leave a note on the couch, saying that I couldn't sleep and went for a run.'

'Ah.'

It was interesting to think of friends who would believe that, and what it said about her.

'But I should start back in a while.'

'Damn.'

She sighed. 'We need to talk.'

'Good.'

'Tell me – do you think elections matter?'

'What? Well, sure. I mean, what do you mean?'

'I mean, do you think they really matter?'

'Hmmm,' Frank said.

'Because I'm not sure they do. I think they're just a kind of theater, you know, designed to distract people from how things are really decided.'

'You sound like some of my colleagues at work.'

'I'm being very scientific, I'm sure.' Her smile was brief and perfunctory. 'You know this futures market I'm supervising?'

'Sure. What, are they betting on the election now?'

'Of course, but you can do that anywhere. What my group is betting on has more to do with potential side-effects of the election. Or, now I'm thinking it's more like causes.'

'What do you mean?'

'There are people who can have an influence on the results.'

'How do you mean?'

'Like, a group involved with voting machine technology.'

'Uh oh. You mean like tweaking them somehow?'

'Exactly.'

'So your futures market is now going bullish on certain people involved with voting technology?'

'That's right. And not only that, but some of those people are my husband and his colleagues.'

'He's not doing what you're doing?'

'Not any more. He's moved again, and his new job is part of this stuff. This group may even be the originators of it.'

'A government agency working on fixing elections? How can that be?'

'That's the way it's evolved. The voting system is vulnerable to tampering, so there are agencies trying to figure out every way it can happen, so they can counter them. They pass that up the chain to be used, and then one of the more politicized agencies takes that information and makes sure it gets into the right hands at the right time. And there you have it.'

'You sound like it's happened already before?'

'I think the Cleland Senate loss in Georgia looks very suspicious.'

'How come that isn't a huge scandal?'

'The best evidence is in a classified study. Meanwhile, since it's been a rumor, it's treated like all the other rumors, many of which are wrong. So actually, to have the idea of something broached without any subsequent repercussion is actually a kind of, what. A kind of inoculation for an event you don't want investigated.'

'Jesus. So how does it work, do you know?'

'Not the technical details, no. I know they target certain counties in swing states. They use various statistical models and decision-tree algorithms to pick which ones, and how much to intervene.'

'I'd like to see this algorithm.'

'Yes, I thought you might.' She reached into her purse, pulled out a data disk in a paper sleeve. She handed it to him. 'This is it.'

'Whoah,' Frank said, staring at it. 'And so . . . What should I do with it?'

441

'I thought you might have some friends at NSF who might be able to put it to use.'

'Shit. I don't know.'

She watched him take it in.

'Do you think it matters?' she asked again.

'What, who wins the election, or whether there's cheating?'

'Both. Either.'

'Well. I should think election fraud is always bad.'

'I suppose.'

'How could it not be?'

'I don't know. It seems like it's been mostly cheating for a while now. Or theater at best. Distracting people from where the decisions are really made.'

'But something like this would be more than theater.'

'So you think it does matter.'

'Well . . . yeah.' Frank was a little shocked that she would even wonder about it. 'It's the law. I mean, the rule of law. Lawful practice.'

'I suppose so.' She shrugged. 'I mean, here I am giving this to you, so I must think so too. So, well – can you help fix it?'

He hefted the cd in its sleeve. 'Fix the fix?'

'Yes.'

'I'd like to, sure. I don't know if I can.'

'It'd be a matter of programming I guess. Re-programming.'

'Some kind of reverse transcription.'

'Sounds good. I can't do it. I can see what's happening, but I can't do anything about it.'

'You know but can't act.'

'Yeah that's right.'

'But you did this. So I'll see what I can do, sure. There must be an activation code tucked in the normal voting technology. There's any number of ways to do that. So . . . maybe it could be tweaked, to disable it. I do have a friend at NSF who does encryption, now that I think of it, and he worked at DARPA. He's a mathematician, he might be able to help. Does your futures market list him? Edgardo Alfonso?'

'I don't know. I'll look.'

'What about anyone else at NSF?'

'Yeah sure. Lots of NSF people. Diane Chang's stock is pretty high right now, for that matter.'

'Is that right?'

'Yes.' She watched him think it over.

Finally he shrugged. 'Maybe saving the world is profitable.'

'Or maybe it's unprofitable.'

'Hmmmmm. Listen, if you could get me a list of everyone listed in my market, that would be great. If Edgardo isn't on the list, all the better.'

'I'll check. He would be discreet?'

'Yes. He's a friend, I trust him. And to tell the truth, he would greatly enjoy hearing about this.'

She laughed, surprised. 'He likes bad news?'

'Very much.'

'He must be a happy guy these days.'

'Yes.'

'Okay. But don't tell too many people about this. Please.'

'No. And the ones I tell won't need to know how I've gotten this, either.'

'Good.'

'But they may need to be able to get back in to this program.'

'Sure, I know. I've been thinking about that. It'll be hard to do without anyone knowing it's been done.' She scowled. 'In fact I can't think of a good way. *I* might have to do it. You know. At home.'

'Listen, Caroline,' he said, spooked by the look on her face. 'I hope you aren't taking any chances here!'

She frowned. 'What do you think this is? I told you. He's strange.'

'Shit.' He hugged her hard.

After a while she shrugged in his grasp. 'Let's just do this and see what we see. I'm as clean as I can be. I don't think he has any idea what I've been up to. I've made it look like I'm chipped twenty-four seven and that I'm not doing anything. I can only really get offline at night, when he expects me to be sleeping. I leave the whole kit in the bed and then I can do what I need to. Otherwise if I dropped the kit it would show something was wrong. So, you know. So far so good.'

'No one suspects you of anything?'

'Not of anything more than marital alienation. There are some friends who know about that, sure. But that's been going on for years. No. People have no idea.'

'Even if they're in the business of having that kind of idea?'

'No. They think they know it all. They think I'm just . . . But it's gone so far past what they can know. Don't you understand – the technical capacity has expanded so fast, no one's really grasped the full potential of it yet.'

'Maybe they have. You seem to have.'

'But no one's listening to me.'

'But there could be others like you.'

'True. That may be happening too. There are superblacks now that are essentially flying free. But hopefully we won't run into anyone like that trying to stop us on this. Hopefully they think they're completely superblack still.'

'Hmmm.' Counter-intelligence, wasn't that what it was called? Surely that would be standard. Unless you thought you were an innermost sanctum, the smallest and newest box in the nesting boxes, with no one aware even of your existence. If her husband was in something like that, and thought his secrets were entirely safe from an estranged wife who did nothing more than sullenly perform her mid-level tech job . . .

They sat side by side in an uneasy silence. Around them the city pulsed and whirred in its dreams. Such a diurnal species; here they were, surrounded by three million people, but all of them conked like zombies, leaving them in the night alone.

She nudged into his shoulder. 'I should go.'

'Okay.'

They kissed briefly. Frank felt a wave of desire, then fear. 'You'll call?'

'I'll call. I'll call your Khembali embassy.'

'Okay good. Don't be too long.'

'I won't. I never have.'

'That's true.'

They got up and hugged. He watched her walk off. When he couldn't see her anymore he walked back up the levee path. A runner passed going the other way, wearing orange reflective gloves. After that Frank was alone in the vast riverine landscape. The view up the Mall toward the Capitol was as of some stupendous temple's formal garden. The smell of Caroline's hair was still in his nostrils, preternaturally clear and distinct. He was afraid for her.


Frank drove back to NSF and slept in his van, or tried to. Upstairs early the next morning, feeling stunned and unhappy, he looked at the sleeve of disks Caroline had given him. Clearly he had to do something with them. He was afraid to put them in his computers. Who knew what they would trigger, or wreak, or report to.

He could put them in a public computer. He could turn off his laptop's airport transmitter permanently. He could buy a cheap laptop and never airport it at all. He could . . .

He went for a run with Edgardo and Kenzo and Bob. When they got to the narrow path that ran alongside Highway 66, he tailed behind with Edgardo, and then slowed a little, and then saw that Kenzo and Bob were talking about some matter of their own, in the usual way of this stretch.

He said, 'Edgardo, do you think the election matters?'

'What, the presidential election?'

'Yes.'

Edgardo laughed, prancing for a few strides to express his joy fully. 'Frank, you amaze me! What a good question.'

'But you know what I mean.'

'No, not at all. Do you mean, will it make a difference which of these candidates takes office? Or do you mean elections in general are a farce?'

'Both.'

'Oh, well. I think Chase would do better than the President on climate.'

'Yes.'

'But elections in general? Maybe they don't matter. But let's say they are good, sure. Good soap opera, but also they are symbols, and symbolic action is still action. We need the illusion they give us, that we understand things and have some control. I mean, in Argentina, when elections went away, you really noticed how different things felt. As if the law had gone. Which it had. No, elections are good. It's voters who are bad.'

Frank said, 'That's interesting. I mean – if *you* think they matter, then I find that reassuring.'

'You must be very easily reassured.'

'Maybe I am. I wouldn't have thought so.'

'You're lucky if you are. But – why do you need reassurance?'

'I've got some disks back in my office that I'd kind of like to show you. But I'm afraid they might be dangerous.'

'Dangerous to the election?'

'Yes. Exactly.'

'Oh ho.' Edgardo ran on a few strides. 'May I ask who gave them to you?'

'I can't tell you that. A friend in another agency.'

'Ah ha! Frank, I am surprised at you. But this town is so full of spooks, I guess you can't avoid them. The first rule when you meet one is to run away, however.' Edgardo considered it. 'Well, I could put them in a laptop I have.'

'You wouldn't mind?'

'That's what it's for.'

'Do you still have contacts with people at DARPA?'

'Sort of.' He shook his head. 'My cohort there has scattered by now. That might not be where I would go to get help anyway. You could never be sure if they weren't the source of your problem in the first place. Do you know what the disks have on them?'

Frank told him what Caroline had said about the plan to fix the election. As he spoke he felt the oddity of the information coming out of his mouth, and Edgardo glanced at him from time to time, but mostly he ran on nodding as if to confirm what Frank was saying.

'Does this sound familiar?' Frank asked. 'You're not looking too shocked.'

'No. It's been a real possibility for some time now. Assuming that it hasn't already happened a time or two.'

'Aren't there any safeguards? Ways of checking for accuracy, or making a proper recount if they need to?'

'There are. But neither are foolproof, of course.'

'How can that be?'

'That's just the way the technology works. That's the system Congress has chosen to use. Convenient, eh?'

'So you think there could be interventions?'

'Sure. I've heard of programs that identify close races as they're being tallied, close ones but just outside the margin of error, so there aren't any automatic recounts to gum up the works . . . Embed a tweak that reverses a certain percentage of votes, you know, just enough to change the result.'

'Might you be able to counter one of these, if you saw it in advance? Some kind of reverse transcription that would neutralize the tweak without tipping off the people deploying it?'

'Me?'

'Or people you know.'

'Let me look at what you have. If it looks like it might be what you think, then I'll pass it along to some friends of mine.'

'Thanks, Edgardo.'

'But here we come to the bike path, let's change the subject. Give me what you've got, and I'll see what I can do. But give it to me at Food Factory, at three, and let's not talk about this in the building.'

'No,' Frank said, interested to see how Edgardo appeared to assume that the building might be compromised. So the surveillance was real after all. Of course he had known that; Caroline had told him. But it was interesting to get data from a different source.

Back at work, showered and in his office, checking the clock frequently and then setting his alarm for three so he didn't forget, Frank saw in an e-mail from Diane that Yann Pierzinski was on the first list for the expanded Grants for Exploratory Research program. He smiled, but then frowned. The new climate studies institute in San Diego had been approved, and the old Torrey Pines Generique facility rented to house it; and Leo Mulhouse had even been hired to run a genetic engineering lab. It all added up to good news, which of course he ought to call and share with Marta.

For a while he found other more pressing things on his list of Things To Do. But it kept coming back to mind, and he found he wanted to tell her this stuff anyway, to hear her reaction – how she would manage to downplay it. So that afternoon, after running down to Food Factory and giving Edgardo the disks, Frank went over and called Small Delivery Systems from a pay phone down in the Metro, thinking to reduce the number of obvious contacts in the hope it would keep their stock down. He asked for Marta rather than Yann.

After a minute she got on, and Frank said Hi.

She greeted him coolly, and he hacked his way through the preliminaries until her lack of cooperation forced him to the point. 'I got it arranged like you asked, I mean I couldn't stay in it directly because of conflict of interest, but it was such a good idea that they did it on their own. There's to be a new federal science and tech center, focused on climate interventions and housed in Torrey Pine Generique's old labs. And Yann and your whole team down there is listed for a big Grant for Exploratory Research too. So now you can go back to San Diego.'

'I can go wherever I want,' she said. 'I don't need your permission or your help.'

'No, that isn't what I meant.'

'Uh huh. Don't be trying to buy me off, Frank.'

'I'm not. I mean, I owe you that money, but you wouldn't take it. Anyway this is just a good thing. Yann and you guys get one of the grants, and this will be one of the best research labs anywhere for what you guys are up to.'

'We already have a lab.'

'Small Delivery is too small to deliver.'

'Not so, actually. We've just gotten a contract from the Russian government. We're licensing the genome for our altered tree lichen to them, and we'll be helping them to manufacture and distribute it in Siberia and Kamchatka this fall.'

'But – wow. Have you had any field trials for this lichen?'

'This is the field trial.'

'What? How big an area?'

'Lichen propagate by wind dispersion.'

'That's what I thought! Have the Russians talked to us or the UN or anyone?'

'The President believes it's an internal matter.'

'But the wind blows from Russia to Alaska.'

'No doubt.'

'And so to Canada.'

'Sure. The spruce forest wraps the whole world at that latitude,' Marta agreed. 'Our lichen could eventually spread through all of it.'

'And what's the estimated maximum takedown from that, do you suppose?'

'Eleanor thinks maybe a hundred parts per million.'

'Holy shit!'

'I know, it's a lot. But we figure there's no way to cause an ice age now, because we can always put carbon back into the atmosphere if we need to. This drawdown at max would only take us most of the way back to before the Industrial Revolution anyway, so the models we run show it will be a good thing, no matter if the takedown goes to one hundred percent of the estimate or not. Or even if it draws down more.'

'I don't know how you can say that!'

'That's what our models show.'

'Any idea how fast the propagation will go?'

'It kind of depends on how we distribute it in the first place.'

'Jesus, Marta. So the Russians are just *doing* this?'

'Yes. The President thinks it's too important to risk sharing the decision with the rest of the world. Democracy could hang up their best chance of a rescue, he apparently said. They now think that global warming is more of a disaster for them than for anyone else. At first they thought it might warm them up and make for better agriculture, but now their models are predicting drought, and cold more severe than ever, so they're bummed.'

'Everyone's bummed,' Frank said.

'Yeah but Russia is actually doing something about it. So quit trying to buy me off, Frank. We're going to be doing fine on our own. We've got some performance components in our contract that look good.'

Villas are cheap in Odessa, Frank didn't say.

'The new center hired Leo Mulhouse to run a bio lab,' he said instead.

'Ah ha! Well. That's good.' She didn't want to give him any credit. No matter what you do you'll still be an asshole, her silence said. 'Okay, well. He'll be good. See you, Frank.'

'Bye, Marta.'


The moment he got off he called Diane, and had to leave a message, but right at the end of the day she called back. He told her what Marta had said, and she was just as surprised as Frank had been, he could tell. Part of him was pleased by this; it meant she had been deceived by Dmitri too, or at least, left in the dark. Not that she sounded like a woman betrayed, of course; indeed, she sounded as if she thought it might be a good development. 'My God,' she said as they finished sharing what impressions they had of the situation, 'things are getting complicated, aren't they?'

'Yes they are.'

A couple days later she confirmed the news to Frank. She had talked to Dmitri, and he had said yes, they were distributing genetically engineered organisms to draw down quantities of carbon fast. It was only a pilot project and they did not expect the organisms to spread beyond Siberia. He wouldn't say over how large of an area the GMOs had been distributed, but he did confirm that one of the lichens had been licensed from Small Delivery Systems.

'Damn it,' Frank said. 'That's Yann. We really need to get him onto our team somehow.'

Diane said, 'I wonder if we can, now.'

'Well, I think he still wants to move back to San Diego. Not that he couldn't on his own, but maybe the center at Torrey Pines will look good to him.'

'Depending on his contract, he may get very little from any

work he's done for Small Delivery. And he may not be in control of his research program.'

'True.'

'Let's keep making the offer. Funding and freedom in San Diego – he may still go for it.'

**Meanwhile, in the midst** of all this, science itself proceeded in its usual manner; which is to say, very slowly.

Anna Quibler liked it that way. Take a problem, break it down into parts (analyze), quantify whatever parts you could, see if what you learned suggested anything about causes and effects; then see if this suggested anything about long-term plans, and tangible things to do. She did not believe in revolution of any kind, and only trusted the mass application of the scientific method to get any real-world results. 'One step at a time,' she would say to her team in Bioinformatics, or Nick's math group at school, or the National Science Board; and she hoped that as long as chaos did not erupt worldwide, one step at a time would eventually get them to some tolerable state.

Of course there were all the hysterical operatics of 'history' to distract people from this method and its incremental successes. The wars and politicians, the police state regimes and terrorist insurgencies, the gross injustices and cruelties, the unnecessarily ongoing plagues and famines – in short, all the mass violence and rank intimidation that characterized most of what filled the history books; all that was real enough, indeed all too real, undeniable – and yet it was not the whole story. It was not really history, if you wished to include everything important that had happened to humans through time. Because along with all the violence, underneath the radar, inside the nightmare, there was always the ongoing irregular but encouraging pulse of good work, often, since the seventeenth century, created or supported by science. Ongoing increases in health and longevity, for larger and larger percentages of the population: that could be called progress. If they could hold on to what they had done, and get everyone in the world to that bettered state, it would actually *be* progress.

Anna was thus a progressive in that limited sense, of evolution not revolution. And for her, science was the medium of progress, progress's mode of production, if she understood that term; science was both the method of analysis and the design for action.

The action itself – that was politics, and thus a descent back into the Bad Zone of history, with all its struggles and ultimately its wars. But those could be defined as the breakdown of the plan, the replacement of the plan by a violent counter-plan. The violence was exerted against the plan; and if ever violence was justified, as being necessary to put a good plan into action, the secondary and tertiary results usually were so bad that the justification could later be proved untrue, the plan itself betrayed by the negative effects of its violent implementation.

Progress had to be made peaceably and collectively. It did not arrive violently. It had to be accomplished by positive actions. Positive ends required positive means, and never otherwise.

Except, was this true? Sometimes her disgust with the selfishness of the administration she was working for grew so intense that she would have been very happy to see the population rise up and storm the White House, tear it down and hand the furniture to the overstuffed fools who had already wrecked the rest of the government. Violent anger if not violent action.

Given these feelings, one obvious opportunity for constructive action had been getting scientists involved in the presidential campaign. Whether or not the SSEEP idea was a good one was very hard for her to judge, but in for a penny in for a pound; and she figured that as an experiment it would give some results, one way or another. Unless it didn't because of a poor design, any results lost in the noise of everything else going on. The social sciences, she thought, must have a terrible time designing experiments that yielded anything confirmable.

So, ambiguous results, at best; but meanwhile it was still worth trying.

Her actual involvement with the election campaign was at third or fourth remove, which was just the way she liked it, and probably the only way that it remained legal. She could certainly talk to Charlie about things Phil Chase could do as a candidate, if he wanted to, that might help him win. Or even propose actions to him that Phil might initiate; after which they could respond however they wanted, and she could go back to the things she did at NSF directly. Whether they did anything or not was their concern; and so she was not actively working for a candidate.

This was partly the usual scientist's disconnect from political action, which was itself partly a realism about doing what one could. In any case she preferred spending that kind of time working on her archeology of great lost ideas in federal science policy. She had already gotten Charlie to convince Phil to introduce a bill to the Senate that would revive FCCSET in an even stronger form, under the guise of being part of a larger 'Climate Planned Response,' or CPR.

Now she was finding the fossil remnants of various foreign aid programs that had been focused on science infrastructural proliferation, as she called it. Some of these were inactive because they were funding starved; others had been discontinued. Anna got Diane to assign Laveta and her team to liaise with the UN's environmental offices, to connect these kinds of projects with funding sources.

'Let's fund them ourselves when we can't find anyone else,'

Diane suggested. 'Let's get a group together to start rating these projects and awarding grants.'

'And Frank would say that group should start writing requests for proposal.'

Diane nodded. 'For sure.'

NSF was now disbursing money at a truly unprecedented rate. The ten billion a year budget goal, only recently achieved, looked like pump-priming compared to what they were now passing out. Though Congress still would not fully fund the repair of the District of Columbia, the right people on the right committees had been scared enough by the flood to start funding whatever efforts seemed most likely to keep their own districts from suffering the same fate. Maybe it was just a matter of politicians wanting to look statesmanlike when the big moment arrived; maybe they were just reflecting what they were hearing from home; maybe the two parties were jockeying for favor in the upcoming election. Whatever the cause, NSF had a supplementary budget this fiscal year of almost twenty billion dollars, and if they could find good ways to spend other federal money, Congress tended to back them.

'They lived through this winter and they've seen the light,' Edgardo said.

Anna maintained that the economy could always have afforded to pay for public work like this – that it was not even a particularly large share of the total economy – but that for so many years they had lived within the premises of a war economy that they had forgotten how much humans produced. Now that it was being redirected a little, it was becoming clearer how much the war economy had drained off.

'Interesting,' Edgardo said, looking intently at her. She very seldom talked about politics. 'I wonder if it will correlate with the carbon economy. I mean, that we blew the fossil fuel surplus on wars, and lost the chance to use a one-time surplus to construct a utopian scientific society. So now we are past the overshoot, and doomed to struggle in extreme danger for some birth-defected smaller version of just-good-enoughness.'

'One step at a time,' Anna insisted. 'By the year 2500 it should all look the same.'

She liked the way she could make Edgardo laugh. It was easy, in a way; you only had to say out loud the most horrible thing you could imagine and he would shout with laughter, tears springing to his eyes. And she had to admit there was something bracing about his attitude. He bubbled away like a fountain of acids – everything from vinegar to hydrochloric – and it made you laugh. Once you had said the worst, a certain sting was removed; the secret fear of it, perhaps, the superstition that if you said it aloud you made it more likely to come to pass, as with Charlie and disease. Maybe the reverse was true, and nothing you said out loud could thereafter come true, because of the Pauli exclusion principle or something like it. So now she exchanged dire prophecies with Edgardo freely, to defuse them and to make him laugh.

You needed a theory of black comedy to get through these days anyway, because there was little of any other kind around. Anna worked every minute of her hours at work, until her alarm went off and reminded her it was time to go home. Then she took the Metro home, thankful that it was running again, using that time stubbornly to continue processing jackets, as she used to before the Foundation had gone into crisis mode. Continuing the real work. At home she found that Charlie had been once again sucked into helping Phil Chase's campaign, an inevitable process now that it was coming down to the wire and they were all doing everything they could; so that he had barely managed to watch Joe while talking on the phone, and had not remembered to go to the store. So off she went, driving so she could stock up on more groceries than could be carried, boggled once again by the destitute look of their grocery store, the best one in the area but sovietized like all the rest of them by the epidemic of hoarding that had plagued her fellow citizens ever since the cold snap, if not the flood. Hoarding was a bad thing; it represented a loss of faith in the system's ability to supply the necessities reliably. While there might have been some rational basis to it in the beginning, what it now meant is that every time she went to the store huge sections of the shelves were empty, particularly of those products that would be needed in an emergency and could be stored at home: toilet paper, bottled water, flour, rice, canned goods. People were storing these in their houses rather than letting them be stored in the store. She was still waiting for the time when every household maxxed, so that when the stores got a shipment they would not fly out the doors.

It also looked like certain fresh foods were permanently in shorter supply than they had been before the long winter. This was a different problem entirely.

So she had to hunt for whatever could be used, buy a few meals' worth of ingredients, some fast stuff, and hurry home to find Charlie still on the phone, vociferating, while also placating Joe about Anna's absence. He had gotten water on to boil, so they were that far ahead. But Nick had spaced on homework and Joe was whining, and Charlie was engrossed in trying to get his boss elected President of the United States, after which things would supposedly calm back down. Aaack!

Oh well; time to heft Joe onto her hip and see if he would help make a salad, while consulting with Nick on math. It would all be better by the year 2500.

Not for the first time, it struck her that things were calmer and more relaxing at work than they were at home. Or rather, that wherever she was, it always seemed like it was calmer at the other place. Was that normal? And if so, what did it mean?

\* \* \*

Back at work, where the calm was again not actually notice-able as such, the climate amelioration projects were still taking up the bulk of their efforts. Carbon capture and seques-tration, cleaner energy sources, cleaner transport: each area by itself was massive and complex, and correlating them was really more than their systems could accomplish. Although Frank had established a model modeling group, to study ways to model their efforts as a single thing.

Meanwhile they continued the work on their own fronts, and reported back to Diane and Laveta. Bioinformatics was still expanding at a tremendous speed, although here as else-where they were running into the same problem they had encountered with the climate: they knew things, but they couldn't act on them. Getting genetically modified DNA into living humans was still proving to be an enormous obstacle.

On the climate front, the North Atlantic project was entrained and happening, therefore out of their hands; and everywhere else, they were running into the tail-wagging-dog difficulty that Edgardo had named Fat Dog Syndrome; the dog was too fat for the tail to wag it, no matter how excited the tail got. They tried to quantify this impression by using cascade math to model ways for distributing money that would perturb other sources of it, finding capital at 'high angles of repose,' venture capital, pension funds, investment banks, the stock markets, futures markets. Indeed, if they could get the markets to invest, they would really be tapping into the economy's surplus value, redirecting it to purposes actually useful. But whether these efforts were finding anything useful in the real world was an open question.

'Big profits in global cooling,' Edgardo said.

'Perturbation.' Anna liked the sound of the word and the concept. 'It's a network, and we perturb it in ways that stim-ulate harmonics.' She thought the math describing this system's behavior was more interesting than the cascade theories, which always went back to chaos theory. Her urge to orderliness

459

made her extremely interested in chaos theory, but the math itself was not as appealing to her as the stuff on harmonics in a network, which tended to describe stabilities rather than breakdowns. Just neater somehow.

'Like cat's cradle,' Diane said once, looking at a diagram on Frank's screen.

'I wish,' Anna said. 'If only we could just stick in some fingers and lift it out into something entirely new! Something simpler. Release a few complications – that used to be a cool move in cat's cradle when I was a girl . . .'

But the truth was, the interlocking networks of human institutions were woven into such a tight mesh that it was hard to get any wave functions or simplifications going. They were tied down like Gulliver by all their rules and regulations. Only the violence of the original perturbation – the flood in Washington – was getting them as much flex as they were seeing; that and the hard winter. Any more than that they were going to have to create by lots of small actions, repeated many times.

So their work went on, under the radar for the most part, unreported in the news. The only exceptions were the most visible and large-scale of the weather projects. For these the public scrutiny was intense, the reaction all over the map. Most of the projects proposed had broad public support. Even the more blatant interventions, like bioengineered bacteria or lichen, had the support of an admittedly smaller majority, like sixty percent. People were ready to try things. The traffic jams and empty stores were getting to them in ways that news reports of distant storms had not.

Phil Chase was noticing that on the campaign trail. 'People are fed up with the disruptions,' he said to his staff. 'Listen to what they're telling us. Too many hassles when things break down. Try anything you can think of, they're saying, to get levels of service and convenience back to what they used to be.' In his speeches he started to say something FDR had said back in the 1930s: 'The solution is to be found in a program of bold and persistent experimentation.'

As a scientist Anna had to like that. They were designing, funding and executing experiments. Compiling a hypothetical candidate's most scientifically defensible positions was just one experiment among all the rest of them. Maybe it would work, maybe it wouldn't, but they would learn something from it either way. She even began to see what she thought might be ripples caused by her perturbations, cascading through the global scientific network of institutions, the agencies and companies and academies and labs – the scientific polyarchy, from individual scientists up to labs, institutions, corporations and countries. Tugging on the cat's cradle, bouncing on the trampoline.

She would go to Frank to talk about amplifying some of these perturbations, also about ways Frank's new projects could sometimes be executed by the already-existing scientific network. Then to Charlie she would talk about what Phil should be proposing in his campaign. Phil was certainly making climate change a major issue – a calculated risk for sure, given the American penchant for denial, particularly of problems caused by Americans. The President himself constantly urged denial as a kind of virtue, and denounced the climate issue as a universal downer – which it was – although he was no longer trying to claim that it was a nonexistent problem.

Phil Chase was not hesitant in bringing up the subject, or in proposing to tackle the problem. Charlie wrote parts of speeches, fed Roy facts and ideas, and discussed strategy on a daily basis. At night he would sit with Anna and watch Phil say things like 'Climate change is obviously real, and byproducts of our economy have had a role in this global warming. Republicans by denying this have compounded the problem, and lost our descendants hundreds of fellow species, and decades of work. Now it's time to do something about it, and I'm the one with the will to do it. We're going to need to work at this, it needs to become a big part of the national project, the focus of our economy. In that sense it is actually an incredible opportunity for new industries. We're on the verge of a truly life-affirming and sustainable global economy, based on justice and nurturing the biosphere, rather than strip-mining and fouling it. I'm ready to lead the way in starting to treat this planet like our home.'

Anna could always tell when Charlie had written what Phil was saying, because Charlie would hold his breath for however long it took Phil to say it. 'Whew! Am I crazy?' he would gasp afterward. 'I must be crazy! Why is Phil trusting me? He's freaking me out here!'

And yet all this seemed to be part of what was helping Phil's numbers; maybe even the main part. He had always polled highest the more he ignored conventional inside-the-Beltway political wisdom. As a Californian politician this was more or less a traditional tactic, reinforced by each subsequent success, as with their recent grandstanding governor. Just go for it, baby! Washington punditry was for girlie men!

Thus now, when Phil was asked about the 'Virtual Scientist Candidate,' he would smile his glorious smile. 'In Europe a candidate like that is called a shadow candidate. I take the people inventing this candidate to be our allies, because if you judge the effect of your vote by rational scientific criteria, then you will never throw it away on a splinter party that doesn't have a chance in our winner-take-all system. You vote for the potential winner most likely to express something like your views, and at this moment I'm that man. So the science guy is *my* shadow.'

His numbers rose again. It seemed to Anna that it was going to be a really close election; so close she could hardly stand to contemplate it.

Edgardo agreed. 'People like it that way. See-saw back and forth, try to get it perfectly level for election day. Confound the polls by sitting inside their margins of error. That way the day itself will bring a surprise. A bit of drama, just for its own sake. Policy has nothing to do with it, life and death have nothing to do with it. People just like a good race. They like their little surprises.'

'They may get a big surprise this time,' Anna said.

'They don't like big surprises. Only little surprises will do.'

On it went. The summer passed, giving them several weeks in a row of weather so cool and pleasant that abrupt climate change began to seem like a blessing. During that time several of the FCCSET programs were linked, and suddenly Department of Energy was on their side – it was actually unnerving – and they were in hot pursuit of what looked like a really powerful photovoltaic cell. Previously the polymers in plastic solar cells had absorbed only visible light, converting about six percent of the sun's energy to electrical power; now researchers were mixing semiconducting nanoparticles called quantum dots into one of the layers, which absorbed infrared light and generated electricity as well. A layering of both yielded an efficiency of thirty percent, and now the mythical ten-by-ten mile array of cells, set somewhere in New Mexico and powering the whole country, was beginning to look like an actual possibility.

Anna went on to her other work, feeling pleased. Perturbation of the network! Cat's cradle, slip and pull! When she went home she would be able to sit there and listen to Charlie's talk about the campaign without getting as anxious and irritated as before – knowing, as she watched the news sprawl across the screen like a giant Jerry Springer show they could not escape, that always underneath it the great work rolled on.

**Anna's great work, however,** was basically a linear process; and it existed in a world with some important nonlinear components, acting in different realms. One morning at home with Joe, Charlie got a call from Roy Anastopholous. 'Roy!'

'Charlie are you sitting down?'

'I am not sitting down, I *never* sit down, but nothing you can tell me will need me sitting down!'

'That's what you think! Charlie I've got Wade Norton on the other line and I'm going to patch him in. Wade? Can you still hear me?'

A second or two of satellite time, and then Charlie heard Wade, speaking from Antarctica: 'I can still hear you. Hi Charlie, how are you?'

'I'm fine, Wade,' resisting the urge to speak louder so that Wade could still hear him down there at the bottom of the world. 'What's happening?'

'I'm on a flight over the Ross Sea, and I'm looking at a big tabular berg that's just come off from the coastline. Really really really big. It'll be on the news soon, but I wanted to call you guys and tell you. The West Antarctic Ice Sheet has started to come off big time.'

'Oh my God. You're looking at a piece of it already off?'

'Yes. It's about a hundred miles long, the pilot says.'

'My God. So sea level has already gone up a foot?'

'You got it, Charlie! I was trying to tell Roy.'

'That's why *I* told you to sit down,' Roy put in.

464

'I had better sit down,' Charlie admitted, feeling a little wobble, as for instance the axis of the Earth. 'Any guesses by the scientists down there as to how fast the rest will come off?'

'They don't know. It's happening faster than they expected. Some of them are running a pool now, and the bets range from a decade to a century. Apparently the goo underneath the ice is the consistency of toothpaste. It lets the ice slide, and the tides tug at it, and there's an active volcano down underneath there too.'

'Shit.'

'So we're talking sea level rise?' Roy asked, trying to get confirmation.

'Yes,' Wade said. 'Hey, boys, I've got to go, I just wanted to let someone know. I'll talk to you more soon.'

He got off and Charlie then explained the situation to Roy. Giant ice sheet, warming, cracking – sliding off its underwater perch – floating away in chunks, displacing more water than it had when perched. If the whole thing came off, sea level up seven meters. A quarter of the world's population affected, perhaps fifty trillion dollars in human and natural capital at risk. Conservatively.

Roy said, 'Okay, Charlie. I get the point. It sounds like it will help Phil in the campaign.'

'Roy, please. Not funny.'

'I'm not being funny.' Although he was laughing like a loon. 'I'm talking about addressing the problem! If Phil doesn't win, what do you think will happen?'

'Okay okay. Shit. My God.' Everything Anna and her colleagues had been doing to restart the Gulf Stream was as nothing to this news. Changing currents, maybe – but *sea level*? 'The stakes just keep getting higher, don't they?'

'Yes they do.'

465

# TEN

## *Primavera Porteño*

Kenzo had run the numbers and found that most seasonal weather manifestations varied by about eight percent, year to year – temperature, precipitation, wind speeds, and so on. Now all that was over. They had passed the point of criticality, they had tipped over the tipping point in the same way a kid running up a see-saw will get past the axis and somewhere beyond and above it plummet down on the falling board. They were in the next mode, and coming into the second winter of abrupt climate change.

The President announced on the campaign trail that he had inherited this problem from his Democratic predecessors, particularly Bill Clinton, and that only free markets and a strong national defense could battle this new threat, which he called climatic terrorism. 'Why, you can't be sure you won't wake up someday to find the world spitting in your face. It's not okay, and I'm going to do something about it. My administration has been studying the problem and getting recommendations from our scientists, and I'm proud to say that on my watch the National Science Foundation initiated this great counter-terrorist operation in the North Atlantic, which will soon restore the Gulf Stream to its rightful flow, and show how American know-how and technology is a match for anything.'

467

*This played well, like most things the President did. He visited NSF for half an hour, and later appeared on the news in a briefing with Diane Chang, the heads of NOAA and the EPA, and his science advisor Dr Strengloft. The President got a great deal of credit for taking on the weather in such a forceful and market-based manner, bypassing the scientists and liberals and striking a blow for freedom and the salt industry. Anna, watching the TV news, hissed like a tea kettle; Charlie threw Joe's dinosaurs at the radiator. The President's numbers went up. Only Diane was calm. She said, 'Don't worry. It only means we're winning. They're all trying to get on our side now. So science is getting some leverage on the situation.'*

*And Phil Chase blew through all the President's claims with a laugh. 'The salt fleet is an international project, co-ordinated through the UN. The part of it we're paying for comes from an appropriation Congress made because of a bill I wrote. The President tried to hamstring this great project up and down the line. Come on! You all know which candidate will work to protect the environment, and it's me, me and my party. Let's turn it into a big party. We can make things better for our kids, and that'll be our fun. That's the way it's always been until now, so you can't let the fear and greed guys scare you 'til you cut and run. The new climate is an opportunity. We needed to change, and now we will, because we have to. What could be more convenient?'*

*This played well too, much to the pundits' private surprise (in public they always knew everything), and now Phil's numbers went up. He was polling neck and neck with the President, and doing particularly well among the boomers and their children the echo boomers, the two biggest demographics.*

*The President's team continued to transpose what was working for Chase into the President's campaign. They began to proclaim the bad weather to be an economic opportunity of the first order. New businesses, even entire new industries, were there for the making! The bad weather was obviously another economic opportunity for market-driven reforms.*

*However, since he had been elected with the help of big oil and everything transnationally corporate, and had done more than any previous president to strip-mine the nation and use it as a dumping ground, he did not appear to be as convincing as Phil. It was getting hard to believe his assertions that the invisible hand of the market would solve everything, because, as Phil put it, the invisible hand never picked up the check.*

*So the election campaign wallowed along in its falsity and tedium, and surprise surprise, as the summer passed it became an ever-tightening race, just as all media hopeful for interested customers might have wished. These summer months were full enough of new weather anomalies and extreme events to keep Phil in the chase, as he liked to put it.*

*So his campaign was doing well, and he kept it up with campaign events all over the world, including a return to the North Pole a year after announcing his candidacy. It was a bit of a throwback to his old World's Senator mode, but he claimed its effect was good, and his team could only follow his lead. 'I have to run on my record, there's no other way to do it. I am what I am.' He started saying that too. 'I am what I am.'*

*'And that's all what I am,' Roy always sang when he said it, 'I'm Pop-Eye the sailor man! Toot toot!' Phil was in fact like Pop-Eye in enough important respects that his staff started calling him that.*

*And Charlie had to admit that since the climate problem was global, campaigning everywhere made a sort of sense. It made Phil and his career and his campaign all of a piece. Meanwhile the President remained resolutely nationalistic, it was always America this and freedom that, no matter how transnational and oppressive the content of his positions. Patriotism as xenophobia was part of his appeal to his base, and it worked for them. But Phil's people had a different idea: the world was the world. Everyone was part of it.*

One unexpected problem for his campaign was that the 'Scientific Virtual Candidate' was polling pretty well, up to five percent in blue states, despite the fact that the candidate was non-existent and would not appear on any ballots. And this of course was a problem for Phil. Most of those potential votes came from his natural constituency, and so it was accomplishing the usual third party disaster of undercutting precisely the major party most closely allied to its views.

Phil looked to Charlie on this. 'Charlie, you have to talk to your wife and her colleagues at NSF about this. I don't want to be accidentally nadered by these good people. You tell them, whatever they want out of this campaign, I'm their best chance at it.'

'I don't want to depress them that much,' Charlie deadpanned, which got a good Phil chuckle, rueful but pleased. His fear that running for President was going to lose him all real human contact (the unconscious goal of many a previous President), was so far proving unfounded. 'Thanks for that thrust of rapierlike wit,' he replied. 'There aren't enough people saying deflationary things about me these late days of the campaign. You are indeed a brother, and we are a real foxhole fraternity, shelled daily as we are by Fox. But don't forget to talk to NSF.' As far as Charlie could tell he was still enjoying himself enormously.

And Charlie did ask Anna and Frank what the plans were for candidate experiment. They both shrugged and said it was out of their hands, the genie out of the bottle. At NSF they talked to the SSEEP team, who were of course already aware of the historical precedents and the negative ramifications of any partial real-world success of their hypothetical campaign. Until preferential voting was introduced, third parties could only be spoilers.

*Frank got back to Charlie. 'They're on it.'*

*'How so, meaning what?'*

*'They're waiting for their moment.'*

*'Ahhhhh.'*

*This moment came in late September, when a hurricane veered north at the last minute and hammered New Jersey, New York, Long Island, and Connecticut, and to a lesser extent the rest of New England. These were blue states already, but with big SSEEP numbers as well, so that after the first week of emergencies had passed, and the flooding subsided, a SSEEP conference was held in which representatives of a hundred and sixty-seven scientific organizations debated what to do in as measured and scientific manner as they could manage – which in the event meant a perfect storm of statistics, chaos theory, sociology, econometrics, mass psychology, ecology, cascade mathematics, poll theory, historiography and climate modeling. At the end of which a statement was crafted, approved, and released, informing the public that the 'Scientific Candidate' was withdrawing from all campaigns, and suggesting that any voters who had planned to vote for it consider voting for Phil Chase as being an 'electable first approximation of the scientific candidate,' and 'best real current choice.' Support for preferential or instant run-off voting method was also strongly recommended, as giving future scientific candidates the chance actually to win representation proportional to the votes they got, improving democracy if judged by representational metrics.*

*This announcement was denounced by the President's team as prearranged collusion and a gross sullying of the purity of science by an inappropriate and unscientific descent into partisan politics of the worst kind. The Scientific Candidate immediately issued a detailed reply to these charges in the form of all its calculation and a description of the analytic methods used to reach its conclusions, including point-by-point comparisons of the various planks of all the platforms, indicating that at this point Phil was closer to science than the President.*

*'You think?' Roy Anastopholous said to Charlie over the phone. 'I mean, duh. I hope this helps us, but isn't it just another of those scientific studies that spends millions and makes a huge effort to prove the sky is blue or something? Of course Phil is more scientific, he's running against a man aligned with rapture enthusiasts, people who are getting ready to take off and fly up to heaven!'*

*'Calm down, Roy, this is a good thing. This is connect-the-dots.'*

*In public Phil welcomed the new endorsement, and he welcomed the voters attending to it, promising to do his best to adopt the planks of the scientific platform into his own. 'Chase Promises To See What He Can Do.'*

*'Try me and see,' Phil said. 'Given the situation, it makes perfect sense. The President isn't going to do anything. He and his oil-and-guns crowd will just try to find an island somewhere to skip to when they're done raiding the world. They'll leave us in the wreckage and build themselves bubble fortresses, that's been their sick plan all along. Building a good world for our kids is our plan, and it's scientific as can be, but only if you understand science as a way of being together, an ethical system and not just a method for seeing the world. What this political endorsement underlines is that science contains in it a plan for dealing with the world that we find ourselves in, a plan which aims to reduce human suffering and increase the quality of life on Earth for everyone. In other words science is a kind of politics already, and I'm proud to be endorsed by the scientific community, because its goals match the values of justice and fairness that we all were taught are the most important part of social life and government. So welcome aboard, and I appreciate the help, because there's a lot to do!'*

*Thus ended the most active part of the first Social Science*

*Experiment in Elective Politics. There would be much analysis,*
*and the follow-up studies would suggest new experiments the*
*next time around, presumably. The committee was there in*
*place at the National Academy of Sciences, and it would have*
*looked bad at that point if anyone inside or outside the*
*Academy had tried to shut it down.*

*Diane, under stupendous heat from Republicans in*
*Congress for appearing to have used a federal agency to*
*support a political candidate, went to the hearings and*
*shrugged. 'We'll study it,' she said. 'We funded an experi-*
*ment in our usual way.'*

*'Would you fund an experiment like that one again?'*
*demanded Senator Winston.*

*'It would depend on its peer review,' she said. 'If it was*
*given a good ranking by a peer review panel, it would be*
*considered, yes.'*

*One of the Democratic senators on the panel pointed out*
*that this would not be the first federal agency to get involved*
*in a political campaign, that in fact several were at this moment*
*working explicitly and directly for the President's campaign,*
*including the Treasury Department and the Departments of*
*Agriculture, Education, and Commerce. While on the other*
*hand NSF had just funded an experiment that had happened*
*to catch on with the public.*

*The debate of the day roared on. The National Science*
*Foundation had jumped into politics and the culture wars.*
*Its age of innocence was over at last.*

**Frank and Rudra Cakrin** continued to spend the last hour of most nights out in their shed, talking. They talked about food, the events of the day, the contents of their shed, the garden, and the nature of reality. Most of their talk was in English, where Rudra continued to improve. Sometimes he gave Frank a Tibetan lesson.

Rudra liked to be outside. His health seemed to Frank poor, or else he was frail with age. On their trips out together Frank gave him an arm at the curbs, and once he even pushed him in a wheelchair that was stored inside the house underneath the stairwell. A few times they went for a drive in Frank's van.

One day they drove out to see their future home. The Khembalis had finalized the purchase of the land in Maryland they had located, a property upstream on the Potomac that had been badly damaged in the great flood. A farmhouse on the high point of the acreage had been inundated to the ceiling of the first floor, and a passing rowboat crowded with refugees from other farms had hacked through the roof to get into the attic. Padma and Sucandra had decided that the building could be made habitable again, and in any case the land would be worth it; apparently it was zoned in a way that would allow most of the Khembalis in the metro area to live there.

So Frank drove out the George Washington Parkway to the Beltway, Rudra peering out from the passenger seat with a lively eye, talking in Tibetan. Frank tried to identify what words he could, but it didn't add up to much – *malam*, highway, *sgan*, hill; *sdon-po*, tree. It occurred to him that maybe this was what conversation always was, two people talking to themselves in different languages, mostly in order to clarify themselves to themselves. Or else just filling the silence, singing ooop ooop.

He tried to resist this theory, so Edgardoesque, by asking specific questions. 'How old are you?'

'Eighty-one.'

'Where were you born?'

'Near Drepung.'

'Do you remember any of your past lives?'

'I remember many lives.'

'Lives before this life?'

Rudra looked down at the river as they crossed on the Beltway. 'Yes.'

'Not interrupted by any deaths?'

'Many deaths.'

'Yes, but I mean, your own deaths?'

Rudra shrugged. 'This does not seem to be the body I used to inhabit.'

Out on the farm, Rudra insisted on trudging slowly up to the land's high point, a low ridge at the eastern edge of the property, just past the ruined farmhouse.

They looked around. 'So you'll make this your new Khembalung.'

'Same Khembalung,' Rudra said. 'Khembalung is not a *place*.' He waved his arm at the scene. 'A name for a way.' He wiggled his hand forward like a fish, as if indicating passage through time.

'A moveable feast,' Frank suggested.

'Yes. Milarepa said this, that Khembalung moves from age to age. He said it will go north. Not until now have we seen what he meant. But here it is.'

'But Washington isn't very north of Khembalung.'

'From Khembalung go north, keep going, over top of world and down the other side. Here you are!'

Frank laughed. 'So now this is Khembalung?'

Rudra nodded. He said something in Tibetan that Frank didn't understand.

'What's that?'

'The first Khembalung was recently found, north of Kunlun Mountains. Ruins located, recently, under desert mountain in Takla Makan.'

'They found the original? How old was the site?'

'Very old.'

'Yes, but did they say a date by chance?'

Rudra frowned. 'Eighth century in your calendar?'

'Wow. I bet you'd like to go see that.'

Rudra shook his head. 'Stones.'

'I see. You like this better.' Indicating the broad sweep of grass and mud under their gaze.

'Sure. More lively. Live living.'

'That's true. So, a great circle route, and Shambala comes to us.'

'Good way to put it.'

Slowly they walked down to the riverbank, a broad swath of mud curving around the ridge and then away to the southeast. The curve, Frank thought, might be another reason the land had been for sale. The natural snake-slither of riverine erosion would perhaps eat away this mud bank, and then the devastated grass above it. Possibly a well-placed wall could stabilize the bank at certain critical points. 'I'll have to ask General Wracke out for your homecoming party,' Frank said as he observed it. 'He'll have suggestions for a wall.'

'More dikes, very good idea.'

On their way back to the van they passed under a stand of trees, and Frank parked Rudra under one to take a quick survey of the grove. Two sycamores, a truly giant oak; even a stand of pines.

'This looks good,' he said to Rudra as he came walking back over the grass. 'Those are really good trees, you could build in several of them.'

'Like your treehouse.'

'Yes, but you could do it here. Bigger, and lower.'

'Good idea.'

Many remote underwater vehicles were cruising the North Atlantic, sending back data that quickly became front page news about the status of the stalled Gulf Stream. At the end of September a hurricane lashed Central America, dumping a great deal of rain in the Pacific, which would increase the salinity of the Gulf Stream further. All systems were go for the salt fleet now converging in the ocean west of Ireland; but in the meantime, with nothing more happening in the Atlantic, the news shifted its attention south, where the West Antarctic Ice Sheet continued to detach, in small but frequent icebergs at its new margin. The big fragment was adrift in the Antarctic Ocean, a tabular berg as big as Germany and thicker than any ice shelf had ever been, so that it had in fact raised sea level by several inches. Tuvalu was being evacuated; further ramifications of this event were almost too large to be grasped. Through October it remained just one more bit of bad news among the rest. Sea level rise, oh my; but what could anyone do?

Frank sat in a room at NSF with Kenzo and Edgardo, looking at data in from NOAA. He had some ideas about sea level rise mitigation, in fact. But now the topic of the hour switched back to the International North Atlantic Current Mitigation Project. Data coming back from the RUVs, white whales, ships, and buoys scattered throughout the Atlantic were encouraging. It was becoming apparent, Kenzo said, that the predictions made by some that a stall in the thermohaline circulation would create negative feedbacks to its continuance had been correct. With the heat of the Gulf

Stream not reaching the far north Atlantic, there had been a resulting southward movement of the Hadley circulation in the atmosphere; this meant a southerly shift in the Atlantic's intertropical convergence zone. Normally the convergence zone was a high precipitation zone, and so with its shift south the rain had diminished in the mid-latitudes where it used to fall, so that the salinity of the balked mass at the north end of the stall had been rising. Even the fresh water cap north of Iceland was not as fresh as it had been back in the spring.

So conditions were ripe; everything was shaping up well for their intervention. The fleet of single-hulled VLCC tankers had been loaded at the many salt pans and ports around the Caribbean and North Africa that had been called upon, and they were almost all at the rendezvous point. The fleet headed north moving into formation, and the photos coming in over the internet were hard to believe, the sheer number of ships making it look like a sure artifact of photo-shopping.

Then the dispersal of the salt began, and the photos got even stranger. It was scheduled to last two weeks, the last of October and the first of November; and halfway through it, three days before the Presidential election, Frank got a call from Diane.

'Hey, do you want to go out and see the salting in person?'

'You bet I do!'

'There's an empty seat you can have, but you'll have to get ready fast.'

'I'm ready now.'

'Good for you. Meet me at Dulles at nine.'

Ooooop! A voyage to the high north Atlantic, to see the salt fleet with Diane!

Their trip to Manhattan came to mind; and since then of course he and Diane had spent a million hours together, both at work and in the gym. So when they sat down that night in adjoining seats on Icelandic Air's plane, and Diane put her head on his shoulder and fell asleep even before it took off, it felt very natural, like part of the rest of their interaction.

They came down on Reykjavik just before dawn. The surface of the sea lay around the black bulk of Iceland like a vast sheet of silver. By then Diane was awake; back in D.C. this was her usual waking hour, unearthly though that seemed to Frank, who had just gotten tired enough to lean his head on hers. These little intimacies were shaken off when the seatbacks returned to their upright position. Diane leaned across Frank to look out the window, Frank leaned back to let her see. Then they were landing, and out of the plane into the airport. Neither of them had checked luggage, and they weren't there long before it was time to join a group of passengers trammed out to a big helicopter. On board, earplugs in, they rose slowly and then chuntered north over empty blue ocean.

Then the northern horizon grew hazy, and soon after that those passengers with a view were able to distinguish the tankers themselves, long and narrow, like Mississippi river barges in their proportions, but immensely bigger. The fleet was moving in a rough convoy formation, and as they flew north and slowly descended, there came a moment when the tankers dotted the ocean's surface for as far as they could see in all directions, spread out like iron filings in a magnetic field, all pointing north. Lower still: black syringes, lined in rows on a blue table, ready to give their 'long injections of pure oil.'

They dropped yet again, toward a big landing pad on a tanker called the *Hugo Chavez*, an Ultra Large Crude Carrier with a gigantic bridge at its stern. From this height the ships around them looked longer than ever, all plowing broad white wakes into a swell from the north that seemed miniature in proportion to the ships, but began to look substantial the lower they got. Hovering just over the *Hugo Chavez's* landing pad, it became clear from the windcaps and spray that the

480

salt armada was in fact crashing through high seas and a stiff wind, almost a gale. Looking in the direction of the sun the scene turned black-and-white, like one of those characteristically windblown chiaroscuro moments in *Victory At Sea*.

When they got out of the helo the wind blasted through their clothes, and chased them upstairs to the bridge's control quarters. There a crowd of visitors larger than the crew of the ship had a fine view over a broad expanse of ocean, crowded with immense ships all carrying salt.

Looking away from the sun the sea was a cobalt color, a deep and pure Adriatic blue, without any hint of the blackness that mysteriously seeped into both the polar seas.

The *Hugo Chavez*, seen from its bridge, looked like an aircraft carrier with the landing deck removed. The quarterdeck or sterncastle under the bridge was tall, but only a tiny part of the craft; the forecastle looked like it was a mile away. The intervening distance was interrupted by a skeletal rig that resembled a loading crane, but also reminded Frank of the giant irrigation sprayers one saw in California's central valley. The salt in the hold was being vacuumed into this device, then cast out in powerful white jets, a couple hundred meters to both sides. The hardrock salt had been milled to sizes ranging from table salt to rock salt to bowling balls, but because a lot came from the salt pans, it was mostly crystalline and pretty fine. In the holds it looked like dirty white gravel and sand. In the air it looked almost like dirty water or slush, arching out and splashing in a satisfyingly broad swath. Between the salt fall and the ship's wakes, and the whitecaps, the deep blue of the ocean surface was infinitely mottled by white. Looking aft, in the direction of the sun, it turned to silver on pewter and lead.

Diane watched the scene with her nose almost on the glass, deeply hooded in a blue heavy jacket. She smiled at Frank. 'You can smell the salt.'

'The ocean always smells like this.'

'It seems like more today.'

'Maybe so.' She had grown up in San Francisco, he remembered. 'It must smell like home.' She nodded happily.

They followed their hosts up a metal staircase to a higher deck of the bridge, a room with windows on all sides that had a view like that from an airport control tower. It was this room that made the *Hugo Chavez* the designated visitor or party ship, and now the big glass-walled room was crowded with dignitaries and officials of all kinds. Here they could best view the long ships on all sides of them, all the way out to the horizon, where more ships were visible only at fore and stern, or by the white jets of salt. Each ship cast two long curving jets out to the sides from its bow, like the spouts of right whales; and every element was repeated so symmetrically that it seemed as if they had fallen into an MC Escher world.

The tankers flanking theirs seemed nearer than they really were because of their great size. They were completely steady in the long swells. The air around the ships was filled with a white haze that drifted down the wake for a kilometer or so before sinking away. Diane pointed out that the diesel exhaust stayed in the air while the salt mist did not. 'They look so dirty. I wonder if we couldn't go back to sails again someday, and just let everything go slower by sea.'

'Labor costs,' Frank suggested. 'Uncertainty. Maybe even danger.'

'Would they be more dangerous? I bet you could make them so big and solid they wouldn't be any more dangerous than these.'

'These were reckoned pretty dangerous.'

'I don't hear of many accidents, given that there are thousands of them out all the time.'

They moved from one set of big windows to the next, taking in the views.

'It's like the San Joaquin Valley,' Frank said. 'There are

these huge irrigation rigs that roll around spraying stuff.'

Diane nodded. 'I wonder if this will work.'

'Me too. If it doesn't . . .'

'I know. It would be hard to talk people into trying anything else.'

'True.'

Around and around the bridge they walked. Everyone else was doing the same, in a circulation like that at any other party. Blue sky, blue sea, the horizon ticked by tiny wavelets, as in a pattern on wallpaper; and then the fleet, each ship haloed by a wind-tossed cloud of white mist. Frank and Diane caught each other by the shoulder to point things out, just as they would have in Optimodal. A bird; a fin in the distance.

Then another group arrived in the room, and soon they were escorted to Diane: the Secretary-General of the UN, Germany's environmental minister, who was the head of their Green Party and a friend of Diane's from earlier times; lastly the prime minister of Great Britain, who had done a kind of Winston Churchill during their hard winter, and who now shook Diane's hand and said, 'So this *is* the face that launched a thousand ships,' looking very pleased with himself. Frank couldn't be sure Diane caught the reference; she was already smiling, and distracted by the introduction of others in the new group. They all chatted as they circled the room, and after a while Diane and Frank stood in a big circle listening to the others, their upper arms just barely touching as they stood side by side.

After another hour of this, during which nothing varied outside except a shift west in the angle of the sun, it was declared time to go; one didn't want the helicopters to get too far from Reykjavik, and there were other visitors waiting in Iceland for their turns to visit; and the truth was, they had seen what there was to see. The ship's crew therefore halted the *Hugo Chavez*'s prodigious launching of salt, and they braved the chilly blast downstairs and got back in their helo.

Up it soared, higher and higher. Again the astonishing sight of a thousand tankers on the huge burnished plate spreading below them, instantly grasped as unprecedented: the first major act of planetary engineering ever attempted, and by God it looked like it.

But then the helo pilot ascended higher and higher, higher and higher, until they could see a much bigger stretch of ocean, water extending as far as the eye could see, for hundreds of miles in all directions – and all of it blank, except for their now tiny column of ships, looking like a line of toys. And then ants. In a world so vast, could anything humans do make a difference?

Diane thought so. 'We should celebrate,' she said, smiling her little smile. 'Do you want to go out to dinner when we get back?'

'Sure. That would be great.'

**Election Day saw winter** return to Washington in force. It was icy everywhere, in places black ice, so that even though everything seemed to have congealed to a state of slow motion, cars still suddenly took to flight like hockey pucks, gliding majestically over the roads and looking stately until they hit something. Sirens dopplered hither and yon, defining the space of the city that was otherwise invisible in its trees. Again there were scheduled brown-outs, and the wood smoke of a million fireplace fires rose with the diesel smoke of a million generators, their gray and brown strands weaving in the northwest wind.

The polls were open, however, and the voters lined up all bundled in their winter best – a best that was much better than it had been the year before. The story of the day became the story of the impact of the cold on the vote, and which party's faithful would brave it most successfully, and which would benefit most from this clear harbinger of another long winter. The first exit polls showed a tight race, and as no one believed in exit polls anymore anyway, anything was possible. It felt like Christmas.

And in fact it was the Buddhist holiday celebrating Dorje Totrengtsel, as it turned out. To celebrate it, and perform a dedication ceremony for their new home in the country, the Khembalis had scheduled a big party for that very day.

Possibly some of those they invited did not make it, because of the meteorological or political complications; but a couple hundred of them did. They gathered in a big crowd under a large unwalled pavilion tent, set up next to the old farmhouse, still empty and in need of renovation.

It took well over an hour for the Quiblers to drive out to the farm, Charlie at the wheel of their Volvo station wagon inching along, Anna in the back with the boys. Joe declaimed a long monolog remarking on the snowy view, and his displeasure that they were not stopping to investigate it: 'Look! Stop! Look! Stop the car!'

When they got to the farm they found Frank was just arriving himself. They parked next to his van and walked around the farmhouse.

Drepung and Rudra were out back on the snowy lawn, steam pouring from their mouths and noses. They were kicking patterns of frosty green out of the thick flock of new snow on the grass. At the center of this improvised mandala stood a blocky shapeless snowman with a demon mask hung on its head, grinning maniacally into the wind. Before it lay a lower block of snow, like the altar stone at Stonehenge. On the flattish top of this mass some of Joe's building blocks were stacked, in two little towers. Two red then green, two red then yellow.

The two men waved cheerily when they saw the Quiblers. They pointed at their handiwork, and watched with pleasure as Joe in his thick snowsuit and boots trundled over ahead of the rest to investigate. They lifted him between them the better to see the two towers his blocks now made. He kicked reflexively at the stacks, and Rudra and Drepung laughed and swung him back and forth, each holding with both hands one of the toddler's mittened fists. When he kicked over one of them, they put him down with many congratulations. 'Ooooh! Karmapa!'

Frank went inside to check on lunch, and came back out carrying two paper cups of a hot mulled cider that he reported had no yak butter in it. He gave one to Anna, who wrapped her hands around it gratefully. Charlie sniffed the steam pouring off it and went in to get one of his own. He spent a while in there talking to Sridar, his old lobbying partner, who had taken on the Khembalis as a client the year before, and was now representing them to Congress and other powers in the capital, with some success and a great deal of amusement. They exchanged the usual sentiments on the election taking place, shaking their heads in the attempt to pretend they did not hope very much.

When Charlie went back outside, he felt again how frigid the day was. Anna huddled against him, nearly shivering despite her bulky coat. The Khembalis and Joe did not seem to mind. Now they were walking around the snow figure in a little march, chanting nonsense together, a string of syllables followed by a big 'HA,' repeated again and again. Joe stomped into the snow as deeply as Drepung, his eyes ablaze under his hood, his cheeks bright red.

'He's getting too hot in his suit,' Charlie said.

'Well, he can't take it off.'

'I guess not.'

'They're having fun,' Frank observed.

'Yes.'

'Joe must be heavy the way he sinks into that snow.'

'Yeah,' Charlie said. 'He's like made out of lead.'

Frank saw Nick standing off to one side and called, 'Hey Nick, do you want to go down to the river and see if there are any beavers or anything?'

'Sure!' They took off down the lawn, talking animals.

Now Rudra stood still, facing Joe. Joe stopped to peer up at him, looking surprised that their march had halted. 'Ho,' he said.

Rudra leaned down and gently rubbed a handful of snow in Joe's face. Joe spluttered and then shook his head like a dog.

'Hey what is he doing?' Anna demanded.

'He's helping him,' Charlie said, holding her arm.

'What do you mean helping? That doesn't help him!'

'It doesn't hurt him. It's part of their little ceremony.'

'Well it's not okay!'

'Leave them alone,' Charlie said. 'Joe doesn't mind it, see?'

'But what are they doing?'

'It's just a little ceremony they have.'

'But why?'

'Well you know. Maybe he's just trying to lower his temperature.'

'Oh come on!'

'Come on yourself. Just let them do it. Joe is loving it, and they think they're helping.'

Anna glowered. 'They're only going to give him a cold.'

'You know perfectly well being cold has nothing to do with catching a cold. What an old wives' tale.'

'Old wives' tales usually contained real observations, smart guy. And it turns out when you get cold your immune system is suppressed, so if there happens to be a virus around you've got more of a chance of catching it, so there *is* a connection.'

'But he's not getting too cold. Leave them alone. They're having fun.'

Except then Joe howled a quick protest. Rudra and Drepung looked startled; then Drepung turned Joe by the shoulder, so that he faced the snowman. Seeing the mask again Joe quietened. He tilted his head, scowled hideously at the snowman, gave the mask back vibe for vibe: no mere piece of wood was going to outscowl him.

Straightening up beside him, Rudra pointed at the demon mask, then up at the low clouds purling overhead. Suddenly he twisted and as it were corkscrewed upward, thrusting himself up and back until he looked straight up at the sky. He shouted, '*Dei tugs-la ydon ysol! Ton pa, gye ba! Ton pa, gye ba*!'

Startled, Joe looked up at Rudra so quickly that he plumped onto his butt. Rudra leaned over him and shouted 'Gye ba!' with a sudden ferocity. Joe scrambled away, then jumped up to trundle down the slope of the lawn as fast as he could.

'Hey!' Anna cried.

Charlie held her arm again. 'Let them be!'

'What do you mean? Joe!' And with a quick spasm she was away and running through the snow. 'Joe! Joe!'

Joe, still running for the river, did not appear to hear her. Then he tripped and fell in a perfect face plant, sprawling down the snow slope and leaving behind a long snow angel. Anna reached him and slipped herself trying to stop. Down she went too; then Drepung joined them and helped them both up, saying 'Sorry, sorry, sorry.'

Rudra stayed up by the snowman, swaying and jerking. He staggered to the snowman, pulled off its demon mask, threw it at his feet and stomped on it. 'HA! TON PA! HA! GYE BΛ! HAAAAAA!'

Hearing this Joe wailed, beating at the snow and then at Anna's outstretched arms. Drepung ventured to touch him once lightly on the shoulder. Joe buried his head in Anna's embrace. Rudra, now sitting on the ground next to the flattened mask, watched them; he waved at Joe when Joe looked over Anna's shoulder. Joe blinked big tears down his cheeks, shuddering as he calmed. For a long time Joe and Rudra stared blankly at each other.

Charlie walked over to help the old man to his feet. Both Rudra and Drepung seemed satisfied now, relaxed and ready to get on with other things; and seeing it, Charlie felt a certain calmness fill him too. He and Rudra went down and flanked Joe and Anna, took Joe's mittened and snow-caked little hands, squeezed them. Joe looked around at the farmhouse and the tent filling with guests, the expanse of snow falling down to the river. Charlie clapped Drepung on the shoulder, held it briefly.

'What?' Anna demanded.

'Nothing. Nothing. Let's go in and see what they have to eat, shall we?'

**Late that afternoon, when** the Khembalis' party was breaking up, and they had heard all about the trip out to see the salt fleet, the Quiblers asked Frank if he wanted to come over for dinner and watch the election returns.

'Thanks,' he said, 'but I'm going to go to dinner with Diane.'

'Oh I see.'

'Maybe I can drop by afterward, see the late returns.'

'Sure, whatever.'

Frank went to his van, drove carefully back to the Khembali house in Arlington. Out in the cold garden shed he changed clothes, trying to think what would look nice. He was going out to dinner with his boss, who would not be his boss for much longer, so that different kinds of hypothetical possibilities might then open. It was interesting, no matter how uneasy he felt whenever he thought of Caroline.

Then one of the kitchen girls called out to the shed from the house door: phone call. He went inside, picked up the house's phone apprehensively. 'Hello?'

'Frank is that you?'

'Yes. Caroline?'

'Yes.'

'Is everything okay?'

'No, everything is not okay. I need to see you, now.'

'Well, but I've got something, I'm really sorry –'

'Frank, *please*! I think he found out about me taking those disks. So I've only got a little time. I've got to initiate Plan B or else. I need your help.'

'You're leaving him?'

'Yes! That's what I'm telling you. I've left already. That's done. But I need help getting away and – you're the only one I trust.' Her voice twisted at the end, and suddenly Frank understood that she was afraid. He had never heard it like that in her before, and had not recognized it.

Frank clutched the phone hard. 'Where are you?'

'I'm in Chevy Chase. I'll meet you at your tree.'

'Okay. It'll take me half an hour or so. Maybe longer with the ice on the roads.'

'Okay good. Good. Thanks. I love you, Frank.' She hung up.

Frank groaned. He stared at the embassy's phone in his hand. 'Shit,' he said. That someone as bold and competent as her should be afraid . . . 'I love you too,' he whispered.

His stomach had shrunk to the size of a baseball. What would this husband of hers do? He picked up the house phone and called Diane's cell phone number.

Maybe she was bugged too. She was doing the same kind of thing Frank was, wasn't she?

'Hello, Diane? It's Frank. Listen I'm really sorry about this, but something has come up here and I just have to help out, it's a kind of emergency. So I need to, I mean can we take a rain check, and do our dinner tomorrow or whenever you can?'

Very short pause. 'Sure, of course. No problem.'

'Thanks, I'm really sorry about this. See there's this,' but he hadn't thought anything up, a stupid mistake, and he was going to say 'something at the embassy' when she heard the pause and cut him off:

'No it's fine, don't worry. We'll do it another time.'

'Thanks, Diane. I appreciate it. How about tomorrow then?'

'Um, no – tomorrow won't work, my daughter is coming

in. Here – oh, wait. I don't see my calendar. Tell you what, let's just say soon.'

'Okay, soon. Thanks. Sorry.'

'No problem.'

End of call. He put the receiver down, stood there.

'Ah fuck.'


He drove over to Van Ness, parked in one of his old spots on Brandywine, walked east into the forest. Slowly he approached his tree, coming to it on the remains of Ross Drive. He saw no one. But then there she was, stepping out from behind a thick oak between site 21 and his tree. He went to her and they hugged hard, clinging tightly to each other.

She pulled back and looked at him. Even in the dark he could see that her nose was red, her eyes red-rimmed.

She sniffed, shook her head. 'Sorry. It's been a very bad day.' She handed him another paper sleeve of cds. 'Here. This is more of their shit. It's a new superblack, working between Homeland Security and DOD. Another strategic support branch.'

Frank took the disks, put them in his jacket pocket. 'What happened?'

'We had a fight. I mean that used to happen a lot, but this time it was – I don't know. Bad. Scary. I'm sick of feeling this way. Really, being around him – it's bad for me. I know better. I can't stand it any more.'

'He didn't find something out?'

'He didn't say anything directly, but I think he did, yes. I don't know. If he found out about me taking the election program . . .' She shuddered, thinking about it. Then: 'It might explain some things. I mean he chipped me again, since I last saw you. New kinds that he thought I didn't know about. They hop on you. When I found them I left them in until today, but I took them out, and then I used his code to

492

get what I could about this superblack onto disk. I don't know how much it'll tell anyone. Then I left.'

'Are you sure you found all the chips?'

'Yes. The bastard. He is so . . . He spies and spies and spies.'

'So, I mean, can you be sure you found everything he's doing?'

'Yes, I ran all the diagnostics, and I saw what he had on me. Now I'm out of there. He'll never see me again.'

The bitter twist to her mouth was one Frank had not seen before, but it was familiar in his own muscles from certain moments of his own break-up with Marta. The wars of the heart, so bitter and pointless.

'Where will you go?' he said.

'I have a Plan B. It's got an ID all set up, a place, even a job. It's not too far away, but far enough I won't run into him.'

'I'll be able to see you?'

'Of course. Once I get settled. That's why I set it up this way. If I were on my own I'd go, oh I don't know. Tibet or something. The other end of the Earth.'

Frank shook his head. 'I want you closer than that.'

'I know.'

They hugged harder. In the darkness of the park it was almost quiet: the sound of the creek, the hum of the city. Two against the world. Frank felt her body, her heat, the pulse in her neck. The scent of her hair filled him. Don't disappear, he thought. Stay where I can find you. Stay where I can be with you.

Frank felt her shudder. It was cold again, not as cold as in the depths of last winter, but well below freezing. The creek rang with the tinkling bell-like sound it took on when all its eddies were frozen over. Caroline's body was quivering under his hands, shivering with cold, or tension, or both. He held her, tried to calm her with his hands. But he too was shivering.

Downstream on the path he saw a brief movement. Black into black. Involuntarily he pulled her to him and around to the other side of the oak next to them.

'What?'

'Look,' he said very quietly, 'are you sure you aren't still chipped somehow?'

'I don't think so, why?'

'Because I think there's someone watching us.'

'Oh my God.'

'Don't try to look. Here, I've got the scanner you gave me.' He thought it over, images of one scenario then another. 'Would he have other people helping him?'

'Not for this,' she said. 'I don't think so anyway. Not unless he figured out that I copied the vote program.'

'Shit. Let's check you right here, okay?'

'Sure.'

He pulled the wand from his pocket, so much like an airport security device. Bar codes in the body. He ran it over her. When he had it against the top of her back it beeped.

'*Shit*,' she said under her breath. She whipped off her jacket, laid it on the ground, ran the wand over it. It beeped again. 'God *damn* it.'

'At least it isn't in your skin.'

'Yeah well.'

'You checked before you left your place?'

'Yes I did, and there wasn't anything. I wonder if there's something about me leaving the house. A tick, they call these. Set to jump when motion sensors go off. Something stuck to the door lintel or someplace. God *damn* him.'

Frank was trying to see over her shoulder, down the path where he had seen movement. Nothing. Feeling grim, he pulled out his FOG phone and called up Zeno's.

It rang twice. 'How does this thing work? Hey, Joe's Bar and Grill! Who the fuck are you?'

'Zeno it's Frank.'

494

'Who?'

'*Frank*. Professor Nosebleed.'

'Oh hey, Nosey! What's happening, man? Did you spot the jaguar?'

It sounded like he'd downed a couple of beers. 'Worse than that,' Frank said, thinking hard. 'Look Zeno, I've got a problem and I'm wondering if you could give me a hand.'

'What you got in mind?'

'The thing is, it might be kind of dangerous. I don't want to get you into it without telling you that.'

'What kind of danger?'

'I've got a jacket here that people are using to tail me with. People I really need to get away from. What I want to do is have them follow the jacket away from me, while I clear out of here.'

'Where are ya?'

'I'm in the park. Are you at your usual spot?'

'Where else.'

'What I was hoping is that I could run by you guys, like I'm playing frisbee golf, and hand off the jacket to you and keep on running. Then if one of you would hustle the jacket out to Connecticut, and leave it in the laundromat next to Dehli Dhaba, I could turn the tables on these people, pick them up when they follow the jacket, and then tail them back to where they came from.'

'Shit, Noseman, it sounds like you must be some kind of a spook after all! So you been out here hiding among us, is that it?'

'Sort of, sure.'

'Harrrrrr. I knew it musta been something.'

'So are you up for it? While you've got the jacket you'll have to move fast, but I don't think they'll do anything to you, especially out on Connecticut. It's more a surveillance kind of thing.'

'Ah fuck that.' Zeno brayed his harsh bray. 'It won't be

495

no worse than the cops. Parole officers stick that shit right into your *skin*.'

'Yeah that's right. Okay, well thanks then. We'll come through in about ten minutes.'

'We? Who's this *we*?'

'Another spook. You know how it is.'

'A lady spook? You got a lady in distress there maybe?'

Sometimes it was alarming how quick Zeno guessed things. 'Are the rest of the bros there with you?'

'Of course.'

'Good. Maybe they can add to the confusion. When we pass through and hand off the jacket, have them –'

'We'll beat the shit out of them!'

'No no no.' Frank felt a chill. 'They could be armed. You don't want to fuck with that. Maybe just go off in two or three groups. Give you some cover, create some confusion.'

'Yeah sure. We'll deal with it.'

'Okay, thanks. See you soon. We'll come in from the creek side and just pass right on through.'

Frank pushed the *end* button. He looked at the chip wand. 'Could this wand be chipped itself?'

'I don't know. I guess so.'

'We'll leave it here. You said in the elevator you were training for a triathlon, right?'

'Yes?'

'Is your husband a runner?'

'What? No.'

'Okay.' He took her by the arm and led her off the path, up into the trees. 'Let's run. We'll go past my park friends and give them your jacket, then take off on the ridge trail north. He won't be able to keep up with us, and after a while he won't know where you are.'

'Okay.'

Off they ran, Caroline fast on Frank's heels. He ran up Ross to site 22, then turned up the trail that ran to the Nature

Center, hurrying the pace so that they would gain some time. Behind him he heard the faint crackle of the pursuit.

They crossed the frisbee golf course, and then Frank really pushed it. At a certain point her husband wouldn't be able to keep up. Once you were winded the will counted for nothing, you had to slow down. As animals he and Caroline were stronger, and out here they were animals. Down the narrow fairway of hole five, leading her between the trees to the left so they wouldn't be seen. Running almost as hard as he could in the dark, Caroline right behind.

Then he was in site 21 and the bros were all standing around, wide-eyed and agog at the sight of them. Even in the midst of his adrenaline rush Frank saw that he would never hear the end of this.

He gestured to Caroline, helped her out of her jacket.

'Hi guys.' He met Zeno's eye. Now more than ever Zeno looked impressive, like Lee Marvin in his moment of truth.

'Thanks,' Frank said, tossing the jacket at him in their usual aggro style.

'Where do you want me to go again?'

'Dehli Dhaba. Drop the jacket in the laundromat next door and get the fuck out of there.'

'Sure thing.'

'The rest of you wait a second and then wander off. Stick together though.'

'Yeah man.'

'We'll beat the fuck out of him.'

'Just keep moving. Thanks boys.'

And with that Frank took Caroline by the hand and they were off again into the dark.

Running down the hole seven fairway he pulled off his down jacket, then passed it back to her. 'Here, put this on.'

'No I'm okay.'

'No you're not, you were shivering already.'

497

'What about you?'

'We run the course out here in T-shirts all the time. I'm used to it. Besides you've got to keep on going after this, right? Whereas I can go home.'

'Are you sure this isn't chipped too?'

'Yes. I've owned it for twenty years, and no one else has been anywhere near it.'

'Okay, thanks.'

She pulled it on as they jogged, and then they started running at full speed again.

'You okay?' Frank said over his shoulder.

'Yeah fine. You?'

'I'm good,' Frank said. And he was; his spirits were rising as he got on the ridge path and led her north on it. Frozen mud underfoot, frigid air rushing past him; there was no way anyone without chips to aid them could track them for long when they were moving like this.

He passed hole eight and turned up cross trail 7, and soon they were out onto Brandywine, and rising to Connecticut.

Just short of the avenue, where there was still some darkness to huddle in, he stopped her, held her. As they hugged he felt for the Acheulian hand axe, there in his jacket pocket against her side.

'What is that?' she asked.

'My lucky charm.'

'Pretty heavy for a lucky charm.'

'Yeah, it's a rock. I like rocks.'

They stood there, arms around each other, poorly lit by a distant streetlight. Her face twisted with distress; why couldn't it be simple? her look seemed to say. Why couldn't they just be here?

But it wasn't simple.

'The Van Ness Metro is just down there,' Frank said, pointing south on Connecticut.

'Thanks.'

'And where will you go?'

'I've got a place set up.' Then: 'Listen, I heard what you said to those guys, but don't you stick around and mess with him,' she said, waving to the east. 'He's dangerous. He really is. And we don't want him to know you had anything to do with this.'

'I know,' Frank said. They hugged again. Briefly they kissed. He liked the feel of her in his jacket.

'Here,' she said, 'you should take your jacket back. I'm going to get in the Metro, and then I'll be into my little underground railroad set-up, and I won't need it. I'll be fine.'

'You're sure?'

'Yes.'

'Okay.' He took the jacket from her, put it on, put the hand axe back in its pocket. 'Where will you go?'

'I'll contact you as soon as I can,' she said. 'We'll set up a system.'

'But –'

'I'll let you know! Just let me go – I have to go!'

'Okay!' Frank said, frustrated.

Then she was off. Watching her turn the corner and disappear he felt a sudden stab of fear. God *damn* this guy, he thought.

He walked north to Dehli Dhaba and passed it, glanced into the laundromat next door. It was almost empty, only a couple of young women folding clothes together at the tables, no doubt UDC undergrads. Caroline's black ski jacket was already there, hanging from the open door of a dryer. No sight of Zeno or any of the rest of the bros. Frank walked down to the corner and stood at the bus stop, then sat on the bench in its little shelter, consciously working to slow his breathing and pulse.

Ten minutes passed. Then three men in black leather jackets approached the laundromat, hands in their pockets. One, a tall, heavyset blond man, appeared to be checking a very heavy watch. He looked at the other men, gestured inside the laundromat. One turned and settled at the door, looking up and down Connecticut. The others went in. Frank sat there looking across the street away from them. The man guarding the door registered him along with the three others waiting at the bus stop, then he turned his attention to the various people walking up and down the sidewalks.

The two men reappeared in the doorway, the blond man holding Caroline's jacket. That was him, then. Frank's teeth clenched. The three men conferred. They all surveyed the street, and the blond man appeared to check his watch again. He looked up, toward Frank; said something to the others. They began to walk down the sidewalk towards him.

Shocked at this turn of events, Frank got up and hustled around the corner of Davenport. As soon as the buildings at the corner blocked their view of him he bolted, running hard east toward the park. Looking back once, he saw that they were there on Davenport, also running; chasing him down. The blond man ran with his right hand in his jacket pocket.

Frank turned on Linnaean, running harder. East again on Brandywine, a real burst of speed, unsustainable, but he wanted to get into the trees again as soon as he could. As he pounded along, gasping, he thought about the man spotting him by way of his wrist device, and decided that his down jacket must be compromised now too. Caroline had worn it, she had been chipped with a tick, these ticks were probably not used alone but in little swarms; she could have had some in her hair, who knew, but if one or more had fallen or migrated from say her hair onto his jacket, he would be chipped himself. That had to be it.

Or maybe he had just been chipped all along.

He flew down the slope to site 21, found it still empty, the neglected fire still flickering. Off with his jacket, off with his shirt. The frigid air hit him and he growled. He took the hand axe out of the jacket and put it into his pants pocket.

He ran up into the mass of trees west of the site, stopped and rubbed his hands over his neck, gently and then roughly; felt nothing. He ran his hands through his hair again, leaning forward and down, pulling at his locks and shaking his head like a wet dog. Tearing at his scalp. Best he could do. Now he had to move again, just in case; he circled around the site and ducked behind one of the big flood windrows, crouched and got a view of the picnic table, between two branches.

He heard them before he saw them, all three men crashing down Ross into the site. They stopped when they saw his jacket and shirt, turned quickly and looked around them, surveying their surroundings like a team that had done it before. Frank felt the tousled hair rise on the back of his neck. His teeth were clenched.

The blond man's hair caught a gleam of firelight. He picked up the jacket, hefted it. Then the shirt. Now came the test. Was there still a tick on Frank? The three men turned in circles, looking outward, and as they did the blond man checked his wrist. Frank stayed frozen in place, waiting for a sign. The blond man's chest rose and fell, rose and fell. He was winded. Frank tried to imagine his thoughts, then fell squeamishly away. He didn't want to know what went on in a mind like that. Plots, counterplots, chipping people – spying on his own wife – out here in Rock Creek Park in the middle of the night, chasing people down. It was an ugly thing to contemplate.

Frank felt the frozen air as if he were clothed in an invisible shirt made of his own heat. Outside that it was obviously cold, but inside his shell he seemed okay, at least for now. When he moved he pushed through the shell, out into the chill.

Up on Ross came the sound of people walking, then Zeno's nicotine voice. Frank shifted down, pulled his phone from his pocket and punched the 'repeat call' function.

'Hey Blood, wassup?'

'Zeno they're back at your picnic table,' Frank whispered. 'They've got guns.'

'Oh ho.'

'Don't go down there.'

'Don't you worry. Do you need help?'

'No.'

'We'll deploy anyway. Ha – too bad you can't call the jaguar out on these guys, eh?'

'Yeah,' Frank said, and thought to add that he was going to be the jaguar tonight; but Zeno wasn't listening. Frank could hear over the phone that he was telling the bros the situation. In the open air their noise had abruptly died away.

Then: 'Hey fuck that!' Andy exclaimed, carrying both over the phone and through the air.

On the phone Frank heard Zeno say, 'Fucking a, Blood, here comes the cavalry –'

Then the forest filled with howls, the crash of people through the forest – and from down near the creek, BANG BANG BANG!

The men at the picnic tables had dropped out of sight. But their conference was brief; after about five seconds they burst to their feet and ran away, south on Ross. Shrieks and howls in the darkness behind them.

Frank took off after them. High howling marked where the bros were in their pursuit on Ross, and thunks and crashes made it clear rocks were being thrown.

Frank darted from tree to windrow to tree, keeping above and abreast of the running men. When they came down the slope to Glover, two of them turned left, while the blond man turned right. Frank followed him, worrying briefly that the two others would come back and jump on the tail of any pursuit. Hopefully Zeno and the bros had already laid off. Nothing to be done about that now. He needed to concentrate on following the blond man.

\*　　\*　　\*

Stalking prey at night, in the forest. How big the world got when you could taste blood. The frigid air cut through the radiance of his body heat, it drove into him, but it was only part of the chase, part of what made him utterly on point. All the hours he had spent out here filled him now, he knew where he was and what he needed to do. It all came down to pursuit.

The trees lining Glover were thick, the ground covered with branches, leaves, patches of new snow. He had trailed feral animals along here before. A human would be both more aware and more oblivious. The blond man was striding rapidly up the road, stopping from time to time to look back. He appeared to be holding a pistol in his right hand. Frank froze when he looked around, then darted from tree to tree, moving only when the man's back was to him. Stay parallel to him but always behind his peripheral vision; be ready to freeze, stop when his head turned; it was like a game, feet lightly thrusting forward, feeling their way to silent landings, over and over, on and on, freezing to check the quarry from behind a trunk, one eye out, as in all the hide-and-seek games any child has ever played, but now performed with total concentration. On the hunt, yes, huge areas opening inside him – he could see in the dark, he could gazelle through the forest over downed branches without a sound, freeze faster than a head could whip around, all with a fierce cold focus. When the man whipped his head around Frank found himself as still as a statue before the blond head had moved even an inch, before Frank himself knew it had moved; and he could barely see it in the dark, just a gleam reflecting distant streetlights through the trees.

At Grant Road the man turned west. He walked out on the street, to Davenport and west toward Connecticut. Now they were under streetlights again, and very few people were out at this hour – none visible at this moment. Frank had to drop back, move across people's front lawns. The man continued to whip his head around to look back from time to time. Frank lagged as far as he could while still keeping him in sight, but still, if he could see the man, the man could see him. His van was one block over, on Brandywine; he could drop down to it on 30th, unlock by remote as he approached, snatch out a sweater and windbreaker, put them on as he walked, then continue out to Connecticut and hope to relocate the man on his way to the Metro. He was out of sight for the moment, so Frank crossed the street and took off in a dash, tearing around the corner and ripping open his van door, getting the clothes on as he took off again west on Brandywine.

He slowed as he approached Connecticut. And there was the blond man, hurrying past him down the big avenue, glowering.

Frank fell in behind him. They were approaching the Van Ness/UDC metro station. At the stop of the escalator the man glanced one last time over his shoulder, a sneer twisting his face, the petulant sneer of a man who always got what he wanted –

Frank snatched the hand axe from his pocket and threw it as hard as he could. The stone spun through the air on a line and flashed past the man's head so close to his left ear that the man lurched reflexively to the right, disappearing abruptly from view as the stone whacked into the concrete wall backing the escalator hole.

Frank ran to it, slowed, looked down into the big oval tunnel, caught sight of the blond man running down the last risers into the station below. Around the opening, pick up his hand axe lying on the sidewalk. It looked the same, maybe a new chip on one edge. There was a deep gash in the concrete wall. He felt it with a finger, found his hand was trembling.

Back to the escalator, down behind a pair of students, pass them on the left. Windbreaker hood over his head? No. Nothing unusual. But it was cold. He pulled the hood over his head, put his hands in the windbreaker's pockets, axe cradled in the right hand. His hands were cold, ears too. Nose running.

Down into the station, buy ticket, through the turnstiles. Look over the metal rail, assuming that the blond man would be going toward Shady Grove: yes. There he was, blond hair gleaming in the dim light of the station.

Frank grabbed a free paper from a trash can, descended to trackside, sat on one of the concrete benches pretending to read. The blond man stood by the track. The lights in the floor flashed on and off. In the dim warmth they felt the first blast of wind from the coming train.

Frank got on the car ahead of the one the man entered. He was pretty sure the man would get off at Bethesda, as Caroline had that first time. So when they rolled into Bethesda he got off a little before the man did, walked to the up escalator ahead of him, took it up without looking back. Through the turnstiles, up the last long escalator, standing to the right as so many people did.

Near the top the blond man brushed by him on the left, already talking on his cell phone. 'We'll find her,' he said as he passed. 'I know she did it.'

Frank stayed on his big riser, teeth clenched. He followed the man across the bus level of the station to the last short escalator, up that. Then south on Wisconsin, yes, just the way Caroline had gone that first time, right on a side street, yes. The man was still talking on his phone, not looking around at all. Barking an order, laughing once. An ugly sound. Frank tried to relax his jaw, he was going to break a tooth. He was hot inside his windbreaker. Breaking a sweat. A few blocks west of Wisconsin the man clapped his phone shut and soon after that turned up the broad stairs of a small apartment building on Hagar, pulling keys from his pocket and shaking his head. He entered the building without looking back.

Frank waited for a few minutes, looking at the building and the street outside. He didn't want it to be over. Suddenly he saw what to do. He went up the steps to the apartment door, jabbed every little black doorbell on the panel to the left of the door, then hustled across the street and stood under a streetlight casting a cone of orange light on the sidewalk and part of the street. He stood under one edge of the light, pulling the hood of his windbreaker far forward. His face was sure to be in shadow, a black absence, like a hit man or Death itself. He thrust the pointed end of the hand axe forward in the windbreaker pocket until it pushed at the cloth.

The curtain in the window on the top floor twitched. His quarry was looking down at him. Frank tilted his head up just enough to show that he was returning the gaze. He held the pose for a few seconds, long enough to make his point: *The hunter hunted.* Hunted by a murderous watcher always there to haunt one's dreams. Then he stepped back and out of the cone of light, into dark shadows and away.

After that Frank walked back out to Wisconsin.

He started to shiver in his thin sweater and windbreaker. Up Wisconsin, back to the Metro.

He felt stunned. Some of what he had done in the heat of the moment now shocked him, and he reeled a bit as he remembered, growing more and more appalled – throwing the hand axe at him? What had he been thinking? He could have killed the guy! Good, good riddance, that would have taught him – except not! It would have been terrible. The police would have hunted for Caroline. They would have been hunting for him too, without knowing they were; but Caroline when she heard about it would have known, and who knew what her reaction might be, he couldn't actually be sure but it was bound to be bad. No matter what, it would have been terrible. Crazy. Leap before you look, sure, but what if your leaps were crazy? He didn't even want to be out there! He had broken a date with Diane to do this shit!

On Wisconsin again. He didn't know what to do. He

wondered if he would ever see Caroline again. Maybe she had used him to help her get away, the same way he had used the bros to help him. Well sure. That was what had happened, in effect. And he had offered to do it. But still . . .

Down into the Metro, nervous waiting, down to Van Ness, out of the Metro. Back in his van Frank changed clothes again. Despite the cold his shirt was soaked with sweat. Pull on his capilene undershirt, thick sweater; in the van's side mirror he could see that once again he looked fairly normal. Incredible.

He sat in the driver's seat. He didn't know what to do. His hands were still shaking. He felt sick.

Eventually the cold drove him to start the engine. Then, driving north on Connecticut, he thought of going to the Quiblers'. He could sit there and drink a beer and watch the fucking election results. No one would care if he didn't say anything. Warm up. Play chess or Scrabble with Nick and watch the TV.

He got in the left-turn lane at Bradley. Waiting for the light he remembered the bros and pulled out his FOG phone, hit resend.

'Hey Nosey.'

'Zeno are you guys okay?'

'Yeah sure. Are you?'

'I'm okay. Hey listen, my clothes I left there at the tables are chipped with some kind of microwave transmitter.'

'We figured as much. So you got parole officers too, eh?'

'Yeah I guess.'

'Ha. We'll dee ex your stuff. But what was with that gal, eh? Don't you know not to mess with parole officers?'

'Yeah yeah. What about you, what was that shooting, who did that? I didn't think you guys were carrying.'

'Yeah right.' Zeno snorted. 'We kill those deer with our teeth.'

'Well there is that.'

'Shit's dangerous out here. I can't hardly keep Andy from popping people in situations like that. Everyone's a gook when he gets excited.'

'Well, it did put those guys on the run.'

'Sure. Better than getting hit in the face with a two by four.'

'Yeah, sure. Thanks for the help.'

'That's okay. But don't do shit like that to us any more. We get enough excitement as it is.'

'Yeah okay.'

**Charlie answered the doorbell** and was happy to see Frank. 'Hey Frank, good to see you, come on in! The Khembalis came over on their way home too, and the early returns are looking good pretty good.'

'My fingers are crossed,' Frank said, but as he took off his windbreaker he looked unhopeful. Inside the entryway he stopped as he saw people sitting in the living room by the fire. He went over and greeted Drepung and Sucandra and Padma, done with their own party, and then Charlie introduced him to Sridar. Again it seemed to Charlie that Frank was unusually subdued. No doubt many of his big programs at NSF were riding on the election results.

Charlie went out to the kitchen to get drinks, and circulating as he did in the next hour, he only occasionally noticed Frank, talking or playing with Joe, or watching the TV. Results were coming in more quickly now. The voting in every state was tight, the results as predicted: the red states went to the President, the blue states to Phil Chase. The exceptions tended to balance out, and it became clear that this time it was going to come down to the western states and whoever was delayed in reporting a winner due to the closeness of the results. Chase had a decent chance of winning the whole west coast, and if some of the late-reporting states went his way, the election too. It was all hanging in the balance.

Charlie sat above Nick on the couch, watching the colored maps on the TV, talking sometimes on the phone with Roy.

Joe was sitting on the floor, putting together the wooden train tracks and babbling to himself. Charlie watched him very curiously, not sure what he was seeing yet. Anna had taken Joe's temperature when they got home, curious at the effect of the snow, Charlie assumed. It had been 98.2; she had shaken her head, said nothing.

Charlie felt a bit drained, perhaps even a bit exorcised, as it were – as if something strange had been inside him as well as in Joe, and Drepung and Rudra's ceremony designed to remove them both. That was a new thought for Charlie – he had not considered the matter in any such light before – but it was certainly true that a feeling of oppression that had been weighing on him for a long time had lifted somehow, leaving a lightness that felt also a bit empty perhaps. He didn't know what he felt.

He saw that Drepung too was keeping an eye on Joe.

Frank sat on the couch across from them, chewing a toothpick and looking tense. The evening wore on. Eventually the Khembalis said their good-byes and left. 'I'll be home in a bit,' Frank said to them.

When they were gone, Frank glanced at Charlie. 'Mind if I stay and see it out?'

'Not at all. As long as it doesn't go on for three months.'

'Ha. It is looking close.'

'I think California will put us over the top.'

'Maybe so.'

They watched on. Eastern states, central states, mountain states. Joe fell asleep on the floor; Nick read a book, lying sleepily on the couch. Charlie went to the bathroom, came back downstairs. 'Any more states?'

Anna and Frank shook their heads. Things appeared to be hung up out west. Frank sat hunched over, eating his toothpick fragment by fragment. Anna sighed, went out to the kitchen to clean up. She did not like to hope for things, Charlie knew, because she feared the disappointment if her

510

hopes were dashed. You should hope anyway, Charlie had told her more than once. We have to hope.

Hopes are just wishes we doubt will come true, she always replied. She preferred waiting, then dealing with whatever happened. Work on the moment.

But of course it was impossible not to hope, no matter what one resolved. Now she clattered dishes nervously in the kitchen, hoping despite herself. Therefore irritated.

'I wonder what's up,' Charlie said.

'Hnn.'

Frank was never a big talker, but tonight the cat seemed to have got his tongue. Charlie always tried to fill silences made by other people, it was a bad habit but he was helpless to stop it, as he never noticed it was happening until afterward. 'Okay, here's what's going to happen,' he said now. 'All the west is going to go for the President except California and Oregon, but that'll be enough for Phil to win.'

'Maybe.'

They watched the numbers on the screens get bigger, barely attending to what they were saying. The minutes dragged by. Anna came back in and sat by Charlie, began falling asleep. Even before the boys had arrived nothing had been able to keep her awake past her bedtime, and now she had ten years of sleep deprivation to catch up on.

Then Charlie clicked away from a commercial to find that NBC was declaring California had gone for Phil Chase, which gave him 275 electoral votes and made him the winner. They got to their feet, cheering. Anna woke up confused, 'What? What? Can it be? Can it be real?' She made them click around and confirm it on the other channels, and they all confirmed it; 'Oh my God,' she cried, and started to weep with joy. Charlie and Frank toasted with beer, got Nick a soda to toast with them. Joe woke up and climbed into Anna's lap as she channel-surfed, being suddenly eager to soak in all the information that she could. 'How did this *happen*?' There were

511

claims of irregularities in Oregon voting machines, apparently, where the margin of victory was especially tight. But Oregon, like California, had voting machine safeguards in place, and the officials there were confident the result would be validated.

Charlie gave Roy a call, and in the middle of the first ring Roy came on singing 'Ding dong, the witch is dead, the witch is dead, the witch is dead, ding dong, the wicked witch is dead!'

'Jesus, Roy, I could be a Republican staffer calling to congratulate you –'

'And I wouldn't give a damn! The wicked witch is *dead*! And our boss is *President*!'

'Yes, we're in for it now.'

'Yes we are! You're going to have to come back to work, Chucker! No more Mr Mom for you!'

'I don't know about that,' Charlie said, glancing over at Joe, who was burbling happily at Anna as she leaned forward to hear the TV better. A traitorous thought sprang into his mind: That isn't my Joe.

' – get yourself down to the convention center and celebrate! Bring the whole family!'

'I don't know,' Charlie said. 'Should we go down to the headquarters and celebrate?'

'No,' Anna and Frank said together.

'Maybe I'll go down there later,' Charlie told Roy.

'Later, later, what's with later? This is the moment!'

'True. But it's a party that will last a while.'

'All night my friend. I wouldn't mind seeing you in the flesh, we need to confer big time now! Everyone in the office is going to get a new job, you realize that.'

'Yes,' Charlie said. 'Advisor to the President.'

'Friend of the President! We're his friends, Charlie.'

'Us and twenty thousand other people.'

'Yes but no, we're in the God-damned *White House*.'

'I guess we are. Jesus. Well, Phil will be great. If anyone can stay human in that job, he can.'

'Oh sure, sure. He'll be human, he'll be all too human.'

'He'll be more than human.'

'That's right! So get your ass down here and party!'

'Maybe I will.'

Charlie let him get back to it. The house suddenly seemed quiet. Joe was still playing cheerfully on the couch next to Anna. She got up, grinning now, and started to clean up. Frank got up to help her.

'This should help all your projects big time,' Charlie said to him. 'Phil is really into them.'

'That's good. We'll need it.'

'He'll probably appoint Diane Chang to a second term at NSF.'

'Huhn,' Frank said, looking over at him. 'Really?'

'Yeah, I think so. I've heard that discussed. He likes what she's been doing, of course. How could you not?'

'I hadn't thought of that.' Frank picked up a plate, looking distracted.

They finished cleaning up. 'I guess I'll be off,' Frank said. 'Thanks for having me over.'

**The drive back to** Khembali House took a long time. Frank chose to drive down Wisconsin and cross the Potomac on the Key Bridge, the shortest route by far, but it was a mistake; the streets were packed with people, literally packed, so that cars had to inch along, nudging their way forward through a mass of celebrating humanity. The District of Columbia had voted nine to one for Democratic candidates for many years, and now a good proportion of the ninety percent were in the streets partying, and cars be damned. Frank had seen this once long before, when he had happened to visit an old girl-friend in D.C. on the Fourth of July, and they had gone down to the Mall to see the Beach Boys. The crowd that day was estimated at 700,000, and when the concert and fireworks were over everyone had left at once. The Metro being over-whelmed, Frank and his friend had walked up 17th and then Connecticut to her place near Dupont Circle, and the entire way they had strolled with the rest of the crowd right down the middle of the street, forcing the helpless cars among them to creep at a pedestrian pace.

This was just like that – a sudden Carnavale, bursting onto Wisconsin. It had the feel of that day in the cold snap when everyone had gone out on the frozen Potomac. The city surprised by joy.

Frank watched through the windows of his van, feeling detached. No doubt it was good news – parts of him knew it was very good news – but he could not feel it. He was still too disturbed by what had happened with Caroline and her husband.

Inching forward, he gave Edgardo a call.

When Edgardo picked up, Frank's ear was blasted by the sound of one of Astor Piazzolla's wild tangos, the bandoneon leading the charge with such scrunching dissonances that Frank's phone screeched. 'LET ME TURN IT DOWN' he heard as he held the phone at arm's length.

'Sure.'

'Okay I'm back! Who is it?'

'It's Frank.'

'Ah, Frank! How are you!'

'I'm okay. So, what happened?'

Edgardo laughed. 'Didn't you hear?' he said. 'Phil Chase won the election!'

Behind his voice the tango kept charging along, and the shifting static in the phone led Frank to think that he might be dancing around his apartment.

'I know that, but how?'

'We will certainly be talking about how this happened for a long time, Frank, and I'm sure it will keep us entertained on our runs. But I predict right now that no one will ever be able to say exactly why this election came out the way it did.' He laughed again, seemingly at the way he could use such innocuous pundit clichés to convey exactly what he meant: *not now*. Of course. And maybe never. 'Meanwhile just enjoy yourself, Frank. Celebrate.'

In the background the tango band twirled on. Frank pushed *End* on his phone; he could tell Edgardo about the new set of disks later. Best not to use phones anymore, as Edgardo had reminded him. He shook his head: his leap-before-you-look strategy was not capable of noticing all the possible consequences of an act. It was not working.

He dropped into Georgetown. It was even more crowded than upper Wisconsin had been, but soon he would cross to

Arlington, and presumably over there it wouldn't be like this. Frank wasn't certain Arlington would be celebrating at all. That would be all right with Frank.

Then just before the Key Bridge traffic came to a complete halt. Downstream to the left he could see fireworks, shooting up off the levee next to the Lincoln Memorial, bursting over their own reflections in the black Potomac. All the celebrants crowding the street and sidewalk were cheering, many jumping up and down. Drivers of cars in front of Frank were giving up and getting out to stretch their legs or join the party. Some of them climbed on the roofs of their cars.

Frank got out too, smacked by the cold into a new awareness of the night and the crowd. Every boom of the fireworks brought another cheer, and all the skyward-tipped faces shone with the succession of mineral colors splashing over them. Frank was seized by the arms by two young women, pulled into their dance as they sang, 'Happy Days Are Here Again,' kicking out in time before him. To keep step he started kicking as well, adding gibbon hoots to the general din. So what if sea level was rapidly rising, so what if there were lichen out there sucking carbon out of the sky – so what if the whole world had just seized the tiger by the tail! They were under a new dispensation, they were entering a new age! Oooooooooooop!

Then traffic was moving again, and Frank had to smooch his dancers and dash to his van. Into its warmth and over the bridge, creeping forward slowly, the fireworks still showering sparks into the river.

Over in Arlington it was entirely different: dark, empty, a little bit spooky. Streetside trees bounced and flailed on the wind. Snow blanketed the big open spaces downtown. Wilson Boulevard was deserted, just as he had thought it might be. There were two countries bound together now, and one of them was not celebrating. A cold and windy night to be sure.

Hard to sustain being out on such a night, if one were not in Carnavale mode. Where would the knitting woman be tonight, for instance? And where was Chessman? Where would the bros sleep on this night? Did it matter to any of them that Phil Chase had won the election? In a system that demanded five percent unemployment, so that fifteen million people were going hungry, without jobs or homes, and an ice age coming on – did any election matter?

By the time Frank drove up to the curb outside Khembali House it was well after midnight, and he was exhausted. All was dark, the wind hooting around the eaves. The house had a presence in the night – big, solid, and he had to say comforting. It was not his home, but it did feel like a place he could come to. Inside were people he trusted.

Through the gate and around the back. Thank God they did not go in for those great Tibetan mastiffs that terrorized Himalayan villages. All was peaceful in the snowed-over autumn garden. Little scraps of prayer-flag flapped on a string in the breeze.

The light was on in their shed. He turned the doorknob gently and urged the door in with its most silent twist.

Rudra was sitting up in bed reading. 'It's okay,' he said. 'No need to be quiet.'

'Thanks.'

Inside it was nice and warm. Frank was still shivering, though it was not visible on the surface. He sat down on his bed, cold hands between his legs and tucked under his thighs. Like sitting on two lumps of snow.

His main cell phone was on his bedside table, blinking. He pulled a hand out and flipped it open to check it. Message from Diane. Called; would call back. He stared at it.

'You also got call tonight on phone in house.'

'What? I did?'

'Yes.'

'Did they leave a message?'

'Qang say, a woman call, very late. Said, tell Frank she is okay. She will call again.'

'Oh. Okay.'

Frank sat there. He didn't know what to think. He could think this, he could think that. Could, could, could, could, could. Diane had called. Caroline had called.

'Windy.'

'Sure is.'

'Good night?'

'I guess so.'

'You are not happy at election result?'

'Yeah, sure. It's great. If it holds.'

'Good for Khembalung, I think.'

'Yes, probably so. Good for everyone.' Except for fifteen million of us, he didn't say.

'And your voyage, out to the salt fleet? Went well?'

'Oh, yeah, sure. Yeah, it was very interesting. We seeded the ocean. Poured five hundred million tons of salt in it.'

'You put salt in ocean?'

'That's right.'

Rudra grinned. Once again the thousand wrinkles in his face reconfigured into their particular map of delight. How often he must have smiled –

'I know I know!' Frank interrupted. 'Good idea!'

Rudra laughed his helpless deep belly laugh. 'Salt to ocean! Oh, very good idea!'

'Well, it was. We may have saved the world with that salt. Saved it from more winters like the last one, and this one too.'

'Good.'

Rudra considered it. 'And yet you do not seem happy, my friend.'

'No. Well.' A deep, deep breath. '. . . I don't know. I'm cold. I'm afraid we're in for another bad winter, whether the salt works or not. I don't think any of the feral animals left will make it if that happens.'

'You put out shelters?'

'Yes.' An image: 'I was in one of those myself, when Drepung found me and brought me here.'

'You told me that.'

'It was filled with all kinds of different animals, all in there together.'

'That must have looked strange.'

'Yes. And they saw me, too. I sat right down by them. But they didn't like it. They didn't like me being there.'

Rudra shook his head regretfully. 'No. The animals don't love us any more.'

'Well. You can see why.'

'Yes.'

They sat there, staring at the orange glow of the space heater.

Rudra said, 'If winter is all that is troubling you, then you are okay, I think.'

'Ah well. I don't know.'

The taste of blood. Frank gestured at his cell phone, put his cold hand back under his thigh, rocked forward and back, forward and back. Warm up, warm up. Don't bleed inside. 'There's too many . . . different things going on at once. I go from thing to thing, you know. Hour to hour. I see people, I do different things with them, and I'm not . . . I don't feel like the same person with these different people. I don't know what I'm doing. *I don't know what to do.* If anyone were watching they'd think I had some kind of mental disorder. I don't make any sense.'

'But no one is watching.'

'Except what if they are?'

Rudra shook his head. 'No one can see inside you. So no matter what they see, they don't know. Everyone only judges themself.'

'That's not good!' Frank said. 'I need someone more generous than that!'

'Ha ha. You are funny.'

'I'm serious!'

'A good thing to know, then. You are the judge. A place to start.'

Frank shuddered, rubbed his face. Cold hands, cold face; and dead behind the nose. 'I don't see how I can. I'm so different in these different situations. It's like living multiple lives. I mean I just act the parts. People believe me. But I don't know what I feel. I don't know what I mean.'

'Of course. This is always true. To some you are like this, to others like that. Sometimes a spirit comes down. Voices take over inside you. People take away what they see, they think that is all there is. And sometimes you want to fool them in just that way. But want to or not, you fool them. And they fool you! And on it goes – everyone in their own life, everyone fooling all the others – No! it is easy to live multiple lives! What is hard is to be a whole person.'